TABOO

Nirmala Govindarajan is an author, journalist, and social sector documentarian. She believes in creating an equal world through her work and writing. *Taboo* is born out of her experience of documenting under-aged girls who are kidnapped, and trafficked. Her novel *Hunger's Daughters* (2018) is inspired by young breadwinners, primarily in Orissa, Jharkhand and Karnataka. Nirmala has authored The *Community Catalyst*, recommended reading for civil services aspirants (2016), and co-authored *Mind Blogs 1.0*, the first blog-to-book format (2010). In 2014, Nirmala co-curated the first edition of the *Times Literary Carnival*, Bangalore and in 2016, she conceptualized and curated the *Literary Lounge* series at the British Council (BCL), Bangalore. Most recently, she has pioneered the *Writer's Yatra* and *Reader's Yatra* interactive writing and reading experiences in offbeat locations. Nirmala dabbles in theatre. She believes in harmonizing with the elements through music and plays the western classical piano and violin.

PRAISE FOR TABOO

'This is a book that blends genres and defies description. Its style is deceptively playful but it conceals as much as it reveals the horrors beneath the surface'

– **Jerry Pinto**, poet and author

'There's music, sex, the scent of forgotten flowers and the search for lost mothers. *Taboo* is a stylized, lyrical, often macabre urban adventure about love, abandonment, power and the persistence of memory. Audaciously defying boundaries to weave in and out of genres, languages, cultures, myths and realities, it tells a remarkable story of today's India and its people'

– **Antara Dev Sen**, literary critic

'*Taboo* travels between places, languages and characters to map a searing and humane story'

– **Hansda Sowvendra Shekhar**, author

'A piercing dialogue embedded in a journey which is nothing less than freedom itself'

– **Yogita Dakshina**, communications specialist

'*Taboo* is a fluid mystery that is waiting to be solved. With an open mind and a keen ear, perhaps you may find the map to the maze ... Undoubtedly, the journey will enchant you'

– **Manohar Prabhu**, poet and musician

'Right from word go *Taboo* grabs you with its raw appeal'

– **Edison Thomas**, Editor-Indulge, *The New Indian Express*

TABOO

A novel

NIRMALA GOVINDARAJAN

PICADOR INDIA

First published 2019 by Picador India
an imprint of Pan Macmillan Publishing India Private Limited
707, Kailash Building,
26, K. G. Marg, New Delhi – 110 001
www.panmacmillan.co.in

Pan Macmillan, 6 Briset St, Farringdon, London EC1M 5NR
Associated companies throughout the world
www.panmacmillan.com

ISBN 978-93-89109-28-3

1 3 5 7 9 8 6 4 2

Typeset in Guardi LT Std by R. Ajith Kumar, New Delhi
Printed and bound in India by Thomson Press India Ltd.

For

My mother Chandra Govindarajan
My first readers Yogita Dakshina and Manohar Prabhu
My inspiration Catherine Raja, and all the survivors of the sex trade
at Freedom Firm and Ruhamah Designs

ONE

PERUMAL AROKYASWAMI IS WELL-VERSED in the art of holding slender beedis between his lips – he tightly drags the native tobacco from the spine of the indigenous Indian cigarette. The government-endorsed, original Vignesh Beedi of unadulterated intoxication is Perumal Arokyaswami's forever favourite brand.

As a lone star from the Far East shimmers with a vengeance in the sky, Perumal Arokyaswami drags the beedi one more time – he is beholden to this native intoxication – he swerves his matted head to face his companion for the night. Moving close to meet her mouth, Perumal Arokyaswami deftly passes the intoxication from his own blackened teeth unto a pair of lipstick red instruments of kiss – the native flavour grabs his companion in her feminine core.

This singular Vignesh Beedi is fortunate, it now rests between a pair of delicious red lips. These lips must have an owner who cares to paint them this alluring shade of red each time the sun goes to bed. The Lady with the Slender Hands wears red, this alluring hue is brightest upon her lips. Her lips, those sumptuous instruments of kiss, are a feast for her lover with the matted head.

But the Lady is not alone with her lover upon this rain-blessed night. The man with blackened teeth and the Lady with the red lips have the rain for company, alright.

Rain, rain, *poda deiyy* groans Perumal Arokyaswami in the Tamil tongue.

Rain, rain, get lost you rascal.

But the rain persists, it brings the Lady and her companion close, skin to skin.

Rain, rain, come back you rascal.

Rain, rain, *vaada deiyy* groans Perumal Arokyaswami in the native tongue of Cottonpettai.

The native tongue of Cottonpettai is Tamil, and this is a perfect setting for lovemaking. This setting has rain, the Lady, and Perumal Arokyaswami, the lovers caressing each other, their near-naked bodies moving to the rhythm of the downpour, and all is seemingly quiet. But not quite – something else is moving upon this rain-blessed night – a human-shaped gunny bag with a rascal inside.

'There's a rascal, and he's moving inside a gunny bag – is he dead or alive?' the frightened Lady and her lover wonder.

The Lady holds her poise despite her fright, and whispers: 'Who can this rascal be?'

Perumal Arokyaswami is tongue-tied, his intoxicated mind has not known Pascal Rebello de Fonseca to be a rascal.

'Pascal Rebello de Fonseca was a wonderful man,' the lover whispers back to the Lady almost trembling in his arms.

This wonderful man loved the Lady with the Slender Hands more than he did his own life – she knows he isn't a rascal. The Lady and her lover, both intoxicated beyond any ability to see reason or the moving gunny bag, heatedly haggle over the 'isn't' and the 'wasn't' until the rain pauses the uncontrollably rising fire within the core of their impassioned bodies.

Their bodies still in contact with each other, the Lady and her lover linger in their own intoxicated thoughts. In the Lady's reckoning, she has known Pascal Rebello de Fonseca ever since she was half a foetus. In Perumal Arokyaswami's reckoning, he has known Pascal Rebello de Fonseca ever since that first rain-blessed night when he shared his *naati,* yes ... country tobacco dosed Vignesh Beedi with the Lady – she, the owner of those tantalizingly slender hands. In fact, Perumal Arokyaswami has known Pascal Rebello de Fonseca much before that night – he is too intoxicated by the stark country flavour of the government-endorsed beedi and the Lady's sumptuous red lips to bring his important past to the present.

Perumal Arokyaswami's past is also his present.

The Lady is present, and her beauty so perfect, Perumal Arokyaswami's masculinity is tense. He grabs the beedi from the pout of the Lady's red lips, drags it deep, permits its perfect flavour to savour his blackened teeth, also fill his entire lean body from his matted head down to his naked toes.

The Lady's near-naked body is tense, she pouts some more, she permits her slender hands accoutred with twelve red bangles each, to grab Perumal Arokyaswami in a tight embrace.

Skin to skin, mouth to lip, Perumal Arokyaswami now holds the naati flavour at grabbing distance from the Lady's pout. The Lady is impatient, she must hold the naati tobacco flavour of Nippanini between her lipstick red, much-practiced pout upon this rain-blessed night – right now! She grabs the beedi between her sumptuous lips, and Perumal Arokyaswami's forefinger follows the naati intoxicant into the Lady's warm and succulent mouth.

Give this naati flavour a pat on its heady back – it is the aphrodisiac that has the red-lipped Lady smitten by the man with blackened teeth.

This naati tobacco is of national importance – it is the celebrated flavour of a town with a permanent Indian postal address in the neighbouring state, the inhabitants of which speak the Kannada tongue.

Upon this rain-blessed night, Perumal Arokyaswami woos the Lady with the naati flavour of small town Nippanini in the tongue he fluently speaks – Tamil. This small town is the source of the world-acclaimed *masculino* Vignesh Beedi. The English word for its Spanish counterpart masculino is masculine, and Nippanini is the richest small town in the Indian Subcontinent.

This beedi from Nippanini is masculine, alright.

'This rugged beedi is a tad too stark for the luscious red lips and delicate lungs of ladies, especially those with slender hands,' deep grunts Perumal Arokyaswami in selfish defence of the masculine-flavoured cash crop. He grunts in arrogant defence of the large-leaved juicy tobacco, this crop the farmer's toil in Nippanini, this small town the currency-rich territory in the Indian State of Karnataka. This small town shares a conscious political boundary with another Indian state. This boundary separates Nippanini from Ajay Nagar, its twin territory. Ajay Nagar has a postal address in the Indian State of Maharashtra, and its inhabitants speak the Marathi tongue.

States are separated by unmarked boundaries and pin-codes in the Indian Subcontinent.

Boundaries have long been crossed, a slumbering fact in the Lady's brain is stirred to the fact that she does not have a permanent postal address anymore. Where there's no home, there's disgrace – the Lady releases herself from Perumal Arokyaswami's tight embrace.

The Lady battles with her past in present tense.

The Lady is homeless, she is consciously chagrined upon this rain-blessed night.

The Lady has grit, she will be called homeless no more, especially upon this rain-blessed night. It pours some more, and her slender hands herald the awakened Rain God –

her red lips utter a threat to the heavens, stirring the resting panic within her sparsely concealed bosom – there's peace no more upon this damp night, the Lady shrieks. Her conscious chagrin fills the street, the entire tier-two city, the sky, also the clouds, and disturbs the awakened Rain God's peace. Perturbed, the clouds spill profuse tears upon this rain-blessed night.

When clouds cry, temperatures drop, and it rains naati beedis in this grade two category southern Indian not-so-big city. Fighting the cold, Perumal Arokyaswami reaches out for his soiled shirt now merged with the Lady's discarded sari, retrieves another naati beedi from the garment's haggard pocket, and lights it. He drags the soul-redeeming tobacco as the beedi steadily warms his skeletal frame which has grown cold in the constant blessed rain.

Upon this rain-blessed night, Perumal Arokyaswami's starving and cold skeletal frame does not have the wherewithal to smirk at the wishes of the consciously chagrined Lady – she, Her Homeless Highness with a red pout. This rain-blessed night, Perumal Arokyaswami's beedi crosses masculine territory, its ultimate naati potency slipping unsteadily into the well-practiced pout of the feminine mouth, and she breathes ...

Breathe in
Breathe out
Breathe high
Breathe higher
Breathe highest...

Perumal Arokyaswami is warm, his light frame is floating in the atmosphere, his own coarse hands gripping the Slender One's soft-as-rose-petal fingers, his heart experiencing the highest bliss.

The time is right upon this rain-blessed night for Perumal Arokyaswami to accompany the Lady with the Slender Hands to bed.

To bed?

But there is no bed.

There is no Pascal Rebello de Fonseca either.

What will Pascal Rebello de Fonseca have to say about the non-existent bed?

'Do not worry Perumal Arokyaswami – nobody knows where Pascal Rebello de Fonseca is, let alone the missing bed,' the Lady consoles her lover.

Where there's a bed, there's a home with a postal address.

There is neither bed stuffed with cotton nor coir upon this Footpath territory. Yet, this Footpath is the most blissful territory for impassioned lovers. Perumal Arokyaswami and the Lady with the Slender Hands, both impassioned lovers upon a well-lit Footpath, are locked in electric embrace.

There is an electric surge – the streetlights glow brighter, creating a perfect setting for a sleep-out under hiding starlight.

This rain-blessed and starless night, surging streetlights throw streams of gleam upon the earth, even the dark sky – there are starry illusions everywhere.

These are illusions of soft cotton stuffed beds, and roofed homes.

Illusions indeed!

These illusions are indeed the disillusions of the now homeless.

These homeless, all self-made stars, call themselves the Fellows of the Footpath.

Every self-made star who has ever smoked the naati beedi of the versatile Vignesh variety walks into this setting, his and her illusion more grandiose with each new drag of the masculino brand.

Suck the masculine beedi together – Perumal Arokyaswami and the Lady with the Slender Hands. Sleep together, his body entwined in hers. Together in the back seat of the large silver-rim-wheeled cycle rickshaw. Back seat, silver rim, rickshaw, et al. – Perumal Arokyaswami's dandy, pride of Cottonpettai, the grade two category southern Indian city. Cottonpettai, the colonially English Lancashire of India in the State of Tamil Nadu – dandy parked with pardonable pride upon the 3 foot wide footpath by the Mettupalayam Railway Station for Erstwhile Steam Engines, downhill Blue Mountain Nilgiris' cash rich crown – the posh Utahkamand.

This 3 foot wide Footpath is the prestigious abode of the homeless in Cottonpettai.

While the homeless return to their starry abode one by one, a gunny bag stirs upon this very Footpath.

How in this wider-than-legally-prescribed Footpath's name can a gunny bag stir?

Regular is a deviant word upon the Widest Footpath of Cottonpettai where Perumal Arokyaswami and the Lady with the Slender Hands are entwined in passionate embrace. The Lady has distinctly passionate ways, especially after her forty-eight-hour-long rail journey from the Twenty Third platform of the Grand Nizamuddin to the foothills of the Blue Mountains in Cottonpettai.

'The Lady with the Slender Hands has been caught

entwined with many men, Perumal Arokyaswami is a poor choice,' dissent the whispers of the Fellows of the Footpath, all returning to their roofless home in twos, threes and sixes after a long day's labour. The gunny bag shows dissent at this poor choice of words, it stirs once more.

The Fellows of the Footpath watch the gunny bag stir, they feel strangely threatened, they whisper no more.

The Fellows of the Footpath, Perumal Arokyaswami and his Lady included, have all the freedom in the world to stir in silence upon this rain-blessed night.

Freedom is in the air. There are whispers in the air too, they stir emotions that have been silenced in fear of truant tongues wagging their displeasure at my pleasure. I stir awkwardly from memories of passionate kisses that have given me no pleasure. The snow-mountain valley, which is now my home, albeit temporary, wears silence in her altitude to match my stirred memories. In silence, I sail Solali Valley's *sin fin territorio* – endless territory on high altitude. In silence, I scour the boundaries of *libertad* in this snow-mountain terrain of Himachal Pradesh. Freedom, yes libertad, is an island on this high-altitude sin fin territorio. Freedom must be savoured, but within the jurisdiction of its tell-tale boundaries. My body is cold, and I am not so certain that libertad can buy me a home, not even a tell-tale shelter.

TWO

JHORU KANBI BADSHAH HAS LEFT HOME. His mother no longer lives in the one-windowed home that he was born into. When he was still a boy of five, Jhoru Kanbi's mother placed a kiss upon his forehead every summer night, blessing him with a fine fortune, conferring her brave son with the royal title: Badshah. When his mother disappeared one *jumme ki raat* after planting a last kiss upon her only son's forehead, Jhoru Kanbi bravely made his own plans. Five jumme ki raats later, he added the royal title of Badshah to his cradle name, and disappeared from his father's faltering sight upon a starless Friday night after the mullah had delivered the special namaz. The now-motherless boy disappeared from his father's sight to become a prince by his own fortune – he had left home to find his *svataha bhagya*.

Twenty-one years later, fortune, yes Jhoru Kanbi Badshah's svataha bhagya, greets him with a kiss. Well-versed in the princely ways of winning over princesses, Jhoru Kanbi Badshah kisses a slender hand wearing twelve red bangles.

Red cannot be ignored.

A winsome princess cannot be ignored.

Instead, Jhoru Kanbi Badshah chooses to ignore two winsome eighteen-year-old belles swaying to Franz Liszt's Spanish Rhapsody stored in the memory of their well-monitored uPods. These belles have stopped to gawk at Jhoru Kanbi Badshah's well-versed kiss – it simply cannot be ignored.

Kiss
Chumban
The simple bliss
Sope ananda
That Jhoru Kanbi Badshah will not miss

Even upon a rain-fed morning.

Upon the hysterical Twenty Third platform of the Grand Nizamuddin – Humongous Railway Station in the Undeniable Capital of India – the simple bliss of a chumban cannot be missed.

But Jhoru Kanbi Badshah cannot continue to kiss, he is hysterical today. The train has just made an excusably hollering and inexcusably late entry into the Twenty Third platform of the Grand Nizamuddin, and this territory falls under the jurisdiction of the Badshah. The hollering train, bound from the Undeniable Capital in the uppity northern region of India to Cottonpettai in the snooty southern region of the same country, has left all the delayed passengers utterly hysterical.

Utterly impatient!

Impatient people running amok

People colliding into each other over and again

People screaming

People gesticulating

People, people, unruly people!

'Stop it people,' growls Jhoru Kanbi Badshah under his kesar aka Himalayan mountain flower scent infused breath.

Breathless, people stop short in their unruly steps.

These people, all passengers bound to a region south of the Undeniable Capital of India, stop and gape at the Badshah as he exudes his mesomorphic self from his perch on the third step connecting the door of the second-class compartment closest to the Supremely Air Conditioned Bogie.

'This is no time to stop and gape, rush to your respective bogies – can't you see the train is already very late!' the Badshah growls once more, simultaneously pleased with his undeniably royal command.

Most people realize once again that they are late, they

dissipate from the Twenty Third platform into their respective bogies.

Within the second-class compartment closest to the Supremely Air Conditioned Bogie, the Lady with the Slender Hands is very pleased that the train is late – she waits for another kiss, surprisingly patient beyond her unregulated temper. Jhoru Kanbi Badshah does not dissolve his passion in wasteful surprise, he regulates his lips for the unregulated act. His lips plant another delicious kiss upon the Slender One's hands.

'*Arre*! A public kiss.'

'*Sarvajanik chumma.*'

'Unforgivable!'

'*Akshamya!*'

The people in the bogies, also the vendors on the Twenty Third platform of the Grand Nizamuddin holler hysterically at the sight of this public kiss.

'Forgive Jhoru Kanbi's insolence,' his entourage of fellow coolies beg excuse for their Badshah's act of private passion upon this public platform.

'This kiss is no act of insolence, it is none of anyone's hollering business upon this busier-than-Cottonpettai's-fish-market platform,' establishes the owner of the twelve red bangles in a voice so soft, yet crisp, also distinctly royal. The hollering people inside and outside the inexcusably late train are dumbstruck, they mind their own respective businesses.

But for the belles with uPods, the owner of the bangles has made her stance abundantly clear to all gawking people who have stopped on the Twenty Third platform of the Grand Nizamuddin to watch this well-versed kiss between a coolie and a Lady.

The belles sigh – this kiss is too important to miss, they simply cannot mind their own respective businesses.

The belles cry – they break into a sudden run.

These belles, all Guides from St. Alphonsious Pre-University College are being strictly monitored by a certain snoopy Master – they shall be repeatedly reprimanded for watching a forbidden kiss.

'Dismiss the forbidden kiss, and proceed to the Twenty Eighth platform to board the Uppity Shuthabdie to Cottonpettai,' the bellowing Master marches with a cane upon the Twenty Third platform, and the belles run faster.

The kiss, an act of naked human passion performed in public view to the tune of the Spanish Rhapsody sounding from the monitored uPods of the belles, lingers long after the Guides have disappeared with the music.

Far away from the Grand Nizamuddin, I fly high, I kiss the sky, I hum the tune of Liszt's Spanish Rhapsody in C-sharp minor to reckon with my lonely state. I have no one to kiss, I am well-versed in the art of *besos* clouds instead. Besos – kissing, *nubes* – clouds. I am well-versed in the art of kissing cold nubes floating above the silence of the sleeping Valley of Solali.

THREE

THE FELLOWS OF THE Footpath have stopped whispering their slander – silence rules the boundaries of love between two beedi-kindred souls upon this rain-blessed night. Silence is the language of love upon the Widest Footpath of Cottonpettai. Love is a Spanish sweet something in Perumal Arokyaswami's cycle rickshaw, which has a prime parking slot on the Widest Footpath by virtue of its dandiness.

By virtue of her kindred heart, *'Mi Corazón,'* whispers the Lady with the Slender Hands, as she silently strokes the lethargic dreadlocks on Perumal Arokyaswami's rain-drenched head. More whispers punctuate their passion-sparked senses which are now beholden to Franz Liszt's rambunctious *Rhapsodie Espagnole* – this classical Spanish tune playing from the Lady's most prized possession, a portable Trillips cassette player of the erstwhile 1962 model. This spontaneous Spanish Rhapsody is punctuated with the many variations of passion between a Lady who has long remained lonely, and a rickshaw-puller who has yearned for the scent of a princess from a distant dream on the Widest Footpath of Cottonpettai ...

Low and high
Bajo y alto
Tender and wild
Oferta y salvaje

Tender and wild lovemaking keeping time with Liszt's Spanish sweet something.

'Corazón, mi corazón,' the Lady declares over and again, her breath keeping time with her aroused passion. This Spanish sweet something translates libertad to her corazón Perumal Arokyaswami, and he moves has matted head from left to right, over and again.

The world is witnessing libertad to the tune of a Spanish Rhapsody.

Journeying uphill towards the peak of the Nilgiris Mountains in the Students' Luxury Bus with leather upholstered streets, halting briefly by the Widest Footpath of Cottonpettai, the same Spanish Rhapsody translates as freedom to two eighteen-year-old belles and a lad of equal age – three uPods playing the tune somewhere deep inside their uniform pockets.

Two eighteen-year-old belles and a boy have just arrived in Cottonpettai from the Undeniable Capital of India – they are set to travel further uphill to camp at Utahkamand, the blue-eyed big town of the Nilgiri Hills. Their uniform pockets are kindred with a certain Spanish composition in C-sharp minor, the tune arousing a passionate kiss between the Lady with the Slender Hands and her lover, the rickshaw-puller, in a tier-two city that lies 2,503 kilometres south of the Undeniable Capital.

Upon this star-kissed night, the belles witness the passionate scene on the Widest Footpath of Cottonpettai, and cry out loud: 'Look, the Lady! Wherever the Lady goes, a kiss follows!'

Yes, the kiss, which could not be missed at the Grand Nizamuddin, has arrived in Cottonpettai!

The belles sigh, the boy cringes, this passionate kiss between the Lady and the rickshaw-puller is too important to miss – hail libertad.

Sigh, libertad is dead.

These belles and boy, two Guides and a Scout, from St. Alphonsious Pre-University College are being strictly monitored – sigh, they shall be reproached for watching a forbidden kiss. This kiss, an act of naked human passion performed to the tune of Liszt's Spanish Rhapsody sounding from their unmonitored uPods, must be dismissed from their monitored minds, and now.

Minds have a way of wandering when uPods decide to sing – the belles and boy leap out of the bus and race uphill Utahkamand, taking freedom in their stride.

The Scout and Guides of St. Alphonsious Pre-University

College wander through the thick Eucalyptus forests of the Blue Mountain ranges with a tune playing from their uPods – this music renders their minds with insane pleasure.

Sshhhh ... these instruments of pleasure must remain in their uniform pockets even as the owl-eyed Master's vision follows the truant Scout and Guides from his lofty position on a leather-upholstered seat in the bus bound to their camp uphill Utahkamand.

See how the Scout and Guides of St. Alphonsious Pre-University College run uphill the Eucalyptus tree and Bison intense Blue Mountain terrain.

See how the Master follows the Scout and Guides with his round-and-big-as-owl eyes.

Hear how the Spanish Rhapsody in the concealed uPods of the reckless Scout and giggling Guides loops into the neoclassical perky refrain of Frisky Emilio – the international rock sensation.

Yippee ... the owl-eyed Master is unable to decipher the perky refrain, his ears are soiled with fungus gathered from his nightly rendezvous to unmentionable locations – he swims tainted waters in the Nilgiri Valley, unknown to his pupils. But the owl-eyed Master must take the reckless Scout and Guides to task – he trains his prying sight between the Eucalyptus maze. The Scout and Guides of St. Alphonsious Pre-University College, upon arriving at the camp uphill Utahkamand, disappear into a forest-hued tent amidst a reclusive cluster of Eucalyptus trees. Here, they rock, then roll to the tune of Frisky's Spanish refrain within the forest-hued tent, their deft movements invisible and inaudible to their owl-eyed, wax-eared Master.

This Eucalyptus Tent is the abode of the Thentodas, indigenous people of the Blue Mountains. The Thentodas have welcomed the Scout and Guides to party in their midst, and dance to a tune strangely familiar to their own tribal instincts.

Yippee ... see this rambunctious party in the Eucalyptus Tent.

The Master cannot see – these Eucalyptus trees are in a maze.

Whoa, what a maze!

Whoa, what a daze!

What ho owl-eyed *abuelo*, game for *tres*?

What ho owl-eyed grandpa, game for three?

No, not three. Then how about the *Cinco Altos!* – the *High Five!* – five is always better than three!

Abuelo ... cinco, seis, seite, ocho

Ocho! Marcha hacia adelante, Sofia

Cinco, seis, seite, ocho

Ocho! Marcha hacia atrás

Cinco, seis, seite, ocho

Seis! Marcha hacia atrás

Whoa!

Grandpa ... five, six, seven, eight

Eight! March forward, Sofia

Five, six, seven, eight

Six! March backwards.

Seven steps backwards, and eight steps sideways the naked flame, over which a newly hunted pig is cooking ...

Watch this pig cooking, its aroma is so novel and so alluring ...

'Fill your stomachs with our native pig delicacy – Awoom, Awaam, Awoom,' beckon the Thentodas.

'Of course, of course, we will, we certainly will,' reply the Scout and Guides unitedly, and let freshly cut slices of the roasted pig glide into their salivating mouths.

'Yummy, yum, yumyum ... how delicious is this native

cuisine,' the Scout and Guides, hungover by the toddy-seasoned pig delicacy of the Thentodas, blurt over and again.

The aroma of toddy over skinned pig wafts all over the place, outside the tent, into the surrounding trunks of Eucalyptus trees, out of their reclusive cluster uphill Utahkamand, and towards the leather-upholstered bus.

Oh, what an unnecessary fuss over a cooking pig! The Master's nose has led him to the forest-hued Thentoda tent, he promptly seeks the lingo of the Scout and Guides to throw the rambunctious indigenous pig cuisine party out of gear.

'Eight steps forward,' the Master bellows in response to Frisky's refrain still singing in the electronic throats of three well-concealed uPods. The Scout and Guides of St. Alphonsious Pre-University College cannot let their passions run amok with Frisky's rhythmic tune for a perky march forward – certainly not now. The crisp march of discipline decreed by the Master is bound by numbers – one, two, one–two–three, looped in a never-ending lack of rhythmic anarchy.

'There is no room for anarchy here, lend yourselves to discipline – now!' bellows the owl-eyed Master once more.

Discipline is vital – it defines the future career of an eighteen-year-old boy studying to be a Suitable Somebody in the Undeniable Capital of India. So is the case of the two Frisky Emilio besotted eighteen-year old belles – they are being groomed to be Suitable Somebodies by an owl-eyed, fungus-eared Master.

'Rest this case,' the Scout and Guides on camp atop Blue Mountain Utahkamand, far away from their homes in the Undeniable Capital of India, unitedly plead.

'This is a case of indiscipline, and you shall be suitably punished,' the Master sternly decrees.

No suitable Scout, nor his counterpart Guide, accoutred

in the blue uniform and white satin-bordered scarf can *marcha hacia adelante*, let alone, *marcha hacia atrás* – they have been suitably punished by their Master! The uPod is suitable neither for the important future of the eighteen-year-old boy nor the same-aged belles. The Master of Sports for Suitable Somebodies, who wears this longwinded title pinned unto his crisply ironed uniform, has secured the future of the Scout and Guides well under his owl-eyed gaze – he must ensure that no boy nor girl under his jurisdiction strays from the beaten path.

'The future wears a blinker – look left, then straight, turn right and left again to keep safe from all sorry. Just skip the *cinco, seis, seite, ocho* for another lifetime of sorry sways to meaningless music!' bellows the owl-eyed Master, loud and not-so-clear for his pupils to hear. The impressionable Scout and Guides of St. Alphonsious Pre-University College cringe under the owl-eyed supervision of the Master of Sports for Suitable Somebodies. Together, the visibly restrained Scout and Guides invisibly wish they were unsuitable nobodies, instead.

The Master of Sports for Suitable Somebodies is indeed very pleased with the obedient restraint of the seemingly restrained, secretly uPod-owning, going to be somebodies at a future date. 'All those who care to be restrained without dissent,' decrees the Master, 'certainly have a date with a disciplined, head-up-in-the-air future.'

Cinco, seis, seite, ocho, my future is a haze. Flip, turn, inside out, my head is upside down – my parachute has a date with my future. *Mi futuro* is my future alone. Whether you get it or not, my future has no date with discipline, my head is upside down

– it is turning around five, six, seven, eight times to the perky momentum of *Cinco Altos!* – come give me a *High Five*!

FOUR

EVERYBODY HAS A DATE with the future. The future is full of dates that cannot be marked on the Calendar of Wannabe This and That Hopes, which hangs on the highest wall of the Twenty Third platform in the Grand Nizamuddin. Only three days ago, two Guides with uPods singing the Spanish Rhapsody, and their Scout counterpart, had thrust this Calendar into a just-kissed coolie's hand even as the inexcusably late train bound to Cottonpettai hollered outside the Twenty Third platform. Wheeling an abandoned step ladder to the far end of the platform, the coolie had hung the Calendar of Wannabe This and That Hopes on the highest wall, writing out his deepest desire in a tongue he has known to speak since early childhood – Marathi. Ever since the day of the fleeting passionate interlude, which was when the Calendar became his medium between earth and heaven, Jhoru Kanbi Badshah has been hoping that the train from Cottonpettai will deliver him a surprise package of slender hands, his to kiss. Yes, Jhoru Kanbi Badshah's chumban in abundant view of going to be Suitable Somebodies, at the beckoning of those sparkling red bangles resting on those slender hands.

Mwah … chumban … what smooth and slender hands, each with twelve red bangles for the coolie to caress and kiss …

But the bangles have remained in Cottonpettai.

Sigh, the bangles have broken on the Widest Footpath in Cottonpettai.

Ayyo, vallazhalgal vondanjipochi.

All twelve red bangles.

Pannandu segappu valazhalgal.

Twelve bangles are now shards of glass.

Pannandu vallazhalgal ippo veen kannadi thoolgal.

Segappu thoolgal.

Red shards.

The Lady with the Slender Hands has left the aristocratic coolie Jhoru Kanbi Badshah's heart in near shards and moved suitcase, Trillips recorder, et al. to Cottonpettai.

In the cosy rexine-covered back seat of Perumal Arokyaswami's cycle rickshaw, dandy upon the Widest Footpath of Cottonpettai, shards of red glass are tell-tale signs of a romantic interlude between a man of no fortune, and a once fortunate woman.

In a cycle rickshaw upon the Widest Footpath of Cottonpettai, there are tell-tale signs of a romantic interlude with a prince.

Who is the prince?

Does this unknown prince have a careless princess to kiss?

In the interlude between river and sky, I, a wannabe princess, plunge into the waters of the icicle-topped Beas, and float in the company of careless jellyfish. Wait, a princess cannot be careless. The jellyfish cannot be careless. The careful jellyfish wears a gelatinous umbrella, food for its sinking body. I cannot be careless, an energy-prepped parachute – yes, a gelatinous umbrella – food for my pining heart, keeps me afloat *en la cielo* ... I have been kept afloat in the sky playing roof to the Valley of Solali. The Beas is suddenly still beneath my feet, the snow mountain river cannot be careless about its meandering boundaries. The Beas is disciplined, it must hug a careful path, and remain within its prescribed boundaries. The river flows beneath my frozen feet as I keep afloat en la cielo, and seek libertad within the meandering boundaries of the blue sky. This blue cielo keeps my frozen feet off the ground, my body bounded to the *azul* aka blue sky so that I do not run back to the prince I pine for before the time is conducive for a passionate interlude between him and I ... My azul eyes are sad, they cry, and the warm tears drench my frozen feet.

FIVE

THE SCOUTS AND GUIDES of St. Alphonsious Pre-University College stand in attention, proud and tall on their white canvas shoe-wrapped feet. They stand braving the summer in an open-to-the-sky field upon this June afternoon in the Undeniable Capital. They stand until they have heard what the Master of Sports for Suitable Somebodies has to say.

'You offspring of somebodies are all here to be deemed suitable to thrive in the capitalist world in the near future – you are all required to follow a strict code of conduct,' bellows the owl-eyed Master.

'Alright,' mutter the future Suitable Somebodies in unison.

'Alright,' bellows the Master, and continues to first address the Guides.

'All you Guides,' the Master decrees, 'must never colour your lips red or any other hue of lipstick. You are, however, allowed to paint your lips with colourless gloss. Talking of gloss, each and every one of you is required to wear your hair in two plaits, and fasten them with red ribbons only – no sparkling headgear whatsoever!'

'Yes Master,' all the Guides, barring one, mutter in unison.

'Master,' cries the one Guide with cropped hair, 'how am I to plait my scant tresses?'

'Wear a red hairband instead, and note that not a single strand of hair brushes the tender skin of your girly face,' retorts the Master.

'Yes Master, I will make every effort to keep my hair off my face,' confirms the short-haired Guide.

'Where there's effort, there's ample gain. I call upon each Scout assembled upon this three-acre ground of the most prestigious St. Alphonsious College to make every effort to keep his shirt buttoned until his neck. Well, almost – you must keep one button loose to be able to breathe,' the Master of Sports instructs with poise.

There's poise when the Master addresses the boys.

These boys, all Scouts of St. Alphonsious Pre-University College are thrilled to be addressed by the owl-eyed Master with such poise – they are indeed superior to the Guides, they beam from eye to mouth.

'Shut your beaming mouths you Scouts,' grunts the Master, dropping his poise. 'Scouts are of course superior to the Guides by a sheer meeting of Y and Y chromosomes. I do not want any Y here touching an X, or mingling with her for that matter, do you hear!'

The Scouts burst into laughter, and the Guides, all bearers of X chromosomes, giggle.

The Master is not impressed, he immediately quells the laughter and giggle – he changes the topic.

'Alright!' the Master says with disguised poise, and continues to deliver his speech. 'Gear up with poise, you have an official invitation to participate in the National Camp for the Braver than the Best along with two eighteen-year-old belles and a blue-eyed lad. These belles and boy, your smarter comrades have already been sent on a special official mission to the Blue Mountains at the behest of a certain Minister for Shelters. For now, this is the only official information you need to be aware of.'

It is now official that the Scouts and Guides will assemble at St. Peter's Friary School, Lovedale Cross, Utahkamand, Blue Mountain Nilgiris, Tamil Nadu in the rain-blessed month of August to be certified Braver than the Best along with the rest. The rest – the azul-eyed Scout and two Guides, their smarter companions – are presently resting after partying in the forest-hued Eucalyptus Tent at the undeniably prestigious National Camp uphill Utahkamand.

'In August, all you Scouts and Guides of St. Alphonsious Pre-University College will board a train to the Lancashire of India aka Cottonpettai from the Grand Nizamuddin aka Humongous Railway Station in the Undeniable Capital, and journey 2,503 kilometres to the State of Tamil Nadu,' decrees the owl-eyed Master.

The Master has left the azul-eyed Scout and two Guides under the care of the priests at St. Peter's Friary, and returned to the Capital to ready the rest of his pupils for the prestigious National Camp in August.

In August, the Master's pupils will mingle with Scouts and Guides from every other Metropolitan City, District Headquarters and Panchayat Block of the Great Indian Subcontinent at the prestigious National Camp for the Braver than the Best, uphill Utahkamand.

The Scouts and Guides of St. Alphonsious Pre-University College are elated, but they will not smile. They cannot smile

– elation is not becoming of future Suitable Somebodies who are all set to embark on the two-day-long rail journey to arrive at the prestigious National Camp. So, the future Suitable Somebodies keep their lips pursed, and together stand at ease. Together, they move their right canvassed feet forward and upward to finally rest their postures in erect attention. The Master of Sports for Suitable Somebodies is at ease, his obedient pupils are together set for the journey uphill Utahkamand.

Downhill Utahkamand, upon the Widest Footpath of Cottonpettai, the Lady with the Slender Hands must pretend that she will not mingle with mere coolies and cycle rickshaw pullers. But the Lady certainly will not mingle with two uncouth eighteen-year-old belles and a boy who call themselves Guides and a Scout from the Undeniable Capital of India – not even under a pretence. These uncouth eighteen-year-olds, en route to their camp uphill Utahkamand, have kept their eyes wide open, and observed her passionate interlude with the rickshaw puller in the most private corner of the Widest Footpath.

The Lady with the Slender Hands is perturbed – she has keen eyes, and in a fleeting glimpse has clearly observed the distinct features of the belles, and especially the boy. The eyes of the Scout are a shade of azul, a distinct hue of blue that the Lady knows from the time her womb had begun to swell nineteen years ago. Training her eyes uphill Utahkamand, the Lady is perturbed some more – the azul-eyed Scout and his two Guide friends are back from their indigenous pig cuisine party uphill – they are fast headed in the direction of the Widest

Footpath of Cottonpettai. The Lady must act fast – the time is raw, and her identity cannot be exposed ...

'No, no, no ... not yet ... in fact, never ...,' the Lady mutters under her naati tobacco-infused breath, and covers her head ... also her face with her paper-thin sari, also Perumal Arokyaswami's bare torso as he lies intoxicated and immovable beside her.

The distance has closed in – the azul-eyed Scout and belles have arrived at the Widest Footpath of Cottonpettai – they stand very close to the no-so-visible Lady. They mutter to each other under their toddy-seasoned pork meat infused breaths – they need to find the Lady.

The Lady speaks from beneath her thin as butterpaper see-through and floral-printed sari. 'I will mingle with suitable names, which have documented association with the aristocracy alone – I do not wear this butterpaper-thin sari over my head for nothing! My own aristocratic face, let alone the crowning glory on my head is not meant for all and sundry to see – go back to your camp uphill Utahkamand,' says the Lady rather sternly.

The Scout and Guides, all going to be Suitable Somebodies, are trained to be obedient, especially to a rather stern and aristocratic voice – they turn to leave.

The Lady sighs in relief – she raises her head to watch the azul-eyed Scout and his companions leave, when suddenly, they turn around. The Scout and Guides have a few questions regarding certain individuals associated with the Lady and their respective positions as documented aristocrats to put forth before they leave.

'Is Jhoru Kanbi Badshah a documented aristocrat?' the belles ask in unison.

'Is Perumal Arokyaswami a documented aristocrat?' the azul-eyed Scout wants to know.

'Is aristocrat Pascal Rebello de Fonseca the Supreme Dictator of all Royal Ragamuffins?' the Scout and Guides question in unison.

The Lady is aghast – she is the lone keeper of the secret of Pascal Rebello de Fonseca's whereabouts, also the goings-on in the lives of the Royal Ragamuffins here and thereabouts. How on earth do these belles and boy have inkling of this secret?

For this secret to remain one, the Lady must maintain silence – she chooses to shun her pretence, and mingle with the rickshaw puller once more.

The Lady will not speak now – all her twelve red bangles are shards of shimmering glass upon the rexine seat of a cycle rickshaw. This Lady has an aristocratic past – she was once a princess. She laid her waist-long locks on golden yellow and shimmering purple silken cushions when she was still a carefully pampered princess in her father's kingdom.

The kingdom the Lady has known was once a simple and blessed home.

Alas, the Lady's kingdom has succumbed to democracy – she was once her father's princess, and she chose libertad to feign her aristocratic status. This princess now prefers to live amidst the aristocratic illusions of the Fellows of the Widest Footpath of Cottonpettai, instead. This Footpath is besotted with a man, and his princely ways. This man is a royal leftover, they say. The Lady knows better than to refute what anyone on the Widest Footpath of Cottonpettai has to say – at least not yet.

The Scout and Guides who have until now been exposed to ideologies that are Right, and Left too, cannot quite comprehend the nonchalant stance of the royal leftover on this Footpath.

Who on earth is the royal leftover?

He, with Left ideologies?

Or, She, with Right ideologies?

Or, She, with Left ideologies, and He, with Right stances?

Left is over Right on the Widest Footpath of Cottonpettai.

Who is Left?

Who is Right?

All that is clear for the Scout and Guides to see is She, the Lady with the Slender Hands, lying on top of He, the rickshaw puller, her face buried in his naked chest, her thin as butterpaper sari covered back leaving both Left and Right ideologies wanting space to breathe.

The Scout and Guides are yet to learn that Left and Right ideologies are siblings who rest in the extended arms of libertad – they are unable to come to terms with the nonchalant political stance of the Footpath dwellers, many of them royal leftovers. Confused, the Scout and Guides abandon their search for the Lady's identity, and return uphill to St. Peter's Friary to rest in the arms of their Eucalyptus-blessed surroundings.

Left and Right ideologies are repelled by Eucalyptus trees – they stay out of the boundaries of the reclusive quarters of the Thentodas as the indigenous tribes of the Blue Mountains unitedly utter Awoom, Awaam, Awoom.

In my reclusive quarters in the Valley of Solali, I perceive Left and Right ideologies from the careless comfort of a *nieve montaña nube* – a snow mountain cloud – they are at loggerheads, they are fierce. I shudder. I see. From this altitude, I come to terms with the comfort that a Lady finds in the arms of a beedi-inhaling rickshaw puller, I shudder. I, a woman, a lady, I *estremecimiento* ... I shudder ... Yes, yes, you heard me right, I estremecimiento on a nieve montaña nube, confused by the upheaval in my comfort zone even as Right and Left ideologies tear the world apart. I see my certain past present my uncertain future from the careless comfort of my self-imposed libertad – am I Right, or Left? I choose nonchalance from the careless comfort of a nieve montaña nube, at least for now – and the snow mountain cloud, my cold bed, comforts my body.

SIX

MY BODY IS COLD inside out. My lips are quivering. My eyes are shut. I have closed my eyes tight in this snow mountain terrain to establish a warm connection with the yellow cushion in my childhood home.

My connection takes me backwards thirty-two years in time, to a day when I am sixteen, and a proud Guide. In my childhood home, upon a sunny day, I rest my chin on my yellow cushion, and read all about a girl who shares my name.

Today, this connection is playing a game of hide-and-seek with my pride, I am no longer a girl of sixteen. Today, my pride trembles along with the bones in my forty-eight-year-old frame as the cold winds penetrate my skin. Eyes closed, I sail in my mind's eye, rising above my nest, into the cold clouds separating my kingdom – my childhood home from the skies. My mind's eye is all pervading. From this altitude, I eye the snow-besotted mountains in the Valley of Solali. This valley town, the heart of Himachal Pradesh, home to the Apple Tree, secret hearth of the Original Kesar flower. I see everything that my heart yearns for, from this snow mountain altitude.

My heart has called it quits with a certain all-pervading eye resident in my mind. My mind has abandoned everything – even the yellow cushion on the red sofa in my childhood home. My mind separates me from Erendira. My heart is heavy, my mind's eye is tired – I descend from my flight, and sit upon a stone bench. This stone bench is no comfort to my frail bones, I grapple with the waning summer sunshine, and yearn to be called Erendira one more time.

Erendira, the girl who took freedom in her stride. I, she, we, who share the same name – me, the woman who found place of pride between the pages of a story that had to be told by Gabriel García Márquez.

I read from the pages of Márquez' rendition of Erendira, an English translation of the original Spanish text composed to the rhythm of the written word by the timeless storyteller. These pages, which have found me after three decades on a stone bench, have knowledgably yellowed between carefully chosen hardbound dictionaries. These dictionaries, my carefully chosen childhood companions, dissolved the barriers between Spanish, Sinhalese, English, Tamil, Marathi, Hindi and Punjabi, also a Thentoda Handbook, all at least half a century old hardbounds, one resting upon the other in an austere Jewish bookshelf with a dozen compartments. These hardbounds were my father's pride. I, their human companion too, was once my father's pride.

I, the bold pride who abandoned the bookshelf to step into Erendira's stilettoes, and perform the Salsa with strange men by the panicked hours of estranged twilight.

With twilight comes a gust of icicle-borne wind, and my fragile pride shivers beneath the sheer garment I accoutre. I hug my fragile pride, now a common sight. My pride is at the mercy of onlookers, all inquisitive about the colour of my skin in the Valley of Solali. The colour of my skin, a dispassionate mix of dark brown and snow white born out of a passionate union is a shade that does not quite match the native human hue of Solali. My skin is visible for all eyes to pry at. I do not care about these intrusive eyes, my fragile pride is cushioned inside my warm and beating heart.

My heart beats for the Prince ... I want to be the Prince's pride.

But my Prince wanders another mountain terrain, I cannot become one with him just yet, I embrace my life in the Valley of Solali.

One with the Valley of Solali, I wear the scent of Kesar, this flower, the pride of the snow-mountain region.

One with the Valley of Solali, time returns me to a carefree day from another decade – I am sixteen, and free. I have abandoned the urban scent of the yellow cushion on the red sofa by the Saint John's Creeper entwined window, and left home to become a princess of *mi fortuna*. My own careless fortune – yes mi fortuna, has left me with no home.

SEVEN

COMFORT IS FOR PEOPLE with careless business practices.

It is Sanyasi Solali Snowmountainwala's business to be careless with his blessings. In the Valley of Solali, this levitating

Sanyasi's blessings are known to comfort traders who are involved in careless business practices. Among them is a certain careless trader with a big moustache thickened with the oil of the nutritious Himachali Badam – he indulges in a business practice that blesses him with a fortune of unmentionable magnitude. This Moustached Traderman's fortune blossoms in the bosom of Solali.

Please note that the Moustached Traderman is known by several invaluable titles – they have all been bestowed upon him by the vice of his various nefarious business practices. But the valuable, Originally Solali Kesar flower which blossoms in these snow-mountain parts, is the Moustached Traderman's most exclusive fortune indeed. She, by virtue of her exotic lineage, has bestowed the Traderman with a title that spells ownership and, in her prime, will go on to fill his already brimming coiffeurs with currency from every corner of the world.

Does the Moustached Traderman own the Kesar flower, the most exquisite and voiceless inhabitant of the Valley of Solali?

Can the Originally Solali Kesar flower be owned in the first place?

The Moustached Traderman likes to be called the owner of the Originally Solali Kesar, and will keep her place of rest a very closely guarded secret.

Stepping aside from the matter under contention, let it be known at this point that it does not matter where Pascal Rebello de Fonseca is ... he is the owner of a very closely guarded secret.

Sshhhh ... Pascal Rebello de Fonseca knows a lot more about the secret Kesar flower than does Manu, chief of the indigenous Gaddi tribe of the snow-mountain Valley of Solali. Pascal Rebello de Fonseca knows a lot more ... with his eyes closed, he can trace the route to the most safely guarded space in which the Originally Solali Kesar, virgin flower of the snow valley grows. Pascal Rebello de Fonseca's eyes also know that the Moustached Traderman's treasury is filled with money from the unregulated sale of delicate Kesar flowers, all cousins of the Originally Solali Kesar.

Getting back to the matter under contention – has the Moustached Traderman found a buyer for the Originally Solali Kesar as yet?

Scented life of the Valley, the Originally Solali Kesar remains unsold and untouched – she is very closely guarded by Manu Gaddi, and the People of the Highest Hill.

This scented life can only be hidden from the human eye. The human nose has its own mind. The Originally Solali Kesar has the rare ability to lure the male nose into these snow-mountains. Once lured, the man in question travels mindlessly around winding snow slopes, across steep inclines, and up a distant path to the Solali Kesar's resting place on the precarious top of the Highest Hill.

If the scent of the snow-mountain Kesar lures you, beware! It is not easy to get past Manu Gaddi, and the People of the Highest Hill as they stand guard to the virgin fragrance of the Originally Solali Kesar. This Kesar is worth her scent in platinum. This Kesar is the Moustached Traderman's fortune. This fortune remains untouched till date under the third-eye supervision of Sanyasi Solali Snowmountainwala. The Moustached Traderman, an ardent disciple of the Sanyasi, will not sell this fortune for all the coiffeurs in the world without the holy man's consent.

Hail the holy man, and his three eyes – he, the keeper of the Originally Solali Kesar.

Hail Sanyasi Solali Snowmountainwala – he, the guy with the third eye who is much wooed by wish-seekers.

'Hail, hail, hail, you top-class holy man, the one and only Shri Shri Shri Shri and Shri Sanyasi Solali Snowmountainwala,' says the Moustached Traderman in a far-fetched sing-song voice to the scale of B-flat minor, and immediately prostrates at the godman's feet.

The Moustached Traderman finds repose at the godman's long-toed feet, he chooses to remain in his prostrated position for all the other disciples to see.

Sanyasi Solali Snowmountainwala is suitably pleased with his disciple's piety, he wiggles his long toes, and places his bare feet upon the Moustached Traderman's near bald head.

The Moustached Traderman feels a chill upon his head, and the cold travels to his neck, all over his back and bottom, down to his heels ... he sighs.

'Oh for the ice-laced blessings of Sanyasi Solali Snowmountainwala – they are so cold, and so comforting, I cannot rise from my prostrated position,' says the Moustached Traderman, once again in a sing-song tone to the scale of B-flat minor, but an octave higher this time around.

Sanyasi Solali Snowmountainwala is pleased some more – he does not speak – he only wiggles his feet in appreciation of the prostrated man's piety, and taps the Traderman's bald head with his long and cold, big right toe.

The Traderman's moustache shudders at the Sanyasi's cold touch, he raises his head, heaves his prostrated body to an upright position, and takes the godman's leave with continued piety.

The Sanyasi flutters his larger than life third eye, and the Traderman slow marches towards his mode of transport – a Humbassador bearing the Indian Ashoka Emblem. Twirling his moustache with his left hand, the Traderman waves goodbye to his fellow disciples as the government sedan departs downhill, leaving behind a trail of smoke.

'Smoke ... such suffocating samoka. Samoka meaning smoke,' *saha* the Sanyasi's disciples as the black and smoggy cloud from the Traderman's Humbassador vanishes around the steep bend.

Saha?

The people of Solali speak a dialect of the Punjabi language, and saha is to them what whisper is to those who speak the English tongue.

There's truth in the saha that fill the Solali air about the Moustached Traderman's other self. Feeling abundantly blessed, the Moustached Traderman is returning home to his palatial bungalow downhill Solali. He has driven away in a modified luxury Humbassador no less than a classic BMW bearing the state emblem of the Undeniable Capital of India, the official car leaving behind a curtain of smoke uphill Solali, and in every other valley through the 309.8 kilometre trail downhill to his palatial home.

Seven hours and thirty minutes away from the motor car infested world beneath the very valley he has made his home, Sanyasi Solali Snowmountainwala will keep the identity of the all-knowing Pascal Rebello de Fonseca under wraps.

I have left the world of cars for a new mundo – I ride the clouds in the Solali sky. In *mi nuevo mundo* ... *si* ... yes ... in my new world, there are snow-dressed mountains. In this new world my identity is under wraps, and I fly higher than the perpetually levitating Sanyasi Solali Snowmountainwala. Mi nuevo mundo is the only world the Originally Solali Kesar has ever known from her resting place upon the precarious peak of the Highest Hill in Solali.

EIGHT

THE WORLD IS OBLATE spheroid for the sake of textbooks. The world, as the Scouts and Guides live it, is rectangular, and lined with long rosewood tables arranged in ten strictly straight rows. Each long table is accompanied by hundred rosewood chairs to accommodate one thousand students in all of the hall with a high and mighty ceiling.

This ceiling stands tall at thirty-two feet from the ground.

This ceiling is an open womb – it carries thirty-two chandeliers with birth certificates dating to the year seventeen hundred and sixty-five. These chandeliers have all travelled to India when the British set up the Raj to rule the Subcontinent with flamboyance.

The British have quit the Raj in nineteen hundred and forty-seven – they have left behind their flamboyance, the chandeliers.

These chandeliers still burn in the year twenty nineteen, and light up all of the 102 feet long, and 12 feet wide rectangular hall – they are now fitted with electric wiring, and host twenty 100 watt Trillips bulbs each.

How befitting these bulbs are of their parent chandeliers – they glow in unison at the click of thirty-two switches. When they glow their brightest, the bulbs light up every corner of the long, and stately rectangular hall.

When the chandeliers glow at 8 p.m., the Scouts and Guides of St. Alphonsious Pre-University College take their rosewood seats, and say their nightly prayers: 'Dear God, make us healthier, wealthier, and somewhat wise; but teach us to always be precise in the way we conduct ourselves as the future Suitable Somebodies of the Indian Subcontinent.'

The owl-eyed Master never fails to make his presence felt at 8 p.m. – all the Scouts and Guides of St. Alphonsious Pre-University College rise to greet their mentor, teacher and gluttonous guide.

The owl-eyed Master has just arrived – he will now lead the proceedings for the night, and direct his pupils to line up by the five long counters with their Chinese porcelain plates in hand.

All five counters in the Royal Rectangular Hall are granite-topped, and lined with four Bunsen burner propped brass-bottomed dishes each.

Each counter is aromatic with two varieties of curry – one meat and the other vegetarian, yet another with cooked Basmati rice, and the last with desi ghee coated chapatti. The aromatic flavours in these brass-bottomed dishes are meant to be savoured by the Scouts and Guides of St. Alphonsious Pre-University College alone, and of course, their owl-eyed Master.

The owl-eyed Master is a meticulous mentor, he has trained his pupils to fill their plates, return to their rosewood chairs, chew their food with mouths closed in deathly silence, and watch Prime Thrive News on any of the thirty-two television monitors propped along the walls of the Royal Rectangular Hall.

Every night at 8 p.m., the Scouts and Guides of St. Alphonsious Pre-University College chew their delicious food in silence, and watch their parents – all Suitable Somebodies being interviewed, followed and/or reviewed on the country's most prestigious Prime Thrive News.

Every night at 8 p.m., the Master of Sports watches India's present Suitable Somebodies with stars in his owl eyes. These Suitable Somebodies are unitedly responsible for the owl-eyed Master's innumerable bank accounts and unmentionable investments in activities that cannot be condoned by law. These Suitable Somebodies are ministers, lawyers, industrialists, bankers and technology honchos in the Indian Subcontinent. They own corporations, also media houses of which Prime Thrive News is foremost in influencing the impressionable population of the Subcontinent.

The future Suitable Somebodies are an impressionable lot – they have grown to comprehend that a Capitalist world is always Right.

This Right world supports freedom of expression, but within boundaries prescribed by those who have a lot of money.

Money equals capital.

Capital equals investment.

The Scouts and Guides have parents – they all have investments aka money.

More than enough money to make an investment or two or three hundred in industries and ventures that generate jobs in various corners of India – some legal, others that cannot be spoken about.

'Never mind what cannot be spoken about, let us speak about how you will all blossom into Suitable Somebodies,' bellows the owl-eyed Master after Prime Thrive News has relayed all the stories that need to be broken to impressionable nobodies in the Indian Subcontinent.

'Yes, yes, what must we do to blossom into Suitable Somebodies ... tell us most honourable mentor, guide and master,' the Scouts and Guides scream in unison.

The Scouts and Guides have been told by their Master of Sports time and again, actually every single night after Prime Thrive News that they need to feel free within their boundaries, blossom into Suitable Somebodies, and create a new world. A Right world. The Master repeats his well-practised speech – he orders his pupils to get right back to their rooms for their post-dinner study hour.

The Scouts and Guides are suitably impressed by Prime Thrive News, they return to their respective rooms with thoughts of their parents, all Suitable Somebodies, including a certain Minister for Shelters who is known by several other names by virtue of his vices. Hail Prime Thrive News – this channel relays their strife to amass wealth come hell, rain, snow and sunshine in order to create a democratic environment for all and sundry in the country.

The azul-eyed Scout and his two Guide counterparts have been exposed to Prime Thrive news too, much like all and sundry in the country. Also, their counterparts from St. Alphonsious Pre-University College who will join them uphill Utahkamand come August.

Uphill Utahkamand, the azul-eyed Scout and two Guides are of rare sensibility – they cannot be fooled by the views on Prime Thrive News. They sit in the Eucalyptus Tent with their thick as Nilgiri forest friends, the Thentodas of rare sensibility, and speak about indigenous means to create jobs.

The Thentodas are thrilled, they salute the azul-eyed Scout and two Guides – Awoom, Awaam Awoom.

Together, this azul-eyed Scout and two Guides are determined to redefine Prime Thrive News with compassionate views on the plight of the once aristocratic Fellows of the Widest Footpath of Cottonpettai, also their friends the Thentodas, when the time is absolutely right.

Prime Thrive News is popular everywhere, even downhill Utahkamand.

Across the street from the Widest Footpath of Cottonpettai, the Fellows and Royal Ragamuffins gather at the popular Kutti Kadai aka Small Shop, and slurp loudly from their glasses of Blue Mountain Tea to catch the news at breakfast hour.

'This is no news, it lacks basic views that have our interests in mind,' the Fellows and Ragamuffins squirm.

'This news lacks views that are pertinent to people who make love on rexine seats,' the Lady with the Slender Hands reiterates, inhaling the essence of fresh dew speckled Blue Mountain Tea, and sipping on the glass with finesse. The Lady simultaneously wears a faint hope in her heart to return to her own childhood world, the other mundo.

Kindly draw your attention to the other world.

Itara jaga aka the other world.

The world of voyeurs with private lives gone public by choice.

Huh! By choice?

Nijamaava?

Really?

De Verdad?

Mi mundo tu world.

My world is your mundo, everything is awry from this stance.

In your world, Pascal Rebello de Fonseca might be declared dead.

When the dead stir, gunny sacks move.

Gunny sacks on footpaths do not feature in Prime Thrive News even when they stir.

Stir this truth, in itara jaga there is nijamave only mi mundo …

Yes, truth is, in the other world, there is really only mi mundo.

Who is in my world … Jhoru Kanbi Badshah and Perumal Arokyaswami?

Jhoru Kanbi Badshah has stopped dreaming of the itara jaga. He is happy to be a coolie numbered as a luggage bearer, his position visible on a steel arm band in his svataha jaga – his own world of parallel tracks.

Perumal Arokyaswami is happy to be a rickshaw-puller, fate tattooed in the indent above his right wrist, nijamave – really, the permanent imprint in his hand is his destiny.

My destiny has led me by the vanity of my free will into my mundo – in mi world of free floating nubes and snow mountain peaks, there is no news of my prince, the love I miss. My vanity is coaxed by my destiny, it directs my attention to my real purpose in the Valley, and I continue to float in search of libertad.

NINE

VANITY IS NEVER FAIR on the Widest Footpath of Cottonpettai – it is dark, and red-lipped. Lips coated with the ultimate colour of heated passion, which is a dark shade of red to accentuate the fair Lady's much-wooed complexion.

This Lady with the Slender Hands wears a dark shade of red upon her lips – she leaves a coloured impression upon her companion Perumal Arokyaswami's cheek, and the mesmerised rickshaw-puller strokes her soft-as-Badam-milk complexion.

A lady's complexion often determines her companions in bed.

The Lady's complexion, the rickshaw-puller notices, is a complex shade of weather-beaten dark – it still determines her companions in bed. He draws his blackened lips close to her face, and breathes into her deliciously pear-shaped ear.

The Lady has had many companions – some Left, and others of the highest Right leanings, especially in the days when her fair as nascent moonlight complexion had not quite been exposed to the naked rays of afternoon sunshine.

Pssst ... nowadays, the Lady's discerning companions of Left views are determined that her waning complexion acquired from consistent exposure to sunlight by mid noon is simply the best.

Who pray are these discerning companions?

The Fellows of the Footpath who are always considered to have politically Left leanings, favour black unlike the Right-approved fair – they are all very discerning. They love the Lady's weather-beaten complexion, a shade closer to black than not – the Fellows of the Footpath rock – literally.

See how the Fellows of the Footpath move.

See how they groove to the rhythm of Frisky Emilo's *cinco, seis, siete, ocho* ... a tune that the Scout and two Guides left back in their hearts en route to their camp uphill Utahkamand.

The Fellows' hearts are wild with unrequited passion – they watch the Lady paint the rickshaw-puller's black-as-night lips with her own bright red instruments of kiss – they groove some more.

Perumal Arokyaswami's black-as-night lips are now red. He draws the shade of his cycle-rickshaw – a detachable umbrella soldered unto his three-wheeled vehicle, to continue his passionate act with his red-lipped Lady love in privacy.

Privacy on an open-to-the-sky Footpath?

Indeed, there's privacy on the Widest Footpath of Cottonpettai! The black of the night gives these Fellows utmost privacy. Much needed privacy in their unsheltered home. And when night befalls, there's moonshine and stardust, and every other celestial hue that the roving planets in the distant skies care to scatter in transit upon their home.

And when the day breaks, their home has an abundance of fresh air and sunshine. Actually, way too much sunshine.

Too much is too little in the Big Mansion. There is only a streak of sunshine in the fully air-conditioned Big Mansion – this sheltered structure – a show-off, the monument of pronounced pride in Cottonpettai. The Baron of Extreme Excess, owner of the Company of Sturdy Steel, is conditioned for little sunshine. This Baron lives in and out of the Big Mansion, his home away from his bigger home with an address in the northern region of the Indian Subcontinent.

Munumunuppus abound Cottonpettai: 'Who in the name of broad daylight is this Baron, we say?'

Munumunuppus ... mutterings ... gossip ... whispers ... sahas ... yes, munumunuppus abound Cottonpettai, and everyone interested in the business of overt passion wants to know who in reality the Baron of Extreme Excess is – his face is perpetually concealed by a pair of pocket dictionary-sized dark glasses.

Pssst ... according to the munumunuppus about town, this Baron is a sucker for extreme excesses – he has special affinity to copulation, money and mansion – he also pines for a lost honey.

Honey?

Ayyo!!!!!!

Oho!!!!!

Honey meaning sweetheart?

Who is the Baron's sweetheart?

Sssshhh ... the Baron's identity cannot be disclosed at this juncture, no matter how far and wide, high and low the munumunuppus go. It may, however, be disclosed that the Baron's Mansion maintains its place of pride ambient in its sparkling marble floors and immaculate white walls, all surfaces scrubbed to sheen by the toil of the Fellows of the Footpath.

My identity cannot be disclosed now – *mi identidad* is non-existent in the snow-mountain Valley of Solali. My identidad in non-existent in Cottonpettai. Mi identity is of no consequence in the Undeniable Capital of India. My identity plays havoc with the Baron's conscience as I rove the snow-mountain valley mingling with all and sundry to gain a glimpse, si, a mere vislumbrar, of the Originally Solali Kesar.

TEN

IT HAS BEEN ESTABLISHED by the Baron of Extreme Excess to all and sundry in the Press, especially correspondents of Prime Thrive News that the Fellows of the Footpath flourish by their mere toil in the Big Mansion. These Fellows flourish more in extreme sunshine by labouring in the Baron's tea gardens uphill Utahkamand.

The Baron of Extreme Excess is a moneyed man – he has provided jobs to all the Fellows of the Footpath. The Baron has more than a greedy streak – he has accumulated lands and tea gardens unofficially acquired by virtue of his high office and his tight fistedness. The Baron never pays the Fellows their full wages.

There's fresh munumunuppu in the air: 'The Baron's heart is black as freshly dug murk. His heart welcomes women by the dozen into his Big Mansion, but never once the Royal Ragamuffins – they are rumoured to share his bloodline.'

'Why, we say,' cry the munumunuppu mongers, 'should the Baron accept the Royal Ragamuffins – they are noisy and spoilt, and give a bad name to the human race – they live alongside the Fellows of the Footpath, and never bother to brush their teeth by moonshine or daylight? Who, for broad daylight's sake, are these Royal Ragamuffins anyway?'

The Royal Ragamuffins, four in number, dressed in black to offset their pale skin tone, do not resemble the Fellows of the Footpath. These Ragamuffins, they have once breathed the air-conditioned oxygen of the Big Mansion, and the Lady alone knows the truth about their concealed identities. Out in the open, the Royal Ragamuffins are full of macho views – they believe that blankets are unnecessary in the damp cold of an August night downhill Utahkamand, thanks to the quality of food they consume.

The Royal Ragamuffins are suckers for food indeed, but they toddy-drink themselves to restful sleep during the rather cold nights on the Widest Footpath of Cottonpettai downhill Utahkamand.

Uphill Utahkamand, there's an icy cold breeze – the Scouts and Guides of St. Alphonsious Pre-University College are gearing up for a night trek.

Downhill Utahkamand, a cold breeze has established its stance. This breeze cannot be bothered by hot-headed, toddy body-warmed Ragamuffins. It does not matter that the Ragamuffins are indeed royal – their lineage is a matter of contention in the Alarmed Hall of Parliament, which has a postal address in the Undeniable Capital of India.

There's more munumunuppu in the night air: 'The Royal Ragamuffins have a special status – they appear on Prime Thrive News every now and then, along with a certain Minister for Shelters who says the Footpath must die. Who on earth are the Royal Ragamuffins, and what in heaven's name are they doing with the Minister for Shelters on his crusade against footpaths, we say?'

'This is no time to discuss the Minister for Shelters and his connection with the Royal Ragamuffins. It is about time to pay heed to the Minister's views about killing footpaths for the sake of upcoming builders, and he has made his stance public on Prime Thrive News, we say!' the munumunuppu mongers make it clear.

The Fellows of the Footpath have all heard the munumunuppus in the air – they stand united – they refuse to let their home die in Cottonpettai, the Lancashire of India.

'Hail Cottonpettai – India's own English Lancashire where the Footpath refuses to die,' the munumunuppu mongers about town declare. 'Hail the Fellows of the Footpath, a brave bunch of men and women – the rickshaw-puller, and his Lady love included.'

By the break of dawn, the Fellows of the Footpath receive a message – they have all been asked to relocate to the Big Mansion at the behest of the Baron who has agreed to shelter them on condition of total-bonded slavery.

Tchhha ...

Tcheeee ...

Yiessshhhh ...

The Fellows of the Footpath will not be bonded – slavery is neither their cup of Blue Mountain Tea nor bright-as-daylight arrack to be consumed at the stroke of midnight in order to give their labouring limbs some sleep.

It is nearing midnight, the time is ripe to sleep.

While the Fellows of the Footpath sleep by the rise of midnight, the Royal Ragamuffins visit the dustbins abounding Chestershire Market in the heart of the Lancashire of India to fill their gunny sacks with means for another buffet meal. The means they find are often dead before they reach the dustbins of Cottonpettai.

The dead never fail to stir munumunuppus.

'These dead means include rotting human flesh,' one faction of munumunuppu-mongers declare.

'Human?' another faction questions in utter aplomb.

'Well, almost human – the dustbins of Chestershire Market have many female foetuses that were once alive,' the munumunuppu-mongers confirm. 'The female foetus can live, only if she is born. When a female foetus is born, she must be protected from scorn – she must not be treated as a piece of meat by men on heat. It is better that a female foetus is dead before she faces scorn – this is what the Baron of Excess strictly believes.'

The Baron is a paradox.

The Baron of Extreme Excess has carefully protected a certain female foetus in her mother's womb. On the day the female child was born, the Baron banished her to a region far away from her place of birth, leaving her to ripen into a belle of delectable flesh and blood.

I was born of human flesh, blood covering my head, and my entire body by the tantric trance of troubled twilight. I was born to be a woman. I was born to touch *la estrellas*. I touch the stars, *si*, I feel the estrellas in a secret firmament hidden in my dreams by night – I need to escape from men they call Suitable Somebodies. Yiekees, by day or night, these men are on constant heat.

ELEVEN

NIGHT IS AN UNBORN DAWN, a forever *feto femenino.* The Lady with the Slender Hands was once a feto femenino aka female foetus in Valle de la Solana, a hamlet in a valley held snugly in the crest of the Pyrenees Mountain Ranges. The valleys of the Pyrenees are no longer home to the Lady's ancestors – her forefathers, none of whom she has met, have long left the land with their kith, kin and entire clan to meander the world in quest of another meal.

Another meal is always a blessing for the Fellows of the Footpath – the Royal Ragamuffins, and the Lady with the Slender Hands included. In response to their hunger pangs, the Boom Clock in Cottonpettai's Chestershire Market chimes nine times – the dustbins are beckoning the Royal Ragamuffins …

Tonight is like every other dark hour in this tier-two city – the Royal Ragamuffins scavenge the best of rotten meat from Cottonpettai's abundant dustbins – it is obvious to the Lady's eye from her place on the Widest Footpath that they have a rather distinguished palate.

The Lady is right, the Ragamuffins recognize the smell of Royal Spice still fresh inside the rotting meatballs they have scavenged in the dustbins of Cottonpettai. These meatballs have been cooked in iron vessels placed over coal fires in the Big Mansion. The Royal Ragamuffins, all four, have mothers they do not recognize. These mothers consumed this Royal Spiced meat, coal fire fresh, when the Ragamuffins were still foetuses inside their abundant wombs in accordance with their father's wishes.

When abundant wombs are not given sanction by the laws of matrimony, their foetuses enter the world as bastards, munumunuppus abound.

The long and wavy-haired Lady knows these munumunuppus to be true – the Royal Ragamuffins are bastards according to vital information buried in a blazing socket in the hippocampus of her skull.

The father aka the Baron of Extreme Excess aka ... well, his third name cannot be revealed as yet the Lady knows, and he cannot be bothered by bastards. In the Lady's reckoning, the Baron of Excess has a son, perhaps a daughter too, sanctioned by the rigourously defined laws of matrimony to show off to the world.

The Baron of Excess believes that daughters are replicas of their mothers – their identities are best kept secret once they are out of the womb.

The Baron of Excess however, according to the notes stored in the Lady's hippocampus, has a special concern for his sons, bastards, and otherwise. The Baron remains invisible to his sons for politically appropriate reasons. He has instead, surreptitiously instructed his Burly Black Cats to keep the dustbins of Cottonpettai abundant with cuisine seasoned with the Royal Spice – this feast is meant to fill the rather large and greedy stomachs of his bastard sons.

Invisible to the Baron's CCTVs, the Lady watches the goings-on in Cottonpettai with a surreptitious eye for bastard sons, and otherwise.

The Royal Ragamuffins have never seen their mothers – they are invisible by day, just like the father they do not know they have. These mothers become visible by night, but choose to stay out of sight of their sons, the Royal Ragamuffins. These mothers, all of them, have borne the foetuses of a powerful and moneyed man in the Indian Subcontinent to beget his muscular sons.

'Who pray are these mothers?' the munumunuppu-mongers want to know – they ask the Lady.

The Lady with the Slender Hands has read much, she says: 'These mothers are erudite, they have travelled all the way from the Pyrenees

'Past the Hebrides

'Crossing continents

'Assimilating, writing, speaking the Colonialese

'Yes! These women even speak the English tongue with the Pekingese

'The Penkingese, a pug

'This pug is a tease

'The pug, a cur

'Its earliest ancestor Shih Tzu is the Lion Dog of China.'

'What on earth is all this mumbo jumbo about pug and tease, and Shih Tzu for India's sake,' the munumunuppu-mongers cry. 'All we want to know, for India's sake, is why the Ragamuffins are known to have a royal bloodline in the first place.'

'Their mothers are like my sisters – the blood flowing through our veins is indeed royal,' speaks up the Lady. 'The Royal Ragamuffins ought to be proud of their lineage, especially begotten from their mothers' ancestry. In fact, one Royal Ragamuffin even has an ancestor from a long weather withdrawn dwelling in the valley of the steppe-sloped Yin Mountains in the southern border of China. This Royal Ragamuffin could well be the descendant of the mighty Tangs.

The Tangs, as you munumunuppu-mongers might want to know, are aristocratic inhabitants of the ancient Yin – you see, we women trace our ancestry to China and Spain and several other nations in between.'

Ancient parameters do not define the present social status of people with aristocratic lineages, and the Lady with the Slender Hands does not resent her past. She simply evokes her past in the present. The Lady with the Slender Hands simply speaks impeccable Español. Spanish aka Español is a tongue foreign to every other *manidhan* aka human being residing on the most prestigious and undoubtedly Widest Footpath of Cottonpettai.

I am at a prestigious high in the sky, practising my vocabulary in every other tongue I care to remember from the dictionaries on my father's Jewish shelf. On this high, I choose an impeccable lengua ... *si* ... an untarnished tongue to communicate with the people who have long left the Pyrenees to speak Colonialese, even with the barking Pekingese. These dogs, *si*, the barking Pekingese, are the favourite pets of the Baron of Cottonpettai.

TWELVE

THE MINISTER FOR SHELTERS has a fetish for barking dogs. His faithful breed of Rajapalayams – all white hounds with an ancestry in the southern region of the Indian Subcontinent

– always accompany the Minister to the Alarmed Hall of Parliament.

The Alarmed Hall of Parliament is twelve times wider than the Widest Footpath of Cottonpettai – it is the country's foremost meeting place for Suitable Somebodies with powerful political profiles – it has an address in the Undeniable Capital of India, and is much visited by the Minister for Shelters.

The Minister for Shelters has a fetish for larger-than-necessary constructions. The Minister encourages other Suitable Somebodies of his ilk to build larger-than-necessary houses, and eventually convert footpaths into their backyards.

At this juncture, is might seem that the Minister for Shelters has a special connection with Cottonpettai.

Well, the Minister has found a twin soul in the Baron of Excess. The latter soul has a Big Mansion in Cottonpettai to his name, and has solely been responsible for rendering certain nobodies roofless. These nobodies have been driven out of their hutments by the Baron of Excess not so long ago, and are now homeless. These nobodies with scant money now live in their new home, the Widest Footpath of Cottonpettai. The Baron is not just greedy, but wealth hungry – he has further used money from the coiffeurs of the Alarmed Hall of Parliament thanks to his twin soul to bribe his Tout. The Baron's Tout, in turn, has used all his wily clout to discourage the impressionable nobodies from investing any further money on repairing their tattered hutments. The Tout is so wily, he has encouraged the people of the Widest Footpath of Cottonpettai to sell their tattered hutments to the Baron's twin soul, instead.

Ever since the Baron has had the Big Mansion constructed in Cottonpettai, the Alarmed Hall of Parliament has been blessed with the Golden Tanjorapura Bells. These Bells break into an excited ring and crescendo each time the Minister for Shelters walks upon the red carpet lining the Alarmed Hall's 10 kilometre-long stretch from its Primary Façade to the Main Meeting Hall where all deals related to shelters and compensations thereof are sealed.

The Minister for Shelters, keeper of the Hall, is in fact a direct beneficiary of the Golden Tanjorapura Bells. Tanjorapura, with its giant Bull Monument is, in fact, the Minister for Shelters' much preferred pilgrimage spot after Shivling.

In Shivling, the ice Linga, manifesto of Lord Shiva, emerges in the season of mysteriously melting snow. Each time the Minister for Shelters embarks upon a pilgrimage to Shivling, he summons a certain Perky Female Pony – one of the many ill-fed means of transport in the Himalayan ranges, and mounts her. The Perky Pony is adolescent and rather weak – she trots unsteadily, and falters over and around the subconsciously melting glaciers of Solali. The Minister for Shelters has a six-feet high, and four-and-a-half-feet wide frame – he revels in the adolescent and menstruating Pony's unsteady trot with a prayer upon his lips to invoke the divine protection of the powerful Shivling. With every right step the Pony takes, confidently balancing the most honourable and pious Minister, a melting glacier disintegrates around the Shivling. This glacier, now one with the mighty Lord Shiva, mindlessly gushes into the fast-flowing Anjuna – this river is the rapidly raging Beas nadi's not-so-silent sister in these snow mountain parts. Despite the melting glaciers and the Pony's unsteady trot, the Minister for Shelters is determined to carry on his overnight journey past valleys wearing plunging necklines and mountains accoutred in brown or white suits of snow all the way uphill from Chandinigarh to Solali, across this hill town, and beyond its invisible geographical separator to Shilving.

Please note that Chandinigarh, a newly proclaimed model Metropolitan city in India, is the Minister for Shelters' native location. In this city, the Minister for Shelters lives in a kilometre-long bungalow christened by a globally travelled and Levitating Sanyasi. When the Minister's house of brick and stone was constructed twenty-five Diwalis ago, a Great Maha Havan with raging fires had been fed with mighty portions of ghee by the Levitating Sanyasi, and the holy man had gone on to christen the Minister's home OneKmBungWow.

Yes, that's how you say it – OneKmBungWow.

'Wow!' abounded the sahas in Chandinigarh upon that holy Diwali day even as the Levitating Sanyasi pronounced the name aloud once more, his voice dominating the firecracker-smitten skies. That day, the people of Chandinigarh, the saha-mongers, repeated the name over and again, but in vain.

The Levitating Sanyasi decided to end the peoples' problem, he explained: 'Say OneKmBungWow as fast as the yearly North Easterly winds scatter your well-oiled, combed and pinned hair out of style, and you will find yourself looping your tongue, and twisting it just right to utter the name of the house of fame.'

'OneKmBungWow ... wow ... wow ... bow-wow ...,' the saha-mongers repeated over and again, until, two and a half decades later, which is here and now, the citizens of Chandinigarh swear by the Minister for Shelters and his palatial house of fame.

Today, the saha-mongers swear by the Minister for Shelters – he has made all the citizens of Chandinigarh prosperous by the power of his Office. The mighty Beas flows all the way down to the State of Punjab, and never fails to inundate the lands of the rich saha farmers.

Chandinigarh is indeed prosperous – it has a shared postal address in the hot 'n' cold Punjab 'n' Haryana territory – these bold states are located in the northern regions of the Indian Subcontinent.

Perumal Arokyaswami's postal address is a closed door. Over three decades ago, this closed door remained open to strangers from 12 a.m. until 12 p.m., round the clock. This same door led the stranger Perumal Arokyaswami to Pascal Rebello de Fonseca's kitchen. The hearth of this home was a coal-fired cooking range, stranger than the rest of the ranges in the Minister for Shelters' Massive Kitchen given its unique environment-comradely design. Pascal Rebello de Fonseca called this cooking range, which chose to keep the carbon dioxide out of breathing range of the cook, the Oxygen Intense Smokeless Chulha.

This Chulha produced no smoke, Pascal Rebello de Fonseco breathed easy.

He breathed, he smoked a joint.

Pascal Rebello de Fonseca smoked up night after every other twilight.

Until one rain-fed night when Pascal Rebello de Fonseca smoked up on a fresh supply of Blue Mountain Utahkamand marijuana, breathed in his kitchen to haze out and witness the smoke from the Chulha slither into a freshly cemented sanitary pipe. The slithering smoke in reality a petrified Python which had travelled in the Baron's sedan all the way from the Himalayan Ranges, had decided to invite himself to Pascal Rebello de Fonseca's kitchen on that rain-fed night – marijuana is dear to all creatures big, small, fat, tall, shapeless, shapely and many other moving creatures, which fall under the gamut of God's creations.

Ever since the long Python meandered into the freshly cemented sanitary pipe that had been installed to make way for Pascal Rebello de Fonseca's carefully secreted ablutions, the man has stopped breathing in his Oxygen Intense Smokeless Chulha equipped kitchen.

Ever since Pascal Rebello de Fonseca stopped breathing in his kitchen, the weathered green door to his house has been permanently shut to Perumal Arokyaswami, and the rickshaw-puller's postal address has been suspect.

I suspect I once had an address. My address, a dead end in a city of dreams, gave me vanity. My vanity ... *si*, mi vanidad has no place in this snow-mountain valley – it has been supressed by a cold wind ... I have been stripped off my identity, mi congelar ... *si*, I freeze. Si, I freeze, I congelar in the cold distance between my lover and I. This distance is uncomfortably cold ... mi vanidad and his vanity have left us – yes, both him and I in a congelar. I freeze as the cold winds parch my torn labios ... mi lips, and mi vanidad.

THIRTEEN

IN THE SWELTERING MONTH of July, cold winds make a sweeping entry into Dundun – they parch the moist lips of *phusphus*-mongers, and tear their frond-thatched tenements – they lift all rubber-slipper-wearing citizens off the carelessly tarred and tardy ground they stand upon. These icicle-borne winds are harbingers of tongue-wagging, yes phusphus, and with it, impending doom.

That's right – there's doom in Dun – these untimely winter winds have gushed into the city via the cervix of a midsummer's day, and are blowing in random unity. '*Aai hai*, our frond-thatched roofs have been blown away by the winds in the forenoon of a sun-blessed day. These winds, they have blown their might over the summer sun – they are demons in disguise, they don't spell good news for anyone – certainly not for us – actually, not even for the Suitable Somebodies of the Indian Subcontinent. After all, if our roofs are blown, and the crops we've sown in their rice fields have all been stung by the icy winds and left to linger until they meet an untimely death, the Suitable Somebodies – all landowners in Dundun – will have no yield – they certainly cannot pay us for our timely labour. No thanks to the untimely winter winds. Aai hai, we are alive, but as good as untimely dead,' there's *phusphusana* in and around Dundun, as local tongues wag freely in the unruly cold air.

Hungered tongues are sharper than freshly sandpapered steel knives – the now roofless phusphus mongers stun the randomly united and raging winds but only for a par second. The icy cold winds can neither be bothered by phusphusana, nor their mongers – they enter every crevice they spy, and rage louder. These stinging winds, they are here on a mission – they must turn Dundun upside down.

Ah, every man, woman and child clothed in coarse native cotton attire and rubber slippers – also every cycle rickshaw plying in the city of Dundun, is upside down.

When everything is upside down, it is inevitable for a Sanyasi to appear on the scene. 'Why on earth is there so much *shooshaa* about Dundun anyway?' a meandering Sanyasi from the nether state would like to know.

'Bah, don't you know,' the phusphus-mongers speak with their heads stuck to the ground, 'Dundun, home to the six-faced clock tower, is an important Indian city – it occupies prime place on the Indian map in the northern belt – it is the capital of the State of Uppercommand, and is cascaded by the lower Himalayan ranges. Dundun is posh – every Suitable Somebody with a political profile at the Centre, also stakeholders of corporations and industries in every nature-blessed part of the Indian Subcontinent has a son or daughter, either or both enrolled in the country's most prestigious institution. Dundun has its nose up in the ferociously blowing and most untimely air – it is home to St. Alphonsious Pre-University College, the country's most prestigious institution – and is serenaded by century old Fir trees.'

This is no time for introductions to esteemed cities and their prestigious institutions – tongues hang loose as the intensity of the winds tighten their vicious reigns over Dundun.

'*Swoosh, swaash, shwaboom* – see how the Fir trees at the circumference of our very own prestigious St. Alphonsious Pre-University College are toppling from their rooted place of pride,' yell the Scouts and Guides of Uppercommand's institution for future Suitable Somebodies. 'It is no use staying rooted to our prescribed spots upon this Grand Assembly Ground, let the winds do their bit, and stand us feet up like the rubber-slipper-wearing populace of Dundun ... at least that way, we get to have some real human fun,' yell the Scouts and Guides who have been bound to live robotic lives, some more.

'Stay rooted, or bury your wind-weathered faces in shame,' bellows a voice above the combined yell of the eighteen-year-old boys and belles – all these teens are wards of politicians, industrialists and their moneyed ilk.

This bellowing voice cannot be ignored – it belongs to the Master of Sports for Suitable Somebodies. The Scouts and Guides of St. Alphonsious Pre-University College voice their fears no more – they unleash all their might, and drive their canvassed feet deep into the windswept ground. But these Scouts and Guides, they simply cannot seem to stand straight.

Nothing is straight upon this windy July day in Dundun – the Fir trees shwaboom some more – some even fall to the ground with thunderous thuds, their age-old roots now hang among the icy clouds.

The Scouts and Guides – they dig deeper, they stand their ground despite the thunderous thuds – they fear the ire of their owl-eyed Master.

The Master of Sports for Suitable Somebodies, on his part, is certainly not pleased with Scouts and Guides who simply cannot seem to hold their canvassed feet upon the ground, they are all swaying out of line for money's sake!

The Master bellows: 'Mind your line!

'Seedhey khadey ho jao iss acche desh ke behaya naujavano.

'Stand straight, you shameless youth of this prestigious country – I, the Master of Sports for Suitable Somebodies, will not tolerate all ye wannabe nobodies.'

The Master's crescendo is dissipated by four chimes from Dundun's half-a-century-old Clock Tower followed by another cold gust of Himalayan wind – he whispers loud enough for his own clogged ears to hear: 'What will the influential parents of these unsuitable somebodies say in the event their sons and daughters indeed want to be nobodies? No, no, this cannot be the case, these have to be somebodies must learn to stand upon their own two feet, and now, but how? Just how upon this unsteady earth am I to steady these wannabe nobodies, and ready them to join their counterparts –the blue-eyed Scout and two Guides at St. Peter's Friary in Utahkamand, to participate in the camp for the Braver than the Best this coming month?'

The Master's bellow and forced whispers, are drowned by another sharp gust of icy mountain wind – he shuts up, and watches the wannabe nobodies sway in dismay.

Where there's dismay, the meandering Sanyasi never fails to appear – he stands by the sidelines of the Grand Assembly Ground of St. Alphonsious Pre-University College, and watches the Master of Sports for Suitable Somebodies fret at the swaying nobodies. The Sanyasi smiles, he enters the Master's mind via telepathy, and finds a crooked thought fraught with lust, that too at this dire hour – chee!

The Sanyasi cringes despite his neutral state of mind.

The Fir trees shwaboom despite their sturdy barks.

The future Suitable Somebodies stay rooted despite the raging winds.

The mongers phusphus some more despite their inverted positions.

'Aai hai, never mind!' the phusphus about Dundun and its nether villages abound in response to the Master's bellow and ensuing whisper. 'Suitable Somebodies – the same bungalow people who own our paddy fields in the villages near and far – cannot be bothered by the unsuitable ways of their teenaged sons and daughters who are known as Scouts and Guides in these Uppercommand parts. The bungalow people's coiffeurs ring with coins of gold – treasure from which the Master of Sports for Suitable Somebodies can be bought and sold, we have been told.'

The Lady with the Slender Hands cannot be sold. She will make love only to those men her own manicured hands will willingly hold.

Perumal Arokyaswami has heard from munumunuppu-mongers that the Lady with the Slender Hands, his lover, has been sold by Pascal Rebello de Fonseca to a certain Moor from the nether regions of Pyrenees. The Moor is said to own a palace of sorts in the natural terrains of Spain – Perumal Arokyaswami does not see truth in what has been said by vagabond tongues. The rickshaw-puller knows only too well the truth that Pascal Rebello de Fonseca had withdrawn all connections with his ancestral land, save the language his forefathers spoke in the valleys of the Pyrenees when he chose to make a home replete with a smokeless chulha in the Indian Subcontinent. Certain Suitable Somebodies with bungalows at the Centre, in Cottonpettai, in Chandinigarh and even in Dundun, have warmed the pockets of munumunuppu, phusphus and saha-mongers to swerve the truth about the Lady's 'commodity' status in the Indian Subcontinent, and Perumal Arokyaswami will not take this gossip lying down.

Gapasapa-mongers are stirring lying gossip in the valleys of Khalaand – Jhoru Kanbi Badshah's mother has been bought and sold, they say in Marathi, their land's much spoken tongue. Jhoru is visiting his hometown on a holiday – there's gapasapa in the valleys about the woman he loves more than he does his status as a coolie – he will not take this slander, lying down. He has spoken the language of these valleys and mountains since his second night in a wooden cradle when his mother had rocked him with her own gentle hands ... Rocking her infant to sleep, Jhoru's mother had stroked his eyes, lulling him to sleep, and dream of being crowned the king of the upper ranges of the grand State of Maharashtra.

Jhoru Kanbi Badshah's infant dreams vanished in his boyhood – two nights after his mother left home, his eyes would shut no more. Ever since, his eyes have been wide open night after day as Jhoru beholds valleys sloping into hamlets ablaze with hearths by the foothills of Khalaand. But Jhoru Kanbi Badshah cannot stop by the foothills of his yet-to-be-conquered territory – he must make the best use of the secret and blatant paths right, left and meandering the Western Ghat mountain ranges to the top, all the way to the epicentre of his dreams. He must make it right to the plateaued top of the Khalaand Range where the mothers and fathers of Jhoru Kanbi Badshah's hamlet, Rozgaarnagar, toil in the Great Aaraamaayu Factory by day. By dusk, the mothers and fathers of Rozgaarnagar walk down the slopes of Khalaand, breeding leeches upon their dry and pealing near-naked feet. Their feet with waning rubber-cushioned slippers holed at the heels are accustomed to the leech-infested terrain of the sloping Khalaand Range. The blood of the people of Rozgaarnagar is food to every crawling leech in search of prey along the slopes of Khalaand, the much-visited Honeymoon Range in the Indian State of Maharashtra.

The air is cold and hot with pregnant passion atop this Honeymoon Range in Himalayan territory. I, a lone *mujer* ... *si*, a woman in these cold and hot ranges, dwell upon the Indian Subcontinent. A mujer, a commodity, the phusphus-mongers in these snow mountain parts say. I, a commodity floating above the Solali sky, yearn for a *luna de miel*. Yes, I yearn for a honeymoon in a city hidden to the roving eye between these snow mountain clouds. In this secret city, I will beso the man I love. My passion is not for sale, and the man I love, my prince, will beso me right back. Yes, my prince, my man will kiss me ... *si*, beso mi in full view of the munumunuppu-mongers roving in a land beneath me.

FOURTEEN

EVERY SINGLE TIME THE Lady with the Slender Hands sleeps with a tattooed man, the munumunuppu-mongers of Cottonpettai declare that she is on a honeymoon.

The Lady has a reputation, there's gossip about town that she is on a perpetual honeymoon with every other man in Cottonpettai.

'Is every other man in Cottonpettai tattooed?' the feminine species of munumunuppu-mongers want to know.

'As far as we know, Perumal Arokyaswami with the dandy cycle-rickshaw sports a tattoo upon his inner hand – this intricate design rests an inch above his left wrist. This tattoo is fragrant, just like the flower it represents – a species of Neelakurinji that grows uphill Utahkamand,' clarify the all-knowing male munumunuppu-mongers of Cottonpettai.

'Then why in Lord Muruga's – the most holy son of Shiva's – name is the Lady with the Slender Hands the ire of such slander?' the female munumunuppu-mongers must know.

'Where there's gossip, there's bound to be slander. Where there's slander, truth is an elusive cousin of the lie that has been spoken out loud and clear for all to hear,' a roving Sanyasi intervenes, and immediately puts all the gossip that has erupted at the Supreme Fish Market in main town Cottonpettai, to rest.

Where there's free gyaan, there's a fresh bout of rain – the shelter-less Supreme Fish Market is about to lose its stench if the munumunuppu-mongers don't act fast.

Fast, faster, fastest, the munumunuppu-mongers of Cottonpettai stop wagging their gossiping tongues – they rush to rescue their dead fish. These fish, all sorted by size and species – pomfret, seer, catla, the tiny nethili variety, sardines, even saltwater mussels, prawns and crabs – are all displayed on dark blue, fungus green, also pale pink plastic sheets which hug the unevenly tarred ground. The ground upon which the munumunuppu-mongers of Cottonpettai display and sell fish and their prawn and mussel cousins, occupies one quarter of the 2.5 metre wide Main Road.

This Main Road is long and wide – it is the perfect riding ground for Roadside Romeos who have played truant from their camp uphill Utahkamand.

Grrr, ghootarrr, sputerrr, whoooz, whizzzz ... the Roadside Romeos race on their hired motorbikes across the Main Road of Cottonpettai, threatening to revive the dead fish, which are fast being stacked into wooden crates by the munumunuppu-mongers – they are in a rush to meet the much talked about Lady despite the rain on this rather hot day downhill Utahkamand.

Cottonpettai is hot and cold upon this near monsoon day. The Lady is stirred by a lone drop from a passing cumulonimbus cloud – the rains that have drenched the Supreme Fish Market are fast racing towards the Widest Footpath of Cottonpettai.

Every time a passing cloud awakens the resting Lady, she is subject to a lewd whistle or two. Every other Roadside Romeo is adept at curving his lips to holler a whistle. Every single time the Roadside Romeos of here and there whistle passion calls to lure the Lady, the atmosphere bursts into the wayward ways and truant colours of pregnant passion.

The Roadside Romeos have arrived along with the rain – they pour their hot and cold passion upon the Widest Footpath of Cottonpettai where the now stirred Lady rests.

'When a Lady is stirred simultaneously by Romeos and rain, she is to be feared,' the Sanyasi whispers, loud enough for both Romeo and Rain God to hear. The Sanyasi, it seems, is omnipresent.

The Roadside Romeos, it seems, are all wannabe Suitable Somebodies – they suddenly find themselves drowned in a multi-hued volley of abuses risen from a stirred volcano. They remain drowned in abuses until the colour of anger – a disturbed shade of flushed red, manifests upon the volcano's chagrined cheek.

The Lady with the Slender Hands is a human volcano – her lips are red hot, she blurts not-so-niceties at the whistling and lewd post-teen Roadside Romeos.

The Roadside Romeos, all clothed in warm jackets and boots, freeze.

The Widest Footpath of Cottonpettai is not just warm, it is hot – it is thundering with the Lady's not-so-niceties upon this pre-monsoon day. Certain whistling Roadside Romeos, all future Suitable Somebodies hovering over the Footpath continue to whistle at the object of their attraction – their post-teen years have taught them little about heeding to any lady's red-lipped telling off. These Roadside Romeos have ears for a certain Master of Sports alone – he has taught them nothing about respecting a Lady upon a Footpath or anywhere else on planet earth for that matter.

There's munumunuppu about town, 'These Roadside Romeos, all children from well-to-do families are all being schooled at the most prestigious St. Alphonsious Pre-University College in Dundun – they simply cannot be bothered about any of those matters which address the proprietary of the Lady's chagrin.'

The Roadside Romeos don't care about losing their reputations to munumunuppus or their mongers for that matter – they have immediate matters of communication to analyse. They have not played truant from the National Camp for the Braver than the Best uphill Utahkamand to dissipate their unchained thoughts on matters like a lady's proprietary for hell's sake – these Roadside Romeos must analyse the nature of their whistling instead. Pregnant passion calls cooed by Roadside Romeos must always abide by the simple law of nature – masculine lust at the sight of a feminine form.

Slurrrp, drool the Romeos. The Lady is a feminine form, she has the figure of a nymph, and the Roadside Romeos must abide by the law of nature – they drool despite the rain, and rev their borrowed motorbikes to raise smoke unto the stirred volcano on the Widest Footpath of Cottonpettai.

The law of nature is not applicable to the Fellows of the Footpath, they have their own mating protocols to follow under the restricted freedom of open skies. The individual's privacy protecting law of India is not in favour of public passion on this Footpath, also its siblings and cousins in various cities across the country. The Constitution does not address the Footpath at all, and certainly not matters of mere passion between people who dwell upon it. The people of the Footpath have no postal address, and the Constitution cannot be held responsible for their lack of privacy in a public space. The Fellows of the Footpath have neither address nor identity, they are poorer than the vote-casting population, which lives in asbestos-roofed homes in urban slums. The asbestos-roofed homes are meant for people who cast votes for the minister of something or the other to earn their postal addresses and, more importantly, their daily wages to meet life's bare necessities.

The Minister for Shelters has stakes in the Asbestos Manufacturing Unit in the moneyed State of Gujarat. Jhoru Kanbi Badshah's grandfather was once a foreman in the same manufacturing unit in Algauv, a small rich town in the State of Gujarat. Only one man is rich in this town, he has a Big Mansion elsewhere in India. All the rest who work in the asbestos factory line live in meagre homes, many with no roofs in the same town. Jhoru Kanbi Badshah's grandfather worked as a duty-bound foreman in Algauv's Asbestos Manufacturing Unit until his lungs refused to recognize the pertinence of oxygen to his own body. Over forty-three years, dark fumes of carbon dioxide invaded thc oxygen in his body, the carnivorous cancer spreading into all the corpuscles, red and white, consuming every organ within its reach. Jhoru Kanbi Badshah's grandfather finally chose to leave Algauv with a somewhat functional organ, three bags, two wives, four sons, five daughters and two grandsons begotten by his first and only married offspring. With three bags, the entire family arrived in Rozgaarnagar at the foothills of Khalaand, and found themselves in an upcountry scenic escapade with an address in the State of Maharashtra. Yes, the entire family arrived without Jhoru Kanbi Badshah's mother.

'Mother?

'Aayi?

'Where is Jhoru Kanbi Badshah's Aayi?

'Hush!!!

'*Shantata!!!*

'Shantata ... hush ... you cannot talk about missing women in the foothills of Khalaand,' the gapasapa-mongers whisper.

In shantata, Jhoru Kanbi Badshah rests his wavy tuft upon the bark of an age-old Magnolia Tree. This tree is like his own mother, his Aayi – she offers him solace on the days he spends away from the Grand Nizamuddin to stopover at Rozgaarnagar. Jhoru Kanbi Badshah never fails to hope that his Aayi will return home to her son one day soon, for him to rest his wavy tuft upon her lap, and find solace.

The gapasapa-mongers hover around Jhoru's resting place, they seem to know all about his early childhood, they say: 'The day Kanbi Badshah turned five, he learnt that his mother had gone missing by a weak negotiation his father made. His father had turned his mother to trade in the small rich town of Algauv. At the age of five, Jhoru Kanbi Badshah knew a thing or two about trade, especially where missing mothers were involved. He knew that his mother would never cook another meal of khaima gravy and sukha roti over the fire upon their humble hearth. How can a traded woman be permitted to cook a gravy of mince and dry bread in the humble hearth of the very man who had sold her to gain his lifelong ration of wheat flour? Jhoru Kanbi Badshah loved the woman who fed him khaima and roti when he was three. Jhoru Kanbi Badshah left home to find the woman who had mastered the art of cooking on a coal hearth despite lashing rains on a distant road in faraway Algauv, in search of his bhagya. Only, in his future, years after leaving home, Jhoru Kanbi Badshah does not remember the name of the distinct road in the asbestos manufacturing town where he lost sight of his mother between the crevices of a wooden door that his little finger could not pry open. Jhoru Kanbi Badshah escaped home through that very main door, when his father had left it wide open on the same day that his now motherless son was to be sent to the Algauv Government School to learn to read and write, and make notes of what he had lost.'

I have lost my *cuaderno* ... mi notebook. I have written in the cuaderno, quite vividly, the distinct details of those passionate nights – eight in a row to be precise, between my lover and I. Those nights now hide in the bosom of pregnant clouds, I decide to play *al escondite*, but not with the love of my life – he has gone missing. The pregnant nubes around me have broken their bubble, it's raining, I tremble, I realize how much I love the man with the tattoo. I love this game of hide and seek that my father and I called al escondite in our ancestral tongue when I was still a girl of six. I am no longer a girl, I play al escondite with the love of my life – I decide to spend this Solali evening looking for passion between the folds of the ready-to-burst cumulonimbus clouds.

FIFTEEN

CUMULONIMBUS CLOUDS ARE WELCOME in the foothills of Utahkamand. The Fellows of the Footpath, the Lady with the Slender Hands included, are smitten by the powerful upward currents of these clouds. When these clouds burst, their abundant waters will align to negotiate a flood, and then come to placidly pool by the foothills of Blue Mountain Nilgiris.

Never mind the mosquitoes, some suspiciously anopheles that hover over this pool of fresh rain water – the Fellows of the Footpath are rather thick-skinned – malaria and dengue are strangers to these parts.

The Fellows of the Footpath know how to take heaven's abundance in their stride as they do the lack of bare living necessities – they dive into the placid pool of clear waters every monsoon midday when they return to their sky-roofed home for an afternoon meal of rice kunji. These clear waters are blessed, they know – they have especially been brought down to Cottonpettai by a transiting cumulonimbus cloud from a certain direction, which by the decree of the Baron of Excess and his band of Royal Ragamuffins, points heavenwards.

A piece of heaven – albeit fluid, is always welcome in Cottonpettai – the Fellows of the Footpath could do with a blessing or two.

Heaven, as the Fellows of the Footpath have come to learn from the Baron of Excess and his trusted band of Royal Ragamuffins, points towards a certain valley in the Himalayan region.

The Valley of Solali is heaven, home to every transiting cumulonimbus cloud. Sanyasi Solali Snowmountainwala floats on a rain-rich cloud – these wholesome bales of ice crystals are furniture in heaven by the decree of his mystic mind. The Sanyasi discovered this heaven by chance when fate found him lying distanced from reality on a bus bound from the newly christened metropolis of Chandinigarh to Manmanali, main town in the heart of Himachal Pradesh. Sanyasi Solali

Snowmountainwala found the distance between reality and levitation comforting in ways that cannot be explained to those who have never smoked the grass of the land – the Solali Weed. This Weed, the candid brand of inebriation with roots in the Himalayan Ranges. This brand of inebriation, in fact, the Sanyasi has discerned, is a racy contender to the Blue Mountain Weed, another feather in Utahkamand's already celebrated hat, er ... crown. When the Sanyasi physically rose from valley to mountain, arriving inebriated by road to main town Manmanali, Snowmountainwala added two prefixes to the lavish name he had acquired enroute to his Himalayan destination. He now wears the godly halo of an anointed levitator, and is widely respected as Sanyasi Solali Snowmountainwala.

Sanyasi Solali Snowmountainwala is a sought-after name in the minister and minstrel experienced heaven called Manmanali, and 10 kilometres uphill from here, all the way through inebriated mountain paths until the Valley of Peace greets you with the scent of Kesar. They call this peace-blessed valley Solali, abode of the man who has stretched the elastic boundaries of heaven to kiss the circumference of earth by means peculiar to candid inhalers of every variety of snow country weed.

Peculiar are the effects of snow country weed – they narrow Sanyasi Solali Snowmountainwala's senses to a secluded mist until his halo snugly embraces his egg-shaped head. Now, no sanyasi can be caught dead eating egg – it is neither vegetable nor dried fresh fruit of the Valley. Sanyasi Solali Snowmountainwala can be caught eating golden freshly dried and salted Badams at sunrise, sunset and the wee hours past the last stroke of midnight.

But, when the Sanyasi takes a puff of the Himalayan weed, he becomes invisible in the Valley of Solali, be it midnight or otherwise.

The monsoon months are here, and the Roadside Romeos have left the streets of Cottonpettai past the stark midnight hour to join their fellow Scouts and Guides under the cover of darkness. The hours past midnight lead to a dainty dawn, yawn into another noon, skip into eventide, and then another 12 a.m. in Cottonpettai. In the thick of darkness, the Lady with the Slender Hands is relieved that the Roadside Romeos have left her alone upon this midnight hour – she dozes peacefully by her lover's side. The Lady is in love with Perumal Arokyaswami. Her heart brims with love for the tattooed man at every hour of the day, and especially by sunset.

Sunset is here, and love is in the Solali air. Love resembles a beetroot – it drips its passionate purple hue between my disjointed dreams in the wee hours of dawn. The sky is a shade of beetroot, *amor* in the dawn-misted Solali sky. Torn away from my lover in his quest for libertad, I fear the hours of twilight – they seclude me from day, and take me into the shade of an unknown night sky. An unknown twilight … a *desconocido crepúsculo* – that's how my father refers to this sunset hour. I know where my father is. I do not know where my lover has gone … my heart sinks in the beetroot hue of crepúsculo, this twilight hour, heavy with yearning for distanced love as I run amok with passion, far away from home, in the nubes hovering over the snow-hugged Himalayan ranges.

SIXTEEN

IT IS RAINING HAILSTONES, and Perumal Arokyaswami's heart is heavy – there is a new demon for the poor to contend with – the Super Minister aka Minister for Shelters aka Keeper of the Alarmed Hall of Parliament has announced a primitive paisa ban in the Indian land. Perumal Arokyaswami is a respectable man – he will follow the decree of the land, but on no account will he enter the Strategic Bank of India. This man simply cannot break his already aching head about fulfilling the supremely stringent regulations involved in opening a savings account – he rests his wavy tuft upon his Lady love's shoulder.

Wandering munumunuppu-mongers are always present at scenes of extreme emotion, they ask: 'How can Perumal Arokyaswami possibly fulfil the bank's supremely stringent regulations? He does not have a postal address – it is absolutely vital for the rickshaw-puller to fulfil these stringent bank regulations in order to be able to open an account. These regulations are absolutely irrevocable, and the Keeper of the Alarmed Hall of Parliament is not about to budge on his decision.'

'That's true,' nods the Lady in assent, and strokes her lover's hair with her slender right hand, 'the Minister for Shelters is absolutely, irrevocably convinced that residents of Indian footpaths are not vital to the development of the nation.'

'Nation? What is nation,' the munumunuppu-mongers ask aloud.

'Nation,' replies the learned Lady, 'is a large body of people associated with a certain territory that is sufficiently conscious of its unity to seek or possess a government, peculiarly its own. If we are indeed united in this territory we proudly call Cottonpettai, no Keeper at the Alarmed Hall of Parliament can indeed provoke us to build shelters of our own, all for the sake of a provisional address to be provided in the Strategic Bank of India!'

'Here's a point of contention,' the munumunuppu-mongers think aloud, 'did Perumal Arokyaswami and the other Fellows of the Widest Footpath of Cottonpettai indeed vote the Minister for Shelters and his fellow members in the Ruling Righteous Government to power?'

The unuttered but understated truth prevails – Perumal Arokyaswami does not have the power to vote. Perumal Arokyaswami does not have a postal address. Perumal Arokyaswami does not have a Voter's Identification Card. Ever since Pascal Rebello de Fonseca's door has remained reportedly 'permanently shut for verification', Perumal Arokyaswami's current postal address remains suspect.

Sanyasi Solali Snowmountainwala's name wears his postal address. He is simply c/o Solali, and bigwigs come to seek his blessings at the Mohini Strength Park, where the Divine Guru levitates under the shade of a Kesar Tree in perpetual half bloom. The Minister for Shelters is a bigwig. This bigwig is enraptured by the supreme powers of Sanyasi Solali Snowmountainwala, and has come to renew his bank of blessings sprinkled by the Divine Guru.

Sanyasi Solali Snowmountainwala blesses the Minister for Shelters, and intervenes in the bigwig's fortune. The supreme Sanyasi thrusts a lucky silver coin into the prostrating Minister's hand, and also a requisition letter.

The Minister feels abundantly blessed, he pockets the silver coin, and reads the requisition letter.

Soon enough, in fact within two hours to be precise, with the Minister's supreme intervention of course, the shelter-less Sanyasi in question, has a Voter's Identification Card!

'Hail the Minister for Shelters, Shri Shri Shri Shri and Shri Sanyasi Solali Snowmountainwala will vote whenever the time is ripe for a poll,' utter the disciples gathered at this opportune time in Mohini Strength Park.

Levitating under his favourite Kesar Tree in half bloom, the Sanyasi speaks in favour of the poll and the Keeper of the Alarmed Hall of Parliament to all his bigwig and small fry disciples visiting Solali from other Indian states, also cities and towns abroad.

His disciples deliver their thanks in unison: 'Extol the poll, it betters the lives of halo-wearing, all-knowing sanyasis.

'Extol Shri Shri Shri Shri and Shri Sanyasi Solali Snowmountainwala.

'Extol the Minister for Shelters.

'Extol the homeless fellows, c/o The Widest Footpath, Cottonpettai, Downhill Utahkamand, State of Tamil Nadu,' the Sanyasi utters in response.

Extol my new home in the nubes. Ensalzar my floating home, it is a notch above the rest. Extol, *ensalzar*, *parattigal*, *stuti*, *prasasa* … I extol the clouds in as many tongues as I have come in contact with by nature of my trade. I sleep on wholesome bales of ice crystals, and ensalzar the moon-smooched stars as I float above the Valley of Solali.

SEVENTEEN

ABOVE ALL ELSE IS the need for shelter, a separator between earth and sky to give privacy to moon-smooched stars. An asbestos shelter will keep Jhoru Kanbi Badshah's father's skin from shrivelling under the intense rays of the mid-morning sun. Mid-mornings in the mountains of the Western Ghats fascinating the landscape of Maharashtra are hot. Mind-numbingly hot in the Indian summer month of May.

'May I come in?' a harsh beam from the mid-morning sun asks, and does not wait for an answer.

The sun does not believe in formalities, but Jhoru Kanbi Badshah's father does. For a start, he prefers to be called Abbajaan – Respectful Father by his truant son Jhoru. From the start, Jhoru Kanbi Badshah has instead preferred to call his father Badtameez Baap – the Arrogant Father.

'*Mere* Badtameez Baap, *darwaza kholo*,' the visiting Jhoru Kanbi cajoles his father to open the door with the gapasapa-mongers in tow.

On the other side of the door, the Badtameez Baap squirms in full gaze of the piercing sunbeam, which has seeped through the hinge. This hinge, which is wide enough to hold a brick through the crumbling door, is also the lone entrance to the Badtameez Baap's single-roomed hutment. Wide-hinged doors crumble when the parent wood has succumbed to the bite of the Insignificant White Worm. The Insignificant White Worm, by natural affinity to rotting wood, has found a happy home in the tiny and big crevices of the Badtameez Baap's door. This door serves as the sole entry to the hutment. The hinge serves as the only window in the humble abode.

'Humility is dead in this abode,' squirm the gapasapa-mongers. 'Imagine, the wife who was traded by the Badtameez Baap is considered dead to this abode.'

Jhoru Kanbi's tear ducts are stirred, he abandons his Badtameez Baap on the other side of the door and the gapasapa-mongers crowded near him to return to the shade of the Magnolia Tree, and cry in peace.

Jhoru Kanbi Badshah returns to this abode whenever his heart pines for his long-traded mother. He returns home every other week via a track he prefers over the rest for its scenic plenitudes, journeying ticketless on Train No. 12247. Ticketless from the Twenty Third platform of the Grand Nizamuddin aka Humongous Railway Station in the Undeniable Capital to Posh Bandra aka Harangued Railway Station in the Deniable Capital of India. But Jhoru Kanbi Badshah never has time to alight at the Posh Bandra Station, saunter the streets, and examine the wonders of Bubambay, the grand metropolis, which has consistently been denied status as capital of the Indian Subcontinent given its geographical distance from the Alarmed Hall of Parliament. This is no time to debate the status of Bubambay on the Indian map – this metropolis does not give leeway to the Minister for Shelters to garner votes. Way too many fellows prefer the footpath in Bubambay – there is neither time nor room to build shelters in this seamless city.

Forget Bubambay for now, it is a not-to-be-bothered-with city. Each time Jhoru Kanbi Badshah makes a trip to Rozgaarnagar, his brief stopover at Bubambay leaves him with just enough time to heave himself into the train bound to Victoria Terminus Know it All Station, which is a twenty-minute commute from Posh Bandra in the Deniable Capital of India. At the Victoria Terminus, there is just enough time for Jhoru Kanbi Badshah to switch tracks, and board the In a Jiffy train, which reaches passengers to unassuming stations along the route from Kashmirila to Kumarikanya, and Khalaand in between. Each time Jhoru Kanbi Badshah alights ticketless in Khalaand, he takes in five breaths of stony mountain air to cleanse the grief in his soul.

Soul cleansed, Jhoru Kanbi Badshah is a stony mountain air certified Full Right Scholar of Counter Abuse. By the way, the gapasapa-mongers who have the unique ability of travelling everywhere, even into Jhoru's thoughts, clarify that a Full Right Scholar is a person who specializes in gaining access to his/her birthright to maternal love, affection, fresh air and food through a well-researched methodology that is gained through life experience, and has no affiliation to any educational institution whatsoever. The Full Right Scholar uses this methodology to counter abuse against him/her, and other people of the ilk, and this definition has been introduced into the activist vocabulary by Coolie No. One: Jhoru Kanbi Badshah himself!

Ever since the day he learnt that his mother had been traded by his father for roti and khaima to feed his additional wives and multiplying offspring, Jhoru Kanbi Badshah let his counter-abuse run pandemonium. Every time he calls out to his Badtameez Baap, abuse loud and clear through the brick-wide hinge of the Insignificant White Worm infested wooden door, there is pandemonium in the single-roomed hutment.

Where population is in excess, pandemonium cannot be ignored. Jhoru Kanbi Badshah's step-mothers, brothers, sisters, and their step siblings – seventeen members in all – adopted into the single-roomed hutment squirm at the emotional excess between father and truant son. But, they all remain tongue-tied because Jhoru Kanbi Badshah, the eldest son, is Heir Supreme to the Badtameez Baap's fortune of ten gold *nagaths*. This truant son is heir to ten gold coins, which his great grandfather, in turn, inherited from his royal Afghan ancestors. It is said in the Badtameez Baap's household, that over a period of two centuries, the royal Afghans, in their turn, inherited the nagaths from their Persian forefathers.

Up here in the sky I have inherited neither *monedas de oro*, nor nagaths – I own a song of passion, which my father played on the century-and-a-half-year-old gramophone, resting on a three-legged stool beside the Jewish bookshelf in my childhood home. I have inherited a faint memory of words from five different tongues, and a famous song … a *famoso canción*. This famous song of the Yellow-billed Magpie, tune of fulfilled passion cascading the snow-mountains of Solali to form an eternal watermark amidst the vivacious ripples of River Beas, is mi famoso canción. This canción takes me to a passionate night with my wavy-haired lover. I sing this famoso canción to match the tone of the Magpie whenever I remember that precious beso … I shared that precious kiss with my prince, the love of my life, upon a winter's night when the stars shone their brightest …

EIGHTEEN

ANOTHER DROP OF RAIN wets the Lady's lips, she feels sappy, she feels love … The Lady with the Slender Hands knows love to be a watermark, un-intrusive and all-pervasive, visible only to the discerning few who recognize a heart when it glows red. Otherwise, love remains invisible to the eye, carefully shielded beneath the tangible cover of clothing and ribcage, the Lady has been told by her knowledgeable father upon a monsoon day in her childhood home.

'Thanks to the Lady's knowledgeable father, sunshine, moonshine or rain, love has a permanent home on the Widest Footpath of Cottonpettai,' whisper the intrusive munumunuppu-mongers. As usual, these mongers have sneaked into the resting Lady's thoughts without seeking her permission, of course – they choose to remain invisible to her watchful eye, they hide behind the Students' Luxury Bus which has just arrived from Utahkamand with a drill of Scouts and Guides.

The Scouts and Guides of St. Alphonsious Pre-University College remain visible to the eye in their well-washed, starched and pressed uniforms – they march down the lofty steps of the Students' Luxury Bus parked across the street from the Widest Footpath of Cottonpettai – with combined pride, they wear their identities for all to see. The munumunuppu-mongers now turn their attention to the future Suitable Somebodies, they declare: 'Their clothing is their identity, their pride. These Scouts and Guides need to stand unified in blue and white, also scarves with half-inch wide red satin lining – after all, this is a clothing combination carefully construed by the Master of Sports for Suitable Somebodies to give identity a sassy image.'

These future Suitable Somebodies are dressed to show off their superior status – they can be identified by their scarves and uniforms during their special expeditions in Indian mountainous regions, north, south, north-north east, and south-south west of the geographical location of their parental homes. For now, they are all lodged in the mountainous regions of Utahkamand to attend the special camp for the Braver than the Best. Right now, they walk past the Widest Footpath of Cottonpettai – they catch the Lady's eye, also her ear.

The Lady is all ears – she hears the Scouts and Guides banter about their expedition atop the moss-besotted mountains of Utahkamand. The Lady is now aware that the students of St. Alphonsious Pre-University College have all rolled down the moss-ridden terrain in slippery raincoats. They have all rolled like tap water washed stones – they have gathered no moss from this damp territory. How sad is that, the Lady feels, especially given the properties of moss. Moss, the Lady knows from her own days as a student, is a tiny flowerless green plant, without 'true roots', which grows in a low round carpet or cushion formation in damp territory.

The Lady's thoughts are interrupted by an iffy eighteen-year-old: 'Why bother to gather moss when the roots are not true to the ground which nurtures them?'

Smart thinking, the Lady inwardly feels, and wonders who the Scout's parents are. 'Roots are for monkeys who care to live by the benevolence of green ...' the Scout continues to exude his intelligence. 'You know monkey aka *bandhar* aka *maakad* aka *korangu* aka *mono* – they all rest atop the same Mighty Banyan Tree under which we make alegre aka merry with the Thentodas every night uphill Utahkamand,' the proud Scout shows off his prowess with language some more.

The Lady feels proud for no explicable reason – she feels an inexplicable connection with the Scout in perspective – she immediately decides to endearingly call him her own *alegre mono*.

I, a creature of mono ancestry, must stay alive – I feed on fruit from the Apple Tree in the Valley of Solali. But this thick snow-white valley speckled with green *manzana* ... *si* ... apples, is not my home. Home is a thick moss-covered mountainous terrain speckled with white mist. Back home, I see eyes of varied shades – brown, black, olive green ... also a shade of blue that my father called azul. These eyes, azul included, are all gathered in a tent of aerial prop roots, which are offshoots of the Mighty Banyan Tree. The azul eyes belong to a body and a head that knows mono from maakad and bandhar, even korangu. I have eyes and a body that I've cared to keep slim – my frame enables me to leap with ease from snow-mountain territory to moss green mountainous regions just the way a merry mono does.

NINETEEN

THE IFFY EIGHTEEN-YEAR-OLD IS indeed a mono. A merry mono who otherwise doubts every decree and norm prescribed by his father. The mono's father is touted to be an important Suitable Somebody who is out to Right all that's Left in the Indian Subcontinent. Upon this monsoon day, the monkey has left thoughts of his ever so Right father tucked away in the Students' Luxury Bus in an inner pocket of his overcoat. The mono has written down all his deepest concerns regarding his father's lack of commitment to the indigenous people of the Indian Subcontinent, and also his doubts regarding his parentage, in a blue diary. The mono does not believe that the woman he now refers to as his mother is indeed the person who bore him in her womb. But without his overcoat, the mono is rather alegre – he is wandering the streets of Cottonpettai on his weekend outing along with his fellow Scouts and Guides from the camp uphill Utahkamand.

'See how the "mono" walks! Mono, haha ... that's exactly how the Lady with the Slender Hands refers to him. This monkey, ya, ya ... mono, he has a regal saunter in his speedy step – he is so alegre. Ya, ya, alegre means merry – that's what I overheard the Lady say to her lover Perumal Arokyaswami. Ya, ya ... and this mono, he seems so merry despite his perpetual iffiness. You know, this alegre mono, he actually has a name, but it cannot be told,' whisper the munumunuppu-mongers about town. 'His name is powerful, it can trigger controversy on the Widest Footpath of Cottonpettai – drive it into your heads that any shame slandered upon this mono's name will put his entire household to blame ... To blame for an indecent name begotten on the streets of Cottonpettai by a certain grooming-to-be-Suitable-Somebody in Dundun's most prestigious educational institution.'

Let the munumunuppu-mongers hush each other up – only time will reveal the iffy eighteen-year-old mono's legal claim to a bilingual, dual cultural name. For now, the pen will tell the story of the eighteen-year-old Scout, and christen him Senor Singh Mono with reference to the context of his bloodline.

For now, the smart-thinking Senor Singh Mono marches down the street which is home to the Widest Footpath of Cottonpettai, and beyond the Baron's mansion to Chestershire Market. Senor Mono, and his fellow Scouts and Guides are here on their official weekend outing to buy the choicest variety of chocolates and biscuits, also imported shoes and sweatshirts to take back with them uphill to their campsite.

'Welcome to Cottonpettai's international variety market – we call it Chestershire – after all Cottonpettai is very English – this tier-two town is called the Lancashire of India,' yells one munumunuppu-monger to another, then one other ... Every monger here is a trader of either clothes and/or shoes, also imported French biscuits and Swiss chocolates, cigarettes, and the occasional Spanish Montecristo cigar.

Senor Singh Mono and his best friends, the two Guides, purchase Swiss chocolates and French biscuits – they prefer the Thentodas' freshly brewed toddy for quick inebriation, to the Spanish Montecristo. Senor Mono's not-so-best friends, the Roadside Romeos, have, meanwhile, pocketed two packets of cigarettes, and God knows how many Montecristo cigars. Senor Mono's other classmates, the Scouts and Guides of St. Alphonsious Pre-University College wander in and out of the many stores, also the Supreme Fish Market for canned tunas, and the Market for Native Factory Spun International Cotton Garments lining the Chestershire Market. Some Scouts and Guides even visit the Main Vegetable Market to shop for fresh and dried exotic fruit.

A merry outing inevitably ends when twilight is only an hour away from moonlight, and the Scouts and Guides march back in the direction of the Widest Footpath of Cottonpettai. The marching Scouts and Guides must board the Students' Luxury Bus, and arrive at the camp for the Braver than the Best, else their owl-eyed Master will let his tongue rant camouflaged expletives.

'How in Blue Mountain Nilgiris' name can an expletive be camouflaged, pray?' the munumunuppu-mongers who have overheard the concern of the Scouts and Guides want to know.

As if in response to their thoughts, the mongers hear one Guide mimic the Master of Sports for Suitable Somebodies aloud ... 'you figs, you funkeys ...', when what he really means is 'pigs and donkeys ...' The Guide's comrades burst into fits of laughter, and so do the munumunuppu-mongers who suddenly find it necessary to invite the future Suitable Somebodies to Cottonpettai's place of attention.

'Welcome to the Widest Footpath, you Scouts and Guides, and importantly the alegre mono,' the munumunuppu-mongers giggle at their own wittiness. 'You have arrived at the launch pad to Blue Mountain Nilgiris, home to the haves, have-nots, also halves by contention of lineage not very unlike the azul-eyed mono amongst you Scouts and Guides,' the munumunuppu-mongers declare.

Eighteen going to be Suitable Somebodies, all Scouts and Guides mentored by the Master of Sports at St. Alphonsious Pre-University College, have arrived at the foothills of Nilgiris. They stand on the Widest Footpath of Cottonpettai, and survey the incline of Nilgiris with brown, black, olive-green and azul pairs of eyes for every hidden path on the tree scanty steam engine rail trail. The eyes of each respective Scout and Guide are pertinent to the lineage the future Suitable Somebody has been taught to lay claim to. Senor Singh Mono, at this juncture, returns his thoughts to his doubts – he permits his azul eyes to rove the Widest Footpath of Cottonpettai, and pauses to meet a pair of globular organs very similar to his own. The Lady with the Slender Hands rolls her azul eyes in disbelief – she is indeed face-to-face with the alegre mono. The Lady thinks fast, she instantly covers her face, also her eyes with her sheer sari. The alegre mono must not stare at a pair of azul eyes for long, this is no time to unearth biological roots and the accompanying truths related to the Scout's lineage. The alegre mono is taken aback by the Lady's sudden rudeness – he chooses to ignore her instantly.

The Lady with the Slender Hands does not care to be ignored. Care to see the Lady? The Lady feels indignantly ignored by an eighteen-year-old wannabe Suitable Somebody whose father has a prestigious job in the Undeniable Capital of India. This eighteen-year-old Scout and his mannerless friends, have no business to be stomping around the private perimeter of her public home, the Lady indignantly feels.

'Stomping monos!

'Where are your modales?

'No manners.

'Modales-less creeps!'

The Lady with the Slender Hands screams.

She weeps, she screams.

Until the modales-less creeps catch the Lady masking her teary face with her slender hands.

In retrospect, why has the Lady with the Slender Hands wept?

One mono cries along with the Lady.

Why has Senor Singh Mono – yes that's the azul-eyed Scout's name – why has he wept?

Seventeen companions huddle around Senor Singh Mono to wipe his uncontrollable tears. The Lady with the Slender Hands has no companions – she continues to spill her controllable tears, now a salty puddle upon the Widest Footpath of Cottonpettai, until the Scouts and Guides have all driven uphill and out of sight in the Students' Luxury Bus.

Perumal Arokyaswami returns to the Widest Footpath by the fall of light.

By the fall of light, the Lady with the Slender Hands sits trite.

Perumal Arokyaswami, by instinct, holds the slender hands by fallen light. Together, the Lady and her lover watch the sun fade into the evening sky, leaving a light trail of orange from the leftovers of its retreating rays.

The rays have retreated, darkness prevails.

The Lady now feels free to rest her head upon her lover's shoulders – she takes a drag of the Vignesh Beedi every now and then, inhaling the masculine tobacco between her profuse tears. No darkness can mitigate her recently kindred love for an alegre mono on the Widest Footpath of Cottonpettai, the Lady cries all night through, and into the wee hours of dawn.

The wee hours of dawn are here, my eyes are puffed, my heart is light. My heart, mi *corazón*. Mi corazón, my prince. Where is mi prince, my love? How light love suddenly feels in this snow mountain territory – I look around, and find my body drifting atop a flying carpet. I am in a trance, I sigh, I cry tears of joy as my flying carpet steers me straight into mi prince's corazón! Love is a wise emotion on a … wait a minute, I remember, yay … *alfombra voladora*, that's right … a flying carpet embroidered with mountain flowers. *Una alfombra de flores* … a florid flying carpet … I take another puff of charas, the intoxicating weed of the Valley of Solali. I sigh, I cry, and through my haze and tears, I watch the pink flores on my alfombra voladora turn black … it is night once more, I am zoning out … bye, bye.

TWENTY

THE LADY WITH THE Slender Hands is the proud owner of an imported alfombra de flores. This floral carpet is the sole reminder of the Lady's royal lineage. Every now and then, the Lady rests her wavy-locked head upon this royal floral bed.

'What a fragrant sight the Lady is with her wavy hair, floral carpet, et al.,' beam the munumunuppu-mongers who can never seem to stop wagging their tongues. The Lady, unmindful of the mongers' tongues, continues to rest her wavy locks upon the floral bed – she falls asleep to dream of the many mattresses, some coarse, others soft, but all of which bear testimony to her varied lovers in the Indian Subcontinent.

The Lady's floral bed in the southern town of Cottonpettai is very unlike the religiously handwoven jute mattress in the northern Valley of Solali.

The bed upon which the jute mattress rests is a lonely place on thunderstorm nights. Sanyasi Solali Snowmountainwala is very lonely upon this disturbed night despite the comfort of the handwoven jute mattress upon which he rests his matted locks. The conventional cumulonimbus clouds doing the rhumba in the night skies above are pregnant with another impending thunderstorm warranting an avalanche in these snow-mountain parts.

An unintended storm often causes an avalanche of alarm in the human body, also in the heart. Sanyasi Solali Snowmountainwala's heart is human, it aches for a certain lady with wavy hair. 'How is the storm treating her tender heart,' he wonders aloud and immediately after levitates in silence to remedy the ache, also its cause.

The Great Southern Express leaves the Twenty Third platform of the Grand Nizamuddin – a storm builds up in Jhoru Kanbi Badshah's heart. His heart misses his mother, beats for a nameless significant other. The Lady with the Slender Hands is not aware that Jhoru Kanbi Badshah has taken her to be his significant other.

Significant people are known to be masters of their own destinies. People become insignificant when their dazzling destinies play hide and seek in dallying daylight.

Truant are ways of dallying daylight.

Let us not dally between beds and hearts, it is time to return to the Lady on the Widest Footpath of Cottonpettai before daylight vanishes behind the cluster of Eucalyptus trees. Here, the scene is set for a game of emotional hide and seek between the male Fellows of the Footpath and the Lady with the Slender Hands.

'Silence! There's mystery between the petals of the flores on the alfombra.

'Silence! There's *misterio*,' the munumunuppu-mongers have picked up some Spanish from the Lady's vocabulary – they feel free to incorporate relevant words in irrelevant sentences.

Meanwhile, there's misterio, er ... mystery in the Valley of Solali, it is time to dally.

It is time to return our attention to the Valley of Solali.

Sanyasi Solali Snowmountainwala stirs in the silence of the night. He has forgotten to levitate to a new height upon this night. At such height, the beady second eye of Sanyasi Solali Snowmountainwala spots a new entity in the mountains, north-north east of the Undeniable Capital of India.

I am an entity in the sky, si, the cielo ... In this sky, I am no star, si *estrella*. I am no bird here, no *pájaro*. I am. *Yo soy*, yes, I am north-north east of the Undeniable Capital of India, I am floating in the Solali sky. This sky has so much oxygen, it makes my head spin. I have spun a yarn about my entity from the comfort of my precarious position in this northern cielo – I? Yo? I, yo, yeee ... who am I? I am who I choose to be in the Solali cielo. I am ... it is way too soon to unravel the mystery of my existence. I exist in the sky, I am not vapour, I am, yo soy, ayyoooo, no no, forget it, my head is hazy, the charas is strong ... forget me not now ... For now, I must hide between the vaporous folds of the pregnant cumulonimbus clouds invading the Solali cielo ... bye bye, find me if and when you can!

TWENTY-ONE

A CERTAIN VISITING SPECIES of winged creatures encircling the Solali sky are together headed on a sojourn to Kumarikanya in the southern-most tip of India. This sojourn is inevitable given the present climatic condition in Solali – all creatures with wings must fly or die.

These ochre-winged creatures, the Greater Flamingoes, have all arrived from Spain to arch their slender necks into River Beas for a feast of Himalayan salmanoids, including a variety of freshwater fish. While hereabouts, these migrant Flamingoes also hope to seek the blessings of a certain holy man residing in these parts. But Sanyasi Solali Snowmountainwala has chosen to levitate, and will not open his eyes, not even the third one located slightly towards the left of the centre of his wide forehead to bless these migrant winged disciples. There are snowstorms upon this warm August month, the Beas is frozen white – the visiting Greater Flamingoes must find bluer waters, and also another sanyasi – preferably one with his feet on the ground. The Greater Flamingoes are quick to grasp the situation – they have a chirpy conference, and arrive at a smart conclusion – they are now set to fly in another direction, to the southern-most tip of the Indian Subcontinent. The people of this nation commonly refer to this tip as Kumarikanya, and also by its other more Colonial name – Cape Comorin.

Cape Comorin dips her tresses, and then her entire face into the Laccadive Sea – she has word from the fish that a certain species of winged creatures with origins in Spain are southward bound, she is rather pleased.

The winged creatures from Solali are quick to think, and quicker to fly. They fly across the Indian Subcontinent in record time touring the States of Punjab, Delhi, Uttar Pradesh, Madhya Pradesh, Andhra Pradesh, and across the Western Ghats encompassing parts of Maharashtra, Karnataka and further down to Tamil Nadu – they hover above the Widest Footpath of Cottonpettai. The Greater Flamingoes, for some strange reason, feel at home in the vicinity of this Footpath – they have heard lilting strains from a Spanish Rhapsody, and a certain Lady with wavy locks whispering sweet nothings to her tattooed corazón. Her corazón, Perumal Arokyaswami's right hand holds his Vignesh Beedi between his slim lips, his left hand strokes his Lady's hair, his eyes take delight in the hovering Greater Flamingoes, a rare treat in Cottonpettai's cloudy skies. The Lady follows her lover's gaze, she gasps in wonder at the Greater Flamencos hovering above the Widest Footpath of Cottonpettai – she engages in a conversation with the winged visitors from her ancestral land. The Lady then goes on to explain the Flamencos' presence in the Cottonpettai skies – these winged creatures have undertaken a rather brave flight all the way from Solali in the nearly northern most tip of the Indian Subcontinent to the country's southern-most helm, Kumarikanya. Almost instantly, his heart, his corazón, the Lady with the Sender Hands, tells her lover the tattooed, and handsome Perumal Arokyaswami, to take a brave trip upon a sailing ship to call it quits with poverty. The Greater Flamingoes hover above the Footpath for just a second more, and then bid farewell to the Lady and her lover at the onset of moonlight.

At the onset of sunrise, Perumal Arokyaswami opens his eyes to capture a great ball of fire descend over the ranges of Blue Mountain Nilgiris yonder – he navigates a kiss upon his Lady's beating bosom. The rickshaw-puller's own heart is beating rather fast, his mind has decided to take a sailing ship from Kumarikanya – India's southern-most conclave of salty waters, and across the Laccadive Sea to the pearl rich shores of Cololomambo, the Undisputed Capital of Serendib.

Perumal Arokyaswami has heard from disputable sources that he has a postal address in scenic Serendib. He has gathered every spare paisa from his rickshaw-pulling toil to broach the disputable topic, and ask for the Lady's hand in marriage. But the Lady has put her foot down and insisted that the rickshaw-puller use every spare paisa hidden beneath the rexine seat of his dandy to sail the Kumarikanya–Cololomambo Streamliner, Coolie Class, to the oyster-washed shores of Serendib. But this saved paisa will not buy Perumal Arokyaswami the Blue Passport, stamp of his citizenship in the Indian continent, his permit to the Serendib.

Perumal Arokyaswami does not own a Maroon Passport, stamp of his Serendib citizenship either, the Lady points out. Perumal Arokyaswami must device a fool-proof plan to travel unnoticed on the Kumarikanya–Cololomambo Streamliner to find his postal address in Serendib, says the disputable source on the Widest Footpath of Cottonpettai.

'Who on planet earth is the disputable source on the Widest Footpath of Cottonpettai?' a nosy munumunuppu-monger states the pertinent question louder than he intends.

'Every single resident upon this Footpath has an identity, but it is disputable,' replies the Lady. 'Every single Footpath resident's identity is disputable for lack of a legal document as prescribed by the Consolidated Constitution of the Indian Subcontinent!'

The munumunuppu-mongers lack sympathy for the people of the Footpath and their disputable identities, they scoot.

The moon has risen one more time – it shines its peace upon the disturbed Footpath in Cottonpettai. Fingers intertwined within his lover's, Perumal Arokyaswami seeks peace of mind – he confides his rather dangerous postal address finding plan to the Lady with the Slender Hands. The Lady is not too pleased, there is trepidation in her love-struck bosom.

Perumal Arokyaswami is pleased by the trepidation in the Lady's bosom, he allows his tongue to meet his lover's downturned lips. He draws her close, and holds the Lady in a tight and smothering embrace, whispering *hadavata* – the Sinhala word for heart – into his corazón's tender ear. Perumal Arokyaswami has much love to bestow upon his hadavata, he must waste no time in adding a definite postal address to his trousseau, and then a passport to ask for the Lady's hand.

The nosy munumunuppu-monger has a sharp ear and a rather long tongue – he states facts about the Lady out loud. 'The Lady with the Slender Hands cannot be won over by a mere postal address in the Serendib. Her Highness has won places in many homes, with postal addresses across the world, in Chandinigarh, even the Undeniable Capital of India. But the postal address which keeps her sane, is the Widest Footpath in the corner most lane where the Lancashire of India submerges its boundaries with Mettupalayam, the Station for Erstwhile Steam Engines downhill Utahkamand.'

'Who is sane?' a toddy-besotted Guide who has snuck downhill Utahkamand with her comrades laughs, and carries on:

'Hehe Haha Hoho Heyhey

'Olayee, Olo,

'Ola!

'Hello!

'*Vanakkam.*

'*Namasthe.*

'Helo?

'Hola!!!'

'Hola', replies her comrade Senor Singh Mono, wiping his tears, beaming pleasantly at all the Suitable Somebodies – Scouts and Guides from across the Indian Subcontinent – they have all gathered by the foothills of Utahkamand, numbers adding up to two hundred and twenty-three upon a not-so-freezing August morning.

Upon this August day, I spot Serendib from the freezing Solali cielo ... brrr ... I am in a *lugar apretado* ... a rather tight spot ... I am in a tight apretado because I see Serendib sailing in the oceans south of India's southernmost tip from my position up here in the northern sky of Solali ... I spot a moving island country, I see ...

TWENTY-TWO

THE MINISTER FOR SHELTERS is in a tight spot. His swollen feet, rendered so by the Solali snow, have left him with a pair of snakeskin leather chappals glued tight unto his unfeeling and blue limbs.

'How in freezing Solali's name will the Minister pay obeisance to his guru, the one and only levitating Sanyasi Solali

Snowmountainwala?' the phusphus-mongers exclaim a tad softer than they usually speak for fear of being pulled up by a politician in power. 'The Minister's chappals are so stubborn, they stay glued unto his blue and frozen feet. The Great Fir Tree by the façade of the open-to-the-sky abode of our very own and holy Sanyasi has a larger than life board glued unto its aged bark. The board sternly decrees clear instructions on chappals, leather and snakes in that order for the Minister and other disciples to take note of.'

With chappals excruciatingly glued unto his feet, the Minister for Shelters limps his way to the façade – he cannot help but stare at the words on the larger than life board – he immediately reads the message out aloud.

'Chappals: Footwear, usually made of leather, designed free-clasped, almost always minus a belt to keep it fastened around the ankle, largely worn by men of politics in India even when it's raining snow in the Valley of Solali. Chappals are finicky, after all they were once living and breathing as the skin of creatures that slithered through the many valleys which define the incline of the Himalayan ranges. The slithering life referred to in this definition of chappals are indeed snakes. Skin once detracted from the snake's body is said to be leather of highest conceivable quality. Chappals that Ministers and other Suitable Somebodies wear are invariably fashioned out of snakeskin leather, and cost a fortune.

'Leather: Material made from the skin of an animal by tanning or any other process to texture it. Snake leather is considered to be an exotic product alongside the tanned material produced from the skin of its reptile cousins, the crocodile, lizard, ostrich, emu, even the mammal camel. No disciple of mine, including a Minister of any rank or order, is permitted inside my abode with leather on his or her feet, frozen or otherwise.'

The Minister visibly cringes – the leather on his chappals belongs to a now dead Indian Python. When the reptile turned six last summer, he was especially slain to fashion a pair of chappals for the Minister. Until last summer, the Indian Python ate rats and rodents, which carried flu into the brick and mud homes of the citizens of India. The now dead Indian Python was imperative in preserving human health, especially among the have-nots in the Valley of Solali.

'Is the life of the Minister for Shelters imperative?' the phusphus-mongers giggle, but very softly.

The slain Indian Python strangles the Minister's swollen feet in death, the politician screams. Sanyasi Solali Snowmountainwala opens his third eye – no, the Minister cannot die … not so soon, not so easily. The Sanyasi immediately descends from his high position of levitation to rescue the Minister for Shelters from the endangered serpent species. The Sanyasi steps outside his abode with a concocted liquid in his brass *kamandal* aka bell-shaped vessel – he orders the Minister to open his mouth. The Minister consumes the liquid – a concoction of snow mountain weed infused with other secret herbs from the holy vessel, and promptly urinates in public.

'*Yiyeessshhh*,' cry out the phusphus-mongers at this public downpour.

'*Aaaaahiisshhh*,' gloats the Minister for Shelters in public – the diuretic concoction of weed and herb has magically reduced the swelling in his feet.

'Hurrah, my feet are free of the suffocating Indian Python,' the Minister gloats some more.

'Free, indeed!' comments Sanyasi Solali Snowmountainwala with a visible smirk upon his pursed lips.

No matter what the Sanyasi decrees, for now, the Minister for Shelters if free of his exotic and suffocating snakeskin chappals. The Minister must return home to OneKmBungWow, asap – these are the Sanyasi's orders. The Minister must prepare for the Ablution from the Wrath of the Indian Python Maha Yagna in the aftermath of having slain a hale and slithering Indian snake in the prime of his reptilian life.

'The Maha Yagna,' the Sanyasi goes on to explain to the gaping phusphus-mongers, and other devotees from Hindustan, Pakistan, Uzbekistan, also a grey French-bearded Moor from Spain, and saffron-attired disciples from every other conceivable country on planet earth, 'is a holy ritual performed in the presence of Agni (fire) by the Big Brahmachari (an agent) to eradicate sins and purify the Main Performer: the Minister for Shelters. Under my aegis, the Minister for Shelters has performed thirty-six Maha Yagnas, each to eradicate a sin he has perpetrated against the law of nature, since the day he assumed office as the protector of shelters for the documented citizens of India.'

The munumunuppu, phusphus, saha and gapasapa-mongers in the southern, central and northern regions of the Subcontinent have declarations to make about certain people living in India.

Aho! Perumal Arokyaswami is not a documented citizen of India.

Ay! The Lady with the Slender Hands is not a documented citizen of India.

Arere! Jhoru Kanbi Badshah is not a documented citizen of India.

Alas! The Minister for Shelters is a documented citizen of India.

Floating seamlessly between the whispers of the August winds, I am no citizen of the land I was born in. I, a citizen of I-don't-know-where, have landed a home in the sky where bricks and stones are unknown. In this sky, there is no footpath to lay my head upon. In this sky, a pregnant cumulonimbus cloud is *mi corona*. I wear my crown ... si, mi corona, like a queen in a Minister's dream.

TWENTY-THREE

THE HALOED AND BARE-CHESTED Sanyasi Solali Snowmountainwala does not wear a crown – he lives like a king.

'The man who roves the Valley of Solali accoutred in nothing but a loincloth is indeed *hamara raja*, our very own king,' declare the phusphus-mongers who hover outside the Sanyasi's open-to-the-sky abode come sun or snow storm.

'Who on planet earth is responsible for making this Sanyasi king?' the visiting Moor from Spain would like to know.

'None other than the Minister for Shelters – he is the moneyed man who lives in a heavenly bungalow right here on planet earth,' confess the phusphus-mongers. 'Thanks to the Minister for Shelters' sorry plight, Sanyasi Solali Snowmountainwala is rather rich with precious currency from Spain, the Serendib and the Mountains of Afghan. In lieu of absolving the politician of all his sins time and again, the

Sanyasi has been suitably rewarded with a brimming bank account perpetually inundated with illegal money, thanks to the Minister's affairs with entities from across the seas.'

'What sort of "*asuntos*" ... er ... I mean "affairs" does the Minister have?' the French-bearded Spanish Moor who was denied a wavy-haired damsel by Pascal Rebello de Fonseca in Cottonpettai over three and a half decades ago, would further like to know.

'The affairs of the Minister for Shelters are sometimes physical. These physical affairs remain secret to the members of OneKmBungWow,' the phusphus-mongers who seem to know everything about everybody say. 'By the way, OneKmBungWow happens to be the name of the Minister's mansion downhill Solali in the rich city of Chandinigarh. The Minister has an immediate family – it includes approximately three permanent members. The Minister's mistresses, however, are not his family – they have not been allowed permanent residence in his mansion, OneKmBungWow. Pssst ... the Minister's mistresses are however granted temporary residence – he entertains them in the secrecy of his plush-bedded private chambers.'

Up north in Chandinigarh, those who seek temporary residence at OneKmBungWow are homeless – they, by personal choice, have decided to forgo access to any Indian Identification Proof either by way of a Blue Passport, Driving Licence, Ration Card, Voter's Identification or even the disputable Aadhaar Document.

The Lady with the Slender Hands has once been a temporary resident at OneKmBungWow – she has forgone this shelter by choice. It is too early to probe into matters of personal choice made by the Lady with the Slender Hands. The Lady does not wish to make a noise about her personal choice.

Down south in Cottonpettai, Senor Singh Mono and his two Guide comrades realize that the Lady cannot be ignored, especially in her silence. The Scout and Guides have played truant from their camp upon this moonlit August night to pry into the asuntos of the Lady.

'Why on earth do Senor Singh Mono and his Guide friends want to poke their not-so-long noses into the silent Lady's affairs?' wonder some munumunuppu-mongers who are out on a midnight stroll.

The answer is complex – Senor Singh Mono cannot quite comprehend the silence that has been maintained regarding matters concerning parentage in his father's ministerial bungalow. Ever since the impressionable Scout's azul eyes met the Lady's equally blue windows to the world, the future Suitable Somebody has made it his life's mission to coax the truth out of his father's perpetually pursed lips regarding his mother's origin.

There's no time for silence indeed – Senor Singh Mono has decided to confront his father regarding his real mother, that too in the presence of his foster *mataji*, asap.

Senor Singh Mono's biological mother cannot be replaced by the foster mataji aka Caretaker his father is legally wedded to. The Caretaker in question can only be a wife, bedmate to his father on the nights that there are no temporary residents in the plush-bedded chambers of the Minister's home.

The Caretaker has made a choice to remain the legal wife of the Minister for Shelters. Is is rumoured that the Caretaker is the only daughter of the Supreme Legal Head of the Indian Nation, and must uphold all that is constitutionally right – she has decided to remain married to a man who loves no one but himself.

The Caretaker has a mind of her own. When her mind will change, turn against the Minister for Shelters, I do not know. What I do know from the position I have taken, is that there is a change in altitude – it has been inculcated by a new layer of winds circulating above the Valley of Solali. These new winds are evasive, and the altitude is higher, also shakier than I have grown accustomed to in these snow-mountain parts. I twirl and swirl in this evasive altitude. Suddenly, I am game to change for altitude. I play a game – I am a *descalzo bailarina*, a bare-footed ballerina twirling on my toes to the natural symphony of the North Easterlies. Sorry, the effect of the charas hasn't worn off fully I guess ... so, ballet is the only sure-footed way to stay firm in the face of impending *cambio* ... si ... *inminente* change ...

TWENTY-FOUR

THERE IS A CHANGE IN the weather by the hills of Utahkamand. Today, the destitute winds from the high-pressure belt of the northern hemisphere wreak havoc in the near southern-most tip of India, giving August in these blue hills a bad name. They call these destitute winds the North Easterlies.

The Scouts and Guides of St. Alphonsious Pre-University College study the weather chart et al., and trace the journey of the destitute winds before they set out on their night crawl. The Scouts and Guides crawl by night to explore the temperament of the jungle. They must adopt the same 'live to let live attitude' of the jungle folk and resident animals, they have been told by the Master of Sports for Suitable Somebodies. For once they agree with the Master of Sports – crawling by night is a natural drug. Better than weed, more dazzling than the aftertaste of the divine drug Magic Mushroom, night-crawling sends blood rush poker straight into an impressionable eighteen-year-old head. When the head is well-fed with one's own blood, the magic is evident – the Scouts and Guides live it up with the jungle folk in silence.

The Master of Sports smells magic in the jungle air – he hopes that the Scouts and Guides will continue to be smelt, and never heard by night. The jungle is kind to the Scouts and Guides from the Undeniable Capital only when the Law of Absolute Silence is strictly maintained.

Thanks to the abnormally long and rather loose tongue of a visiting Moor in Solali, there is much ado about a certain missing Lady in the Undeniable Capital of India. Her mother country Spain, wants the Lady with the Slender Hands back, asap.

'ASAP!' The phusphus and the munumunuppu-mongers simultaneously repeat … 'as soon as possible!

'What is possible is left to the whims of the Indian Diministry.

'The Indian Diministry comprises a board of Unsuitable Ministers for Suitable Posts.

'Shake up the Diministry if possible!
'As Soon As Possible!
'ASAP!'

Please lend me a hand, asap! My hand is shaking, my *paracaídas* ... you know mi parachute is collapsing ... Mi paracaídas and I are a combined entity. The turmoil in the sky is unsettling our combined centre of gravity. Fasssttt ... cielo ... heaven ... I know I am making no sense, but this is unsettling. Faster than fassst, please ... my parachute and I have merged with icy ripples ... River Beas is in my mouth for cielo's sake! Lend me a hand, fasssttt. Faster than fasssttt ... how can I swallow this *bullicioso rio* ... you know? No, you don't ... bullicioso aka rambunctious, *rio* aka river. Help is not forthcoming from where I speak, there is no hand to separate me from the icy rio's ripples, I swallow the rambunctious river they call Beas in these snow-dressed parts. I swallow the pride of this snow-mountain state ... I guess I can swallow anything after inhaling so much charas – bah!

TWENTY-FIVE

THE LADY WITH THE Slender Hands must swallow her pride. The Lady must leave the royal confines of the Widest Footpath, Cottonpettai, Tamil Nadu. The Lady has been looked in her azul eyes by a certain training to be Suitable Somebody for cielo's sake, she takes a deep, long drag from a fresh Vignesh Beedi, but to no avail. The Lady is not herself – she realizes she hasn't ignited the beedi, she sighs.

She sighs, she cries, she holds the unlit naati beedi between her lipstick red pout – the Lady with the Slender Hands is frazzled, she decides to confide in Perumal Arokyaswami.

What one decides to do, seldom coincides with one's action.

There is action in Chandinigarh – the Minister for Shelters wanders here and there, barefooted, to appease Dev Nagraj the Snake Lord. The here and there includes temples for every single God who has played a significant role either in the Mahabharatha or the Ramayana, also snake holes, Neem and Banyan trees, public parks and private wells. If one watchfully wanders the streets of the most well laid out double capital and union territory of India, yes Chandinigarh, one is bound to find a snake hole by the Bombastic Banyan Tree right in the middle of this posh city.

Sanyasi Solali Snowmountainwala once sat under the same Bombastic Banyan Tree to offload his stress in a puddle of puke, the discomfort emanating from his food-bereft stomach and then out through his long unwashed mouth. The now Sanyasi Solali Snowmountainwala was then called Puke Paaghal, his constant ablutions earning him the name of a vomiting madman. The sole difference between then and now is the Sanyasi's origins. Then, nobody knew where he came from, they couldn't care less, they shunned him, and simply called him Puke Paaghal. Now, nobody knows where he comes from. In fact, people couldn't care less where he comes from, they offer him obeisance, and simply call him the one and only holier than holiest Shri Shri Shri Shri and Shri Sanyasi Solali Snowmountainwala. You see, the big difference between then and now is the name, and the Sanyasi title alone.

The name is of consequence in matters of matrimony. The name is of consequence in matters of singlehood. When Puke Paaghal decided to give his name up, he chose to be called the celibate Sanyasi Solali Snowmountainwala, despite his continued interest in his long-dead wife.

This Sanyasi is now an ascetic, a monk, a man who has given up all worldly desire, especially lust, to attain nirvana.

Each time Sanyasi Solali Snowmountainwala remembers the Lady with the Slender Hands, he attains nirvana. Time accumulates memories, which surface on lonely nights in the Solali snow.

I feel lonely in the cold texture of the raunchy ripples of Rio Beas … I remember those raunchy nights when I slept, my hand upon the *Príncipe*'s hand … I feel the texture of his flesh, the Prince, si, my Príncipe is near.

TWENTY-SIX

PONDERING THE EQUATIONS OF life back in the environs of Rozgaarnagar, Jhoru Kanbi Badshah rests his head against his favourite Magnolia Tree, and contrary to his firebrand personality, quite resignedly, reconciles to the fact that he indeed was never a prince. But his mother did not bestow Jhoru with the title of Badshah for nothing, his firebrand head counters him. A Badshah is an Emperor, and the entire world is always at his beck and call – he counter-reasons his own reconciled thoughts. Jhoru is a Badshah because his mother said so, and he is not about to give up his title for the sake of peace in his Badtameez Baap's pitiable home. Jhoru Kanbi Badshah believes, deep inside his flappy heart, that his mother is not dead. How on earth is a Badshah to bring a long-dead mother alive ... he is, after all, no Sanyasi who wears a third eye upon his broad and all-knowing forehead. The Magnolia Tree, who has listened to Jhoru's quandary in silence, now sends a solution in response – she drops a stem of her golden leaves upon the Badshah's turbaned head.

Jhoru Kanbi Badshah is now an enlightened coolie – he has decided to listen to what his Badtameez Baap has to say, fully well aware that his biological father's verbal diarrhoea is bound to leave a loud and astoundingly indignant stench, given his fallen entity as a wife-trader. Jhoru and his childhood friend, the Magnolia Tree, spout a poem on the fallen entity in question.

'Fallen entity ... Jhoru's father is a *gira hua insaan*.

'When an entity falls, trees are at stake.

'When an entity falls, death by disappointment is inevitable.

'Where there is death, there are coffins.

'Coffins are made of wood.

'Wood from trees.

'Nature's grief – trees are at stake!

'But whose life is at stake?

'The Badtameez Baap continues to have a life.'

Jhoru Kanbi Badshah, who has arrived at his father's home, stands face-to-face with an almost rotten front door – he continues to listen to his Badtameez Baap in silence. The Badtameez Baap is hysterical, he continues to brandish evocative expletives regarding his son's parenthood.

'*Aai, hai* ... the Badtameez Baap has just called his son a *harami*,' the gapasapa-mongers of Rozgaarnagar and every other hamlet in Khalaand have emerged out of the thick jungle to exclaim so loud, the skies thunder.

The 'bastard' son has the last hysteria. Standing on the other side of the open slat, the son brandishes his only weapon called Will in the manner of the invincible Emperor that he is, and whispers a vow to the thundering cumulonimbus clouds.

The cumulonimbus clouds have heard that Jhoru Kanbi Badshah will find his mother and call the Badtameez Baap's expletive a con, asap – they thunder some more.

'But how will Jhoru Kanbi Badshah find the woman he has lost close to two decades ago to a trade rumoured to be most unbecoming of a mother?' the gapasapa-mongers ask aloud.

The how is immaterial ... the Will is the only material, albeit intangible, which Jhoru Kanbi Badshah must harness to find his long-lost mother, the thundering cumulonimbus clouds seem to respond. The clouds make an additional effort and break into rains immediately – they drench the Western Ghats, indulging every crevice in the eighteen ways uphill to the premises of the Aaramaayu Factory that Jhoru Kanbi Badshah will meander by the might of his renewed Will to commence his search for his long-traded mother.

Mothers can be traded for *khaima*.

Mothers can be traded for *meen khozhambu*.

Mothers can be traded for *carne de cerdo salada*.

No beef mince, no fish curry, nor salted pork can bring back the traded mother to her hearth. She is still flesh and blood, and has a traded place on the Minister for Shelters' head. The traded mother is a feather on the Minister for Shelters' political topi … This topi, a cap, a psychedelic embellishment, prominent with red and purple stripes, is a perpetual feature on the Minister's near bald head.

A topi is meant to cover all that which cannot be displayed in public.

The emotion which perplexed my hormones on a tender night between dreams, bed and a feather-light cielo in the distant Solali sky cannot be displayed once more. The same emotion now dances over *aguas turbulentas* … si, troubled waters. My Príncipe, I worry, is treading troubled waters, and my emotions are in a turmoil. There's another rumbling in the cielo … listen … the waters are troubled in this snow-mountain state. I must cross these troubled snow-mountain waters to return to that tender night between dream and bed, and distant Solali cielo – I need help, I need charas …

TWENTY-SEVEN

PERUMAL AROKYASWAMI NEEDS TO cross the troubled waters hugging the southernmost tip of the Indian Subcontinent to return home to Serendib. Home, a mere notion in the rickshaw-puller's mind. Home, a place once candidly described by a rain-washed black and white photograph, carefully tucked into the pocket of his almost white shirt. Today, this white shirt is Perumal Arokyaswami's most prized possession. Prized and not priced, because he cannot ascribe a value to it. Priceless, because this white shirt is the last remaining piece of cloth from a childhood gone awry when his father left the near six-year-old Perumal Arokyaswami to fend for himself under the mercy of a cumulonimbus cloud.

When Perumal Arokyaswami was nearly six years old, and alone, mercy arrived in the form of a marzipan. Yes, a Spanish *mazapán* ... an almond and honey infused energetic and soothing marzipan was held right under his tender nose by the Good Man of Cottonpettai. That day, the near-six-year-old Perumal Arokyaswami wiped his wet eyes, and gulped the delicacy, mazapán tenderly handed to the abandoned boy on a steel plate by Pascal Rebello de Fonseca.

Yes, Pascal Rebello de Fonseca was a good man.

Pascal Rebello de Fonseca is still the Good Man of Cottonpettai according to certain not-so-specific sources.

But getting back to that night, Pascal Rebello de Fonseca adopted a near-six-year-old boy of foreign origin into his home. That night, Perumal Arokyaswami came to be c/o Pascal Rebello de Fonseca.

Memories are made of quaint emotions from that night – they refuse to die today.

Resting his head upon the frazzled Lady's naked shoulder, today, Perumal Arokyaswami remembers the first mazapán he had ever tasted. Today, Perumal Arokyaswami rebels against fond memories of Pascal Rebello de Fonseca, the man who is being discussed as dead by not-so-specific sources. Today, Perumal Arokyaswami allows the somewhat fond memories of a rain-fed day in Kanandy – Hill Station Queen of Serendib to resurface. In the silence of these memories, the rickshaw-puller hears distinct drumbeats. The drumbeats sound louder with every new pound, and six loin-clothed men whip their *gata berayas* in unison. These six gata berayas have all been handmade in Serendib's Kurugabala hamlet. These six gata berayas have travelled far from their birthplace – they boom for all ears to hear in the backyard of the Great Peace God Temple Monastery in Serendib's holy mountainous town, Kanandy.

Perumal Arokyaswami's ears hear the inevitable beats
Loud beats
Louder beats

Until six-year-old Perumal Arokyaswami's heart beats for his homeland.

Perumal Arokyaswami keeps his eyes closed. He dreams, he stumbles into the inner sanctum of the Great Peace Temple Monastery where his mother is stringing a garland of Nil Manel – the Blue Water Lilies of mountain country Serendib ... fragrant fruit of its sister tree, the juicy rambutan.

'Yum ... may I have another rambutan, just one more please?' Perumal Arokyaswami utters aloud with his eyes closed, head still rested upon his Lady love's bare shoulder.

'Rambutan, what's that?' quivers the Lady with painted red lips.

'Rambutan,' the rickshaw-puller replies in near wakefulness, 'is a fruit with a smooth hairy exterior, and a fleshy, translucent, mellow pink interior. The rambutan has a sweet acidic taste, much like the fresh grape of Cottonpettai. A close cousin of the sweet lychee, the tropical fruit rambutan is an oval shaped 3 cm to 6 cm long berry, found in Southeast Asia – the Philippines, Malaysia, the Serendib included.'

'In fact,' Perumal Arokyaswami ventures to add, 'the rambutan is as exuberant in the Serendib as is the Kanandyan dance metred with the rhythm of gata berayas.'

The Lady is suitably entertained, she wants more food for her soul: 'So, what pray are gata berayas?'

The sound of gata berayas whispered in his ear by a certain Lady, his love, immediately pulls Perumal Arokyaswami out of his dream. The rickshaw-puller shudders, and moves closer to his Lady – he buries his disturbed head in her near-naked bosom, and mutters ... gata berayas ... Mava ...

'Mava?' the Lady prods ...

'Yes, Mava ... my Amma ... my Mother ... I see her face so clearly ... she wears a blue-stoned stud on her right nose, she makes garlands of Nil Manel ... the gata berayas grow louder ... I rush into her lap, she gives me a rambutan to distract me from my fear. I am petrified ... six Kanandyan dancers whip their gata berayas in unison ... I am shattered by the sound their whips eke out of the hides of dead goats ...' Perumal Arokyaswami sobs.

The Lady strokes her lover's head with her slender right hand, moistens his dark lips with her tongue, draws him closer to her near-naked bosom, and prods Perumal Arokyaswami to speak his sorrow out: 'What have dead goats got to do with gata berayas?'

'Hides of dead goats cover the two apertures of the oval-shaped gata berayas,' the rickshaw-puller mutters through his sobs. 'Gata berayas are the native drums of Serendib ... they are hollowed with jackfruit wood.'

Da drida da, drida da ... strumming a rhythm on jackfruit wood, I coax my erstwhile Krishna Tara brand of sitar, twin soul of the Strumaha FG 820 natural acoustic guitar, to stir passion into the melancholic mountains surrounding Solali. Strum stir, stir strum. I *rasguear*, I stir, I strum, I *remover*. Music knows no boundaries, no language either ... cliché ... never mind ... I just strum to stir emotions lying motionless after the repercussions of that tender night. My Príncipe and I, we are emotional equals ... si, we drift aimlessly by ourselves in the aftermath of our intense passion on that tender night ... Si, rasguear equals strum. Stir equals revolver.

TWENTY-EIGHT

THE NIGHT IS DEEP, and Senor Singh Mono readies to stir the silence in the Mettupalayam Railway Station for Erstwhile Steam Engines – he lowers the black case slung across his left shoulder, and unzips it to retrieve his Strumaha FG 820 natural guitar. Senor Mono takes two-and-a-half minutes to tune his acoustic instrument – he breaks the silence with the A-minor chord. He strums, he dramatically transposes the rhythm to the chord of E-minor, he sings along in his butter-edged, but macho voice ... *Your breath is hot, I love your tender caress/Cool Carolina/My coolest hot brothel ballerina/I simply cannot desist the way you groove* ... And his companions, the two Guides, groove to Hokuto Del Pazo's composition *So Groovy*, they twist unsteadily, and attempt to twirl on their leather-booted toes. Together, the Scout and Guides enter the stationary train with the Erstwhile Steam Engine, and bring rhythm to the sleeping Mettupalayam Station Guard's raunchy dream.

The raunchy momentum in the rexine seat of the cycle rickshaw on the Widest Footpath of Cottonpettai is suddenly groovy. The Lady is stirred by the momentum of the Hokuto Del Pazo strum and croon by a voice which is almost as groovy as the twenty two times Golden Guitar Music Award winning Spanish-Japanese fusion rock icon. The Lady, a Spanish brothel ballerina in her own right, grooves lying down, and grinds her near-naked body into her lover's. The Lady is oh *So Groovy*, she simultaneously wishes to come eye-to-eye with the butter-voiced singer, strumming and stirring the sleeping Guard in the Mettupalayam Railway Station, also other Fellows resting nearby on the Widest Footpath.

The Scout engrosses his Guide comrades with some more strumming and crooning – he simultaneously wishes to come eye-to-eye with the azul-eyed Lady when she has untangled from her romantic momentum with her lover, the rickshaw-puller.

'What on earth is a certain Scout and two Guides doing at this unearthly hour in the Mettupalayam Station for Erstwhile Steam Engines?' some roving munumunuppu-mongers who do not care to shut eye ask rather aloud.

'The Scout and his Guide comrades have played truant – they have braved a night crawl all the way from Utahkamand, stealthily moving through the Blue Mountain jungles, and downhill to the Mettupalayam Station, giving melancholy the slip,' exclaims a certain munumunuppu-monger who traverses the Nilgiris by night in search of healing herbs.

'Melancholy?' certain munumunuppu-mongers repeat.

'Yes, the Scouts and Guides of St. Alphonsious Pre-University College are pre-disposed to melancholy – this emotion is a subtle retaliation to imposed discipline,' the night-time monger further explains.

'Discipline?' the other mongers exclaim.

'Why is discipline so overrated? The Scouts and Guides of St. Alphonsious Pre-University College have reverently led discipline by the elbow, straight out of the confines of daylight, into the regime of the night. So, every night they crawl, literally, under the dense cover of sleeping Neelakurinji flowers,' the night-time monger explains, and promptly rests his case.

The night is young, the Lady who is transported to a land of reverie by the butter cool voice and the fragrance of the not-so-distant Neelakurinji flowers, croons a dreamy poem she has made up on the spot. She croons to the scale of F-major with her lipstick red mouth ...

'Neelakurinji ... blue flowers of the Queen Mountain

'Dress the slopes of Utahkamand, these flowers blossoming in unison every twelve years

'These flowers have a musical dent, they resound in this mountain range with a tender lilt of purple

'This tender lilt, a soft rock song

'This song, Oh! So Groovy ... aye, I the coolest hot brothel ballerina from the very Spanish-Japanese Hokuto Del Pazo's song

'I, the Lady with them azul eyes

'The same azul eyes that the truant Scout from uphill Utahkamand sports

'Upon his Greek God, sorry Spanish God like face

'The Scout is a Spanish Dios ... yeah God ... yeah Ama a Dios ... yeah Love Dios

'The butter-voiced Senor Singh Mono who has played truant from his camp uphill Utahkamand to groove in the Mettupalayam Railway Station, and rove the streets of Cottonpettai ... aye

'Aye ... ha, aha, haaaa'

Sigh ... the aye feeling Lady has fallen asleep, that too, with her azul eyes closed. The singing Scout arrives at the Widest Footpath of Cottonpettai in the deep of the night with his guitar, Guides, et al., only to find the Lady's eyes shut to the world.

The Scout is so near but yet so far from learning the truth about his real mother – let us not probe Senor Singh Mono's parentage at this early juncture, that too upon a deep and dark night such as this.

This night is like no other, light ripples rumble in the belly of Rio Beas. Eee, hee, Rio Beas is inebriated – this river has consumed snow-mountain weed. I am high on weed. I am high up in the cielo. I am high down here in this rippling river they call Rio Beas in the dark of a night ... I am on weed. Aye, weed will take me far away from this deep night, and transmit me into the arms of dawn. A new dawn is waiting to hug me and dry my soaking body, clothes, et al. By the way, where are my clothes? In my Príncipe's hands, I see ... I see my clothes in my Príncipe's hand, I need a hug to cover my bare body. Aye, the dawn is here, and I have just received a very, very *abrazo, apretado cálido*, aye, a very, very, warm, tight hug ...

TWENTY-NINE

THE SUN IS ROUND and surprisingly hot at 37 degree centigrade upon this monsoon day – the time is ripe for a hug on the Widest Footpath of Cottonpettai.

'Hug me tight,' a feminine voice whispers.

'Hug who?' a masculine voice whispers back.

'Hug the Lady with the Slender Hands. Hug me tight,' quivers the Lady for the second time, louder, her voice caressingly audible, despite the blaring traffic. Perumal Arokyaswami hugs the Lady really apretado.

Really apretado … *realmente* tight. Perumal Arokyaswami's throat is tight. His throat holds sadness in its pit even as he hugs the Lady with the Slender Hands upon the Widest Footpath in the Lancashire of India.

Perumal Arokyaswami is really sad because India does not share borders with Serendib.

Serendib is an island.

No man can live as an island, the scriptures decree. Perumal Arokyaswami must take a sailing motorboat, and ride the salted waters of the Indian Ocean, past the Laccadive Sea and onwards to the island of Serendib upon a suitably warm day such as this.

The sun is round and not so surprisingly hot at 37 degree centigrade upon this August morning in Chandinigarh – warm days have a special effect on the Minister for Shelters' tongue.

That's right, warm days can reverse the Minister for Shelters' cold temperament towards the Lady with the Slender

Hands. His heart is wild with passion for the Lady, mother of his questionable heir. His heir, to his chagrin, sports distinct physical features that have been modelled in the Lady's womb. The heir's blood is bold and red with Spanish roots. By the law of the Indian land, there is impurity in the heir's blood.

'Why then has the impurity of Senor Singh Mono's blood been overlooked by law?' the saha-mongers have their concerns.

'This impurity,' pleads the Minister for Shelters to all those wagging tongues which care to lend their ears to a drunk politician, 'can well be overlooked. After all, I planted this wild seed under the influence of a Spanish Rhapsody, 'tis in my reckoning, a melody of pure impurity.'

The saha-mongers aren't so certain they can take a drunk politician's word at tongue value, let alone his justification for planting his wild seed under the influence of a Spanish Rhapsody.

This story is in the midst of turmoil – no facts can be taken at tongue value. Especially facts related to the parentage of Senor Singh Mono.

No matter what the facts are, Senor Singh Mono's name has been documented in the Indian census, he is the legal heir to OneKmBungWow with an address in posh Chandinigarh. This heir is rich and poor at once. Rich in currency, poor in emotion.

Back in his camp uphill Utahkamand, Senor Singh Mono's emotion is sad and happy at once – he knows by instinct that he is physically close to his biological mother. And then, there's the other mother, the Caretaker.

Rafting in the bullicioso Beas, I, a *madre* ... a mother topples over indignant rio waves. I swim, I breathe, I rise, I topple until the indignant waves swallow *mi autoestima,* aye my self-esteem has just disappeared into the belly of the rambunctious Rio Beas.

THIRTY

THE MAIN MANDI IN the valley hamlet of Rozgaarnagar is loud with negotiation – famers of this lower Khalaand terrain are busy trading their self-esteem. This isn't good news, the farmers' fertile lands are their self-esteem, and these near paisa-less people have just sold their dhal and roti to the owners of the Aaraamaayu Factory. This is ugly news – the Aaraamaayu Factory has an address on the highest ranges of Khalaand, and belongs to a family of Land Gobblers.

'*Arere* ... the farmers of Rozgaarnagar have discarded their self-esteem, they have thrust their fertile fields ... soul of their lives ... food source of Khalaand into the hands of the Land Gobblers. These mindless farmers, they have traded their self-esteem for a price. This price they do not realize, will not yield them two square meals when the currency notes they have earned in exchange for their self-esteem disappear in less than a month. Arere ... the farmers of Rozgaarnagar have exchanged their precious fertile lands for a price. Alas ... the price the farmers hold in their labour-hardened hands will feed their larger than ten mouth families for just over a month. Alas ... the farmers have sold their stomachs to men who will bring down the hill to spite the precarious hold of nature over man, woman and Indian Python,' yammer the gapasapa-mongers with uncontrollable disdain over the negotiation that has just taken place at Rozgaarnagar's Main Mandi.

It is time for an imperative digression – when nature loses control over man, hungry women give birth to malnourished children.

Jhoru Kanbi Badshah is all of twenty-four years today – this man is a child in the lap of Nira, tributary of the sinewy Bhima river that drifts through the Khalaand ranges.

'Jhoru is a child

'Jhoru *eka mulaga ahe*

'Nira, carry your child to Bhima,' yammer the gapasapa-mongers who have decided to follow Jhoru everywhere.

'Bhima, is my mother with you?' asks the forlorn Jhoru.

'What on earth is Jhoru Kanbi Badshah's mother doing with the River Bhima?' the gapasapa-mongers are aghast.

Jhoru Kanbi Badshah has heard from sources on the banks of Nira that his mother is constantly accompanied by Bhima.

Bhima has a questionable reputation in Khalaand. Why does a sinewy river, source of crops and life giver, have a questionable reputation in these parts of the Western Ghats? The Bhima in question is a man fondly named after the sinewy river by his great grandmother when she heard the baby boy's cry slide over the slopes of Khalaand, and merge into the Nira on a hot summer's afternoon. This Bhima in question is now over five decades old, and is certainly not visible to Jhoru Kanbi Badshah's eye in the dense forests that define Khalaand.

Jhoru Kanbi Badshah's search for his mother must stop for the day.

As afternoon submerges into twilight, Jhoru Kanbi Badshah can no longer control his tears. He weeps for his mother, his tears spilling into the Nira, salt to salt, as the river ultimately joins the sea.

Rio Beas will flow into the waters of Sutlej after journeying 470 kilometres before the Red River converges with the Indus to then spill itself into the Arabian Sea by Rachikar, the capital of India's neighbouring country. The Red River is Sutlej's other name. Floating in Rio Beas, *yo ver rojo* … I see red. I see rojo in the middle of a dark, and blue night … I have darned good eyesight I say … I see red in the middle of a bullicioso rio.

THIRTY-ONE

'RED IS THE SPECIFIC colour of murder, left right left.

'Red is the specific colour of passion, left right left.

'Murder is passion gone astray, left right left.

'Bring passion back to its glory, left right left.'

Let red be the colour of passion, and passion alone, right right right …

The Scout and his two Guide comrades from St. Alphonsious Pre-University College have escaped their camp in the wee hours of night, they are marching downhill Nilgiris, and are chanting their slogan of passion just loud enough for their Thentoda friends to hear.

The Thentodas respond from the thick of the forest: '*Awoom Awaam Awoom*, let red be the colour of passion, and passion alone.' The Thentodas repeat the refrain their big city friends have chanted one more time to confirm their solidarity, and promptly disappear into the thick of the night.

This night, the Scout and two Guides from St. Alphonsious Pre-University College have escaped from their camp uphill Utahkamand to spout slogans in favour of a certain entity who wears red in her attitude on the Widest Footpath of Cottonpettai. Whew ... this Scout and two Guides are visibly red in the deep, dark hours of the night ... they have spouted slogans and marched at once. They have marched by the wee hours of night, in silent left right movement, whispering slogans about the colour red, and quite breathlessly, arrived at the foothills of Utahkamand in a tizzy.

By the foothills of Utahkamand, each future Suitable Somebody's face is flushed a passionate shade of red. This shade matches the colour of the Lady's lipstick red pout.

Senor Singh Mono has led his comrades on this secret march to observe the Lady with the Slender Hands from close quarters. He has chosen the deepest hour of the night for this activity in the hope that his intent will remain secret to his owl-eyed Master.

Senor Singh Mono is not aware that in the darkest corners of the night, the Fellows of the Footpath keep a wakeful eye for prowlers, especially those who wish to remain secret to the human eye.

The darkest corners of the night induce the Senor and his friends to wonder whether the Fellows of the Footpath are indeed human. Because, from what they know, a human is expected to sleep indoors, not under a starry sky upon a Footpath in the Lancashire of the South, for heaven's sake.

The Fellows of the Footpath are babbling in various foreign tongues for heaven's sake, the Scout and Guides listen.

'For *swarg*'s sake.'

'Your swarg is not my heaven.'

'Your heaven is not my cielo.'

'Your cielo is not my *paralokam* ...'

Perumal Arokyaswami has found cielo on earth, he whispers into his Lady's naked ear. The rickshaw-puller has understood under the starry sparkle of the sky, that his heaven, yeah ... his paralokam lies awake while the Lady's cielo sleeps.

Watching the Lady with the Slender Hands sleep peacefully under the starry sparkle of the night, Senor Singh Mono's tender heart finds swarg. The azul-eyed Scout's heart visits the same heaven where his mother once held him to her bosom, rocked him on a cumulonimbus cloud and showed him her starry cielo. His heart is warm, the Scout sways from side to side, his Guide friends sing the traditional folk lullaby *Hush Little Baby Don't You Cry* in tandem.

Perumal Arokyaswami can catch the movement of an errant fly in the darkest corner of the night, he has neither missed the sight of the swaying Scout, nor his *Hush Little Baby* singing Guide friends.

Perumal Arokyaswami can neither ignore the movement nor the singing of a certain Scout and two Guides who have marched down Blue Mountain Nilgiris to spy upon the Lady, his love.

Perumal Arokyaswami sees red.

Red equals anger.

Anger equals murder.

Murder of the azul-eyed Scout's intent to get closer to the Lady, Perumal Arokyaswami's love.

The rickshaw-puller wastes no time, he pulls his Lady closer, and signals to a spying munumunuppu-monger.

Suddenly, the night is still no more, there's munumunuppu everywhere – by the Widest Footpath of Cottonpettai and uphill Nilgiris in the camp for the Braver than the Best – alert!

'Alert Senor Singh Mono and both ye Guide comrades – the Master of Sports for Suitable somebodies has heard from roving voices in the Blue Mountains that certain future Suitable Somebodies are up to no good.

'Alert Senor Singh Mono, you will soon face inquisition by the Master of Sports for Suitable Somebodies,' assures the spying munumunuppu-monger in the deep of the night.

In the deep of the night, I face the road to Chandinigarh, mi heart is pounding in rhythm with Rio Beas. Mi heart is weak. Mi face is pale … My heart, mi face. Mi corazón, mi *cara*. Mi pale cara reflects the rhythm of mi corazón. Mi corazón, mi pale azul eyes …

THIRTY-TWO

THE LADY WITH THE Slender Hands watches a fledgling ray of the Cottonpettai sun glide over Blue Mountain Utahkamand – a streak of light gently settles on her pale complexion. The Lady is pale. The Lady is strong. There is no strength in blood, especially in the Lady's world where all her relations by marriage, parentage, kinship, and birth have forsaken her.

Upon the Widest Footpath of Cottonpettai, the Lady's strength is her complexion.

'Ayyo, today, the Lady's strength, her complexion, is rather pale,' comment some very long-nosed munumunuppu-mongers.

'Never mind,' retorts the Lady aloud, 'my strength is Perumal Arokyaswami.'

'Never mind,' retorts the Lady softly, and for her own ears she utters, 'my strength is Sanyasi Solali Snowmountainwala.'

This worshipful morning, Shri Shri Shri Shri and Shri Sanyasi Solali Snowmountainwala wears a pale glow, his skin lightened by the nourishing properties of Kesar. This skin-nourishing mountain flower has a heady fragrance – it promises to make all dark objects fair, with an added glow.

Sanyasi Solali Snowmountainwala is an object of his own creation. He is worshipped by ministers, tourists and others who have imagined the Supreme Power to be an object.

The Supreme Power is objectified in gold, silver, bronze, metal, wood, also stone infused by holy verse chanting worshippers with the flesh and blood of the Creator. Sanyasi Solali Snowmountainwala walks in flesh and blood as the Supreme Power, the Creator of all life forms, objects, snow-mountain weed, and also a brand of tobacco. Sanyasi Solali Snowmountainwala sits unmoving in his sanctum like a gold figurine clothed in saffron, folds of the sacred cloth adorned by His Holiness neatly pleated to conceal substances that the human eye must not catch sight of. The Sanyasi's stillness is determined by the dosage of snow-mountain weed, which is closely tucked between the neatly pleated folds of his saffron robe.

Also tucked beneath the folds of the Sanyasi's saffron robe is a pack of the supremely masculino Vignesh Beedi. The supreme tobacco brand has travelled far from its manufacturing unit, and all the way to Solali within the folds of a white handkerchief in the Minister for Shelter's Black Briefcase.

The Black Briefcase is of supreme importance, it contains important deeds in the form of rubber-stamped papers, and intoxicants in the form of the very potent Vignesh Beedi.

The Minister for Shelters recommends those commodities which benefit him directly via indirect business practices – he carries his recommendations in the Black Briefcase held snugly unto his sagging chest.

'The Minister for Shelters is here with his Black Briefcase, et al.,' there's rather loud phusphus in the Solali air, 'the politician sighted in these snow mountain parts has an indirect stake in the Vignesh Beedi manufacturing unit. In fact, the Minister's name is carefully concealed in the Partnership Deed – it travels with him everywhere, even to the toilet in his Black Briefcase.'

Meanwhile, in Cottonpettai, the munumunuppu-mongers concede they have learnt of a certain Partnership Deed, which defines the Lady's fortune.

'Deed indeed!' murmurs the Lady with the Slender Hands.

The Lady knows only too well that her signature reflects in the Partnership Deed – she is the owner of a flourishing business – she is the Baroness of Beedis. This Lady has begotten this title from a life she cannot return to.

'Cannot, or will not?' the munumunuppu-mongers want to know.

I cannot return to my yellow pillow, I am the Baroness of Beas. I, a Baroness intoxicated by a stray beedi which has slipped out of the Black Briefcase, and landed itself in mi *casa*. Yay, my home, mi casa is c/o any street in Solali … all are welcome to come share this very masculino beedi with me in my snowy drawing room.

THIRTY-THREE

THE LADY WITH THE Slender Hands holds a half-smoked Vignesh Beedi between her red lips, and announces in a convent school educated drool: 'Welcome to the Bandaranaike International Airport.'

'*Ayubhuvan* to Sundaranaike International Airport,' Perumal responds.

'The Cololomambo International Airport has two other names – Sundaranaike and Kamalanayake. Write down the address of the International Airport, Perumal Arokyaswami,' coaxes his Lady love.

The rickshaw-puller holds an unlit masculino beedi between his blackened lips, he writes as his Lady love dictates: Sundaranaike International Airport, Cross Country Friendship Road, Kamalanayake 11455, Serendib.

'Learn to say welcome in Sinhala Perumal Arokyaswami,' another voice deeper than the Lady's prods the rickshaw-puller from a not-so-visible corner of the Footpath. 'Ayubhuvan,' says Perumal Arokyaswami in a not-so-deep voice, giving the 'u' an 'o' twist, recalling the pronunciation from a distant day in his boyhood.

But who is instructing Perumal Arokyaswami in the tongue of his Motherland? The 'who' remains a shadow in a not-so-visible corner of the Widest Footpath of Cottonpettai. The who in question could either be alive or dead, only time will tell.

This is no time to chase a shadow.

Time is transient on the Footpath – seconds leap into hours – Perumal Arokyaswami navigates his tour to his Motherland with inputs from his Lady love and the beedi dragging shadow of 'who'.

This 'who' has a special effect on the rickshaw-puller. Perumal Arokyaswami's heart is flushed with tender loving care – he feels one with his special family – he closes his eyes and, in his immediate dream, leaps into the blue-green waters of the Laccadive Sea, and beyond it, swims into the uterus of the Indian Ocean.

The Indian Ocean is blue-green – her uterus is fertile with pearls of exalted variety.

The dance of blue-green feathers in the lower ranges of the Western Ghats is a celebratory sight for the citizens of Rozgaarnagar – the Peacock is a common sight in these parts.

The dance of the Mor, the national bird of India, is an uncommon sight in these parts.

The Peacock features as India's national bird in every primary school textbook, even in the rural hinterlands of this rather large country with 1,847,454 square miles of land area.

Rozgaarnagar is a rural area, but no hinterland. Few are aware that Rozgaarnagar is indeed a village fast extending its built-in area into the nearby forests to establish itself as a respectable town. By decree of the Minister for Shelters and others of his suitable ilk in the Alarmed Hall of Parliament, an Indian town can be deemed respectable only in the event it has more concrete than trees. So, this near town has every facility a respectable wage earner dares to hope for. The Provision Store at the main intersection of Rozgaarnagar and the Bubambay–Punone Highway has every ware ranging from plastic buckets to sachets of Suryasilk shampoo, also all shapes of aluminium vessels that a householder in these parts can safely hope for.

This near town is steadily losing its need for the potter's wheel to spin vessels of clay to store fresh rain water – the florescent green plastic bucket hanging from the ceiling of the asbestos-roofed Provision Store must find a place in a Rozgaarnagar house.

This near town has little care for its hibiscus flowers and henna leaves – these indigenous herbs washed human hair clean for three generations before the original inhabitants of Rozgaarnagar were invited to join the Aaraamaayu Factory as respectable wage earners.

But Rozgaarnagar has not been granted the status of a town by the Government of India. The original inhabitants of Rozgaarnagar – the adivasis called Khalkholis – must continue to live as their ancestors did – off the lurching forests defining the perimeter of its territory on all four sides.

At this point the gapasapa-mongers interrupt: 'But, Jhoru Kanbi Badshah's Badtameez Baap is not an original inhabitant of Rozgaarnagar – he can neither live off the forests like the Khalkholis, nor find respectable employment at the Aaraamaayu Factory.'

Getting back to the facts, for over fifty years now, the original inhabitants of Rozgaarnagar have been looking into wood-framed mirrors precariously fastened on their raw, unbaked mud walls, and adjusting their moustaches grown long and luscious with the fertile properties of the tall mehendi shrub.

Mehendi is the indigenous nomenclature for henna – every time a Khalkholi twirls his moustache, he utters a rather loud prayer to this shrub.

The nomenclature of the juicy red apples of Himachal Pradesh varies by the soil of the land. I bite into the juicy Kulkulu manzana, this royal apple, the crown … si, the *corona* of a neat pile of similar fruit displayed in a shop in the Central Market of main town Manmanali, the big landscape downhill Solali. I bite the juicy corona down to its core. The Kulkulu crown is a juicy red manzana, a rojo apple – this, the prime attraction in the Central Market of Manmanali.

THIRTY-FOUR

KULKULU IS THE TOWN you meet by the gentle curve of River Beas downhill Manmanali. Kulkulu is the yardstick of a premium countryside town, English style. Kulkulu is alive in the stomach of the Himalayan ranges – it has enough food, sunlight, water and snow to shield its succulent apple trees from the sweaty turmoil of incessant heat.

Heat is a condition that causes sunstroke during the months of June and July, even in the midst of August in the Undeniable

Capital of India. With no further clues on Bhima's whereabouts, Jhoru Kanbi Badshah has returned ticketless on Train No. 12247 to the Grand Nizamuddin from the Victoria Terminus, to perform his coolie duties in the Undeniable Capital.

Jhoru Kanbi Badshah has the mettle of a warrior – he cannot be bothered about sunstroke. He has spent his earliest years in the sun-intense town of Algauv, day after dawn soaking in the afternoon rays – the heat averaging 42 degree centigrade round the year, a soothing touch on Jhoru's skin, much like morning dew on a nascent leaf.

Jhoru Kanbi Badshah is still a nascent leaf – he has a tender heart beneath his toned chest. Jhoru's heart is burdened, he stands still, the afternoon heat pounding upon his head, hot rays seeping into his skull in the Undeniable Capital. This afternoon, Jhoru Kanbi Badshah hopes beyond hopelessness – he wants his sun-soaked skull to burst in hell.

Jhoru Kanbi Badshah deserves to be in hell, a voice inside his heated skull resounds – he falls faint in full view of all his Coolie Comrades assembled for a game of rummy upon the Twenty Third platform.

'Hell on earth,' Jhoru's Comrades yell.

There's hell for passengers on the Twenty Third Platform as thirty-two coolies, all Jhoru's Comrades, run pell-mell.

They run to rescue Jhoru Kanbi Badshah from his own hell.

The Coolie Comrades awaken their brother in profession from his faint – they thulp the depression out of Jhoru Kanbi Badshah's sun-burnt skull – they lead the son of a traded mother back to his mission.

There's phusphus everywhere: 'Yay! Jhoru Kanbi Badshah is back on track on the hysterical Twenty Third Platform of the Grand Nizamuddin. He will find his mother, and bring his father on track – the Badshah has pounded his fists upon a steel trunk, and firmly sworn his intent to his Coolie Comrades.'

Thirty-two coolies agree that Jhoru Kanbi Badshah has a firm idea. This idea is the child of rage. Rage is contagious in the afternoon heat. Thirty-two coolies, Jhoru included, sign a pact in rage to wipe the Badshah's father's name off the records of the living, they will show no mercy.

Mercy is the soul of Solali. Sanyasi Solali Snowmountainwala's mercy drifts in River Beas, all the way to Kulkulu.

I drift along the highway, my body floating in Rio Beas. I drift, I am not dead. I drift, I am alive. *Mi deriva*, I drift. I simply deriva alongside a dried log of snow-mountain Sal wood – it has escaped from its pile while in transit on a tractor … we *tránsito* together. Together, log of snow-mountain Sal wood and I tránsito from Manmanali to Kulkulu.

THIRTY-FIVE

FRESH AUGUST RAINS ARE visited by the noon sun – seven colours first amalgamate, and then come unmixed to fill the Kulkulu sky. A rainbow in the not-so-far sky is always a good omen in these parts – the time is ripe for the Mountain Men to use their sickles and probe their rain-fed lands in search of the principal seed of this much Bollywood-filmed valley. But the principal seed under probe, the Originally Solali Kesar is hard to unearth in rain-fed lands that lose themselves in layers of snow even when the sun shines brightly.

The Mountain Men probe the lands deeper, they ask: 'Remember where the Originally Solali Kesar rests?'

'The Kohinoor of Himachal, the Original Kesar, rests in a silent nook deep in the snow-redeemed forests uphill Solali,' whispers the oldest Mountain Man with the whitest moustache in the group.

'The Mountain Men now have a clue, they will soon take on the uphill task of locating the Originally Solali Kesar,' the info-scavenging phusphus-mongers linger around, and spread a rumour.

This rumour is a rascal, surpassing the Mountain Men who are all trudging at donkey's pace – it jumps the line to the top of a hill, which is not quite the highest in these snow mountain parts.

After an hour's trudge, there's mischief cooking upon the Little Hill. This Hill, the meeting point of the Mountain Men, also all Manu Gaddi's lesser known cousins – their moustaches not as lavish as his.

'Who in the rainbow upon the Kulkulu sky's name is Manu Gaddi?' a long-nosed phusphus-monger would beg to know.

'Well, he is the man who guards the Originally Solali Kesar along with the others, we beg you to recall. Together, the main man Manu Gaddi and the others are called the People of the Highest Hill,' whisper the Mountain Men for all their comrades to clearly hear, and register in their wool-capped heads.

When the Mountain Men whisper loud enough, the women of small big town Kulkulu are all ears. Today, their ears have gathered a secret no one dares to talk about in the lower ranges of the State of Himachal Pradesh. This secret must be kept, snuggled close to their wombs, and made warm with the glow of an earthen oil lamp the women hold snugly under their embroidered pherans.

In the valleys of Himachal where draughts of wind blow cold almost all through the year, the Mountain Men, their women too, wear the loose and flowing woollen pherans – these garments styled at the waist by a luigi, the customary multi-hued sash. When the cold draughts blow, men do what their women follow – they keep their hands warm by cupping earthen lamps beneath their pherans.

The earthen lamps must shine all night.

The Kulkulu Valley sleeps by night.

So ja mere laal by night.

Sleep my little lad by night.

For when the day breaks, the night will retreat into a shell.

And you will lose the secrets known to the night alone if you don't dream alright.

Why is there such a hue and cry about the night?

Ask the women of Kulkulu Valley – they cry, they sing, they keep the secret of the Mountain Men close to their wombs by day and by night. Their children, now grown to run alongside the Beas in their hometown, the Kulkulu Valley, have heard their mothers' sobs while still foetuses in their wombs.

I hear the mothers' sobs. I hear the river gush. The river cannot digest such sorrow in its gush. The river must simply flow. The river I call Beas. The Beas is melancholic in these parts. The *melancólico* Rio Beas flows by Kulkulu. The melancholic Beas carries me upon his burdened shoulder over boulder, pebble and rock. Sometimes skirting the rock, at others engulfing the tiny pebble, but always frisking rapidly with the secret of the Kulkulu women, Rio Beas flows incessantly.

THIRTY-SIX

A SECRET MUST BE honoured for its desired solitude – a gust of Eucalyptus-perfumed winds sweep the Widest Footpath of Cottonpettai in consent. The Lady with the Slender Hands has a secret to keep. The secret rests in her throat, she calls this hiding place the Adam's apple.

It is easy for the Lady with the Slender Hands to conceal her secret, the Adam's apple, as a biological rule, does not showcase itself prominently upon a woman's neck – she relaxes.

It is not so easy for the Lady to conceal her secret, especially when the Adam's apple, breaking all biological rules, loses its composure, and protracted sorrow bursts into sudden tear. The Lady breaks down.

When the Lady with the Slender Hands sheds a tear, rest assure Perumal Arokyaswami is very near. He is so near, the Lady chases the tear right back to her Adam's apple where her sorrow can shut-up and remain a secret.

Senor Singh Mono has met swarg in the Lady's eye, he has a secret to keep in his Adam's apple. Every Scout and Guide on camp in Utahkamand has a secret to keep under the strict surveillance of a tool called Controlled Emotion, and Senor Singh Mono simply cannot be seen wearing passion for all to see upon his fair-complexioned face. Neither Scout nor Guide, as per the Law of Extreme Discipline in the St. Alphonsious Rule Book, is permitted to shed an undue tear – not even let loose an unwarranted word flying out of pitch in random temper from their near-eighteen-year-old mouths. In fact, not even think an undue thought, deviant to the calm nature that civilized people are called upon to sport. In short, no Scout nor Guide from St. Alphonsious Pre-University College can step outside their calm façades in public view. Certainly not in view of the Master of Sports for Suitable Somebodies.

There's gossip all over the Indian Subcontinent: 'Suitable Somebodies – past, present or future – are required to be civilized 24/7.

'*Siṣṭa sampanna, sabhya, civilizado* ... yeah these Scouts and Guides camping uphill Utahkamand are required to be civilized round the clock, according to their owl-eyed Master.

'Perumal Arokyaswami does not have a postal address, he cannot be *śiṣṭa sampanna* for the Lady's sake.

'Jhoru Kanbi Badshah does not know where his mother is, he cannot be *sabhya* for the Lady's sake.

'The Lady with the Slender Hands paints her lips bright red, she cannot be *civilizado* for the sake of the men in her life.

'The Minister for Shelters lives in OneKmBungWow – he has fathered a son he acknowledges as his own, and lives with a woman who does not colour her lips – he is certainly civilized for the sake of his high position.'

Civilized people have large homes and families – one wife is mandatory, one son is inevitable to carry the bloodline into another generation and crown it with the Minister for Shelters' immortal name.

Uphill Utahkamand, Senor Singh Mono is suddenly perturbed about the nature of his bloodline. There are rumours in the campsite uphill Nilgiris that his bloodline is mixed, his roots are fragmented by diverse cultures, and his genes are not becoming of an original Aryan.

An Aryan man is considered to be the highest order of flesh and original blood upon the Indian Subcontinent. An Aryan man is tall and well-toned, fairer to the eye than his counterpart Dravidian from the southern region of India. Fairness and Loveliness, the master brand of Indian creams can convert a Dravidian into an Aryan by continuous usage. By historical evidence, the fair-skinned reign supreme. So, it is imperative for all dark-skinned Indians to turn fair.

Sanyasi Solali Snowmountainwala is not an Aryan man, but is rumoured to have an ancestral connection with the fair-skinned humans from the Western world – he reigns supreme.

'But,' exclaim the phusphus-mongers, 'Sanyasi Snowmountainwala's skin is barely visible to the eye. His beard extends from chin to eye, salt and pepper hair joining his eyebrows. Eyebrows pointing towards his mane. Mane of matted hair, black and grey all over. A divine sight, the Sanyasi of Solali is clothed from head to toe with hair and saffron cloth all over.'

'Hush ...' some more phusphus-mongers yell out in panic, 'there's a tremor in Manmanali, let us all go over to the very edge of the bridge, and jump into the ever-flowing River Beas.'

'Stop yammering in panic,' counters a rather old and respectable phusphus-monger, 'there's a far more important tremor to address. Our revered Sanyasi's prime disciple – the Minister for Shelters – has a son named Senor Singh Mono camping at an address uphill Utahkamand, in a location down south of our country. This Senor has a tremor in his heart, he hides a secret concerning his original bloodline in his Adam's apple.'

'What a thing to say ...,' counter the yelling phusphus-mongers, wide-eyed, 'does Sanyasi Solali Snowmountainwala know about the tremor in Senor Sigh Mono's bloodline?'

'Senor Singh Mono's secret is hard to conceal, or so my munumunuppu cousins reveal,' states the old and respectable phusphus-monger. 'The young Senor must escape the routine of Utahkamand, conceal his identity with a peppered beard, and travel across the length of the Indian Subcontinent to seek visitation with Sanyasi Solali Snowmountainwala.'

The old and respectable phusphus-monger's munumunuppu cousins spread the word for a certain azul-eyed Scout to hear – Senor Singh Mono prepares for his travel across the Indian Subcontinent to first arrive at Manmanali, where the heavens are reconstructing the abode of Gods – the tremors increase.

Tremors have side effects. The Mountain Men of Kulkulu know a certain Sanyasi in Manmanali who shifts from the left side of his wooden stool to the right, and rolls his head backwards –

his lifeless eyes meeting the cumulonimbus cloud in the near blue sky when questioned about the Originally Solali Kesar.

When the Mountain Men share a secret on the hill, the Kulkulu women hear it in their homes. The secret knows that the best place to snuggle in the cold is the warm womb of a Kulkulu wife.

I am a wife in the Kulkulu Valley, my husband's identity is a secret I keep warm in my Adam's apple. I am urged to keep my secret well-fed, I eat a Kulkulu manzana, and bite into its black seeds. I spit the seeds into the tremor disturbed and haphazardly rippling Rio Beas – aye, a new Apple Tree is sown in a fertile river bed. The apple is the staple food of Kulkulu. Will the manzana, aye ... the apple, the staple of Kulkulu, bear fruit in the perennially fertile comfort of the rio's bed?

THIRTY-SEVEN

THE MINISTER FOR SHELTERS plunges his five foot, nine-and-quarter inch long and endomorphic body into the plush comfort of his silken bed – he draws a velvet pillow beneath his near bald head, and promptly snores.

When the Minister snores, OneKmBungWow experiences a mild tremor. The Caretaker and the Support Staff at the ministerial residence panic, they run helter-skelter until they briefly stop to peer into the Minister's inner chamber. They witness the politician prostrated upon his silken bed with his eyes shut and mouth wide open, his snore shaking the sanctity of the very foundation of OneKmBungWow – all those who have stopped to peer, panic, barring a brave lady. The Caretaker is brave, she heaves a sigh of relief, the Support Staff follow her action – together, they decide to reconfirm that the ground beneath their feet is indeed shaking because of the Minister's snore. Moving closer to the Minister, the Caretaker – his legal spouse according to documented sources – runs a Peacock feather over his face, beneath his nose, and into his nostrils to confirm that the politician is indeed sleeping. The politician squirms with his eyes shut and mouth wide open – the Support Staff heave a sigh of relief, and vamoose off to their respective rooms.

The Minister for Shelters is unperturbed by the melee – his eyes, still shut, flutter rapidly in all directions, the pounding rate of his heart increases, he dreams a powerful dream, and snores louder until a volley of sahas invade his deep slumber.

'Fie upon the Minister for Shelters, his so-called son Senor Singh Mono's bloodline is questionable,' the mongers saha so loud, the Minister's snores are muted, his powerful dreams and busted, and his half-open eyes witness the earth shaking beneath his silken bed.

'An earthquake, save my pure soul,' the Minister for Shelters screams first, and then opens his dreaming eyes wide enough to find that all is still around him.

The Minister heaves a sigh of momentary relief, he springs to his pedicured feet; he summons No. 1, his senior-most and loyal Support Staff, and orders him to call his trusted Lawyer Latif – fast!

'Yeah, yeah summon Lawyer Latif fast, ye Minister with a pure soul indeed,' the saha-mongers prod the politician from the other side of his bedroom window. The Minister squirms, but decides to keep his foul mouth shut for a change – he vamooses off to his Main Chamber to meet the lawyer in question.

Lawyer Latif is a clean-shaven and clever man – he has arrived at OneKmBungWow with the required Memorandum of Understanding aka MoU intended to secure Senor Singh Mono's future.

It must be made amply clear at this point that a secure life for a future Suitable Somebody implies enough money for the Scout in question to buy a valley and embellish it with a castle, its décor suitable to accommodate revellers who pay for their stay is Euro, in Dollars, Yen, and even Rouble. Lawyer Latif has meticulously worded the MoU in favour of the most Suitable Somebody, Senor Singh Mono, and further added clauses to amply ensure that the landed party entering into the agreement does not find himself manoeuvring a misunderstanding with the Minister. In Lawyer Latif's experience, when a misunderstanding with the Minister cannot be cleared by word, deed or money, blood is spilt. The Minister for Shelters does not hesitate to discharge a detractor off his flowing blood, especially when the misunderstanding cannot be resolved in the former's favour by word, signed deed and, of course, a hefty bribe in the form of feminine flesh.

The Minister for Shelters utters the final word in matters concerning property anywhere in the Indian Subcontinent. The Minister owns lands everywhere in the country, also prime tobacco fields in Ajay Nagar with an address in the State of Maharashtra. The Minister can choose to own valley and lake, river and hill, all he needs to do is utter his avaricious heart's desire, and the assets that belong to India's masses will be his.

The Minister's assets across the length and breadth of India will be inherited by his one and only son Senor Singh Mono, or so Lawyer Latif's updated MoU contesting all matters of bloodline indicates. The Minister is pleased, he calls for a Press Conference in the Public Hall of Chandinigarh, and announces Senor Singh Mono his one and only son, as his true blue heir.

No. 1 travels eight hours by road from Chandinigarh uphill Manmanali to hand Sanyasi Solali Snowmountainwala the Press Release announcing Senor Singh Mono as the Minister for Shelters' only son. The Sanyasi smirks, he knows only too well that the Minister for Shelters has a bag of secrets, its contents gorier than the Royal Ragamuffins' gunny sacks of rotting meat from Cottonpettai's prised dustbins. These contents are abandoned skeletons from past deeds.

The phusphus-mongers have read the contents of Sanyasi Snowmountainwala's thoughts, they recite:

'Past deeds.

'Past seeds.

'Past forward.

'Past present deeds.

'Deeds from past seeds sown on inebriated nights.

'These seeds are now full-grown men.

'Men of flesh and blood.

'Royal blood.

'Four Royal Ragamuffins.

'Royal seeds of the Minister for Shelters, if you please.

'The Minister for Shelters is very careful with his seeds – he sows them only in royal territory.

'How many homes does this Minister have? How many names does the Minister for Shelters sign under?'

'This is no time to question the multiple personalities the Minister for Shelters sports. Sanyasi Solali Snowmountainwala will unravel each mask the Minister wears when the time is conveniently conducive to spell out the many names that the father of several unclaimed sons misuses according to his convenience. Right now, the Sanyasi must use his third eye to set right the plight of the Mountain Men assembled on the Little Hill in Kulkulu for the Minister for Shelters is all set to steal the raised land from beneath their very feet.'

Time deserves a break, especially in the Kulkulu Valley where I have stopped to overhear the secret of the Mountain Men – I eavesdrop. My Adam's manzana wells, this secret of the Mountain Men is too harsh to wear in silence around my neck. I *llolar*, and my tears meet the rippling Rio Beas. I cry secretly into Rio Beas. My llolar cannot be heard by the Minister for Shelters in Chandinigarh. I cry, si, I llolar some more, and hope my Príncipe opens the door to his corazón once more.

THIRTY-EIGHT

NO. 1 OPENS THE SAL wood-carved front door of OneKmBungWow to let in four Royal Ragamuffins, all residents of the Widest Footpath of Cottonpettai. These Ragamuffins have once again been summoned by the Minister for Shelters to dine at OneKmBungWow, their air tickets borne from Cottonpettai to Chandinigarh by the host himself. The Ragamuffins cannot comprehend the reason for such royal treatment time and again – they are happy to be the most wanted Fellows of the Footpath. The Minister for Shelters camouflages the real reason for this royal treatment, he claims it is an act of charity for the betterment of these already charming and enthusiastic teenaged boys living on a tier-two city footpath with other not-so-happening people.

The Minister's reason is immaterial to the very materialistic Royal Ragamuffins – they are simply happy to fly from Cottonpettai to Chandinigarh, and consume the choicest butter chicken, chocolate chip ice cream and five-year-old scotch whiskey, which the politician himself has brought back from the Duty Free Store at the Toronto Pearson International Airport. Once the Ragamuffins have been pleased with ample food and drink and allowed a night's rest, they are woken up early by No. 1 to be taught discipline by the Minister for Shelters.

The saha-mongers have inkling of the politician's intent, they whisper: 'The Minister for Shelters is inculcating discipline into the four Royal Ragamuffins with special help from Staff No. 1. These Royal Ragamuffins will watch over the Widest Footpath of Cottonpettai, abode of important foreign dignitaries the Minister for Shelters personally knows.'

Perumal Arokyaswami is considered a foreign dignitary on the Widest Footpath of Cottonpettai. His ancestors are from Serendib, a foreign land not too far from Kumarikanya in the southern-most tip of India – it rests across the Laccadive shores.

Perumal Arokyaswami must return to Serendib for good, remark the Chandinigarh return Royal Ragamuffins in unison upon a moon-fed night in the darkest corner of the Widest Footpath. Perumal Arokyaswami is perturbed by this remark –

he grasps the Lady's slender hands tight, and gapes in silence at the moon. The Royal Ragamuffins are perturbed by the rickshaw-puller's silence, they have been strictly disciplined by the Minister for Shelters to knock the calmness out of Perumal Arokyaswami's life – they must do so, asap.

The Lady is shocked to hear the Royal Ragamuffins speak their minds to Perumal Arokyaswami under the spell of the moon. The Lady knows only too well that the Minister for Shelters has 'disciplined' his secret agents to speak where their tongues must remain tied.

The Lady cannot be controlled by the Minister for Shelters, leave alone his secret agents who call themselves the Royal Ragamuffins – she burns their egos upon this cold night with her fiery gaze. The Ragamuffins find their pumped-up egos in smithereens, they empty their brandy bottles into their expanding stomachs, and pretend to fall asleep at once.

The Lady pretends to fall asleep at once – she closes her kohl-lined eyes, and keeps her pear-shaped ears open to eavesdrop on the now whispering Ragamuffins.

Eyes closed, I continue to float in the rapids of Rio Beas. The rapids toss me up in the moonlight, they bring me near the Little Hill in Kulkulu where the Mountain Men are whispering their woes – I keep my *ojos* closed and *orejas* open, I eavesdrop upon their whispers. Yes, my eyes ... mi ojos are closed, and my ears, mi orejas are open as I strive to stay afloat in the rapid Rio Beas.

THIRTY-NINE

THEIR EARS HAVE HEARD an untoward news – the citizens of Rozgaarnagar run amok. Loose-tongued gapasapa-mongers run amok over the ranges of Khalaand, their mouths delivering news to all and sundry in hill and valley from the desk of the Cheap Operating Officer aka CheapOO of the Aaramaayu Factory. The monsoon rains are here, and the CheapOO has decided to shut down production of the Factory's Hyper Healing Products for two whole months. Each year, production comes to standstill as the machines are thoroughly oiled to withstand hyperactivity in the ensuing ten months, and the walls of the Factory smeared with green grease from the Healing Products, are whitewashed. During these two months of renovation, the daily wage earners aka all the citizens of Rozgaarnagar must depend upon their savings for their everyday meals. The CheapOO has firmly established that when there is no work, there is certainly no wage. Each year, when the two dreadful work-down months near, the daily wage earners find their not-much-to-talk-about savings in the Strategic Bank of India disappear within three days – they apply for fresh loans they pledge to repay.

The citizens of Rozgaarnagar simply cannot fill their stomachs and their rising needs with their daily wages anyway. Today's needs were yesterday's luxuries in the near big town of Rozgaarnagar.

Today's needs include the inevitable mobile phone. Where there are mobile phones, top ups are necessary. But who are these necessary people the citizens of Rozgaarnagar are conversing with?

'Pssst ...,' say the gapasapa mongers, 'the Badtameez Baap makes a necessary call from his mobile phone to Jhoru

Kanbi Badshah every evening, soon after sunset, for a reason that cannot be disclosed. The other daily wage earners of Rozgaarnagar make necessary calls to their daughters. The daughters of the people of Rozgaarnagar have been married off at the onset of puberty to wage earners in other industrial small towns, Algauv included.'

'Why is it necessary for the daily wage earners to call the daughters of Rozgaarnagar every day?' a rather young and not-knowing son of a gapasapa-monger would like to know.

'Their daughters, their parents have learnt from the womenfolk of the Badtameez Baap's household, can well be traded in the asbestos town,' the all-knowing gapasapa-mongers care to explain.

'Traded?!' the young gapasapa son exclaims.

'Jhoru Kanbi Badshah's mother was traded in the asbestos town – that's all your young ears need to know for now,' an elderly gapasapa-monger admonishes rather sternly.

All gapasapa-mongers who have lived over two decades of earth life are aware that the daughters of Rozgaarnagar, fresh as Winter Lilies, can well be traded in the year long summer town of Algauv. Business, the moneyed believe in this asbestos town, can never be complete without Winter Lilies – these fragrant creations are cool elixir for men on constant heat.

The heat is stifling in Rozgaarnagar this year – mobile phones, all Yeskia 1100s, are among the fastest selling necessities at the small big town's Provision Store.

Each night, the people of Rozgaarnagar say a prayer for the owners of the small big town's necessary blessing – the Provision Store. The owners of the Store are entities the people of Rozgaarnagar do not know. The owners have more than one Provision Store. The owners are conglomerates, pioneers of a retail chain equipped with every product one needs to survive upon planet earth.

A levitating Sanyasi discourses: 'Planet earth does not require mobile phones. Voices carry via telepathy if you care to align with the pulse of the planet under contention.' The people of Manmanali, Solali, even Kulkulu Valley have gathered in thousands – they are transfixed by Sanyasi Solali Snowmountainwala's discourse on affairs concerning planet earth's well-being.

I am transfixed by the sound of my voice. I hear my voice playing over and again in my husband's head. My *marido* ... si, mi husband knows from my voice that I am not dead. I am alive in Rio Beas, its pebbled banks my bed. I sleep on my *cama*, si, mi bed on the banks of Rio Beas with my head firmly resting upon planet earth.

FORTY

UPHILL UTAHKAMAND, THE NIGHT is deep, and the Master of Sports for Suitable Somebodies has his head firmly resting upon the wooden bed in the camp for the Braver than the Best. This man of extreme discipline does not believe in mattresses, especially the soft variety into which his firm head can get lost in sleep forever.

'A sunken head is considered dead,' proclaim a band of high-on-arrack night-time munumunuppu-mongers upon arriving swaggeringly at the Widest Footpath of Cottonpettai. 'Uphill Utahkamand, from where we're arriving like knights with a swagger in our steps, the Master of Sports for Suitable Somebodies does not want to be caught either dead, alive or sleeping, hehe, haha, hoho!'

'Who is dead?' the half-awake Lady with the Slender Hands must know.

'Pascal Rebello de Fonseca is considered to be dead, hehe, haha, hoho,' swagger the arrack-high munumunuppu-mongers some more.

The Lady has not seen Pascal Rebello de Fonseca dead. The Lady believes only that which her kohl-lined eyes have seen, she chooses to ignore the munumunuppu-mongers despite the trepidation in her near-naked chest.

The munumunuppu-mongers are high on country toddy they call arrack downhill Utahkamand, they choose to peer into the Lady's kohl-lined eyes, and leer at her inner beauty.

'This Lady, the princess of the Widest Footpath of Cottonpettai ... she sleeps on the other end of the Footpath in her lover's arms – *aman da*, yes man, she wears kohl, yeyeye, yoyo, oho!' leers an unsteady and high-on-arrack Royal Ragamuffin who has been awakened by the swaggering mongers.

'Aman da, yes man,' says another equally high-on-arrack and unsteady Royal Ragamuffin, 'this Lady, she wears kohl, the Indian mascara. This foreign-looking Lady wears kohl, the hallmark of eye make-up in India, also other countries with geographical boundaries lying east of Europe, yayay, yoyo, oho!'

The Lady never fails to add a layer of kohl to her fish-shaped eyes. This black layer guides her vision, believes the much sought-after Lady. Her vision tonight tells her to lie quiet, and listen to the political undertone speaking through the tongues of the four rascal and drunken Royal Ragamuffins.

The Royal Ragamuffins are stupid.

Stupid men seldom have a vision.

Vision finds comfort only within the boundaries of kohl-lined eyes. The Lady with the Slender Hands has her eyes fixed on the Royal Ragamuffins in the dark of the night. The Ragamuffins are sloshed on arrack, they do not see her open eyes. The Lady's kohl-lined eyes are hidden from all leering sight as the playful moonlight caresses the skin under her sheer printed veil.

Such is the mark of a princess, moonlight her gentle ally when enemy troupes invade her courtyard. The Lady, a princess by birth in a distant land she does not remember, exudes a distinctly Her Highness demeanour in her own courtyard called the Widest Footpath of Cottonpettai.

Perumal Arokyaswami has a strong suspicion that the Lady he sleeps with every night is not of Indian origin.

Where there's suspicion, the swaggering munumunuppu-mongers butt in with a poem, they sing: *'Two foreigners to the Indian soil lie arm in arm, their near-naked bodies entwined like snakes by moonlight, and sunshine on an Indian footpath.'*

Who is an Indian?

An Indian is either born in the geographical boundaries marked on the world map called India, or given citizenship by migration.

Migration is an unsettling term on the Widest Footpath of Cottonpettai – all its sleeping and half-awake residents squirm whenever the word rings in the air. Perumal Arokyaswami, in particular, is deeply perturbed – he has no recall of his migration to India. The rickshaw-puller's thoughts are random and perturbed – he knows he is an Indian by sweat and toil. A cycle–rickshaw-puller must sweat and pant, and only rant in private when he transports his customer from one market to another. The Lancashire of the South is well-acclaimed for its clothes market. Perumal Arokyaswami has few clothes to call his own.

Clothes cannot keep me warm in the zany Rio Beas, I freeze in its frigidly cold and fluid body. My body floats like a wooden log dislodged from its companions now riding the same truck further uphill. My body is not dead, I swim, I float, I search for my companion in vain. *Dónde es mi compañero* ... where is my companion, I ask over and again, my hoarsened voice thicker than the incessantly pelting snow.

FORTY-ONE

SENOR SINGH MONO'S BLOOD is thicker than the fresh August raindrops drenching his face – he has decided to embark upon his mission with a companion, actually two. No mission is easy without appropriate company, he has learnt from the experience of being a respectable Scout. Senor Singh Mono's mission, he has decided, will have a force of three. Two Guides have decided to keep Senor trustworthy company all the way from Cottonpettai to Manmanali. From Manmanali, the threesome force – one Scout and two Guides

– will travel by foot to the destination where Sanyasi Solali Snowmountainwala sits upside down at all times, barring when he needs to pee.

Uphill Utahkamand, the Scout and Guides surreptitiously fill their backpacks with a set of clothes, and importantly their uPods to keep them company on the long-and-not-too-certain-of-the-desired-outcome journey ahead of them.

uPods fed with Frisky Emilio's hits will keep the Scout and Guides on track as they launch upon their meandering quest across the Indian Subcontinent for the straight truth.

A Frisky Emilio tune is all over Blue Mountain Nilgiris, the munumunuppu-mongers have adapted the lyrics, they sing:

'Hey, cinco, seis, seite, ocho – get back on track!
Cinco, seis, seite, ocho
Ocho! Marcha hacia adelante, Scout and Guides
Cinco, seis, seite, ocho
Ocho! Marcha hacia atrás

Five, six, seven, eight
Eight! March forward, Scout and Guides
Five, six, seven, eight
Six! March backwards.

Forward march, Senor Singh Mono, do not look back!'

Senor Singh Mono will not look back. He has convinced the Guides – two eighteen-year-old belles in love with Frisky Emilio's perky beats, that the journey from Utahkamand to Manmanali will not bring them back to their fate.

The Guides who have agreed to play truant from the camp for the Braver than the Best would like to know what fate has in store for them, they ask their Scout comrade.

'Ask fate, why me?' beams Senor Singh Mono, and in a more serious vein declares with a sudden surge of hope in his rapidly beating heart, 'You Guides can hope for the best in life, you need not confine yourselves to those silly rules that have been framed to turn you into Suitable Somebodies, after all!'

The Scout wears hope in his heart, it can bring his mother back to his father's door, after all. Senor Singh Mono wears this hope upon his face, his wide-as-the-Pyrenees Ranges smile says it all.

For some strange reason, Senor Singh Mono is deeply drawn, wide-as-the-Pyrenees Ranges smile, et al. to all things Spanish.

For now, the Spanish numbers cinco, seis, siete, ocho will set the pace for Senor's journey along with his Guide comrades to their desired destination.

'For now, you Scout and two Guides, just cinco, seis, siete, ocho – do what you like best,' cheer the munumunuppu-mongers.

Just doing what he likes best, the Master of Sports for Suitable Somebodies decides to let his curiosity travel ahead of his toes. Uphill Utahkamand, the Master awakens from deep slumber – he follows three sets of shoe prints with his owl eyes, simultaneously sniffing the scent of future Suitable Somebodies with his long, crooked and pointed nose.

Of all the woes, the newly escaped Senor Singh Mono and his Guide comrades now need to contend with a long, crooked and pointed nose.

The long and crookedly pointed peak of the Kulkulu hill is happy to be noticed by land grabbers. This hill is prime land. I sit still upon this hill. The *viento*, si, the wind blows over the Kulkulu hill. I sit still in the Kulkulu viento. Today, the viento, si, the Himachali *hawa* is furious – it slaps me hard across my naked face.

FORTY-TWO

THE NAKED RAY OF Utahkamand sunlight is harsh and gentle at once upon this pre-monsoon morning. Senor Singh Mono and his Guide comrades have walked all night over harsh terrain, unnoticed, to escape from the camp for the Braver than the Best. At the break of dawn, the Scout and Guides have found themselves face-to-face with a harsh truth. Truth is, the Master of Sports for Suitable Somebodies has poked his long, crooked and pointed nose into their well-guarded escape plan. Yes, the Master plans to separate the trio. Senor Singh Mono and his Guide comrades cannot be separated from each other by their Master or any other – such is the gentle truth about trust between three discipline-abandoning post-teens, they think on their toes.

'Whoa ... trust the Scout and Guides to come up with an escape plan alternate to the one the Master of Sports has discovered,' whisper the trailing munumunuppu-mongers at the break of dawn.

Uphill Utahkamand, the Master of Sports is unaware that the three future Suitable Somebodies have caught his long, crooked and pointed nose prying into their well-guarded secret. Their alternate plan will of course be a secret kept locked between six lips. Three mouths defined by six brown-red lips will remain locked until their owners – Senor Singh Mono and the two Guides have actually embarked upon their journey.

For now, the threesome has returned to their staring point – they sit with mouths sealed shut by an oath of supreme secrecy made in Senor Singh Mono's private tent.

For now, the perks of being the Minister for Shelters' favourite son are supreme. A private tent in a public camp is an inevitable perk that comes automatically to the legal son of a Minister in the Indian Subcontinent. Senor Singh Mono thanks his fortunate stars back in the camp for the Braver than the Best uphill Utahkamand, also his father, the Minister.

It is not always that sons born to the same Minister become legal heirs to their father's property.

Downhill Utahkamand, the four Royal Ragamuffins, all illegally begotten sons of a certain Minister, are not documented citizens of the Indian Subcontinent – they enjoy the perks of an undisciplined existence on the Widest Footpath of Cottonpettai. This Footpath is now under dispute, the Baron of Excess with the biggest Mansion in Cottonpettai claims to have bought off this public space for his private use. The Royal Ragamuffins, by virtue of their undocumented parentage have been accorded the status of Indian citizens – they have special permission to roll on the Baron's so called private property as they please.

The Royal Ragamuffins have taken it upon their muscular shoulders to do as they please – they rebuke Perumal Arokyaswami, their fellow Footpath dweller, a foreigner upon Indian soil to bloody well return to Serendib, and now.

The August showers rain down in response – the seething Indian soil around Cottonpettai turns tepid, and the four Royal Ragamuffins continue to shower abuses at the resting rickshaw-puller.

'Ayyoo,' yelp some lurking munumunuppu-mongers, 'see how the Royal Ragamuffins squirm! They have been rebuffed by Perumal Arokyaswami – the man from Serendib has remained tepid, eyes cold as evening mist in response to the verbal threats of four Royal Ragamuffins!'

A tad over twenty years in age, and muscular, the four Royal Ragamuffins are invariably heated by Perumal Arokyaswami's tepid response. They take a not-so-secret oath to vent their chagrin by prowess of their muscular power.

Muscles and brains do not co-exist when the emotion of power intervenes. The four Royal Ragamuffins swear by the strength of their muscular power that they will give Perumal Arokyaswami a heated blow below his belt, and render his manhood extinct when the time is ripe for them to act. For now, they are not too certain the Minister for Shelters will abet such a ruthless and unthinking act – the Royal Ragamuffins turn off the heat in their heads, and take swigs of scotch from their brown brandy bottles.

'What a strange phenomenon meets our eyes, the Royal Ragamuffins have stopped themselves from an unthinking act,' observes a wise old munumunuppu-monger. 'A ruthless act is punishable by law, especially if blood is shed, limbs rendered limp, muscles and bones beaten to resemble a dish of mashed potato topped with tomato sauce in a countryside dhaba – the Royal Ragamuffins have saved themselves from imprisonment by a thinking act, I say!'

'What on earth is a dhaba?' a rather muscular and unthinking munumunuppu-monger asks aloud.

'A dhaba,' replies the wise old monger, 'is a hotel on an Indian highway found more abundantly in the northern regions of our Subcontinent. These dhabas serve spiced Indian curries to go with a range of dripping-in-oil breads and white rice for those who cannot digest wheat, and its poor cousin maida. But, at this point, what might be more pertinent for your ears to hear is that poor, unacknowledged half-brothers cannot be allowed to mingle with going-to-be Suitable Somebodies. There's a certain Minister for Shelters who lives in Chandinigarh – he is calculative, he cannot allow two half-brothers to become one. In the event of such oneness, the Minister for Shelters will be split in half, perhaps quarter, one hundred, one million parts by our very own four Royal Ragamuffins who will stake claim to his properties scattered all across the Indian Subcontinent, including Cottonpettai, by virtue of being his illegal sons. And then, the Minister will be forced to disown his manhood to prove that he has no sons, legal or illegal.'

The Lady with the Slender Hands makes her presence felt on the Widest Footpath of Cottonpettai, she laughs out loud at the wise old munumunuppu-monger's rendition of the Minister's foreseeable plight to prove his manhood otherwise. From the turn of gossip, the Lady knows only too well that neither she nor her lover, the rickshaw-puller, can be disowned by the Indian Subcontinent, let alone be shunned by a foolish Minister who panders to a certain sanyasi uphill Manmanali in Solali with the hope of being washed off all his increasing sins.

I cannot be disowned by the winds of Kulkulu. The winds are angered by my tears, my well-hidden fears. The vientos are determined to slap my fears, control my tears. The winds of change are here. Yes, the vientos of *cambio* are here. Cambio … si, change! Yes, si, change is near.

FORTY-THREE

CHANGE YOUR ATTITUDE, Jhoru Kanbi Badshah – do not wear anger upon your folded sleeve. Jhoru Kanbi Badshah has read this refrain over and again, in fact, every evening on his touch screen mobile phone. The Badtameez Baap is trying hard to discipline his truant son from behind the shackles of his own, unforgivable sin with a safe tool called the traditional mobile phone – the saddened father types out the same message to Jhoru every day after sundown.

The mobile phone is only a tool. Jhoru Kanbi Badshah is only a coolie on duty at the Grand Nizamuddin. A coolie with a missing mother whom he simply cannot seem to find. No way, this saddened coolie will not tolerate his Badtameez Baap's disciplinary act – no, not even for another day.

Another day in Rozgaarnagar means more hungry mouths to feed. The Badtameez Baap does not have a single paisa, let alone the princely sum of Rs. 15 with which to purchase a kilogramme of downgraded rice to feed his hungry wives and hungrier children – he has got the gapasapa-mongers' tongues wagging …

'Hoy, hoy, his ill-begotten children.

'Illegal children.

'What are the rights of illegal children?

'Ask the fathers who sired them, unmindful of their rights.

'Unmindful acts of procreation cannot be ignored, even by the perpetrators. These perpetrators, the Minister for Shelters, the Badtameez Baap included, will not be ignored by their illegally begotten sons.

'Do these unmindful men want the attention of sons they simply will not acknowledge?'

Sanyasi Solali Snowmountainwala is omnipresent, he hears everything everywhere, and to the best of his knowledge, sons tend to pay attention to their respective fathers. Especially those sons, including Jhoru Kanbi Badshah, who have decided to take law into their hands. Jhoru, the Sanyasi knows only too well, will use his father like a radar to find his missing mother against all laws that tell him to lay off the complex search. His traded mother, he does not understand, is caught in a complex family web. This web, her emotional territory, as she angers and tears, laughs and sneers, holding dearly onto the flimsy threads of life.

'Life,' intrude the phusphus-mongers into the Sanyasi's thoughts, and repeat the Holy Man's discourse aloud for all to hear, 'is of the conscious and sub-conscious mind, of God, of soul, of emotion, of emotionlessness, of seeking the mountains for escape from societal ties.'

Escaped from societal ties, Sanyasi Solali Snowmountainwala is pleased that his discourse is being heard, and repeated – he lets his soul hang upside down. Every soul has a conscience. The Sanyasi's conscience cannot be caught hanging upside down amidst snow-mountains where everything seems downside up – he decides to stretch his limbs instead, and embarks on a walk to ponder matters of identity and crisis.

Upside down, downside up, *ultam pultam, dubackdoom* … I toss my emotions into the rambunctious Rio Beas, and blabber incoherently. My identity is a crisis, my life is upside down … I need a drag of charas to calm me down … I retrieve the joint the Sanyasi has personally rolled for mi aching corazón, and smoke up … ultam pultam, dubackdoom, mi *vida,* si … my life is suddenly downside up ... I lay my emotions to rest upside down, my anger and tears hanging precariously on a snow-mountain nube in the Indian State of Himachal Pradesh ... si, this is vida ...

FORTY-FOUR

THERE IS A DEFINITE THREAT to the Minister for Shelters' well-concealed emotions in OneKmBungWow – his minions might suddenly find his eyes brimming with tears. The Minister cannot rest until he has stood upside down, trampled his fears, squashed his tears, and run amok at the behest of his guru Shri Shri Shri Shri and Shri Sanyasi Solali Snowmountainwala. He summons his Humbassador, drives uphill Chandinigarh to Manmanali, and beyond the town's Central Market to Solali.

The Minister for Shelters is en route to Solali where the Sanyasi with the open third eye hangs upside down to perceive mountains, trees, hill men and women too, downside up.

Of course, the women of these hills do not fancy being watched downside up. Sanyasi Solali Snowmountainwala cannot be perturbed by what the women think – he has no one else to please but himself in this scenic mountain town.

Solali is of international importance – it is home to a deemed university, a hydroelectric plant and a wood-cutting unit. The Originally Solali Kesar, of course, is its erstwhile inhabitant with many eyes, national and international, seeking the flower's secret hideout. The Originally Solali Kesar, under the given circumstances of unwarranted discovery by intrusive eyes, is currently pleased to be guarded by Manu Gaddi and the People of the Highest Hill.

Yes, the Originally Solali Kesar can think. In fact, this petite Kesar breathes, and occasionally talks.

'What's going on in these snow-mountain parts where a Kesar, a delicate flower, is said to talk?' some unsuspecting disciples speak out loud.

'Well, the going will only get more convoluted until the Originally Solali Kesar is actually found,' the Sanyasi who hears and sees everything everywhere, mutters to himself, and continues to bless all lost people who are here to find purpose in life.

Once lost and now found people in the mountain ranges of Himachal Pradesh are reluctant to return to their respective towns, cities and other near-urban geographical areas with a large number of motorcars. In the mountain ranges of Himachal Pradesh, lost people tend to find hope in pristine pebbles, River Beas' ripples, even Sanyasi Solali Snowmountainwala's stubbles.

'Stubbles?' a bunch of newly found disciples quiver. 'Where on earth has Sanyasi Solali Snowmountainwala's thick-as-a-sparrow's-nest beard disappeared to morph into mere stubbles?'

Of course, the phusphus-mongers have the answer: 'The Sanyasi shaved it for a cause – he does not want to be found. At least, not found easily by the Minister for Shelters.'

'Are they not as thick as thieves – the Minister for Shelters and the now beardless Sanyasi with a nascent stubble?' the disciples with newfound souls would like to know.

'Not really, the Sanyasi is not what he seems,' the phusphus-mongers giggle.

Sanyasi Solali Snowmountainwala's identity has been carefully established over the past twelve years with his thick-as-a-sparrow's-nest beard.

Beard … *daadi* … In Tamil, in Marathi, in Hindi too, daadi is the accepted word for the revered beard.

The much-revered *barba*, which the Sanyasi has carefully nurtured with every exotic oil extracted from the Himachali almond and the native olive of Spain, speaks of his youthful vitality.

Barba in Spanish refers to the same beard, without which the Sanyasi looks rather weird.

I wear a nose ring, I feel weird. I am a bride, the nose ring is my identity. I am a Kulkulu bride … I wear an embroidered pheran – this wedding costume a garden of ethereal silver flowers besotted by spring. I wear silver earrings to match the garden on my pheran. This garden is my identity, and I wear it for all to see … No matter what I wear, my identidad tells me I am a stranger in these parts. Mi identity as a Kulkulu bride is being watched closely by the hill men and their wives from a safe distance, their presence in these parts hidden to my eye. Never mind, kill mi identity. My identity is dead, so go take a plunge in the rambunctious Rio Beas because you don't know who I really am.

FORTY-FIVE

THE RAINS HAVE LET up in Cottonpettai, the noon sun shines brightly, and the Fellows of the Footpath are transfixed – they have just heard a man construed to be dead, speak. When the dead decide to speak up, the living see nightmares by daylight.

Pascal Rebello de Fonseca is a nightmare for all those who have arrived at the inevitable conclusion that he is dead.

Noon moves closer to sundown, Perumal Arokyaswami snuggles up to his Lady – he strokes her bare arms, and whispers into her naked ear: 'Is he dead?'

'Is who dead?' the Lady responds.

'Is Pascal Rebello de Fonseca dead?' Perumal Arokyaswami screams out rather loud, his voice gruff with the mature essence of authentic Vignesh Beedi rising above the winds that have gathered over the Widest Footpath of Cottonpettai upon this twilight hour.

The Lady chooses to gaze at the rising swirl of winds, also into the fading light of day in response to her lover's louder than intended query.

Of course, mystery looms large over the supposed death of Pascal Rebello de Fonseca who simply disappeared into the fading light of day when Perumal Arokyaswami was away on a pilgrimage last December, the holy month of Karthika.

Last December, Perumal Arokyaswami, accoutred in black, wore beads around his masculine neck, and walked barefoot up the Holiest Hill, the mountain abode of Lord Murugan in the State of Kerala.

Lord Murugan is Lord Shiva's son, according to mythological sources.

Lord Murugan has many holy abodes, including some on mountain tops in distant jungles in the heartland of Serendib. Perumal Arokyaswami had no recollection of the Murugan Temple, the sanctum where he was given his name, until Pascal Rebello de Fonseca took him under his foster care. Pascal Rebello de Fonseca went on to raise him in the faith he was born into, and Perumal Arokyaswami has, since the age to fifteen, made a week-long pilgrimage to the Holiest Hill on every month of Karthika, not missing a single year in between.

Pascal Rebello de Fonseca is a man of distant connections, distinct roots. His own roots find their origins in Spanish territory – Pascal Rebello de Fonseca's ancestors discovered Serendib upon a lucky day in the twelfth century. Pascal Rebello de Fonseca's earliest ancestor was called a Sephardi Jew with immediate connections in Spanish territory. The Lady with the Slender Hands knows Spanish. She knows even more about Pascal Rebello de Fonseca, but is not about to disclose anything to anybody, not even to her lover Perumal Arokyaswami.

Jhoru Kanbi Badshah knows where to run when his head is in a tizzy, he returns to Rozgaarnagar to rest his wavy tuft upon his foster mother, the Magnolia Tree, where the world is suddenly serene. In this world, Jhoru's heart is thankful – he looks heavenwards, and salutes the royal Afghan, his ancestor. This Afghan, the same man who has left his Supreme Heir with a treasury of ten gold nagaths. Jhoru, by virtue of his birth as the firstborn son of the Badtameez Baap, is Supreme Heir to the nagaths which are presently in strict custody of the latter. The latter, the Badtameez Baap, is in strict custody of his ill-begotten sons who will not allow him to part with Jhoru's inherited fortune.

Jhoru Kanbi Badshah is in strict custody of his need. His need, an emotion called greed. His greed, born out of a deficit. Jhoru Kanbi Badshah is in deficit of affection from his mother. His mother, the woman he cannot seem to find in a hurry given his limited resources. Jhoru is immensely perturbed, he hugs the Magnolia Tree, his foster mother, and makes a petition to the heavens: 'Bring my Badtameez Baap to repent for his past sin. The sin of trading my precious mother for *rupayya* – bring her right now!'

I give sin a bad name in Kulkulu, I have a dark *secreto* to keep. Yes, I have a secret, a dark secreto to keep. I have a son, si, a *hijo*, and I have kept his birth a secreto all these years. I am dying to blurt out the secreto born out of my adolescent sin with the Minister for Shelters, but no thank you.

FORTY-SIX

SENOR SINGH MONO IS dying to make an exit right now from the camp for the Braver than the Best in Blue Mountain Utahkamand, but there's the long-nosed and owl-eyed Master to contend with.

The Master of Sports for Suitable Somebodies is not just a man with owl eyes and a long, crooked nose, he has a rather crafty head – he has deprived many families of their wives. Senor Singh Mono has wind of the owl-eyed Master's vice, his ears perk up to listen to a conversational aside by a lurking munumunuppu-monger.

'Listen clearly to this aside ... Jhoru Kanbi Badshah's mother was once a respectable wife,' blurts a grey-haired munumunuppu-monger.

'What exactly does respectable connote?' Senor Singh Mono butts in with a question to the munumunuppu-monger's astonishment.

'Err ..., okay, so to answer your question ... society prefixes the adjective "respectable" to an individual's name in order to illustrate that he or she is correct. Preferably, always correct,' replies the old monger, and continues to blurt out some more asides about the owl-eyed Master. 'The Master of Sports for Suitable Somebodies is always correct, he wears respectability on his sleeve. His sleeve is respectable. His sleeve is long. Very long. Always long. About fifteen batches of students before you, yes, all former Scouts and Guides of St. Alphonsious Pre-University College have been intrigued by the length of this Master's long sleeves – so you too, had better show some aplomb, Senor!'

'What pray does the Master of Sports for Suitable Somebodies conceal beneath his sleeves all the way down to his wrists?' asks Senor.

'A few unmentionable tattoos starting from his shoulders all the way down to his wrists,' replies the munumunuppu-monger.

'Whoa ... the Master has tattoos ... that too unmentionable ones under his long sleeves ... this is a vital clue ... it will certainly lead me to my biological mother,' yells Senor Singh Mono, signalling his two Guide comrades to march to the Frisky Emilio refrain, he plays the rhythm on his uPod.

'Cinco, seis, seite, ocho

'Ocho! Marcha hacia adelante, Profesor!

'Cinco, seis, seite, ocho

'Ocho! Marcha hacia atrás, Profesor!

'Five, six, seven, eight

'Eight! March forward, Teacher ... er ... Master!

'Er ... march backwards, Master of Sports for Suitable Somebodies,' yell the Scout and two Guides with newfound glee. They have a vital clue – they trace the owl-eyed Master's shoe prints, and follow the rather long trail to River Pyraka, uphill Utahkamand.

'Pssst ...' says the old munumunuppu-monger, 'Senor Singh Mono and his two Guide comrades are three steps ahead of their owl-eyed Master. The three eighteen-year-olds have caught their Master in the buff, waist above, swimming in the deep, bold waters of River Pyraka which flows 19 kilometres uphill from the main town of Utahkamand.

'Senor Singh Mono and the two Guides on the threshold of their Solali mountain escapade have relied on their dear Thentoda friends, the respectable jungle folk of Utahkamand. Where the Master's shoe prints ended suddenly, the Thentodas appeared to lead the threesome to the peak of Moogambobettu Mountain where River Pyraka first swells, then tapers northwards, and swerves westwards to meet the Glen Abend dam. Thanks to the Thentodas, the Master of Sports for Suitable Somebodies has been caught full body tattoo swimming in 'off human limits' waters in the Pyraka and Glen Abend dam fed hydroelectric plant.

'The Scout and two Guides have caught their owl-eyed and tattooed Master performing an unsuitable act. One man's unsuitable act will help a threesome's pact to unveil the mystery of a missing biological mother,' the old munumunuppu-monger decrees.

I am a mother, I am a child. The Originally Solali Kesar is a child in the womb of Solali, and Rio Anjuna is her amniotic fluid. Rio Anjuna, prime tributary of the bullicioso Rio Beas, flows boldly in the Valley of Solali. This rio, she is warm despite her cold fluidity. I am a mother, I am cold despite my warm body. I am a madre, I have a *matriz*, si, I have a womb. I, a madre, wash my womb in the cold warmth of Rio Anjuna.

FORTY-SEVEN

THE WOMB IS THE most abused part of a woman's body, especially when a lady has been coaxed into a compromising position by the Minister for Shelters. The Royal Ragamuffins, all four of them as a matter of disputable fact, have slept, played, swum, floated and turned cartwheels in the cushion of the life-supporting amniotic fluid for nine months, each in a different woman's womb. In his youth, the Minister for Shelters preferred to coax a different woman, almost always of foreign origin, into a compromising position, on each of those lonely nights when he had no land deals to settle.

On each of those lonely nights the Minister for Shelters is said to have plunged in naked desire, and planted a wild seed in a foreign womb. The Minister's wild seeds are now full-grown men with common ancestors from their paternal side – they call themselves the Royal Ragamuffins of the Widest Footpath of Cottonpettai.

Every man and woman living on the Widest Footpath of Cottonpettai has ancestors. The Lady with the Slender Hands and Perumal Arokyaswami have ancestors from the same country, which by the way, is not the Indian soil. But the two, the Lady and the rickshaw-puller, are neither related by blood nor marriage.

Given their foreign identities, Perumal Arokyaswami does

not believe the Lady with the Slender Hands can remain secure on the Widest Footpath of Cottonpettai without a legally sanctioned marriage to endorse their union.

The Lady has had past experiences that do not permit her to believe marriage can bring her back the same respect she had grown accustomed to before her womb had become home to a foetus. Perumal Arokyaswami persists, the Lady does not wish to be pushed out of her choice. At least not right now, when nothing must come between the Lady's wish and the irresistible kiss. Perumal Arokyaswami drags the unlit end of his masculine Vignesh Beedi, and proceeds to kiss the Lady with the Slender Hands ... his gleaming cycle rickshaw their rexine bed of passion under the shimmering afternoon sky.

This afternoon is like any other upon the Widest Footpath of Cottonpettai, the sun shines on its inhabitants as they go about their businesses. The business people of the Footpath sell lost electronic gadgets found in parks and other public areas, including the Main Vegetable Market, the Supreme Fish Market and the Market for Native Factory Spun Cotton Garments well within the radius of Cottonpettai.

This afternoon is not like any other upon the Widest Footpath of Cottonpettai – the Lady and her paramour Perumal Arokyaswami are performing an act that is acceptable only when day disappears into night.

The moneyed people of Main Town Lancashire continue to shop for found electronic gadgets in full view of the slanderous act, which by unrecorded Indian law, is permitted only by night.

The Lady with the Slender Hands is a woman of instant emotion – she will keep her passion alive until the moneyed people stop gaping at her private act of intimacy.

Intimacy is a secular act as the Lady makes her independence known in public.

The public has passed dissatisfactory statements regarding the Lady's independence.

The public has failed to notice that the Lady with the Slender Hands is not alone in her independence.

It takes two to negotiate a well-versed kiss in a cycle rickshaw, unmindful of prying public on the Widest Footpath of Cottonpettai.

It takes two to feel the imbalance of hormones triggered by touch. This imbalance has been enthused by an emotion between my man and I, while we slept, and dreamt freely between earth and sky. Si, mi *hombre*, yes, my man and I lay down to dream, and touch each other to trigger passion. This passion between mi hombre and I was triggered while we dreamt our own dreams, and reached out to each other in the dark of the night under the star-studded sparkle of the naked cielo ... I open mi ojos tonight to stare into the naked sky, mi hombre is nowhere in sight. I close mi eyes once more to witness mi hombre and the cielo, all drifting in the sleeping Rio Beas – no end to this dream is in sight.

FORTY-EIGHT

IN THE NORTHERN REGIONS of the Indian Subcontinent, sleeping on the edge of a fledgling rainbow, Sanyasi Solali Snowmountainwala is oblivious to the furore growing inconsistently louder as a mob of chattering novices walk uphill Manmanali.

'Pssst ...,' whisper the phusphus-mongers, 'these novices have pledged their boyish pranks and playtime of *lagori*, also snow-mountain cricket to serve the upside down man with the almost always sleeping third eye. Lagori, as the novices play it, is a game of seven stones that are carefully picked by boys under the age of fourteen from the bed of the rambunctious River Beas. These pebbles are to be knocked down by an apple, preferably a half ripe fruit of Kulkulu variety to cause minimal harm to the natural stones of Beas. Snow-mountain cricket, as the novices play it, requires one piece of drifting wood procured from the rambunctious River Beas, and of course an apple, preferably a raw fruit of Kulkulu variety to ensure that the edible ball travels far enough to score boys under fourteen years of age boundaries, adding up to four runs at one shot.'

In the southern regions of the Indian Subcontinent, the Royal Ragamuffins have crossed respectable boundaries to hatch a murderous plan. They plan to murder a man on the Widest Footpath of Cottonpettai.

Their plan has been overheard, there's incoherent munumunuppu of varying detail mentioning people who live on the Widest Footpath of Cottonpettai, and others who have never visited it.

'Too bad for the plan.'

'Too good for the man who cannot be murdered yet.'

'Good, man, murder – run for your life Senor Singh Mono.'

'*Nalladhi, manidhan, kolai* – run for your life Perumal Arokyaswami.'

'*Achha, aadmi, khoon* – run for your life Master of Sports for Suitable Somebodies.'

'*Changle, manusa, khoona* – run for your life Badtameez Baap.'

'*Bueno, hombre, asesinato* – run for your life Pascal Rebello de Fonseca.'

Pascal Rebello de Fonseca did run for his life on a quarter moon night. No one knows whether he still has life.

Everyone knows the rest of the above-mentioned people are alive. No one knows who the Royal Ragamuffins are planning to murder. Everyone knows their murderous plan has been overheard. Everyone knows that overheard plans are incongruent with details that are almost never factual.

Sanyasi Solali Snowmountainwala thrives on factual details. From the sound of the pounding in his sleeping head, he has factual proof that the mob of novices is an apple's throw away. Sanyasi Solali Snowmountainwala decides to sit head upright to gain a third eye view of the mob – he sees an army of fourteen-year-old boys, all indigenous inhabitants of the snow mountains, pelting the air with half-ripe apples and pebbles from the River Beas.

The Sanyasi decides to first feed and rest the boys before he gets down to addressing the reason for their angst.

I rest my pounding head upon a pebble in the bed of Rio Beas. This pebble, my water pillow. This water is cold, it shakes mi out of mi *sueño*, si, my dream. Mi sueño is dead. Am I dead too? A dead bride in Rio Beas? Am I a *muerto novia* … a dead bride in the cold Rio Beas?

FORTY-NINE

SOMEONE HAS DROPPED DEAD in Chandinigarh, there's phusphus everywhere.

'Dead?'

'She is dead.'

'Dead!'

'All that is alive is dead.'

'Dead is a lonely word.'

'All those who are lonely are dead.'

'Senor Singh Mono's Caretaker has dropped dead.'

'The Caretaker had dropped her wifely duties to return home to her mother last evening. No one knows how the Caretaker dropped dead, instead ...'

'The Minister for Shelters has dropped his plans to visit Solali, and returned to OneKmBungWow half way through his sojourn.'

'Senor Singh Mono has dropped his plans for the secret escapade with the two ready-to-run Guides, to return home to OneKmBungWow.'

'OneKmBungWow wears tragedy in its façade. Chandinigarh must wallow in this tragedy ... after all, the Mistress of OneKmBungWow was a Mahaan Stree ...'

'A Mahaan Stree is a Great Lady of supreme reputation and power. Power, which comes with wealth and/or marriage to a wealthy man. The Caretaker was married to a wealthy man.'

'The Minister for Shelters is a wealthy man.'

'How does a man become wealthy?'

'This question cannot be answered at this dire hour of tragedy, let the wealthy Minister of Chandinigarh wallow in self-pity.'

Chandinigarh is a perplexed town. The phusphus-mongers are perplexed by the sudden dropping dead of the hale and healthy Caretaker – they begin to sing praises of the Mahaan Stree.

'Balle Mahana Aurata,' sing the four Royal Ragamuffins in praise of the Caretaker, only to be hushed by the citizens of Chandinigarh.

Balle Balle is a purely Punjabi phrase with no parallel translation in any other spoken language – it is meant to depict sheer happiness. There is no happiness in the Caretaker's death. The four Royal Ragamuffins have decided to stifle their happiness for a change.

With the Caretaker's death, change is inevitable in OneKmBungWow. The Minister for Shelters has welcomed change ever since he decided to coax different women into compromising positions on lonely nights.

'The Minister for Shelters is lonely.'

'Dead is a lonely word.'

'Is the Minister for Shelters dead?'

I have no shelter in Kulkulu, I shiver in the summer viento. Summer in Kulkulu is colder than the hottest day in Cottonpettai. I long for a summer day in Cottonpettai. I long for a *verano día* in Cottonpettai. From English Valley Kulkulu to the Lancashire of the South, I long for a verano día … I long for a summer day.

FIFTY

IT IS A LONG summer day, and Sanyasi Solali Snowmountainwala has found a poem written on a piece of paper – he assimilates the words carefully for his third eye to register.

Longing for a Summer Day in Cottonpettai
Winter woollens stifle her day
Day is just another word in the Valley of Kulkulu
Before you utter 'here comes the sun' in Kulkulu, the valley sleeps.
Cottonpettai never sleeps.
The sun never sets in Cottonpettai.
Especially for the rich landlords and business barons of Cottonpettai.
Barons and landlords rich by cotton
Cotton a rich crop
Cotton a cash crop
Cash crop of Chandinigarh in the Indian State of Punjab
Cash crop of Algauv in the Indian State of Gujarat
Cash crop of Cottonpettai in the Indian State of Tamil Nadu
Cotton, the sunshine crop
Cotton for the poor
Cotton for the rich
Cotton for Perumal Arokyaswami who smokes the cash crop of Nippanini and Ajay Nagar
Tobacco the cash crop of the Indian State of Maharashtra
Tobacco the cash crop of the Indian State of Karnataka
Tobacco for the rich
Tobacco for the poor
Masculino tobacco for the Lady with the Slender Hands
Holding an active Vignesh Beedi, tobacco at its potent best on the Widest Footpath of Cottonpettai.

Here comes the sun in Cottonpettai.
Sun, sun, sun.
Sun, son, sun,
Son in the sun.
Where is the Lady's son?
Who is the Lady's son?
It is time to return to the sleeping Valley of Kulkulu where there is no talk of a son.
The sun shines briefly in Kulkulu.
Bask in the Kulkulu sun
Until winter woollens stifle her day in the Valley of Kulkulu.

I feel stifled in my embroidered pheran, garment of exotic woollen from the Valley of Kulkulu. Woollen sheared from the *oveja* ... si, the sheep, which graze the valley and drink the waters of Rio Beas to digest their meal. Oveja reared for their fine wool at the Fur and Animal Breeding Station located at a latitude of 31.58 degrees north and a longitude of 77.20 degrees east. Animals bred in natural captivity downhill Kulkulu in lowland Gracia. I am a *cautivo natural* ... si, a natural captive of the snow mountains. These mountains are now mi casa, si ... my home, yet I am restless.

FIFTY-ONE

HOME IS RESTLESS WITH emotions gone awry between the Caretaker and the Minister for Shelters. The just recently declared dead Caretaker's anger is vocal on the unmade master bed in OneKmBungWow. Nothing perturbs the Minister for Shelters more than tell-tale signs of lovemaking visible for all his staff to witness at the break of dawn on his master bed. The Minister resembles an irate snow-mountain cloud hovering over an arid desert – all citizens of Chandinigarh relate this phenomenon to deep sorrow at the loss of a good housekeeper called a spouse.

The Minister for Shelters loses his composure, he weeps at the sight of his unmade bed. He weeps because this sight, the unmade bed, is not the way he remembers leaving it before embarking upon his sojourn to Solali.

The Caretaker has left the Minister's bed unmade by choice. The Caretaker, it has been implied by phusphus-mongers in OneKmBungWow, has used the Minister for Shelter's private double bed in his absence. The Caretaker, it is being whispered, loud enough for the Minister for Shelters to hear, was on the unmade bed with a man, who is not her legal husband.

The Minister for Shelters is the Caretaker's legal husband.

The Minister for Shelters is a man.

The Minister for Shelters has never coaxed the Caretaker, his legal wife, into a compromising position on his master bed.

Of course, the Minister for Shelters has no recall of his coaxing abilities on those inebriated nights when the amount of liquor he consumed directly impacted his actions.

The Minister for Shelters is inebriated almost on every other night when matters pertinent to lands and shelters thereof have been put to rest with his best interests duly factored into bond-papered agreements.

Agreements are precursors to disagreements in OneKmBungWow.

Disagreements lead to unmade beds in OneKmBungWow.

Unmade beds distress the Minister for Shelters who is

as sober as a dented steel cycle rickshaw wheel – he sits mournfully beside the dead body of the Caretaker.

Perumal Arokyaswami weeps like a distressed cumulonimbus cloud at the sight of dented steel – he has just fallen off his cycle rickshaw right at the centre of the Supreme Fish Market in Cottonpettai. The shining wheel of the cycle rickshaw is dented. Perumal Arokyaswami's pride is dented. The shining wheel is his pride. This wheel is made of steel. Steel, a rare jewel upon the Widest Footpath of Cottonpettai.

'*Yewww* ...,' observes a sly munumunuppu-monger, 'Cottonpettai is breathless with vanity.

'Vanity precedes a fallen foreigner.

'Fallen foreigner Perumal Arokyaswami weeps, he is utterly distressed!'

I have a new name downstream Kulkulu, they call me a fallen foreigner. Hi, I am *caído extranjero* ... si, a fallen foreigner drifting in distress downstream Rio Beas, and beyond it to lowland Gracia. Si, you can call me a caído extranjero. Actually, you can call me anything, but only if you happen to be my Príncipe. Just call me, I will stop drifting, and change my course.

FIFTY-TWO

THE COURSE OF THE vivacious River Pyraka is determined by the deep lefts, and deeper rights that the ranges of Blue Mountain Nilgiris have formed in an effort to show off their daring and dangerous, yet caring personality.

The peaks and troughs of Blue Mountain Nilgiris are part of a larger family of ranges called the Western Ghats which join the contours of the Indian Subcontinent all the way from the States of Gujarat to Kerala, covering Maharashtra, Orissa, Karnataka, Tamil Nadu, the Union Territory of Goa, too, along its course.

Traversing the course of the Blue Mountains, its indigenous people, the Thentodas, follow the Pyraka through its meandering lefts and sharp rights, praising this water body – source of their food, quencher of their thirst, this river their life-giver.

'Awoom, Awaam, Awoom,' the Thentodas praise River Pyraka at its deepest and furthermost point, they dip their long-haired heads, also bare their chests in its cool waters – they come face-to-face with a pair of hands that do not quite resemble the indigenous texture of their own people.

'What the Awoom!' the Thentodas exclaim in combined flabber-fluster. 'Who in the holy Pyraka's name do these tattooed hands belong to, we say – Awoom, Awaam, Awoom.'

There is no place where the munumunuppu-mongers fail to pry – they reach the scene of discovery, they cry: 'The Master of Sports for Suitable Somebodies does not know that he has been watched near-bare-bodied and swimming in the depth of River Pyraka, his red-bordered tattoos highly visible by fading daylight for all the Thentodas of Blue Mountain Nilgiris to see. This Master's tattoos carry secrets from a distinct day in his youth. These secrets are screaming to be discovered in the territory of the Thentodas.'

Downhill Utahkamand, Perumal Arokyaswami stretches his hands – he wears his tattoos with the secret pride of a freshly anointed king.

'Alas, what false pride,' the senior munumunuppu-monger exclaims, 'Perumal Arokyaswami can neither be a king in Serendib nor a ruler in the Indian Subcontinent.'

'But why can't a rickshaw-puller be a king?' a rather young and dunderheaded munumunuppu-monger questions out of turn.

'Turn your nascent ears to this: Serendib and India have been declared as democratic nations. Kings, as I might point out to dunderheads, have no place in democratic nations,' replies the senior monger with poise.

'So why am I hearing that a certain Minister for Shelters who owns a rather big bungalow in the city of Chandinigarh is living like a king?' the dunderhead asks with a smirk.

'*Awwwwooch*, the Minister for Shelters ... well, he is no less than a king,' says the senior monger. 'In fact, even as we speak, I have word from fellow saha-mongers that the Minister for Shelters is a widower now that the Caretaker has been declared dead. Yes, a widower waiting for his dear and legal son Senor Singh Mono to appear on the scene of death, and perform the last rites for the Caretaker. It is staunchly believed in Chandinigarh that last rites performed by a legally begotten son will ensure smooth passage of the just-declared-dead person to the nether world.'

'Is this nether world called Solali?

'Or is it called Serendib, a world in an island?

'Or, better still, is it called the Widest Footpath of Cottonpettai where the Caretaker can acquaint herself with other people who have been declared dead to the living world?' the dunderhead makes an effort to show off his prowess with wordplay.

'The Fellows of the Footpath are dead. The Fellows of the Footpath have no legal documents to prove their identities. But the Fellows of the Footpath serve the living. The living, including the Minister for Shelters, have well-documented identification cards to show off their citizenship to established authorities anywhere on planet earth,' says the senior munumunuppu-monger, deftly deviating from the topic under contention.

Suddenly, piercingly, Perumal Arokyaswami's voice splices the conversation – he cries to the open skies: 'The Widest Footpath of Cottonpettai is on planet earth for heaven's sake.'

The open skies hear the lament of a man with a dented wheel of steel. This wheel sets his neatly washed cycle rickshaw in motion every day and other night to transport passengers to their intended destinations. This wheel is Perumal Arokyaswami's sole means to earn rice, curry and the occasional fish from the stagnant lake halfway uphill Utahkamand. This wheel feeds Perumal Arokyaswami and the Lady with the Slender Hands as well. Alas, this wheel is now dented.

'Who on planet earth has dented Perumal Arokyaswami's wheel of steel?' the munumunuppu-mongers wonder in their own thick heads.

I had a will of steel until that winter night when he touched my hand, and his flesh lingered on my naked skin until the break of dawn. When a will of steel melts, the human body morphs into a fluid jellyfish. I, a jellyfish in Rio Beas. The touch from that winter's night so real, a romantic interlude between a jellyfish and a prince. Perumal Arokyaswami is not a prince ... a príncipe cannot romance a *gelatina pez* ... I repeat – a prince simply cannot romance a gelatina pez, si ... a jellyfish!

FIFTY-THREE

HAIL JHORU KANBI BADSHAH – he is no longer a prince. This prince is now the Emperor of a territory that does not belong to him in the first place.

Jhoru Kanbi Badshah rules the entire territory between Platform No. Fourteen and Platform No. Twenty Three in the busy railway station of the Grand Nizamuddin – he has earned his kingly title by the sweat of his toil. This self-crowned king has several coolie disciples – he fights for their fundamental rights whenever time from his coolie duties in his platform territory permits.

Hail the Minister for Shelters, he is a Voted Head and self-crowned king – he can grant citizenships to people with suspect parentage at his will. But alas, he has withheld the citizenship rights of the four Royal Ragamuffins in lieu of their suspect parentage to save his own reputation from slander.

Never mind, the four Royal Ragamuffins find excitement in death – they have been invited by the Minister to the Caretaker's funeral, despite their suspect parentage.

The Caretaker's death has caused much excitement among the citizens of Chandinigarh. The citizens aka saha-mongers have gathered at street corners, they can also be found at the Main Square, the Balle Football Stadium, even the big Peepal Tree near the Chandinigarh Government School. In every corner of this posh city, the citizens are discussing the nature of the Caretaker's death in whispers.

Whispers seldom remain within the boundaries of a gathered group.

When whispers travel beyond the boundaries of a gathered group in Chandinigarh, they morph into new sentences which have no congruence with the original news whatsoever.

The khakhi-clad law enforcers of Chandinigarh are enraged.

Enraged, they tour the city, and scream into their handheld loudspeakers, '*Phusphusana mana hai.*'

The citizens of Chandinigarh turn deaf ears, the instruction bellowed in Hindi cannot control the wild whispers enveloping the city. These wild whispers are akin to an inebriated *toofaan* – a violent Indian storm that is slandering a certain Minister's reputation must be put to rest.

The law enforcers are further enraged – they bellow above the rising toofaan of whispers: 'Saha mana hai.'

No saha, no phusphusana, not even whisper can be crushed by the intoxicating effects of the wild toofaan which is shaking up the Minister's reputation at Chandinigarh's public mourning points. The saha, the phusphusana, the gossip rises above the instructions bellowing through the handheld speakers, and explodes in the politician's ears, he squirms.

The exploding gossip is bound to upset the political superiority of the Minister for Shelters at the State, and most certainly at the Centre. The Centre responds to public furore when whispers travel beyond four solid walls, into the streets, enter public places, ride buses and trains on highways to bigger cities, and finally arrive at the metropolis in question – the Undeniable Capital of India.

The Centre works in haphazard ways with high-handed ministers orchestrating the affairs of the country from the heads of rectangular glass-top tables. It is too hot for high-handed ministers of the Centre to step out during the months of May, June, July, August, September, and most of October, up until Diwali, the festival of lights, which sometimes finds a date on the Indian calendar in November. In December, the high-handed Voted Heads, including a certain Minister for Shelters, must take official holidays, and travel to warmer regions. The seaside in the Union Territory of Goa somewhere close to the stomach of the Indian Subcontinent located at a latitude 15.49 degrees north, and a longitude of 73.83 degrees east, is a much-recommended region by ministerial holiday advisors for its sun, its shine and its nonchalant attitude towards high-handed ministers.

The snow mountains of Solali are high-handed – they do not care a Dollar, in fact not even a Euro, for my compromised emotional plight. The snow mountains of Solali have never melted to a warm human touch which has lingered beyond the night – how will they empathize with my emotional plight – I need a drag of charas, please. The high-handed Solali mountains are emotional tonight, the snow has begun to melt from the highest peak visible to my azul eye. My heart melts as I watch the snow invading the sparkling Rio Beas and jerks its frisky fluid momentum. I wear my melted heart, si, mi *derretido* corazón on the long sleeves of my bridal pheran. My derretido corazón watches the disappearing snow from the comfort of the long sleeves of my bridal pheran. Mi corazón pounds fast and loud at the sight of this natural divorce – how can the snow leave the Solali mountain bare?

FIFTY-FOUR

THE LADY WITH THE Slender Hands has undergone a natural divorce.

A natural divorce does not require legal sanction from any court of law on planet earth.

In fact, a natural divorce does not require sanction from the other partner in confluence with whom the Lady with the Slender Hands once begot a dark-haired son with eyes the colour of azul – this blue the same as the hue of the ocean that separates India from Serendib.

This son has eyes like his mother, hair like his father.

This son is confused because his mother, the Caretaker, is dead.

The Caretaker's eyes are now permanently closed. When her eyes were open, they were not the colour of the ocean playing host to oil ships, luxury liners and motor boats, also fishing coracles between India and Serendib.

Senor Singh Mono must lift the now permanently shut Caretaker's eyelids one last time. Senor Singh Mono must understand why the Caretaker's eyes do not match the colour of his own pair of windows to planet earth.

Planet earth is taking a nap upon this summer afternoon. The intense atmospheric heat has left the planet limp, taking all the oxygen-inhaling creatures across its intricate web of latitudes and longitudes on its midday dreaming tour.

Jhoru Kanbi Badshah awakens from his midday nap to find the Twenty Third platform of the Grand Nizamuddin shaking. Passengers, fellow coolies and tea vendors are all shaking with newfound fear. The four Royal Ragamuffins, bored out of their non-existent wits, have fled the scene of the Caretaker's impending funeral, and decided to invade the peace within the geographical territory of the Twenty Third platform with a bout of bullets, their inebriated hands shaking dangerously. Passengers to and from the length and breadth of the Indian Subcontinent run pell-mell as bullets targeted in haphazard directions, fly at random intervals, instilling fresh fear among the temporary inhabitants of the Grand Nizamuddin.

The Emperor cannot be perturbed by random bullets. Even less so by four stupid and random Ragamuffins who seem to have left all common sense back in the perturbed wombs of the mothers who begot them. Jhoru Kanbi Badshah, the ruling Emperor of the entire geographical territory between Platform No. Fourteen and Platform No. Twenty Three in the Humongous Railway Station of the Grand Nizamuddin, is all set to spank the four Royal Ragamuffins one by one.

First, Jhoru Kanbi Badshah must shout out a strict order for every Ragamuffin on the platform to hear.

'*Apne nakli goliyon se bhare, asli bandhookon ko neeche phenko,*' shouts the Emperor, instruction strict and loud in the Indian tongue of the territory, clear for every Ragamuffin to hear.

The four Royal Ragamuffins are taken aback – they drop their fake guns with newfound fear.

Fear is now a recognized sentiment on the Twenty Third platform of the Grand Nizamuddin, thanks to four Royal Ragamuffins with neither identity cards nor brains to save their skins in dire time.

I recognize fear in the melting snow territory. I wear my *temor*, si, mi fear upon my ashen face. The snow melts some more, my temor increases, my ashen face turns rojo, my ojos spurt tears. Newfound tears are tell-tale signs of hidden fears ... these hidden temors lying dormant beneath the snow, on the surface of the Solali mountains ... Mountains hiding manzana trees, Silver Oak, Badam branches and Kesar buds – Himachal's natural wealth hidden beneath the layer of deep winter snow. Beneath the layer of temor upon my ashen face, I wear a shield of grit. This grit, my weapon against the natural enemy. The enemy, the man to whom I have given a natural divorce. The *enemigo*, mi enemy now mourns the death of his legal wife. What a plight – the enemigo is left with no wife, neither natural nor legal.

FIFTY-FIVE

IT IS LEGAL TO dance on the Widest Footpath of Cottonpettai. The Lady with the Slender Hands grabs Perumal Arokyaswami in a quick embrace, she hums the *La Cucaracha* deep in his cone-shaped ear, and lets her tongue swirl and dance around his naked neck. The aroused couple – the Lady and the rickshaw puller – they embrace the traditional Spanish composition like natives to the land where the score in A major scale belongs.

The score in A major belongs to Mexico.

This is a revolutionary Spanish score.

This score they call *La Cucaracha* in Spanish is known as *The Cockroach* in English parlance.

The tune is set in Spanish parlance on the Widest Footpath of Cottonpettai – *Pa, pa, pa, paaa paa, pa pa pa, paaa paa, pa pa, pa pa, pa pa, paaa* ... and can be emulated on string, percussion and the keyboard with equal cockroach grace.

With grace, the Lady with the Slender Hands sways. With grace, she sings the upbeat *La Cucaracha* in the Spanish tongue from its pre-revolutionary days, and her lover, the rickshaw-puller, repeats the strain in the English tongue.

Lady: *'De las patillas de uno moro'*

Lover: *'From the sideburns of a Moor'*

Lady: *'tengo que hacer una escoba'*

Lover: *'I must make a broom'*

Lady: *'para barrer el cuartel'*

Lover: *'to sweep the quarters'*

Lady: *'de la infantería Española.'*

Lover: *'of the Spanish infantry.'*

'Of the Spanish infantry,' repeats the lover Perumal Arokyaswami in impeccable English tongue, a language foreign to the other Fellows of the Footpath.

The Fellows clap, the Lady with the Slender Hands calls Perumal Arokyaswami's tongue revolutionary. The Lady then goes on to croon the lyrics of *La Cucaracha* for its post-revolutionary standpoint.

'Listen to the Lady croon with her lover, the rickshaw-puller,' says a one-hundred-and-one-year-old munumunuppu-monger, 'there's a revolutionary standpoint on the Widest Footpath of Cottonpettai, years after the political upheaval in Mexico,'

Lady: *'La cucaracha, la cucaracha'*

Lover: *'The cockroach, the karapaambuchi'*

Lady: *'ya no puede caminar'*

Lover: *'can't walk anymore'*

Lady: *'porque le falta, porque no tiene'*

Lover: *'because it's lacking, because it doesn't have'*

Lady: *'Marihuana pa' fumar.'*

Lover: *'Marijuana to smoke.'*

'*Ayyo* ... there is no marijuana to smoke on the Widest Footpath of Cottonpettai,' join in the other Fellows of the Footpath.

'Let us dance the Karapaambuchi instead, and smoke the Vignesh Beedi,' responds the Lady with the Slender Hands.

The cockroaches of the Widest Footpath of Cottonpettai aka the Fellows, and the Lady with the Slender Hands end the dance party with a double pack of Vignesh Beedis.

'Hail Vignesh Beedi.

'Hail *La Cucaracha.*

'*La Cucaracha,* there is a revolution in the Lancashire of the South.

'Watch out for the Fellows of the Footpath – they have tasted marijuana under the spell of *La Cucaracha* to the scale of A major,' declare the watchful and musically knowledgeable munumunuppu-mongers.

I see a cucaracha swimming belly upwards in the now snow-laden Rio Beas. The cucaracha knows no fear in the Beas. The

Beas, brimming with the snow cover of the Solali mountains, carries me in its icy belly alongside the cucaracha – we both drag a fresh supply of charas laced with hashish from the neighbouring country of Everestpal. The cucaracha and I, we survive the stinging cold of the snow mountain. The cucaracha is revolutionary, and so am I. I swim the cold tide with a cucaracha ... I am a revolutionary bride in the Kulkulu valley ... hehe ...

FIFTY-SIX

UPON THE AUSPICIOUS DAY the Caretaker became a bride, she wore a splendorous silken attire of sheer red richness embellished with golden tassels. Her bridal attire – a kurta and pajama they call a feminine Punjabi suit – was resplendent with precious stones, and a sheer georgette veil trailing six yards after every step she took around Agni on the day of her wedding.

Agni is the auspicious Fire God who sanctifies weddings and births – also deaths – in the Indian Subcontinent. The Minister for Shelters looking almost dapper in a golden sherwani they call a masculine Punjabi attire walked around Agni, followed by his bride, and her six-yard-long sheer georgette veil.

Veil embellished with a thick golden border running around its corners ...

The same veil, in all its grandeur, now runs around the Caretaker's body, her lifeless frame resting in the front garden of OneKmBungWow for all the saha-mongers of Chandinigarh to view.

Sahas rest in the Rose buds of red, white, yellow and orange hue accoutring the front garden like a natural wreath.

'Phusphusana mana hai ... do not whisper in the front garden,' the Minister for Shelters' Burly Bodyguards are up and about, digging into their hand gun holsters for their weapons in the absence of the Royal Ragamuffins.

Alas ... the Burly Bodyguards have lost their guns – the Royal Ragamuffins have disappeared with the deathly weapons loaded with fake bullets – there are sahas going haywire in Chandinigarh.

There are not-so-loud thuds on the Twenty Third platform of the Grand Nizamuddin – four Royal Ragamuffins who have escaped a funeral in Chandinigarh have dropped their deathly weapons loaded with fake bullets in response to a loud shout.

Jhoru Kanbi Badshah is a revolutionary upon the Twenty Third platform – he has made his stance on terrorism clear with a loud shout.

'He is brave, he is wise, the title of Emperor is for the Badshah to keep,' the phusphus-mongers of the Undeniable Capital of India have spread the revolutionary word to their gapasapa cousins in the Khalaand rangers.

'Sabhash, Beta,' beams the Badtameez Baap the same evening over a call to his truant son Jhoru Kanbi Badshah.

The phusphus-mongers repeat: '*Sabhash, beta* ... congratulations son ...

'Son of a Badtameez Baap, the latter with no face to show his legal heir.

'This son is triumphant to be declared a Warrior of Peace by the Centre in the Undeniable Capital of India.

'This son, the Emperor, the man called Jhoru Kanbi Badshah.'

Meanwhile, his lost mother celebrates her Badshah's victory as she rests in peace amidst a melee of voices and unwanted noises.

❧

The Minister for Shelters is lost. The Minister for Shelters has gone missing. Missing from the front garden of OneKmBungWow. Missing from the side of his dead bride. The dead bride must be secretly pleased, the buds of orange, red and yellow Rose bushes phusphus.

The citizens of Chandinigarh are secretly pleased to learn that the Minister for Shelters has gone missing from OneKmBungWow.

❧

Uphill Manmanali, Sanyasi Solali Snowmountainwala is secretly pleased to learn that the citizens of Chandinigarh are clueless about the Minister for Shelters' whereabouts.

The novices are pleased to notice that Sanyasi Solali Snowmountainwala smiles, and wears a constant mischievous sparkle within his right eye. The Sanyasi's left eye remains firmly shut, the thick lid limp from a thwack.

The thwack a ruffian act by a rogue apple, which came flying through the snow-mountain sky a few steps ahead of the approaching novices.

The rogue apple of hybrid Kulkulu variety was a mere fruit in the right hand of a novice, all of eight years in biological age until 122 seconds ago. The half-ripe rogue apple now wears a dent upon its greenish exterior thanks to its sudden clash with Sanyasi Solali Snowmountainwala's left eye.

The eight-year-old novice has spotted the rogue apple, he lets out a squeal of joy. Joy accompanied by a mischievous sparkle in Sanyasi Solali Snowmountainwala's third eye. The Sanyasi's third eye has the notorious reputation of emanating a mischievous sparkle when all is well with the novice world.

I am a novice in the wool-shearing trade. I close both ojos … I close my eyes tight as a blade shear travels below the layer of wool on a pregnant sheep's body, touching the oveja's trembling skin, giving both unborn lamb and mother-to-be a frightful roller-coaster vision of hell. I am in hell, si, *infierno* – it is not far from the Kulkulu Valley – it is called the Fur and Animal Breeding Station. I, a bride in hell, not far from the Kulkulu Valley. A bride, a novia in infierno is a common sight in the Indian Subcontinent. No one notices me in Gracia, I am a common sight in and around the terrains of Kulkulu Valley.

FIFTY-SEVEN

LEECHES ARE A COMMON sight in the Khalaand rains – they feast on the Badtameez Baap's bare feet today. The Badtameez Baap has bothered to venture out on this monsoon day in the Western Ghats to find food for his famished family.

This monsoon mid-morning is like any other waterlogged day in the sloping terrain of Rozgaarnagar. The workers who earn their daily meal in the Aaraamaayu Factory are at a loss of words upon this monsoon mid-morning, they look each other in the eye. The eye accepts what the heart will not – the people of Rozgaarnagar decide to talk to their daughters in Algauv.

The skies darken the horizon by the early twilight hour in Rozgaarnagar, the hills and valleys surrounding it as well. The skies are perturbed by the consequence of the calls which the citizens of Rozgaarnagar are about to make to their daughters in Algauv.

'Why are the citizens of Rozgaarnagar perturbed about their daughters?' a very young and knive gapasapa-monger questions.

A senior gapasapa-monger prefers to read the words written by a wise youth of the region:

'The Daughters of Rozgaarnagar

These daughters
They are young
They are all under the age of twenty-one
All under the beady eyes of men
Men who are not their fathers
Men who are not their brothers
Men who are not quite their husbands
But they are under the beady eyes of men, alright
The alright men of Algauv
Men with muscular hands
Muscular hands entwine themselves into the dainty hands of the daughters of Rozgaarnagar.'

The senior gapasapa-monger concludes the letter with his own thoughts: 'It is about time the citizens of Rozgaarnagar make calls to their daughters – they are presently under the beady eyes of the *snãyuňcã purusha* of Algauv.

'Yes, under the beady eyes of the muscular men of Algauv.'

Sanyasi Solali Snowmountainwala has eyes for the inappropriate. From his elevated place on a snow mountain, the Sanyasi's all-pervasive third eye sees the inappropriate actions of the muscular men of Algauv – they entwine their slimy-as-oiled-rubber hands into the dainty limbs of the daughters of Rozgaarnagar. By the way, the daughters of Rozgaarnagar are the newly wed wives of Algauv.

'Can girls under the spell of beady eyes and inappropriate touch remain daughters and wives for long?' the phusphus-mongers of the snow-mountain valley would like to know.

I long for his touch, the man I call husband in my bridal pheran. I watch the oveja, si, the sheep in Gracia's Fur and Animal Breeding Station – they do not long for the touch of the blade shear. The blade shear brings the fear of death. Death so near. Is death near? I cannot lay upon my deathbed before I have felt his warm touch. My husband's warm touch, si ... his *calentar toque* has brought changes to my matriz. The calentar toque of the man I call husband consumed my body, and filled my matriz ... mi womb. Husband, the man who is father to my son ...

FIFTY-EIGHT

SENOR SINGH MONO IS a son. A son with a father suddenly gone missing. A son with a dead mother. This mother is not his own in blood. This mother's eyes are not the colour of his windows to planet earth. Or does the colour of his mother's eyes match that of his?

Senor Singh Mono is in deep quandary, he must open his declared dead mother's eyelids.

The citizens of Chandinigarh share Senor's quandary, they run pell-mell, and behave difficult. The Burly Bodyguards are alert, they must save the Roses – orange, red and yellow too, from the difficult citizens of Chandinigarh. The red and yellow Rose bushes phusphus are being squashed by citizens filling every available gap between the thorns on the hundred bushes flowering in the front garden of OneKmBungWow. They are destroying the Caretaker's budding red and yellow Rose bushes phusphus, right from the root of their finicky parent plants.

The Burly Bodyguards cannot register the simple fact that the Caretaker, legal wife of the Minister for Shelters, the guardian of OneKmBungWow with its front garden of Roses, also Senor Singh Mono, et al. is now lying dead.

Burly Bodyguards will simply guard despite pell-mell, et al. They will guard the Roses in the front garden come hell, rain, death, saha, phusphus, munumunuppu, also gapasapa.

Well, death has come, and the Burly Bodyguards simply cannot seem to register this blatant fact of life.

Miles away from Chandinigarh, the Lady with the Slender Hands has learnt of the Caretaker's body – she has understood fully well that death is life gone out of steam. She continues to croon *La Cucaracha* in full steam, especially for the delight of the Fellows of the Footpath. The Lady with the Slender Hands is a crooning cucaracha upon the Widest Footpath of Cottonpettai. She has long given up her name, call her the Lady with the Slender Hands or *La Cucaracha* or *Di Karapaambuchi* –

she has risen to fame solely by the magnificent flush of passion upon her lips. The Lady, lips painted red, night after day upon the Widest Footpath of Cottonpettai lures every man in sight, including a certain Minister for Shelters who is missing from Chandinigarh.

Red is the colour of a woman who has won life in death.

The Caretaker wears red, she is dead to life. Her eyes reflect the colour she wears. The Caretaker's eyes are red. The citizens of Chandinigarh spot red.

Red, the colour of danger.

Danger, the act of a collapsing son.

Son, the legal heir of the Minister for Shelters.

The legal heir to OneKmBungWow has collapsed notwithstanding the red hue of the Caretaker's eyes.

All eyes, including the Caretaker's, are on Senor Singh Mono.

Sanyasi Solali Snowmountainwala opens all his three eyes, suddenly – he has spotted red in the Caretaker's vision despite his remote location. The vision the Sanyasi beholds opens secrets that were never meant to be unravelled in the first place.

The novices, all boys lurking around the Sanyasi, cannot keep secrets hidden under thick tufts of hair. The novices, all boys under the age of fourteen, pledged to 'sanysihood' are bald – they are now beholders of a secret pertinent to a woman declared dead in Chandinigarh.

Senor Singh Mono must pledge his curly black-brown tuft, the crowning glory upon his masculine head, to the Caretaker's spirit, and go bald right away, declare the citizens of Chandinigarh.

Senor Singh Mono does not rebel the declaration – consumed by fear, he has lost his consciousness in full view of the red-eyed and declared dead Caretaker.

'Downhill Manmanali, in the posh city of Chandinigarh, a spirit has been born out of Senor Singh Mono's fear. Fear not ye bald-headed novices of the valleys of Kulkulu and Manmanali,' bellows Sanyasi Solali Snowmountainwala.

The novices promptly shrivel with fear.

I watch the oveja shrivel with fear. They fear the blade shear, the sheep bleat aloud. I promptly grab the shear from the shearer. The shearer wears a pheran, the length of the garment hiding his toes. The shearer must flee, but he cannot run. He lifts his pheran above his ankle to unravel his feet, and flee. Alas, the shearer's feet have no toes. No toes, no flee. My toes are numb ... si ... I have *entumecido* toes, I must flee ... I must *huir* now. How on planet earth will I huir – I mean flee – when my numb toes refuse to comply with the signal from my mind?

FIFTY-NINE

MIND IT, THE THENTODAS, all original inhabitants of the forests surrounding Utahkamand, do not support acts of crime. When the honour of a woman is at stake, the perpetrator of the crime is almost certain to embrace death if caught by a Thentoda in this Blue Mountain territory.

The Thentodas have caught the Master of Sports with tattoos from head to toe, barring his face. They spot some more tattoos upon the owl-eyed scoundrel's torso as he heaves himself above the depth of River Pyraka to grasp a breath of clear air.

'Awoom, Awaam Awoom,' the Thentodas thunder in fearsome tenor, they have understood from the tell-tale tattoos upon the Master of Sports' body that he has been involved in the act of trading daughters and wives, ever since the senior-most indigenous tribe members have first witnessed him in lustful transaction over two decades ago.

A fresh bout of August rains consumes the aghast ranges of Blue Mountain Nilgiris, the Thentodas respond with a thunderous Awoom, Awaam, Awoom.

The Master of Sports is beyond aghast, he shudders – he suspects his end is near. This Master, he hangs his head down, hoping that his face disappears into the fast swelling Pyraka, giving his impending end a miss. The rains tear the skies and pound the Master's head harder.

The Thentodas are thrilled, they praise the rains and Pyraka the river, their life-giver, they chant in their native tongue.

'Aiyaaa waiyaaa Pyraka ... Aiyaaa waiyaaa aiyaaa waa ... Aiyaaa, thenpuchiin sathiyama aiyaaa waiyaaa ... Thenpuchi nam Daivam ... Inda manidanai naam dhandipom!'

Munumunuppu-mongers wandering the Blue Mountain ranges have wind that the Thentodas have sworn by their *Daivam* aka God. Their Daivam is the Honeybee, which keeps the Thentodas fed through the deepest winters of Blue Mountain Nilgiris. By the divine intention of the Honeybee, the Thentodas have decided that the Master of Sports must hang his head down in shame by the Main Square of Utahkamand.

The Thentodas firmly believe that a crime is considered dead only when the perpetrator sheds all his accumulated titles, including his clothes, also his tattoos, and parades through the crowded square of Utahkamand, giving up every physical manifestation of his criminal act. They will scrape the tattoos off his chest with country spades, if needed. They will scrape this criminal clean of all his dirty acts. But first, the criminal must be brought to the Main Square of Utahkamand by sheer force of his own mind.

The criminal in captivity of the Thentodas has a mind – it is infested with layers of fungus accumulated over fifty years. The Master of Sports for Suitable Somebodies must first clear the accumulated fungus from his mind. Until then, the Master's criminal act will not be brought to public gaze in the Main Square of Utahkamand. The Thentodas are very particular that the mind of a criminal must return to the logic of emptiness before it is re-infused with good thoughts.

Meanwhile, the kind Thentodas do not believe in keeping their captive hungry, they stuff a fresh rambutan into the Master's mouth – the latter bites into the fruit which is more abundant in the neighbouring country of Serendib. This rambutan is an antidote to diarrhoea, a physical condition during which one cannot stop running to the loo soon after every poo.

The Master of Sports for Suitable Somebodies has just consumed an entire rambutan, he needs to poo instantly. The Master for Sports is petrified. It is widely known among those who have been petrified, that the need to poo is an inevitable fallout of this extreme emotion.

Love is the resultant emotion of Raag Bihag – I press, pull and pluck the string of the sitar to emote the *amor*-arousing *krintan* in the establishing notes of the raag. Love, hiding from the sunlight in the Solali Valley, and crouching deep inside my heart, stirs – my hands follow the emotional amor trail as I strum *sa mama ga pa, ..., ni ..., nisa*. I blush as the strum of notes gather steam from that night when I, a woman, carelessly loved the man I now call my husband. Why does amor show its true colours only on the other side of day, in the deepest hour of night? Why does amor hide deep inside my heart, warmed by my pheran, refusing to shake hands with sunlight? A cumulonimbus nube masks the sunlight caressing Solali, and I find myself among a group of boys, all under fourteen years of age with bald heads grouped together like a flock of sheared sheep in Solali. I remember the bald sheep, all freshly sheared ovejas in Gracia. I remember a lot of things ... *yo recuerda amor* ... si ... I remember love.

SIXTY

LOVE IS A LUNATIC emotion among the tobacco-growers of the twin towns of Nippanini and Ajay Nagar. The Minister for Shelters is a lunatic on the prowl in this tobacco-rich region – he has fled the stoic cremation ceremony of the Caretaker, his legal wife, to set matters of love right.

After all, the Minister for Shelters first understood the complexities of the lunatic emotion of love in the twin tobacco towns of Nippanini and Ajay Nagar. The Minister was once a significant tobacco grower. He tended to the large and juicy masculino tobacco leaves through numerous seasonal vicissitudes of failed monsoons and excessive rain showers from the time he remembers playing road lagori as an eight-year-old son of a rich farmer.

'Laud the Minister for Shelters, his heart beats for the verdant *thambakhu* – tobacco – fields of the rural landscape in the jurisdiction of the twin towns of Ajay Nagar and Nippanini,' whisper a bunch of gapasapa-mongers who are at the just declared widower's heels.

The Minister is unaware of followers in these parts, his heart beats faster – he walks through the rural tobacco stretches which he has wandered from early childhood to his nascent manhood. This rugged rural tobacco variety, best suited to roll out the masculine Vignesh Beedi, is rather finicky – it does not care to withstand the wilt of thirst. This beedi variety tobacco staunchly flourishes when the rainfall is liberal.

The Minister for Shelters is mesmerised by the liberal flowering of yellow tobacco buds. These yellow flowers bring back liberal memories of love in the rural tobacco fields.

'Memories of love ... *athavani of prem,*' whisper the gapasapa-mongers, 'Ah ... how the Minister for Shelters longs for the liberal dose of love the rural tobacco fields provided him in his youth ...'

In his youth, the Minister experienced love – it was as liberal as the trending monsoon showers which have begun their journey from the southern-most State of Kerala, and are travelling northwards into Andhra Pradesh, inundating the tributaries of River Krishna in the rural surroundings of Nippanini in Karnataka and Ajay Nagar in Maharashtra, along the way.

This heady combination of rain and tobacco fills the Minister's heart with more love. Tobacco, the nose-up-in-the-air cash crop of India, never fails to set a spring in the Minister's step. Tobacco, the crop with zero tolerance for moody cumulonimbus clouds, never fails to fill the Minister's heart with pride.

'The Minister is not very unlike the tobacco crop – he has zero tolerance for moody cumulonimbus clouds which affect the masculine content of the tobacco adversely, when they shower less or more water than they are absolutely required to,' whisper the gapasapa-mongers some more.

This masculino tobacco, as a rule of its genetic inclination, does not withstand rainfall in excesses, nor sunshine for that matter – the Minister is proud of its stance. Sunshine is abundant in the Deccan Plateau with a grid of latitudes and longitudes converging bang in the belly of the Indian Subcontinent. Ajay Nagar and Nippanini are the star tobacco regions in this Deccan grid.

The Minister for Shelters is a star, prestigious first citizen of this region – he wanders these tobacco fields with careless abandon.

The masculine tobacco, a prestigious kharif crop, is sowed ceremoniously between the months of May and July, alongside jowar, bajra, rice, maize, cotton, groundnut, jute and hemp – some food crops, others cash yields.

The tobacco crop, of course, is a cash yield.

The Minister for Shelters takes all responsibility for the cash yielded from tobacco – this crop the crown of the kharif season when the swell of its enormous leaf expands, and thrives on ideal iron and phosphorus balanced soil, nourished by the monsoon-inundated rivulets of River Krishna.

The Minister for Shelters takes in the essence of a Vignesh Beedi, his act hidden to public eye by an enormous tobacco leaf.

The gapasapa-mongers drag their respective beedis and say out loud: 'Tobacco, the flourishing crop, grown in the temperature and rainfall-ideal Extremadura Valleys of Spain.

'*Tabaco*, the lifeblood of the Lady with the Slender Hands – she has untraceable ancestors in Spain.

'Tobacco for tabaco.

'The Minister for Shelters loves his tobacco.

'The Minister for Shelters is the slave of a lunatic emotion.

'*Lunático* love has turned the Minister for Shelters into a slave.

'The Lady with the Slender Hands is a lunático revolutionary of love dancing with careless abandon, and romancing with a moneyless rickshaw-puller upon the Widest Footpath of Cottonpettai.'

I trust the dried Tobacco Flower sleeping in a cloth pouch tucked in the inner layers of my pheran to revive the lunático emotion of love. This Tabaco Flower, once a fresh bud thriving on a deep green plant, is now the essence of a mature Vignesh Beedi. My beedis sleep with the yellow Tabaco Flower in a well-concealed cloth pouch. Ouch, where on planet earth is my pouch? The bald novices of Solali have never seen a pouch in their young lives, they unanimously declare. I dissolve into the mob of novices, I deserve to find the pouch, my treasure. The *tesoro* in my pouch is worth its weight in lunático emotion. The treasure in my pouch is called love. The lost tesoro is mi amor, si, my love.

SIXTY-ONE

THE MINISTER FOR SHELTERS is lost. Rumours are rife in the front garden – saha-mongers whisper that the Minister for Shelters is lost in search of love. Senor Singh Mono must find his lost father before the Caretaker leaves OneKmBungWow for the very last time, never to return in her physical form.

Will the Caretaker keep her dead word never to return?

The Caretaker, when she was still alive, once left OneKmBungWow vowing never to return to the *veshyalay.*

Phusphus travels from Rose bud to jackfruit ripened in its parent tree in the front garden – 'OneKmBungWow is a brothel,' confirm the citizens of Chandinigarh. 'Brothel aka veshyalay aka OneKmBungWow aka the private abode of the Minister for Shelters! But it turns out that the Minister for Shelters is lost elsewhere in search of love.'

Love is a taboo emotion in the upper hills of Nilgiris where the Scouts and Guides of St. Alphonsious Pre-University College are on special camp. The Master of Sports for Suitable Somebodies has allayed the surge of blossoming love between the Scouts and Guides with a ban. This ban prohibits the to-be Suitable Somebodies, all girls and boys from respectable homes, from embarking upon night crawls together.

But where is the man who has imposed this ban on adolescent hearts gurgling with the emotion of love?

The Master of Sports for Suitable Somebodies is doggy-pedalling in the deep waters of Pyraka – there is a ban on his re-entry to land. The Thentodas' eyes, adding up to ten in number, pry into the soul of the Master of Sports.

They find the spot empty, the Master of Sports has no soul.

'A Master with no soul is training Scouts and Guides in the hills of Utahkamand to be Suitable Somebodies – bravo, indeed!' jeer some prying munumunuppu-mongers.

Amidst all the melee in Chandinigarh, Senor Singh Mono has word from the Scouts and Guides that the Master of Sports for Suitable Somebodies has sold his soul. For now, the Caretaker's soul must exit planet earth along with her dead body. Senor Singh Mono is in deep distress over matters concerning dead and sold souls. To top it all, his biological father is a lost soul.

The soul is lost.

The lost *alma* wanders masculino tobacco fields.

The Minister for Shelters' lost athma finds solace in the potent Vignesh Beedi.

The potent Vignesh Beedi is the essence of the fattened tobacco crop of the Deccan Plateau – it brings solace to the Lady with the Slender Hands.

The solace of a lost soul is purely dependent on the potent Vignesh Beedi.

Perumal Arokyaswami feels lost – he bends his matted head towards a pair of reddened instruments of kiss, and tastes the lingering tobacco, masculine essence of the Vignesh Beedi upon the lips of the Lady. This thambakhu has the lingering aftertaste of discarded love upon the Lady's sumptuous red lips.

Alas! I have discarded the last remnants of love, masculine fragrance from a distant tabaco field in the Deccan Plateau. I fall into the rippling Rio Beas hoping to disappear with the last remnants of amor into the deep blue-green sea. The Indian Ocean beckons my lost soul into its blue-green womb. My womb, si, my matriz reminds me of a child I once begot in love. Mi amor lives in the eyes of my child.

SIXTY-TWO

JHORU KANBI BADSHAH LIVES in the eyes of his mother. His mother has spent nights and days, and the minutes bridging afternoon and twilight, crying for the child her eyes have not beheld since the first day she was traded.

Algauv is abuzz with the banter of traded daughters plaiting their long and black tresses as the sun-drenched afternoon nears the twilight hour. The daughters of Rozgaarnagar are the prized catches of the snãyuňcã purusha aka muscular men of Algauv. The snãyuňcã men of Algauv are immensely proud of their prized catches. These muscular men wear their pride in their arms. Red-bordered tattoos embellish the arms of these snãyuňcã purusha for all to see whether they care to, or not.

These special tattoos showcase the masculinity of men who trade their wives for money.

The Thentodas trade honey for money.

Honey is not just the nectar produced by its parent bees as the Thentodas know it. It is an endearing term a man calls his wife or lover and vice versa, as Suitable Somebodies and the muscular purusha of Algauv know it.

The muscular men of Algauv, too, trade honey for money.

The wives they call honey.

Honey aka *shahad* aka *madhu*.

Madhu aka Latha aka Sarla aka Kamla aka Vimla aka the daughters of Rozgaarnagar.

Shahad aka then

Then aka honey

Honey, the lifeblood of the Thentodas

Honey, bloodbath in Algauv.

When a muscular man trades his honey, there is money involved. Where there's money involved, a bloodbath is inevitable.

There is no money in Rozgaarnagar this season. The men and women of Rozgaarnagar have made a series of inevitable, inter-state phone calls to their daughters. The daughters of Rozgaarnagar wear their emotions on their free-flowing sari pallus.

The daughters of Rozgaarnagar have free-flowing emotions, they cry. The inevitable calls from Rozgaarnagar have left the drains of Algauv overflowing with emotion. The wives of Algauv shed their tears into the drains.

Drains, the homes they have been married into.

Homes, where snāyuňcā purusha come at the fragile hour past twilight, and leave before the clock aka Big Ben clangs twelve times at the stroke of midnight in Algauv Mandi.

The wives of Algauv hang out by the drains bordering the Mandi. The muscular men of Algauv hang out with them for an hour or two, and reward them lavishly for their physical time together and apart. This reward will pay for some more tattoos on the hands of the men who have married the daughters of Rozgaarnagar.

Tattoos are prominent designs on human skin, made possible by an indelible ink penned into the dermis, which is the live tissue beneath the epidermis. Tattoos are usually permanent – among the muscular men of Algauv, they are symbols of indelible sexual lure.

The muscular men of Algauv lure the moneyed purushas of their town into availing sexual favours for a price. These sexual favours are granted by their newly wed wives.

The tattooed men of Algauv have made their private wives public. The wives of Algauv sell their flesh in the public Mandi.

The Badtameez Baap's flesh is rotting. The flesh upon his hands made stale by unwashed needles entering his dermis to leave indelible marks of sexual favour in the form of red bordered tattoos is fast beginning to act in his disfavour.

I must act before the clock in the Main Market of Solali chimes at the midnight hour. My pouch is still missing, I must act now. I act, I pretend, I invite the bald novices for a hushed meeting. The novices act when silence rules the atmosphere. The novices, all boys under the age of fourteen, are terribly hungry for noise. Let's make a noise about the missing pouch, I urge the boys. The *chicos*, si the boys, scratch their *calvo cabezas*, si bald heads, and open their mouths wide. I stand aside, and watch in triumph – the urged calvo chicos, all eighty-three bald boys say 'yayyy' in unison. Eighty-three bald novices are inexplicably elated to say the 'yayyy' word. Yayyy is the snow-mountain cousin of the word hurrah.

SIXTY-THREE

AMONG ITS LONG LIST of restrictions, uttering the word hurrah at the camp for the Braver than the Best is strictly prohibited. Today, the camp is lifeless, the Scouts and Guides have retreated to their respective tents to whisper hurrahs among themselves.

The Scouts and Guides of St. Alphonsious Pre-University College on camp in Blue Mountain Utahkamand are happy to hear that the Master of Sports for Suitable Somebodies has gone missing. A Thentoda song wafts through the heady Blue Mountain air, the Scouts and Guides listen:

Then Thena
Then thana
Then puuchi then kudutha idam
Pyraka karaiodum
Paaduvom aaaduvom
Then thena
Then thana

The Thentodas sing the '*Then Thena*' – they talk of the honeybee, which gives them their nectar by the banks of River Pyraka where every man, woman and child of their tribe dances and sings.

The Scouts and Guides are on an instant high, each teen dances to this song.

Song and dance are essential ingredients for the balanced growth of Scouts and Guides, all around eighteen years of age.

'Gao, nacho, khul ke jeeyo iss desh ke layak noujavano,' the Scouts and Guides feel free to sing in unison.

'Fell free to sing, dance, live it up Scouts and Guides, all future Suitable Somebodies of the Indian Subcontinent – your errant owl-eyed Master is not about to return anytime soon,' a passing munumunuppu-monger prods. The Scouts and Guides repeat the strain, they sing ... *'Gao, nacho ...'* their voices now loud and clear in the jungles abounding Utahkamand. The regaled jungles carry the joyous song over the swaying Eucalyptus trees, and across tea gardens into the countryside ... Song swirling back into the deep crevices of the Blue Mountain Nilgiris, and plunging into the heaving waters of Pyraka causing a beat to skip in the owl-eyed Master's heart.

River Pyraka is heaving with million palpitations. These visible palpitations resemble the trepidations of the Master of Sports' heart at the sound of song and dance in the camp for the Braver than the Best. The Master of Sports for Suitable Somebodies is battling with an unsuitable heart. The Master's heart beats fast, it pants. His heart beats slower, it tires, panics, and turns cartwheels in the cold waters of Pyraka. His heart stops beating.

'Whoaaaa,' yelp some prying munumunuppu-mongers, 'the Master of Sports for Suitable Somebodies has had a heart attack. The watching Thentodas have heaved him out of the cold waters, and taken the Master into their custody. The Master of Sports' recovery is inevitable under the custody of the Thentodas. The Thentodas are the custodians of the forests of Utahkamand. These custodians – every man, woman and child in their tribe – will ensure that all animals and human

beings who have made these forests their temporary and permanent homes are safe.'

The Royal Ragamuffins have been let off by a custodian of peace Emperor Jhoru Kanbi with a warning–they have boarded the immediate and crowded passenger train to Chandinigarh. These Ragamuffins, they feel safe in a crowd. Four is a crowd. Upon arriving at their destination, the four Royal Ragamuffins merge into the expanding crowd gathered at the main entrance of OneKmBungWow.

Where there is a crowd, there is confusion.

Where there is confusion, there is lack of clarity.

There is lack of clarity regarding the disposal of the Caretaker's body adorned in bridal finery, et al. in the continued absence of the Minister for Shelters.

Absence makes the heart grow fonder. The Lady with the Slender Hands is increasingly growing fonder of Perumal Arokyaswami. The cycle rickshaw puller too, is growing fonder of the Lady – he is happy in his present state. This state of kisses, caresses and dances to the A major high note of *La Cucaracha* is all that a rickshaw-puller with no postal address in the Indian Subcontinent cares about at this point.

'How can a man with origins in the Serendib embrace life, kiss and dance carefree when his identity is a potpourri of nationalities, one by birth, another by residence, and a third by historical connections?' a munumunuppu-monger ponders in his own lice-infested head – he scratches it vigorously.

'What on earth in identity?' another munumunuppu-monger with more lice in his head cares to know despite the itch in his scalp.

'Identity refers to those physical, emotional and geographical characteristics which come together to define an individual as a unique entity,' the monger with fewer lice in his head replies.

As Perumal Arokyaswami's heart brims with more love for the Lady, he is emotional about his lack of identity. Identity begets family. Family begins with bringing home a wife. Perumal Arokyaswami has no home. He cannot bring home the Lady as wife until he procures an identification card – a passport perhaps from the Indian Subcontinent.

'Alas ... Perumal Arokyaswami must first establish his Indian roots like a Dandelion extending its contractile roots longitudinally into the soil. The rickshaw-puller must connect his roots to a memory which brings Perumal Arokyaswami to the inevitable fact that he is irrevocably in love with the Lady in his arms ...' observes a rather erudite munumunuppu-monger – he goes on to recite an impromptu ditty:

'Love, a Dandelion

'A Dandelion riding the winds of Blue Mountain Nilgiris

'Winds carrying the Dandelion downhill Nilgiris to Cottonpettai

'Dandelion from a wayside cluster in Wellington

'Wellington, the Military Town neighbouring Utahkamand

'Utahkamand, where love, soothing to the touch, rides the emotional petals of a Dandelion called the Lady

'Dandelion ... si, the Lady lying head heavenwards upon the Widest Footpath of Cottonpettai

'Perumal Arokyaswami lying head heavenwards upon the Widest Footpath of Cottonpettai

'Perumal Arokyaswami's left palm, the Dandelion's pillow

'Vignesh Beedi in Perumal Arokyaswami's right hand

'The beedi slips into the Dandelion's mouth – she and her lover bond over forgotten roots, memories of which do not manifest in their newfound state of detachment

'Detachment is sexy, it is foreplay to forgotten roots

'Perumal Arokyaswami gasps, roots suddenly not forgotten

'Perumal Arokyaswami remembers his roots from a distinct rain-fed day in a Murugan Temple in a less-trodden forest hill in Serendib.

'Perumal Arokyaswami remembers Pascal Rebello de Fonseca

'The time is ripe for Perumal Arokyaswami to don black beads, and a dhoti.'

'What ho is a dhoti?' the munumunuppu-monger with fewer lice stops scratching his unwashed for twenty-three days head to ask this rather important question – he has a special interest in clothing.

'A dhoti is a rectangular piece of cloth available in white, also colours, checks and a hotchpotch of floral patterns. This four metre long cloth is worn like a wraparound skirt by men across the Indian Subcontinent, even in some African nations,' the erudite monger cares to explain.

Walking freely in the Valley of Kulkulu and uphill Manmanali, Sanyasi Solali Snowmountainwala drapes his four metre long dhoti around his face. His face must stay well-concealed from Manu Gaddi and the People of the Highest Hill guarding the Originally Solali Kesar.

But the dhoti unwraps itself from the Sanyasi's face for a brief moment, and there's phusphus in the air:

'Sanyasi Solali Snowmountainwala is a Moustached Man.'

'The Minister for Shelters is a Moustached Man.'

'The Master of Sports for Suitable Somebodies is a Moustached Man.'

'Pascal Rebello de Fonseca's photographs show that he is a Moustached Man.'

I remember Pascal Rebello de Fonseca. I remember the Minister for Shelters. I know Perumal Arokyaswami. I have met Jhoru Kanbi Badshah. I am a woman, I have no moustache. I am a woman, I have lost my identidad. I am ... *yo soy.* Yo soy ... I am a woman who knows Sanyasi Solali Snowmountainwala from a *verano tarde* ... si, a summer afternoon in Chandinigarh. That summer afternoon in Chandinigarh gave me a new identity ... I have a brand new identidad – verano beckons. Summer beckons me home as I wander the always cold Valley of Solali.

SIXTY-FOUR

THE ORIGINALLY SOLALI KESAR has never seen summer. The resting place of this highly sought after Kesar flower is a cold nest.

Saha-and phusphus-mongers wandering the Valley of Solali know the nest to be a warm and comfortable home for new born fledglings. This home is usually constructed by the fledglings' parents, foundation laid with utmost care, and the phusphus-mongers relate what they think they know:

'The Originally Solali Kesar has parents.

'The four Royal Ragamuffins have parents – they have not built them nests.

'The four Royal Ragamuffins have incredible skills – they all ran before they walked.'

The four Royal Ragamuffins are said to have wings on their sturdy feet. Sahas abound that the Minister for Shelters is a scoundrel – their feet retreat with the speed of lightening from OneKmBungWow.

The four Royal Ragamuffins must find their mentor, they will not have him unduly called a scoundrel by riff raff.

'Riff-raff people these – the so-called reputable citizens of Chandinigarh,' confirm the Royal Ragamuffins in whispers among themselves.

Riff-raff whispers fly.

The citizens of Chandinigarh are advanced in the ways of capturing flying whispers. The citizens of Chandinigarh pounce on the four Royal Ragamuffins and beat them to pulp.

The four Royal Ragamuffins, despite their Himalayan strength, are no match for a million citizens of Chandinigarh. They groan and moan, pleading for sympathy until the million citizens of Chandinigarh take no pleasure in beating pulp to dough.

Senor Singh Mono takes no pleasure in pain. He takes the Royal Ragamuffins – all four scoundrels simultaneously groaning in pain to the inner premises of OneKmBungWow.

The citizens of Chandinigarh simultaneously whisper in the outer premises of OneKmBungWow. There's saha all over the place as the citizens of Chandinigarh fall over each other, bump into the Burly Bodyguards, stumble over the enclosure where the body lies, and rub shoulders with the declared dead Caretaker.

The Burly Bodyguards are aghast.

The Burly Bodyguards are useless scoundrels.

The Burly Bodyguards have allowed four scoundrels who have stolen their weapons to create unnecessary furore at the Grand Nizamuddin, into the inner premises of OneKmBungWow!

The Burly Bodyguards have all overlooked one million citizens, to rub shoulders with the dead Caretaker in the outer premises of OneKmBungWow.

The Burly Bodyguards, the Royal Ragamuffins, the citizens of Chandinigarh are all scoundrels.

Scoundrels aka *badmaash*.

These badmaash Burly Bodyguards are sure to lose their prestigious jobs. Wait until the badmaash Minister for Shelters returns.

A badmaash here, a scoundrel there

Here and there ... *idhar udhar*

The scoundrels run *thithar bithar* ... here and there ...

The Caretaker's body is moved by this aimless thithar bithar of scoundrels.

There's gapasapa elsewhere: 'Here, there, see how aimless he is – the scoundrel runs.'

'This badmaash is an aimless Minister for Shelters.'

'The Minister for Shelters has rediscovered the aimless scent of love in a tobacco field hiding in the bosom of the Deccan Plateau – he is deeply moved.'

Jhoru Kanbi Badshah is deeply moved by the distinct force of his own voice. This is the voice of the Saviour. Jhoru Kanbi Badshah is no longer an Emperor, he is God, voice his fellow coolies on Platform No. Twenty Three. This platform is now host to the star of the Grand Nizamuddin – Jhoru the Coolie has saved the lives of at least one lakh passengers en route to their desired destinations from four preposterous idiots who call themselves the Royal Ragamuffins.

The citizens of Rozgaarnagar have news of Jhoru's brave act – he is a star, they must follow him. This star, their Saviour. The Saviour they call Jhoru Kanbi Badshah.

'A Saviour is born – the daughters of Rozgaarnagar can stop painting their lips red in Algauv,' decree the gapasapa-mongers who have brought the news to Khalaand's hamlet in the first place.

I wear rojo ... si, red upon my lips. My red labios go unnoticed in the snow-mountain valley. In the valleys abounding the snow territory of Himachal Pradesh, in Kulkulu, in Gracia, also in Solali, every other pair of lips is red – it is the natural hue of these instruments of speech and kiss. The women of the valleys wear their pherans and their red labios with the poise of apples nurtured and matured to ripeness in snow-mountain territory. A basket of Kulkulu apples travel past the Main Market of Solali upon the head of a hill man – I take a deep drag of mountain charas. This man belongs to the tribe of people guarding the Highest Hill. *Yo seguir*, si, I follow this man, quietly – hush ... *silencio*! I signal the trail of calvo-headed novices who have decided to seguir me as I follow the man to the Highest Hill. Together, the novices and I leave a trail of exclamations to keep our pursuit silent ... we say, and repeat ... Silencio! Hush! Silencio! HUSH! The last hush is so loud ... silencio ... the man of the hill is looking back.

SIXTY-FIVE

THE FOUR ROYAL RAGAMUFFINS seem to have a Head ... hush. Never mind the hush, the Head is missing, if not dead. The four Royal Ragamuffins, it emerges from whispers in the inner sanctum of OneKmBungWow, are extremely unclear regarding the life and death matters of their Head. The four scoundrels simply follow orders whether the Head is alive or dead. The orders are disseminated by a voice, which is heard by the Royal Ragamuffins over their mobile phone, a SUAS technology super gadget manufactured in the Far East outside the borders of the Indian Subcontinent.

Senor Singh Mono hears a voice in his head. The Royal Ragamuffins are certainly important to the affairs of OneKmBungWow, a voice among the riff-raff assembled in the outer premises shouts out this information is a shrill and distinct drawl akin to a sanyasi's all-knowing metre. Senor Singh Mono is deeply troubled by the voice inside his head, also the other shrill drawl outside OneKmBungWow.

It is essential for the citizens of Rozgaarnagar to voice their concerns regarding matters of seasonal employment at the Aaraamaayu Factory. A voice which has recently arrived from the Undeniable Capital of India has so proclaimed. The citizens of Rozgaarnagar are only too willing to follow Jhoru Kanbi Badshah's voice which is sensibly rich with relevant advice. This is the advice of the newfound Saviour – the citizens of Rozgaarnagar will act upon His word.

'The Saviour is here.

'The *Rakshanakartha* is here.

'This Saviour is the Rakshanakartha of the simple citizens of Rozgaarnagar,' proclaims a wise gapasapa-monger.

'What pray are the traits of a simple citizen?' a rather fashionable monger wants to know.

'Simple,' says a wise monger, 'defines that, and only that which has no complications.'

Complications are the outcome of the simplicity of the citizens of Rozgaarnagar. The citizens are in a complicated mess, thanks to their minds which probe nothing below the surface of a matter. When matters are not sifted by the mind, they tend to complicate the functioning of the body – the citizens of Rozgaarnagar are utterly weak, they tend to fall at every step. The citizens have had no meal to eat for a fortnight in the hills of Khalaand. The citizens of Rozgaarnagar, all have near fractured legs.

The citizens of Chandinigarh, all have near fractured egos. Their egos dangle in disdain for Senor Singh Mono. The young heir of the Minister for Shelters, they notice, has much disdain for the Caretaker, his legal mother.

The citizens obviously fail to notice the illegal goings on in the inner premises of OneKmBungWow.

When curiosity rises, sahas abound: 'What goes on in the inner premises of OneKmBungWow, pray? Senor Singh Mono has never addressed the Caretaker as his mother, never in public, and certainly not in the inner premises.'

The Lady with the Slender Hands has never heard from the son she coaxed out of her womb upon a biting cold winter's night in Chandinigarh. The Lady is resting her head upon a loose cobblestone on the Widest Footpath of Cottonpettai – she is dealing with troubled thoughts.

The munumunuppu-mongers who know their Spanish recite: 'The trouble is loose

'Deep trouble on a *suelto* cobblestone

'Knock the *suelto* trouble off your head, dear Lady

'Suelto *problema,* si, loose trouble must be removed from the head before it becomes a tumour

'A tumour that leaves you dead

'Coax the trouble until it comes loose from your head!'

The Lady's head is coaxed out of its deep and distant thought by the Fellows of the Footpath. All the inhabitants of the Footpath must attend the Maha Mangalam Holy Sojourn Meet, and bid goodbye to Perumal Arokyaswami as he prepares to walk barefoot into the night.

Barefooted in black on his yearly sojourn to the Murugan Temple on the distant hill.

The Murugan Temple on a hill is not in India.

The Murugan Temple can be reached by foot from the shores of Cololomambo, capital city of Serendib.

Perumal Arokyaswami has purchased a Coolie Class ticket aboard the streamlined vessel bound to Serendib. The vessel will cut, glide and slide over the waters of the Indian Ocean once it has passed the Laccadive Sea.

'Does Perumal Arokyaswami have an identification proof – a Red Passport, if not a Blue one, to legally travel across international waters?' the curious munumunuppu-mongers query.

My passport is red, mi *pasaporte* is blue. My passport is in every hue my eye chooses to see. Soda, lemon, ginger, pop; I want the Blue Passport on top. Soda, lemon, ginger, pop; I want the Red Pasaporte on top. There is no Soda Man in Solali. There is a Soda Man by the Widest Footpath of Cottonpettai. A Soda Man in the Indian Subcontinent sells a drink of lime laced with ginger and coriander. The drink is further topped with spice and crushed ice in hot and temperate climatic zones. My passport has turned green – this, the colour of multi-celled algae at the bed of the snow-crushed Rio Beas. I am *feliz*, si … I am blissful in this snow-mountain territory because I see my pasaporte in every hue I care to perceive after taking a long drag of charas.

SIXTY-SIX

THE MINISTER FOR SHELTERS is in blissful comfort as he rests his head against the bark of a Tamarind Tree bang in the middle of his tobacco fields. He plucks a blissful Yellow Tobacco Flower, shuts his eyes and hums a tune, until an SMS interrupts his rhythm.

The Minister for Shelters reads this message – he is immediately shaken out of his comfort, he crushes the Yellow Tobacco Flower in his palm.

Extreme comfort inevitably leads to discomfort, the Minister has abandoned the scent of the Tobacco Flower to hurry back home, and fulfil his legal duties towards the Caretaker. The power of the Tobacco Flower, the Minister for Shelters does not realize on his hurried journey back home, can last beyond its physical beauty, past its life's tenure.

The Minister for Shelters boards the next flight to Chandinigarh – he feels extreme discomfort in the Comfort Business Class seat.

Back in Chandinigarh, irate saha-mongers speak up: 'The Minister's seat is determined by riff-raff

'Riff-raff cast their votes in inebriation.

'Inebriation fed into their bodies with money.

'Money from the Minister for Shelters' abundantly full, and overflowing coiffeurs.'

The Royal Ragamuffins are very loyal to the Minister, their Head. They are increasingly displeased with the riff-raff in Chandinigarh, and all the damage their gossip is causing the most respectable Minister for Shelters who has arrived right in time for his wife's departure.

Unmindful of the Minister's arrival, the citizens of Chandinigarh shriek: 'Will the dead Caretaker speak one last time?' The citizens shriek with grief – their throats turn hoarse as the appointed hour for the Caretaker's *anthim sanskaar* nears.

The saha-mongers find the dire need to discourse on the importance of the anthim sanskaar aka last rites to facilitate the Caretaker's gateway to heaven:

'Last rites are essential for a speedy entry into the gates of heaven.'

'Heaven, a place larger than OneKmBungWow.'

'The Caretaker must get to this heaven somehow.'

'But ... how now?'

Amidst all the melee, the Caretaker's body has gone missing, and no one knows how.

Since no one knows how, every chattering lip in Chandinigarh goes silent.

Algauv is silent tonight. The husbands of Algauv's wives are silent – they have decided in their thick heads to keep their bread-earning women indoors. There is wind of a Saviour in this now windless town of Algauv located at a latitude of 21.41 degrees north, and a longitude of 72.20 degrees east in the Indian Subcontinent.

Algauv has restricted entry to the winds of change, their speed curbed at its perennially salted shores. 'Algauv must thrive on its asbestos manufacturing line, and that alone,' the only rich man with a bungalow here, and also a Big Mansion elsewhere in the Indian Subcontinent decrees.

Asbestos from the wrecks of ships come to Algauv to meet their end from distant shores. From France and Spain, even Serendib, the aged ships must sail to their graveyards on the shores of Algauv with an address in the Gulf of Kambhat in the State of Gujarat. These aged ships must sail one last time.

How will I sail the cumulonimbus nubes to heaven without a pasaporte? Where on earth is my pasaporte? Earth, my present home in heavenly Solali. Heavenly … si, Solali is the celestial abode of Shri Shri Shri Shri and Shri Sanyasi Solali Snowmountainwala – he has a third eye, and I need to access it fast to find my missing pasaporte. I am here, but is the

Sanyasi with the third eye in Solali at this moment? Where, where, where ... nowhere ... Sanyasi Solali Snowmountainwala is nowhere to be seen. Has the Sanyasi disappeared from the sight of mere mortals? I am a mere mortal with no pasaporte for a trip to heaven. It is not yet time for me to die, my missing pasaporte is an invisible sign from the cielo above.

SIXTY-SEVEN

THE CARETAKER'S BODY HAS gone missing – Senor Singh Mono has filed an F.I.R aka First Information Report. The Double Superintendent of the Chandinigarh Police Force has arrived at the scene of crime – he has personally verified the F.I.R.

The crime of stealing the dead body of the Minister for Shelters' wife is an offensive act – it can cause irreparable damage to the tender sentiments of the bereaved.

The act can be termed criminal, only if the Caretaker's declared dead body has actually been stolen. Practical measures must be taken to find the missing body of the dead Caretaker – this seemingly impractical F.I.R is imperative.

There is a practically impractical question regarding the declared dead Caretaker's intentions. The saha-mongers confer: 'Did the Caretaker rise from her dead stance unable to bear the noise pollution in the premises of OneKmBungWow? Or, did a certain vagabond stranger scoot with the Caretaker's body amidst all the melee in the city?'

The Double Superintendent of Police overhears the gossip, he contemplates: 'A vagabond is always a stranger in a new city. A stranger is always a prime suspect in a crime which has taken place in broad daylight, and in full public view.

A vagabond is almost always the prime suspect in a scene of daylight crime.'

'Pssst ...,' whisper some saha-mongers into the Superintendent's flapping ear, 'a levitating stranger, a vagabond, was last seen in the vicinity of OneKmBungWow.'

A mob grows distinctly louder in the vicinity of the Widest Footpath of Cottonpettai. The Lady with the Slender Hands is distinctly perturbed by the approaching mob screaming obscenities at Perumal Arokyaswami.

Screaming obscenities at Perumal Arokyaswami is a moral crime in the event he has embarked upon a barefoot pilgrimage, accoutred in black neck downwards to his big toes to pay obeisance to Lord God Muruga.

A man on a barefoot pilgrimage must be revered like God by one and all decree the Fellows of the Footpath. Together, fish vendors, coconut hawkers, flower sellers, rag pickers and other unemployed Fellows who comprise the joint population of the Widest Footpath of Cottonpettai stand ferociously close-fisted, legs askance, bodies set to punch the mob which is hobbling at a pace destined for those inebriated by country toddy. Perumal Arokyaswami's holy name cannot be maligned by obscenities – the Fellows of the Footpath will guard their comrade's reputation fiercely.

The fiercely advancing toddy-inebriated obscenity-spewing mob comprises seasonal workers from the Baron of Extreme Excess' Company of Sturdy Steel, with a manufacturing unit recently established in Cottonpettai's Special Economic Zone. The mob is furious that Perumal Arokyaswami has indented the Company, and in turn the Baron of Extreme Excess himself. How can Perumal, a mere rickshaw-puller, point fingers at the Baron, their Lord God who has cut their wages by half, but provided salt to their everyday meal. The rascal rickshaw-puller, the Baron's mob declares, has no business to slap Cottonpettai's largest hearted man with a legal notice seeking to replace his tardy wheel of steel, that too immediately. After all, Perumal Arokyaswami did not have any business to fall, cycle, rickshaw seat, steel wheel, et al. at the Supreme Fish Market of Cottonpettai, the mob cries.

Perumal Arokyaswami, it must be noted at this mob-yelling point, did not have any business falling off his cycle rickshaw because the wheel of steel, manufactured at the Baron's Company, was on warranty.

My pasaporte does not come with a warranty. My pasaporte is my identity, but I do not have the document with me. I am not *gratis* ... si, I do not have a pasaporte to set me free. I can tell you who I am only when I am gratis, si, I must be free to speak, you see.

SIXTY-EIGHT

THE THENTODAS ARE FREE to wander the forests of Blue Mountain Utahkamand. They know all there is to be felt, seen and heard in the darkness of the forest night to stay out of the way of jaywalking animals.

Jaywalking is the art of sauntering on a city road, head up in the air, shoulders relaxed, legs taking slow lingering steps, cerebellum in complete nonchalance to traffic and domestic animals. In the Nilgiris jungle, most animals are well-versed in the art of walking narrow and broad paths, including the complete stretch along the railway line which transports the train from the Mettupalayam Railway Station for Erstwhile Steam Engines in the vicinity of the Widest Footpath of Cottonpettai to Utahkamand and back every day. These animals are also well-versed in the art of jaywalking the Cottonpettai highway on which buses, lorries and private cars ply, that too, without being hit and left nearly dying or most certainly dead.

Few other animals who do not fall into the 'most' category are also accustomed to jaywalking the forests of Blue Mountain Nilgiris – but, they are not well-versed in the art of staying out of hitting range of speeding vehicles which are not visible to the naked eye. Only the sixth sense is equipped to detect these vehicles from a non-relatable distance, and few animals use it in time to escape being knocked off.

The Lady with the Slender Hands' sixth sense shows her that Perumal Arokyaswami is all set to meet danger in the shin. The Lady's sense is telling her that the cycle rickshaw puller will be socked in the shin sooner than later. With her eyes shut, the Lady can clearly see her lover's tibia newly dislocated from its parent body, shuddering like a vagabond splinter. The Lady shuts her eyes tighter to access her sixth sense further, and is somewhat relieved – in the future, Perumal Arokyaswami's tibia has not been separated from his body, it has only been fractured, and the fibula on his right leg has not suffered the impact of the socking.

The Thentodas can fix a fractured tibia like they would the broken wing of a Dove.

The Dove flies ... Pura parakidi
Pura vizhindidi ... Awoom, Awaam, Awoom
Awoom, Awaam, the Dove falls.
Pura ... Awoom, Awaam, Awoom
Awoom, Awaam ... the Dove
Awoom, Awaam ... Pura parakidi
The Dove flies ... Awoom, Awaam, Awoom.

Sing the Thentodas about a Dove they have rescued from the constraint of its broken wing.

This Dove has brought them a letter from their brethren across the Indian Ocean.

Across the Indian Ocean, Serendib waits for the delayed Dove, and a response from the Thentodas.

The Dove is now homeward bound. Visible to the human eye, the Dove has a multi-hued wing. The Thentodas have woven infant Peacock feathers into the Dove's broken wing. This Dove now resembles the Indian National Bird.

I see a Dove. The *Paloma* ... si, the Dove sees me. The Paloma drops the letter he has carried in the folds of his multi-hued wing from across the Indian Ocean into my frozen hands. The message in the letter is warm. The warm words settle in my throat. My throat is stifled, I cannot utter the words that I must immediately speak. I must *hablar* … si, I must speak before the novices disappear from sight. I hablar – the novices do not hear me speak. The novices are at a game of snow-mountain cricket. The game demands they scream. From Solali to Kulkulu, the snow-mountain valley resounds with the novices' scream.

SIXTY-NINE

THE CITIZENS OF ROZGAARNAGAR scream, their thunderous voices erupting a landslide in Khalaand. The citizens have been told that their daughters must please men other than those they have married. Each daughter from Rozgaarnagar, their parents hear, must close her eyes and permit her naked body to please a man whom she has not slept with before.

Each night, a daughter of Rozgaarnagar cries for no one to hear. She cries after her intercourse with a man she has never known in the drains surrounding the Big Ben in Algauv Mandi.

On this night, Jhoru Kanbi Badshah has wind of these cries – he will not tolerate them anymore. Jhoru, the Emperor, directs the citizens of Rozgaarnagar to fall on their knees and raise a united voice to the ancient trees, their Gods.

The citizens of Rozgaarnagar fall on their knees and worship the age-old trees – the Jhadas of the Western Ghats.

'Jhada majhe Deva … ye, ye, ye
Ye, ye, ye … tree my God
Jhada Deva, ye
Tree God, come … ye
Come and save our daughters, ye
Our muli need us, ye
Our muli, our daughters, they will come back home to us, ye Deva

To light the hearths of Rozgaarnagar, ye Deva
Deva ahe yethe, there is light.'

'God is here, there is light,' reveals the newly enlightened Jhoru Kanbi Badshah pointing skywards to the topmost tip of the oldest Jhada in Rozgaarnagar.

The oldest Jhada kisses a cloud – the citizens of Rozgaarnagar watch wide-eyed, open-mouthed, knees glued to the soil of Khalaand – they believe this sight to be a miracle – it shows them how their daughters can overcome their fates in the drains of Algauv and reach for the skies.

The four Royal Ragamuffins believe that a miracle has evacuated the Caretaker's body from the premises of OneKmBungWow. The Royal Ragamuffins reveal their combined belief in miracles thanks to their upbringing in the land of the Thentodas – they try their best to convince the investigating Double Superintendent on duty in Chandinigarh. The investigating cop gapes at the four Royal Ragamuffins in disbelief – he threatens to put them behind bars with their beliefs, et al. in the same police station where an F.I.R. for the missing Caretaker's body has been filed. The four Royal Ragamuffins decide to shut up, they do not believe in bars.

The Scouts and Guides of St. Alphonsious Pre-University College decide to venture on a night crawl in the forests surrounding Blue Mountain Nilgiris. The night promises to reveal a secret. This secret, the Blue Mountain night reveals, will lead them to the Originally Solali Kesar.

The Originally Solali Kesar, the Scouts and Guides have learnt, is as dainty as a new born Solali dew. This dew of snow-mountain territory is as precious as a diamond ... In pursuit of this diamond, people spill red. This red, they call blood.

Yo ver rojo – I see red. A novice has been hit by a half ripe rojo apple on his calvo head. His head is now red. Red, the colour of blood. This novice has blood, like you and I. This novice cannot be dead. This novice is muerto, his fellow bald friend believes at the sight of red upon his comrade's calvo head. The little boy cries, 'The novice is dead.' The crying novice wants to be the little boy that he still is, not a future saint in snow-mountain Solali. I do not see Sanyasi Solali Snowmountainwala anywhere. 'Turn your attention to the bleeding novice, please,' says a voice I can hear but cannot see. I must *oír* what I see. I must *ver* what I hear. Oir – hear, ver – see! I see what I hear.

SEVENTY

'HEAR THE MINISTER FOR Shelters out,' his entourage of Buxom Secretaries plead. The citizens of Chandinigarh have no time to hear a fumbling Minister, they will not heed to the Secretaries' palpitating pleas.

The pleas have left the Buxom Secretaries breathless, they palpitate some more.

The Ministry of Chandinigarh is increasingly breathless with the rising footfall in its air-conditioned premises. The panting bevy of Buxom Secretaries order the attendant to make more tea and cater to the angered feet scuffling in the corridors of the Ministry.

The attendant serves many cups of tea. The cups cannot be counted, they sit on top of each other in a rectangular tray. The attendant balances the tray, cups of tea et al. – he resembles a ballerina on cooking duty for foes who must be turned into friends.

In the Ministry, fair-weather friends are more fearsome than ferocious foes. Friends and foes are all cold and unfeeling about the Minister for Shelters' personal tragedy. The attendant must warm their unfeeling hearts with hot black tea.

The Ministry of Chandinigarh has one attendant. He caters to five hundred and sixty citizens, all of whom have managed to enter the air-conditioned premises of the Chandinigarh Ministry in one simultaneous step forward, and right into the Secretaries' chamber. The attendant is old, perhaps eighty-three earth years in age, say his birth records gone missing in Chandinigarh. The birth record is buried in the rubble that was once the attendant's shelter in Chandinigarh. The attendant to the Minister for Shelters has no roof over his white-haired head.

The saha-mongers open their mouths to speak: 'White for peace

'White for an ageing attendant

'The white-haired attendant has managed to restore peace in the Ministry of Chandinigarh

'The angered footfall is drinking black tea served by the white-haired attendant

'Black tea they call *kala chai*

'Kala chai to bring peace to feet that fell in the Ministry of Chandinigarh upon hearing that the Minister for Shelters has returned to his hometown after a brief sojourn in an unknown location.

'By the way, the location remains unknown because the Minister for Shelters has chosen to remain mum upon his return to Chandinigarh.

'The Minister for Shelters will now silently mourn the death of his wife, the Caretaker of OneKmBungWow.'

Now is the most appropriate time for all the citizens of Chandinigarh to refrain from phusphus, and go mum. Whispers do not beget action against crime the way silence does, the citizens must know.

The Thentodas maintain silence as the Master of Sports for Suitable Somebodies surely and steadily recovers from his heart gone cold in the heaving River Pyraka. The Master of Sports speaks – the Thentodas squat on their haunches with upturned ears, and listen.

The Thentodas have learnt a secret.

Awoom, Awaam, Awoom, the secret rests in their throats.

Throats home to a secret that must remain mum under the present circumstances, decree the Thentodas in a hush.

Awoom, Awaam, Awoom, *oru rahasyam* Thentodas' *thondaigalil toongihindranai.*

Awoom, Awaam, Awoom, a secret sleeps in the Thentodas' throats.

A sleeping secret must be allowed to rest until matters pertinent to its source are investigated with natural care, decree the Thentodas.

I must keep the face behind the voice I have heard secret. The secreto face has never been seen before by visiting travellers, and people on escapades to Solali. The bleeding calvo novice has seen the face that Manu Gaddi and the People of the Highest Hill safely guard from public view. I must guard my secret. My secreto must remain in my corazón while I wipe the bleeding head of the near muerto novice. I will be as near muerto as the novice if I let the secreto slip out of my mind, and into my tongue. *Mi lengua* quivers with secreto fright. Mi lengua, my tongue. Mi corazón, my heart. Mi lengua is in my heart as the bleeding novice quivers, I am faced with a snow-mountain terrain challenge.

SEVENTY-ONE

THE SCOUTS AND GUIDES of St. Alphonsious Pre-University College have a challenge at hand – they must contact Senor Singh Mono, asap.

All phones, mobiles and otherwise, have been cut off in Blue Mountain Utahkamand – there is absolutely no contact in these ranges. The network is damp in these mountain ranges with perpetually bursting cumulonimbus clouds making contact with the world outside the camp for the Braver than the Best impossible. The cut-off-from-the-world going-to-be Suitable Somebodies are bursting with an emotion they have been told to curb as honourable Scouts and Guides in the Indian Subcontinent. In the dark of a damp and network-bereft Utahkamand night, the Scouts and Guides of St. Alphonsious Pre-University College wear fear, the curbed emotion, upon their teenaged faces. Many Guides visibly burst into tears. Many more Scouts wear the tears beneath the surface of their reddened faces.

Where there is no network, reddened fear is inevitable.

Fear is a footloose emotion in Utahkamand.

The Master of Sports for Suitable Somebodies has nothing to fear, he has bared his footloose secret to the Thentodas.

The Thentodas are the keepers of law in the jungles abounding Nilgiris – they mete out justice by nature's decree, and that alone.

The Thentodas, keepers of peace in the jungles, turn up where they are needed most – they manifest out of the green cover at times of dire need …

Awoom, Awaam, Awoom, the Scouts and Guides of St. Alphonsious Pre-University College hear the song of the Thentodas loud and clear.

Where there is no network, only the voices of the peacekeepers ring loud and clear.

Awoom, Awaam, Awoom, the Thentodas are clear, they are near.

They are near the camp for the Braver than the Best in Blue Mountain Utahkamand – the cut-off-from-the-rest-of-the-world Scouts and Guides have nothing to fear.

Near the hamlet of Rozgaarnagar, careless bullets fired from AK-47s – all assault rifles – are heard. The citizens of Rozgaarnagar perk up – the careless bullets are summons from the CheapOO implying that there's a sudden out-of-season order for the Hyper Healing Balm. The bullets are meant to free the citizens' heads and hearts of all care for their loved ones, and scuttle impromptu towards the Aaraamaayu Factory to make an unseasonal buck or two.

'The season of labour has begun, dear citizens of Rozgaarnagar. Put on your clothes, drop your troubled thoughts in the deepest valley you can find, and run to the Aaraamaayu Factory dear young and old citizens!' announces a gapasapa-monger with a loud and booming voice.

Together, separately, sliding, slipping, falling, rising, running, stumbling, the citizens drop their troubled thoughts instantly, and assume the eighteen precarious paths to the Aaraamaayu Factory uphill Khalaand.

'*Thamba* ... stop ... *rukhiye* ..., do not run – not separately, not together,' screams Jhoru Kanbi Badshah in a pitch nearing the B flat major range, his voice ringing over the raging bullets of the assault rifles in the valleys abounding Khalaand.

The citizens of Rozgaarnagar, accustomed to the threat of raging cartridges from AK-47s, do not thamba. The citizens do not stop, they are quick to run, fast to slip, slide, fall and rise to brave the eighteen uphill and steep paths to the epicentre of their dreams on the plateaued top of the honeymoon Khalaand Range – the Aaraamaayu Factory.

The citizens slip and slide to rise and run for fear of the same rifles – these weapons have assaulted their now dead kith, kin and comrades from nether hills in a violent effort by the CheapOO and his goons to coax them out of their homes, towards the epicentre of their dreams. The now dead people of Khalaand were driven to rest forever by the bullets screaming out of the assault rifles. The now dead people had all slept through the threatening sounds of the bullets when it was time to meet their dreams.

These assault rifles, the potent bullets included, have all been acquired with clout from a Ministry, which sanctions properties in off-bound territories in the Indian Subcontinent – the topmost hill in Khalaand is one of them.

I tread in off-bound territory, my bare toes are stung by newly melted snow. I have wrapped the newly bleeding calvo novice in my snow-bathed pheran, my skin draped in sheer cotton rags fit for summer breeze. The breeze is iced in Solali, I freeze. I *congelar* in Solali. I freeze, si, I congelar in Solali – my skin stands in attention to the colder than ice wind. My slim cotton rags expose my skin to Manu Gaddi and the People of the Highest Hill. My skin is a random shade of light and dark, a complexion not native to the Indian Subcontinent. I wear a random smile, practiced to perfection to conceal my identidad. I wear an *aleatorio onreír* upon my icy breeze washed face … si, mi random smile will conceal my identidad.

SEVENTY-TWO

SANYASI SOLALI SNOWMOUNTAINWALA WEARS a random smile. The smile conceals his identity – he continues to walk scot-free on the main streets of Chandinigarh.

Sanyasi Solali Snowmountainwala walks.

A citizen walks behind him.

Another citizen joins the two.

The two are followed by three more.

More and more citizens join the line.

The line of followers grows.

It grows until all the citizens of Chandinigarh are followers.

Followers who need direction from Sanyasi Solali Snowmountainwala, the man who wears a random smile upon his emotion-bereft face in Chandinigarh.

The Fellows of the Footpath are agitated by a random smile. The smile the Lady with the Slender Hands wears upon her agitated face in acceptance of Perumal Arokyaswami's fractured tibia does not seem to synchronize with the seriousness of the situation at hand. This combination of agitated face and random smile unnerves the remaining Fellows of the Footpath. The Lady, of course, cannot reveal that she has been prepared for the situation given her advanced sixth sense – she continues to wear the random smile. The remaining Fellows of the Footpath, of course, do not subscribe to the rather uncommon sixth sense. The Fellows solely subscribe to what the world wears on its façade.

The world is a façade.

The Widest Footpath of Cottonpettai belongs to this world.

The Widest Footpath of Cottonpettai is a façade.

Façade is illusion. Illusion results in deception. The deceived enjoy the results of an illusion, which has purely been created to give flavour to the story of the Lady, her lover, and the other Fellows of the Widest Footpath of Cottonpettai.

The Fellows of the Widest Footpath of Cottonpettai lead a flavoured existence. The Lady with the Slender Hands is the prime source of their existence.

Existence, as the people of Cottonpettai know it, is a lifestyle adopted by people, depending on their sensibilities, sensitivities and, most importantly, cultivated sensualities.

The Lady with the Slender Hands has flavoured the 'free

from social pressures' lives of the Fellows of the Footpath with her cultivated sensuality. The citizens of Cottonpettai, who otherwise do not live on the Footpath, are enamoured by the refined ways of the Lady. They wonder from the air-conditioned comfort of their four-wheeled motorcars about the existence of such an unmistakably lissome and erudite Lady residing on the Widest Footpath of Cottonpettai.

But the munumunuppu-mongers about Cottonpettai notice otherwise. 'Today, the otherwise calm Lady's existence is shaken,' they say.

'Today, the Lady sings a sad song with *raro* gusto.

'Raro gusto meaning superior taste – such is the flavour of the Lady's sad song.

'This song reveals all that has gone wrong with Perumal Arokyaswami's tibia.'

'How, oh, how will Perumal Arokyaswami *caminar* to the Murugan Temple? How will he caminar ... we mean, how will Perumal walk barefoot up the rugged and stony path to the Murugan Temple on a distant hill in Serendib?' one Footpath Fellow would like to know.

'Why, with his muscular legs toned to expert 'stony uphill walking' shape from pedalling the cycle rickshaw day in and night out,' the remaining Fellows of the Footpath respond.

I cannot respond to nature's call. Nature's call cannot be subdued for long, it makes me twist and bend in convoluted postures that catch the attention of Manu Gaddi and the People of the Highest Hill. *Mi piel*, si ... my skin, *mi giro*, si ... my twist both are the talk of the Highest Hill of Solali. *Mi piel*, a unique shade of light and dark, is in a giro, and the cold snow-mountain *vientos* blow. I freeze until mi piel is the lightest shade of dark because my blood is turning *frío* ... si, cold.

SEVENTY-THREE

A COLD, DARK NIGHT in the forests of Blue Mountain Utahkamand has many possibilities for a light-hearted rendezvous with a suitable partner.

The munumunuppus in the air reveal that certain Suitable Somebodies have decided to go on joint rendezvous with prospective partners.

Unmindful of the munumunuppus in Utahkamand, the Scouts and Guides of St. Alphonsious Pre-University College have decided to hold hands and banter through the night. This act of pairing between a boy and girl, the Master of Sports has strictly told the future Suitable Somebodies, is most unbecoming of Scouts and Guides. The Scouts and Guides care no more for the strict instruction – the Master of Sports cannot keep a beady eye on their rendezvous anymore. The Master has been missing from the camp in Blue Mountain Utahkamand for two nights and three days – he has left the Scouts and Guides entrusted under his beady eye by Prominent Parents in the Undeniable Capital of the Indian Subcontinent, to do as they please.

The Prominent Parents – barons of steel and ministers for this, that and otherwise inconsequential to the Indian Subcontinent's wholesome progress, included – are blissfully unaware of the recent turn of events at the camp for the Braver than the Best. The Prominent Parents are also blissfully unaware that the beady-eyed Master of Sports cannot be trusted with their offspring – they continue to thank their lucky stars for such a fine mentor to their children.

'Beware the Master of Sports for Suitable Somebodies,' announces a gruff-voiced monger in the forests of the night. 'This Master, he has a beady eye for intimate goings-on, which are none of his business in the first place, really!'

Senor Singh Mono has a beady eye on the Royal Ragamuffins, their ruffian actions speak louder than their garbled words. The Royal Ragamuffins have turned the inner premises of OneKmBungWow into an adventure sports arena. The four Ragamuffins have decided to make good the missing body's absence with a game called Find the Dead Caretaker with a Provided Clue. They have turned OneKmBungWow inside out and upside down to plant suitable but grossly misspelt and illegibly written clues on chits under the sofa, between the Caretaker's clothes in the larger than life cupboard inside the Minister for Shelters' inner chamber, also on top of the sophisticated chimney in the Massive Kitchen of OneKmBungWow.

The clues are written by four clueless Royal Ragamuffins.

The clues lead the Royal Ragamuffins into larger than life cupboards that strictly belong to the residents of OneKmBungWow, and them alone.

The Royal Ragamuffins do not have a clue about the exclusivity of private spaces given their public home on the Widest Footpath of Cottonpettai – they wander the inner premises of OneKmBungWow like heirs to the vast and posh properties of the Minister for Shelters.

The four Royal Ragamuffins, all wannabe heirs, scream and scowl.

The Ragamuffins, all four, stand in front of the Ego Mirror inside the secret chamber of the Minister for Shelters like heirs supreme, and preen.

They preen, they sing: '*Attawatta, Jottapotta,* we are hot, we are smart, we are full of brawn.'

They sing, they grin, they scowl: 'Attawatta, Jottapotta, we are tall, we are handsome, ayooweee, see how we resemble the Minister for Shelters!'

They sing, they stare beady-eyed into the Ego Mirror: 'Attawatta, Jottapotta, why do our features match those of the Minister's?'

Senor Singh Mono does not have an answer to this why. When Senor Singh Mono does not have an answer, he orders an apple pie from the catalogue of OneKmBungWow's Massive Kitchen.

'Let the aroma waft, and fast, for there is another why looming like an apple pie in Senor Singh Mono's head,' the saha-mongers whisper.

My head is reeling, my feet are sore. Mi cabeza kisses mi feet, I faint. My head rests on my frozen feet. My cabeza, si ... mi head is dead ... or so I think until I blink. My gaze meets a head that is not mine. This cabeza belongs to Manu Gaddi – my head still rests upon my quivering shoulders. I scream, and mi cabeza hurts some more. My head is sore in the icy Valley of Solali, I scream no more.

SEVENTY-FOUR

THE SCOUTS AND GUIDES of St. Alphonsious Pre-University College scream together. Their combined scream so loud and filled with 'fanger', awakens a sleeping Viper in Blue Mountain Utahkamand.

Fanger is an emotion that consumes adolescent boys and girls when they break rules for the first time – it is a combination of fear plus anger. Fanger is an emotion which leaves you fighting between your fist and your head. Your fist wants to punch the cause of your anger. Your head reels from fear of the cause which caused you the fanger in the first place.

A sleeping Viper recognizes fanger as an emotion which a future Suitable Somebody alone can emit from his or her throat until it hurts, and leaves the screamer speechless.

The Scouts and Guides holding hands with their crushes for the first time in their adolescent lives are speechless at the sight of the awakened Viper. The Viper, speechless by biological disposition, hisses back at the Scouts and Guides, and vanishes to a quieter nook in Blue Mountain Utahkamand to continue snoozing.

The Scouts and Guides remain speechless, they sigh. They suddenly miss the Master of Sports for Suitable Somebodies, they sigh again.

Elsewhere in the blue ranges of the Nilgiris, the Master of Sports for Suitable Somebodies suddenly feels a gush of warm liquid in his nearly dead heart, he sighs. This sigh is an expression of relief, as more blood gushes in full force pumping the Master's heart back to life.

'Awoom to the Master of Sports' heart
'The heart so red
'Red the colour of passion ...

'Look how passion is a rekindled emotion in the Master of Sports' heart,' some lurking munumunuppu-mongers comment.

'Awoom, Awaam, Awoom,' sings the Master of Sports in a rather squeaky voice. Along with his saviours, the Thentodas, the Master sways his head from side-to-side with as much vigour as his recently warmed cold heart will permit.

The sun blazes at 36 degree centigrade in and around Cottonpettai – the heat masks the foothills of the cold Blue Mountain Nilgiris in the Mettupalayam Railway Station for Erstwhile Steam Engines until the waiting passengers break into sudden perspiration.

These passengers, all bound for an uphill sojourn to Utahkamand, are taken aback by the manic heat by the foothills of a cold mountain. These passengers, all accoutred in superior cotton and diamond finery set in gold, perspire some more. They squirm, they perspire, they exude the manic temperament of the heat. These passengers have no choice but to fish out their silver-rimmed hand fans and wish away their perspiration, before the heat stops them in their tracks.

The tracks are gleaming in the manic sun. The tracks will take these squirming, perspiring, fanning passengers uphill Nilgiris to Utahkamand in the high first-class bogie of the Erstwhile Steam Engine dandy.

I am visibly squirming, shivering, even perspiring in the perennially snow-mountain town of Solali at the base of the Highest Hill. Manu Gaddi is cold, his eyes crisp as alert flakes of snow on the Highest Hill of Solali. His eyes pin me down to the frozen earth. I feel the frozen *tierra*, si ... the earth move under my feet. I remember the pop star Dianne Queen, I croon: *There's a grasshopper squirming under my feet – I feel it, There are stars dropping from the skies – I feel them ... I feel Manu Gaddi's cold eyes melt the snow under my feet, the tierra moves*. I close my eyes, and wish the earth swallows me, I scream – the tierra moves. Manu Gaddi's gaze is no longer on me, he turns 180 degrees in the direction of the scream to face the top of the Highest Hill where the Originally Solali Kesar rests. I open my eyes to meet the depressive sun, I am no longer in *humano* company. My only human company at the bottom of the Highest Hill has fled to the top.

SEVENTY-FIVE

JIBBER-JABBER IS RIFE that Perumal Arokyaswami has fled to his native country Serendib, abandoning the other Fellows of the Footpath in the Indian Subcontinent. When a man goes missing, jibber-jabbers are evitable.

The Fellows of the Widest Footpath of Cottonpettai, the Lady with the Slender Hands included, have chosen to avert jibber-jabber by spreading a responsible rumour. Rumour has it that Perumal Arokyaswami is in constant touch with his comrades on the Footpath via the para-psychological medium of telepathy.

Telepathy pays no heed to physical space and time, it manifests whenever and wherever it rightfully should.

Jhoru Kanbi Badshah must right the wrong that mires Rozgaarnagar's daughters – he switches to telepathy mode to connect with the Thentodas on the southern side of the Western Ghats.

Gapasapas crop up everywhere: 'Via telepathy, our Saviour Jhoru is now aware that a certain Master of Sports for Suitable Somebodies is responsible for trading Rozgaarnagar's daughters.'

Sanyasi Solali Snowmountainwala gazes at an apple-sized crystal ball, and comes eye-to-eye with a daughter of Rozgaarnagar – she is now a resident of Algauv. His followers, all citizens of Chandinigarh, also gaze into the crystal ball.

The ball is blank.

The citizens of Chandinigarh gaze into Sanyasi Solali Snowmountainwala's blank third eye. The third eye does not wear a layered tunic like his two other windows to the world do. The third eye has no fibrous outer tunic, nor cornea, nor sclera. The third eye is matter of fact – it exudes no emotion like its tunic-wearing siblings called the tear spilling left and right eyes.

The third eye is naked.

The third eye looks at the object or person it is gazing at with no strings attached to the heart or the mind of the beholder. What Sanyasi Solali Snowmountainwala sees with his third eye is but the absolute truth. The citizens of Chandinigarh are all for truth. Sanyasi Solali Snowmountainwala speaks the absolute truth. The citizens of Chandinigarh begin to phusphus about the absolute truth.

There is phusphus in Chandinigarh about the daughters of Rozgaarnagar, all wives of tattooed snãyuñcã purusha spending sleepless nights in the drains surrounding the Big Ben in Algauv Mandi.

I spend another sleepless night in Solali. This night is lonely, I tussle between my dream and reality. I toss, I tussle. *Yo sacudida* ... si, I toss. *Yo pelea* ... si, I tussle with my corazón which beats quite loudly for the man who has left me high and dry. I shiver in a high mountain valley, my throat dry for want of water, my corazón paranoid for the man who has left me. Mi corazón beats for a man I met on a tobacco field in the Deccan Plateau. Mi corazón must return to Serendib, where it belongs. But who on planet tierra is in Serendib? The tierra is round, I remind myself. But the earth is oblate spheroid, not round. What goes round may not come oblate spheroid. I mince words on *firma* tierra ... si, the firm earth is not round. This night is cold and lonely, I shiver in my scant attire, I mince words, I pelea with my emotions, I blabber on planet earth. I blabber and jibber-jabber until I fall asleep on planet tierra – I am oblivious to this snow besotted night in Solali.

SEVENTY-SIX

SERENDIB IS OBLIVIOUS TO Pascal Rebello de Fonseca's name.

'Do not take his *nama* in vain,' yells Perumal Arokyaswami, pronouncing name in a tongue foreign to his own. The citizens of Serendib are perplexed by Perumal's accent, they ask in their native tongue Sinhala: '*Oyāgē nama mokakda?*'

Perumal Arokyaswami remains silent, he will not reveal his nama in his home country.

'What is your name?' repeat the citizens of Serendib in English, urging Perumal Arokyaswami to break his silence.

Those who gossip in Serendib are called ōpādūpa-mongers, they speak: 'Silence is golden if Perumal Arokyaswami has a Red Passport – it will indicate that he is a citizen of Serendib.

'Silence is blackened coal if Perumal Arokyaswami has a Blue Passport – it will indicate that he is an Indian citizen.

'Silence is of no consequence if Perumal Arokyaswami has no passport at all.'

The citizens of Serendib find no passport on the silent Perumal Arokyaswami's person. The cycle rickshaw puller's presence is of no consequence in Serendib. Perumal Arokyaswami is free to continue his journey to the Murugan Temple on a distant hill in a less-trodden forest in Serendib.

In silence, Perumal Arokyaswami remembers his promise to Pascal Rebello de Fonseca – he hobbles in the direction of his ultimate destination, his gait a tad slow given his recently broken – and fixed – tibia.

The rickshaw-puller hobbles until the wind carries a whisper, and delivers it in his ear. '*Vāsanāva,*' whispers Pascal Rebello de Fonseca into Perumal Arokyaswami's right ear – his recently fixed tibia on the same side of his body freezes. 'Good luck,' reiterates Pascal Rebello de Fonseca's voice into Perumal Arokyaswami's right ear – his recently fixed tibia on the same side of his body unfreezes. Perumal Arokyaswami has come to terms with the fact that good luck, yes Pascal Rebello de Fonseca, is on his side in Serendib.

Downhill Utahkamand, the Lady with the Slender Hands rests her back upon the rexine seat of Perumal Arokyaswami's cycle rickshaw, and lets her sixth sense transport her to Serendib – she sees Pascal Rebello de Fonseca whispering into Perumal Arokyaswami's ear, and smiles.

Uphill Utahkamand, sixth sense tells the Thentodas that the man with the fixed tibia is making steady progress towards the distant hill in Serendib.

The Thentodas raise their hands skywards and sing: 'Awoom, Awaam, Awoom, lift the man with the fixed tibia to the distant hill

'That hill so precious
'That hill so thick with proof
'Proof of Perumal Arokyaswami's undocumented identity
'Awoom, Awaam, Awoom – here's to lost and found identity.'

My identity is questionable. Manu Gaddi questions my identity. My identity must remain secret to the guardian of the Originally Solali Kesar on the Highest Hill of Solali, I remain silent. It is important to remain silencio ... si, I must keep silent despite Manu Gaddi's prying eyes. Manu Gaddi's eyes are prominent, I see them clearly at the bottom of the Highest Hill. Manu Gaddi's eyes are blazing rojo ... si, they are red balls of anger at the peak of the Highest Hill in Solali. Rojo is the most visible ball of anger upon a white and snowy slope.

SEVENTY-SEVEN

THE FOUR ROYAL RAGAMUFFINS are suddenly shocked by their visible resemblance to the Minister for Shelters. They always take matters which shock them seriously. The Minister for Shelters has trained the four Royal Ragamuffins to suspect reasons causing them shock under every single circumstance that throws them off balance.

The four Royal Ragamuffins know they have lost balance when their heads feel light and their mouths produce laughter without any documentable reason. Preening at their reflections in the Ego Mirror once more, the four Ragamuffins laugh uproariously, heads swaying from left to right, up and down in frenzied momentum, their feet running amok in the inner premises of OneKmBungWow.

The four Royal Ragamuffins are visibly shocked, they can neither control their heads nor their mouths – in fact, they can't even stop their running feet from going amok.

Within a matter of ten minutes, phusphus travels via open mouths in Chandinigarh, the Minister for Shelters is visibly shocked in his Ministerial Chambers. The four Royal Ragamuffins have exhibited their peculiar reaction to sudden shock, which the Minister alone understands.

The Minister for Shelters' already saddened face registers the shock he feels. The shouting citizens in the Ministry register the shock on the Minister's face. The citizens simmer down, and look equally saddened.

Phusphus travels via the shut lips of the citizens of Chandinigarh – Senor Singh Mono learns of his father's intense shock at the peculiar behaviour of the four Royal Ragamuffins.

Senor Singh Mono misunderstands the reason for his father's shock. He thinks his father's source of woe is the Caretaker's missing body.

'Focus on the missing body, please,' scream the citizens of Chandinigarh lurking in the outer premises of OneKmBungWow, interrupting the Senor's thoughts.

Senor Singh Mono has no time to waste, he puts on his powerless spectacles – he must focus on the missing body, and the Caretaker alone. Focus begets answers. The golden telephone with a wooden dial rings in the Main Hall of OneKmBungWow – Senor Singh Mono answers the call.

The four Royal Ragamuffins continue to wander the inner premises of OneKmBungWow – they laugh aloud while Senor Singh Mono writes down a vital clue in his Groovy Green Book.

I converge my eyes to the tip of my nose, and laugh rather aloud for a woman of small frame. Manu Gaddi's eyes continue to look rojo. I converge my eyes closer and laugh some more – my small frame wobbles like a skeleton inebriated on Solali weed. Manu Gaddi's eyes begin to lose their rojo at the sight of a laughing skeleton. Manu Gaddi's eyes are no longer red, the colour of chagrin. The red has vanished – I have worked my silly laughing mojo on the rojo-eyed Manu Gaddi. My mojo is happy, I laugh some more. Rio Beas is tickled by my loud laugh, it flows haphazardly, frothing the rocks resting on its chest with mirth. I am tickled by Beas' mirth, I laugh some more. A loud laugh is contagious in snow-mountain Solali. Manu Gaddi is tickled, he decides to laugh. Hahahahahahahahhahahahhaa ... laugh out loud when rojo is averted. I have averted Manu Gaddi's anger for the time being. Or so I think until Manu Gaddi's eyes begin to glow rojo, the same angry red I thought I have averted. I laugh some more until my eyes begin to glow rojo. My eyes and Manu Gaddi's are both rojo – yes, red, the colour of anger is also the ultimate shade of fear. I fear anger standing at the foot of a distant hill in Solali.

SEVENTY-EIGHT

'FEAR NOT DEAR CITIZENS of Rozgaarnagar, your daughters shall return to their parental homes in Good Time,' Jhoru Kanbi Badshah decrees.

The citizens of Rozgaarnagar nod their sad heads in assent, they salute Good Time.

'Good Time stands still in Khalaand,' the gapasapa-mongers comment, and continue to ask a profound and pertinent question. 'Still waters run deep, where is Bhima?'

Ever since Jhoru Kanbi Badshah has assumed the role of Saviour, he acts before he thinks – he marches with the citizens of Rozgaarnagar to the banks of the sinewy River Bhima.

Bhima is still, his masculine waters are deep in contemplation. Jhoru Kanbi Badshah stands still, accompanying the river in his contemplation.

Contemplation stirs still emotions. The citizens of Rozgaarnagar cannot stand still, they follow Bhima to his merging point with River Nira. Jhoru Kanbi Badshah's eyes follow the citizens of Rozgaarnagar, until they meet Bhima.

Bhima, the man Jhoru Kanbi Badshah's mother was last seen with.

'Bhima, a man?' a young gapasapa-monger asks open-mouthed.

'Bhima, a river, also a man!' an old gapasapa-monger clarifies, and blinks, only to miss Jhoru Kanbi Badshah taking a mighty leap forward. The monger blinks one more time, and between the fraction of a wink and shut eye, he catches the Saviour pinning Bhima, the man who was until then resting beside the river, his namesake.

Good Time is aroused, it begins to manifest in Rozgaarnagar as Jhoru Kanbi Badshah marches Bhima by the scruff of his ageing neck to the hamlet in Khalaand.

'Who on earth in the name of the mighty Western Ghats is Bhima?' many unknowing citizens would like to know.

There are answers floating in the air, thanks to some all-knowing mongers: 'Awoom – the Thentodas worship the tallest trees of the Western Ghats.

'Awaam – the Thentodas know a man who calls himself Bhima.

'Awoom, Awaam, Awoom, the time is near for Bhima's doom.

'Good Time is near.'

The citizens of Rozgaarnagar are pleased – they nod their less sad heads, they salute the approaching Good Time.

'It is too soon to be pleased, dear citizens of Rozgaarnagar – mysteries remain half resolved yet,' points out Saviour Jhoru.

The citizens of Rozgaarnagar stand still.

Still emotions run deep.

Deep down, they know they must rescue their flesh-harassed daughters stranded in the drains surrounding Big Ben in Algauv.

From the foot of the Highest Hill in Solali, I look hard into the deep valley. I see life in the city of Chandinigarh, the phusphus of its citizens is controlled by a sanyasi who is sitting with his right foot on his left thigh. I look harder still, and realize it is the same sanyasi with the prominent third eye. The third eye has been nurtured in the snow Valley of Solali over weed and good deed in equal measure as the calvo novices whisper to each other. The novices! Where have the novices disappeared? The foot of the Highest Hill in Solali is hardly the appropriate place to contemplate sanyasis on sojourn and missing novices! I am a lady, I must present myself in appropriate ways, always. I, a lady with scant robes. 'I am a *dama*, bring me my robes,' I yell above the loud silence of the Valley. No one hears *mi grito* – my yell is a mere whisper in the loudly silent Valley of Solali. I yell no more.

SEVENTY-NINE

THE LADY WITH THE Slender Hands cannot yell – she is choked with tears that block her larynx. The Fellows of the Widest Footpath of Cottonpettai blink in silence – they cannot understand why the Lady is unable to yell.

The larynx acts as a vestibule between silence and noise. This vestibule allows what the human head thinks, to be heard. The Lady with the Slender Hands thinks – she comes in contact with an emotion buried bellow her belly. In this region, her foetus found the emotion of unconditional love. Here, her foetus slept and swayed to urban pop lyrics until he came out into the world as a baby.

Senor Singh Mono loved pop music when he was still a foetus – there is an unconditional beat of happiness in the rhythm of this genre of songs. Senor Singh Mono needs happiness, only the unconditionally soothing beat of the great pop star Frisky Emilio can redeem his sorrowing soul, which yearns for his two mothers – one dead, and the other missing.

How do young sons deal with absent mothers?

They *cinco, seis, seite, ocho* in the absence of their fathers.

Cinco, seis, seite, ocho
Ocho! Marcha hacia adelante, Sofia
Cinco, seis, seite, ocho
Ocho! Marcha hacia atrás
Cinco, seis, seite, ocho
Seis! Marcha hacia atrás

Forward march! Senor Singh Mono runs forward and backward, and totally amok with the four Royal Ragamuffins in the inner premises of OneKmBungWow.

The music loops, it plays *cinco, seis, seite, ocho* – the rhythm runs amok until it stops. Senor Singh Mono stops while the four Royal Ragamuffins continue to run amok.

Senor Singh Mono remembers his mission halted midway given the sudden demise of the Caretaker. He must pick up the dangling strings of the mission right away – he calls his two Guide comrades.

Cinco, seis, seite, ocho ... seis, marcha hacia atrás – I have strings attached to my past. I was a lady with delicate mannerisms in the past, I must learn to be human. A human can do what a lady cannot. A human can scream louder than the silence of snow-mountain Solali. I scream. The scream echoes over the mountains into the valleys of Kulkulu, surrounds Gracia, and rides Rio Beas to the town of Chandinigarh. Sanyasi Solali Snowmountainwala grabs my scream, and binds it in the retina of his third eye. The sensitive to light retina which rests behind the third eyeball accesses impulses via the optic nerve to see a visual image in the brain. Sanyasi Solali Snowmountainwala's brain sees me in trouble. His brain transmits my form into his third eye. His third eye finds me in the crystal ball sitting in front of him.

EIGHTY

SANYASI SOLALI SNOWMOUNTAINWALA'S CRYSTAL ball is no longer blank. The citizens of Chandinigarh find a troubled human in the crystal ball. This human happens to be a lady who has recently abandoned her delicate mannerisms to make herself heard.

The lady has been heard.

There's phusphus in Chandinigarh: 'A lady is in trouble in snow-mountain Solali.'

Trouble follows the Minister for Shelters from the Ministry into Chandinigarh's High Street, also the Biggest Bylane of the city, thereafter to the outer premises of OneKmBungWow, and walks inside the house in mourning alongside his honourable self.

Trouble ruffles the tongues of the citizens of Chandinigarh some more. They saha: 'Aha, oho, ya, ya, no, no hey ho ... the Minister for Shelters is rubbing shoulders with trouble!'

'In fact, trouble is one step ahead of the Minister for Shelters,' sahas in the inner premises of OneKmBungWow announce the arrival of calamity.

Senor Singh Mono announces the Minister's arrival to the four Royal Ragamuffins still running amok. The Minister takes quick steps towards his Inner Chamber, the Royal Ragamuffins are slow to grasp sahas – all four of them mingle their steps, trip over each other's bare toes, and fall flat in front of the man the Ego Mirror has clearly indicated they resemble.

The Minister for Shelters stops short in his quick steps. He chooses to keep mum about the mismatched mingle and ensuing fall of the four Royal Ragamuffins until all the saha in Chandinigarh stops.

Senor Singh Mono is suitably surprised by his father's choice to keep mum over the fall of four full-grown boys who clearly have no business to run amok in the inner premises of OneKmBungWow when the house is still in mourning.

The four Royal Ragamuffins have stopped running amok, OneKmBungWow mourns in silence. Pin drop silence.

Silence ... not quite. Scream ... thud ... silence.

Yes, a scream tears through OneKmBungWow louder than the pounding silence – the Minister for Shelters' once steady but now shaking Burly Bodyguard loosens the grip on his double-barrelled shotgun SxS – the weapon falls down with a thud!

'Thud ... scream ... silence once again ... what's rocking

OneKmBungWow for heaven's sake!' the saha-mongers wonder aloud. There is prolonged silence.

The Minister for Shelters has chosen to stay mum despite the thud and the prolonged silence until he is called to act further.

There is no further reaction from Manu Gaddi – he has chosen to stay mum in reaction to my crystal ball stirring scream. I have chosen to ignore Manu Gaddi, either mum or staring rojo with anger at my shivering frame – I start my ascent to the top of the Highest Hill in Solali, alone. The Highest Hill is vehemently high – I miss my comrades, the calvo novices. But where are the novices? They have promised to accompany me on the journey up the Highest Hill once their comrade, the near muerto novice has rested enough to regain the blood rush inside his calvo head. I turn back with the hope of seeing a calvo novice, but find my pheran lurking behind me, instead, si ... Si, si, si ...my bridal garment is following me up the Highest Hill in Solali – strange, but true.

EIGHTY-ONE

PERUMAL AROKYASWAMI STANDS AT the foot of the not-so-trodden hill in a distant forest in Serendib. He stands still, fixing his gaze at the peak of the distant hill until his tibia feels a rush of fresh blood. This blood rush is no simple surge, it makes his taut tibia come unstuck – there's magic in the air. Perumal Arokyaswami's pursed lips come unstuck – he smiles wider than he did when Pascal Rebello de Fonseca vanished after whispering into his ear. Perumal stands just a moment longer to smile and whisper a silent prayer for the sake of this most important journey, before his unstuck tibia leads him uphill.

Perumal Arokyaswami stops for a moment longer to shut his eyes and remember the Good Man of Cottonpettai who had taken him under his loving care when all hope of returning home to this distant hill was lost.

Eyes now open and deliberately treading uphill, a voice rings in Perumal's ear. 'You shall not make the journey up the less-trodden hill in Serendib alone, you will have jumbo elephants to guide you to the root of your identity,' Pascal Rebello de Fonseca had once said to Perumal Arokyaswami over a smokeless chulha-warmed mazapán.

On a less-trodden hill in Kanandy where there is neither food nor water in sight, the combined taste of almond and honey energizes Perumal Arokyaswami's tongue – these flavours are fresh from the distinct memory of a Spanish mazapán. That mazapán, an almond and honey flavoured marzipan – this food, mercy showered upon an orphaned boy by the Good Man of Cottonpettai. The Good Man they call Pascal Rebello de Fonseca.

The orphaned boy, now a man with an injured tibia has braved the cumulonimbus cloud stirred waters between India and Serendib to meet his roots on a less-trodden hill.

The cumulonimbus clouds are pleased, they shower their blessings on Perumal Arokyaswami in a remote forest, home to the blessed Murugan Temple of Kanandy.

Kanandy, the Hill Station Queen of Serendib.

Perumal Arokyaswami accesses a somewhat similar memory of a rain-fed day in the backyard of the Great Peace God Temple in Kanandy, Isle of Serendib. It is a memory from a day when he was not quite six years old. The memory is somewhat fond, he hears the pulsating sound of approaching gata berayas until his misty eyes meet those of the lead percussionist's.

Perumal Arokyaswami is taken by surprise – he has not been told by the whisper in his ear that he is to meet six percussionists with their gata berayas, et al. en route to the top of the least-trodden forest hill in Serendib.

Surprise, when it meets any individual, is an eye-opening occurrence which takes place when one least expects it. The occurrence can be good or otherwise, depending on how wide the eye has been opened. This eye under contention is an inner vision. This vision, the sight of Perumal Arokyaswami treading up a less-trodden hill in Serendib has been brought to Sanyasi Solali Snowmountainwala's third eye for review.

Meanwhile, Perumal Arokyaswami is soaked to the skin by a sudden downpour – this rain storm leads the rickshaw-puller along with the gata berayas and jumbos who seem to have arrived on the scene out of the blue, to the vision of his lost past now resting not so far away upon the least-trodden hill of Serendib.

The Highest Hill of Solali is steep, I must wait for my pheran to keep pace with me. I watch my pheran move steadily. I smile at what I see, I watch my pheran move unsteadily. I frown at what I see – my pheran is now the head gear of the near muerto novice. I hope the novice will not be muerto before help arrives from Chandinigarh. I must keep the near muerto novice *viva.* I must keep the near dead novice alive, si, he must remain viva in this snow-mountain terrain.

EIGHTY-TWO

THE WIVES OF ALGAUV are alive – they wear prayers upon their lips at the crack of dawn. These wives are daughters of God-fearing parents – they pray at the birth of a new day, come what may.

A new day in Algauv is a reckless bustle of discarded asbestos on wheels. The steel wheels of horse-drawn carts are all dented. The dead weight of discarded asbestos cannot be borne by rusting steel. The friction of rusting steel upon kutcha roads pockmarked with dents by three-tonne trucks cannot be borne by ill-fed horses. The ill-fed horses are alive on a somewhat nutritious dose of hay fed to them on the sly by the wives of Algauv.

The wives of Algauv buy the hay with the surplus coins they have carefully knotted into their slippery synthetic saris. These coins are the same surreptitious gifts from men who visit them by night in the drains surrounding the Big Ben. These coins, the wives save for the ill-fed horses which spend nights by the same drains, watching over the daughters of Rozgaarnagar as the women win bread money in not-so-respectable rupees for their snãyuňcã purusha. The daughters of Rozgaarnagar have learnt to be sly for fear of being burnt in their delicate palms with butts of unextinguished Vignesh Beedis – the horses, their well-wishers, neigh in pain.

The wives of Algauv, once daughters of Rozgaarnagar, wear the stamp of Vignesh Beedis upon their palms. They conceal their abused palms inside the folds of their synthetic saris. These are the same synthetic saris which the citizens of Rozgaarnagar, parents of the wives of Algauv, have gifted their daughters in medium-sized kit bags. These saris are their prized wedding trousseaus.

These prized trousseaus are special packages wrapped to order by the keepers of Rozgaarnagar's Provision Store – saris packed in a gradation of colours varying in brightness and synthetic texture. The synthetic texture the new wives of Algauv call nylon. Nylon, a material which has undergone a chemically fabricated process to render the saris slippery to the touch and glitter with artificial sheen.

All that glitters in Algauv is not gold, but for a daughter from Rozgaarnagar. Jhoru Kanbi Badshah's mother was once a glittering wife of Algauv.

A glittering wife is worth a gold mine if she is monitored by a snãyuñcã purusha day and night.

Day or night, Jhoru Kanbi Badshah will watch all that glitters with a discerning eye. At this twilight hour between day and night, he spots a gold mine – he brings Misfortune by the scruff of his ageing neck to Rozgaarnagar.

There's random gossip all over the Indian Subcontinent regarding a certain person called Misfortune.

A gapasapa-monger says: 'This gold mine is indeed a man they call Misfortune – he has brought much woe to the citizens of Rozgaarnagar.'

A phusphus-monger adds: 'Misfortune must be kept under lock and key until the Originally Solali Kesar is located.'

A saha-monger ventures to convey: 'Senor Singh Mono will leave the closely guarded premises of OneKmBungWow by the break of moonlight, giving the slip to Misfortune.'

A munumunuppu-monger has the last word: 'Two Guides, both training to be Suitable Somebodies, have given the slip to Misfortune. The Guides are no longer in Utahkamand, they have fled the Blue Mountains to meet a fellow Scout headed on a mission to a distant hill in Solali.'

I hear voices, I turn around to see visitors in the Highest Hill of Solali. Visitors are welcome only if they have given Misfortune the slip. I slip, I lose my grip on the newborn pines which have stretched their small limbs to take a peek at the truant sun. I must regain my grip before the hard-to-find sun, si, the truant *sol* disappears in the embrace of a pregnant cumulonimbus nube. I slip, I grip the nearest speckled rock covered with nascent snow. The rock is soft, it moves. I tighten my grip on the moving rock, so soft and luxurious to the touch. The rock retaliates with a growl. I spontaneously howl louder than the growl. The speckled rock resembles a snow leopard, eyes wide open, whiskers erect, all four paws geared for pounce on the perpetrator. I, the perpetrator, destroyer of the snow leopard's siesta, howl louder than the growl. I come to sudden terms with the fact that the rock which resembles a snow leopard is indeed a Himalayan Cat. I loosen my grip, I *resbalón*, si, I slip – the visitors watch me resbalón – my frozen body comes to rest at their feet. I have spotted three pairs of booted feet, all accoutred for a long trek in knee-deep snow on a distant hill in the State of Himachal Pradesh.

EIGHTY-THREE

THE THENTODAS HAVE TAKEN a long trek by day in the deep forests of Blue Mountain Nilgiris.

They trek, they sing, they brandish their flutes styled out of wayward Bamboo trees. These hand-carved flutes are special, they produce the distinct hum of the honeybee when they are swirled. These flutes are doubly special – they are three feet long, and serve as walking sticks when the terrain is unconducive for natural balance. The Thentodas are known to balance the terrain naturally, by means of unnatural acrobatics that are exclusively practiced by the jungle folk, their ancestors, their kith and kin, also the four-legged mammals hereabouts. The Thentodas have crossed the unconducive terrain, they swing their flutes which now serve as walking sticks to stir a melodious whir in the atmosphere with their trademark sound Awoom.

'Awaam, Awoom, Awaam, the primary folk of Utahkamand, the Nilgiris jungle savvy Thentodas are here,' announces the handlebar-moustached Driver of the Erstwhile Steam Engine urging the slow train to a halt.

The Engine, accustomed to the Driver's easily excitable nerves, falters to a yawning halt in the middle of what seems like nowhere.

Awoom, Awaam, Awoom, the rising melody of a dozen Bamboo flutes stir the curiosity of passengers in the high first class bogie of the Erstwhile Steam Engine in the middle of nowhere. The curious passengers snake their jewelled necks outside the windows, expecting to see Bison in the middle of nowhere.

'The Thentodas are not Bison.

'Bison, the four-legged animals called Gaur, with shining brownish-black complexions and two classic outward bending horns, share the jungles of Blue Mountain Nilgiris with the honey-tapping Thentodas.

'The Thentodas have two legs each.

'Their legs so supple and so strong – they climb rocks beyond human reach.

'The Thentodas have two hands each.

'Their hands so nimble, they heal incurable diseases of the heart and mind.

'Mind what you think of the jungle-savvy folk,' the Driver explains, and goes on to admonish the diamond-brandishing elite, his handlebar moustache nodding in agreement.

Stranded in the middle of nowhere, the diamond-accoutred elite deem it necessary to mind their powerful tongues – they cannot afford to return to the Undeniable Capital of India minus their heirs.

The munumunuppu-mongers have ventured into the elite people's heads and heard their thoughts, they announce: 'Their heirs are fans of the Thentodas.

'Awoom, Awaam, Awoom, here come the Thentodas.'

The passengers in the high first class bogie of the Erstwhile Steam Engine adjust their superior cotton attires to welcome the Thentodas, whatever this so-called jungle-savvy species might be.

The diamond wearing elite are unaware that their disdain for jungle-savvy folk is being monitored by the Thentodas who have stopped for a water break in the vicinity of Hillgroove Station, midway to Utahkamand.

The Thentodas have a balm for disdain – their healing hands will extend treatment to the diamond-wearing elite when they least expect it.

Of course, the diamond-wearing elite in high-profile cotton wear do not expect the hands of the Thentodas to touch them at all. They are not aware that the Thentodas have hands in the first place.

Alas ... the diamond-wearing Suitable Somebodies from the Undeniable Capital of India have never heard of God's closest earthly comrades – the Thentodas.

'Never mind, where the elite are concerned, ears are meant for diamonds, not hearing,' squirms the Driver of the Erstwhile Steam Engine, eliminating a crystal of diamond dust from his handlebar moustache.

Diamond dust in reality is a cloud kissing the ground, its body comprising minute ice crystals. The diamond dust of icy particles is a rare phenomenon – it is distinct in appearance in an otherwise cold but sun-scorched region.

Munumunuppus fill the air: 'Hail the *vyara* dust, Awoom, Awaam, Awoom.

'The vyara dust is the Thentodas' diamond accoutrement.

'Awoom, Awaam, Awoom – the Thentodas wear diamond around their necks, their belly buttons, their shins and their ankles, too.

'Please note that the Thentodas are richer by diamond dust than the elite of the Undeniable Capital of India travelling to Utahkamand in a high-class Erstwhile Steam Engine bogie.'

Diamante dust clouds the distance between me and the suddenly awakened Himalayan Cat. I stand on tip toe and reach for the icy crystals that form the membrane of the diamond dust in snow-mountain Solali. Bless this diamante dust, I am no longer visible to the invasive eyes of the Himalayan Cat. Bless this diamante dust, Manu Gaddi cannot see me sprawled at the feet of one Scout and two Guides. I am a *princesca* deemed queen with a diamond dust-speckled crown at the foot of the Highest Hill in Solali – my Super Special Task Force aka SSTF comprising one Scout and two Guides has arrived.

EIGHTY-FOUR

PERUMAL AROKYASWAMI, A PRINCE deemed king with a diamond dust-speckled crown upon his rain-soaked head, majestically walks up the distant hill in Serendib to the sound of receding gata berayas.

This diamond dust is a near cosmic phenomenon in Serendib. The six percussionists gape at the *diyamanti* dust – they allow their gata berayas to recede until there is dry leaf drop silence.

In silence, Perumal Arokyaswami and the male percussionists walk tenderly between colonies of blissful Neelakurinji flowers – the men are happy given the extravagance of the cumulonimbus clouds – they are happier to see a downpour of rare icy crystals of diyamanti dust.

'Blissful Neelakurinji flowers ... see these happy blue flowers blossomed to a tender lilt of purple after twelve long years in a distant hill in Serendib,' declare the opadupa-mongers who spread gossip all over Serendib.

These flowers, they dress the rugged path to the top of a seldom-trodden hill in Serendib and all the way to the top where the Murugan Temple is lit by a single oil lamp. Perumal Arokyaswami treads the Neelakurinji-smitten path wearing a diyamanti dust crown upon his simmering head – nothing has changed in these parts since he has last seen it.

Perumal's head is simmering with memories that have decided to surface on this not-so-easy but ethereal journey to a long-lost day in his distant past.

The distant past is now present.

The six percussionists, overwhelmed by the present spectacle of diyamanti dust crowned Neelakurinjis begin to sound their gata berayas. The six percussionists cannot seem to resist keeping their feet in step with the beats growing ruggedly louder with the tempo of their nimble hands. The six percussionists sway to the Kanandyan dance, their lissome gata berayas exploding with renewed passion for an ancient art form.

The gata berayas take Perumal Arokyaswami back in time – he is now the owner of a newfound memory brought to surface from old occurrences that have been buried in a deep socket of his hippocampus.

'Hippocampus,' intervene the scientific-minded opadupa-mongers, 'is that part of the human brain, which, along with its counterpart the cortex, aids memory.'

Memories surge, and eight *Elephas Maximus* enter Perumal Arokyaswami's hippocampus.

Err ... not quite – these eight Asian Elephants aka Elephas Maximus with tall heads to enhance their already high statures are sharing 'far above the shoulder' space with Perumal Arokyaswami, each mighty mammal sporting a crown of diyamanti dust.

The percussionists are stunned, they bring their dancing feet and nimble fingers beating a cosmic rhythm on their gata berayas to a sudden pause – they permit a fresh spray of diyamanti dust to settle upon their bare shoulders.

The rhythm has suddenly died – Perumal Arokyaswami's hippocampus pauses in its speedily rewinding track down memory lane – the voice of Pascal Rebello de Fonseca whispers a precise instruction in the rickshaw-puller's left ear.

I have given the Scout and two Guides precise instructions. The Guides must first take the shortest path to the peak of the Highest Hill in Solali, while I find myself some clothes to wear. The Scout must first locate my missing pouch. The pouch has more than the memory of a romantic interlude between the Minister for Shelters and me in a tabaco field in the heart of the Deccan Plateau. The Yellow Tobacco Flower in the pouch is accompanied by a Nil Manel, a Blue Water Lily from a holiday to Serendib during my childhood years in the distant past. The Scout is rather pleased to be of special assistance to me, I recall his face from a day in my not so distant past – rewind my hippocampus to my *pasado*. Mi pasado, si, my past is full of memories I must bring to the present to save the Originally Solali Kesar.

EIGHTY-FIVE

THE MISSING CARETAKER'S PAST is not etched in the Minister for Shelters' hippocampus. The Minister is feigning memory loss in the inner premises of OneKmBungWow where matters have gone way out of hand, beyond his sharp mind, and above his clever head. Matters of the declared dead Caretaker's past must be brought to the present attention of the Double

Superintendent of the Chandinigarh Police Force investigating the F.I.R. with details of her disappearance. The Minister for Shelters has no option but to comply with the Superintendent investigating the Caretaker's whereabouts.

The four Royal Ragamuffins, despite their not so active hippocampi, are aware that the Caretaker's past is not to be talked about under the present circumstance. The Minister for Shelters has had a word with his bastard sons about the dire consequences of raking up the declared dead Caretaker's past.

'But how can a declared dead Caretaker's body go missing?' bemuse the citizens of Chandinigarh, their continuous sahas regarding the whereabouts of the missing corpse is filtering through the slats of closed and barred windows that dress the walls of OneKmBungWow.

Sanyasi Solali Snowmountainwala has arrived at the scene of crime and heard all the sahas – he is not about to divulge the whereabouts of the Caretaker's body – the time is not quite ripe for disclosures. However, the time is ripe for Sanyasi Solali Snowmountainwala to disappear from Chandinigarh within the fraction of a second.

A fraction of a second has elapsed – Sanyasi Solali Snowmountainwala is gone. Within the same fraction of a second, sahas erupt all across Chandinigarh that a bearded sanyasi with a prominent third eye has disappeared as suddenly as he had appeared when the Caretaker's body was still lying in front of OneKmBungWow.

This saha overwhelms the citizens of Chandinigarh awaiting the return of the Caretaker's body in the outer premises of OneKmBungWow. Wasting no parsec, the citizens spill the beans through the window slats and deliver the phusphus straight to the Minister for Shelters' sharp ears.

With his ears on the matter, the Minister for Shelters must grab the attention of Sanyasi Solali Snowmountainwala's third eye.

'The third eye alone will reveal the fate of the Minister for Shelters when the Caretaker's body makes a statement,' a saha monger reveals.

'How in heaven's name can the Caretaker's body, dead for over seventy-two hours now, speak?' trembles the Minister who has wind of this fresh and scary saha.

There are terrible thoughts running in the Minister's mind, he speaks to himself: 'This is no time to debate about the larynx of the Caretaker's dead body. The larynx is but a sound box, a messenger to a thinking mind. Does the dead Caretaker's mind think?'

The Minister for Shelters is overwhelmed by the activist Caretaker's ability to make a noise about women's rights without uttering a sound from her larynx, even in death. But the Caretaker's dead body has made no noise on women's rights, wrongs or otherwise, at least not yet ...

The Minister for Shelters is losing his ability to cope with the missing dead body of his legal wife. He must enter the sphere of Sanyasi Solali Snowmountainwala's third eye to cope with impending nightmares regarding his dead wife making a silent noise about preserving women's rights.

There is no more time to lose over bemuse – the Minister for Shelters summons his four bastard sons in the noted absence of his legal heir, to enter the Sanyasi's third eye by hook or crook. His mind made up to salvage a losing battle, the Minister for Shelters leaves no hook or crook unturned to make his presence felt where it immediately matters. He presents himself in front of Sanyasi Solali Snowmountainwala's third eye of his own accord – the Minister's bastard sons have been of no help whatsoever.

I see eye-to-eye with Senor Singh Mono, I sigh. His eyes, a mysterious shade of blue, which my ancestors of Spanish origin wear in their perplexed expressions. Senor Singh Mono wears a perplexed smile as I look him in his blue eye. My ojo and his eye are the same vivacious shade of azul. All is azul in Solali between Senor Singh Mono and I, until a rojo manzana lands with a soft thud upon my wavy-haired head.

EIGHTY-SIX

ALL IS WELL IN Jhoru Kanbi Badshah's head – Bhima will lead him to his mother.

All is well in Rozgaarnagar – the citizens will walk together with Jhoru Kanbi Badshah to meet his long-lost mother.

All is not so well in the Badtameez Baap's household – fear is rife that his traded wife will banish his enlarged family upon her untimely return. In lieu of their fear, the other family members of the Badtameez Baap's household refuse to accompany Jhoru Kanbi Badshah and the citizens of Rozgaarnagar on 'Mission Find the Missing Mother Who Is Now a Traded Flower Upon Another Man's Chest'.

Leading the entourage of citizens who have decided to follow Jhoru Kanbi Badshah, the Saviour remembers one evening when he was still a boy, and his mother held a flower between her teeth.

This flower was a Gulaab.

Gulaab, a Rose.

Rose, the colour of passion.

Passion the colour red.

Red petals strewn all over the bed.

The same bed where she became wife to the Badtameez Baap on an unfortunate night in November, remained as cursed to the lady after seven wedded years to Jhoru's father.

Seven years after her marriage to the Badtameez Baap, the scoundrel had traded his own wife, Jhoru's mother to a snãyuňcã purusha – he sported a distinct tattoo upon his chest.

Rose petals serenading the distinct tattoo shaped as a Tobacco Flower upon the heaving chest of the snãyuňcã purusha.

The tattoo, a distinct vision which remains in Jhoru Kanbi Badshah's heavy chest.

This vision, a sight from the night his mother was traded to the man with a tattoo upon his hairy chest.

This night, when Jhoru Kanbi Badshah, not quite six years in age, watched the Gulaab slip from his mother's mouth as the man with the tattoo grabbed the Rose with his sharp-as-a-razor-blade teeth.

Sharp teeth tearing the Rose, biting into his mother's flesh.

Jhoru Kanbi Badshah, the little boy of almost six, watched the Rose petals fly across the bed and settle upon the Tobacco Flower once his mother had been taken ...

That night, Jhoru Kanbi Badshah's mother screamed one last time, pleading with the Badtameez Baap to intervene, as her husband and tied up son watched her whimper through the slats of the broken and mended window in a house with an address in the farthest corner of Algauv.

It is another day in the farthest corner of Rozgaarnagar.

En route to the source of the sinuous River Bhima with an entourage of citizens behind him, Jhoru Kanbi Badshah's chest is heavy with this secret from the same day his mother was traded.

The rojo manzana which has touched my head leaving a visible bump, has sent my chest racing with emotions that have forgotten to rest. My chest panicks with yearning for the child my womb once carried. I carried the foetus on tip toe for fear of being caught wandering pregnant by wagging tongues. Senor Singh Mono is no foetus, but he triggers the emotion of love in my chest with his azul eyes. My ojos are moist, they open and close to find solace between sleeping emotions that simply will rest no more. Si, yes, I mean *ninguno* ... no, I cannot rest until I reach the top of the Highest Hill in Solali.

EIGHTY-SEVEN

THE LADY WITH THE Slender Hands cannot rest until she hears from Perumal Arokyaswami – she watches the Fellows of the Footpath as they roll on their backs, hands and feet up in the air, merrily guffawing at the stars in the distant sky. The Lady is amazed at how the Fellows are always out of control in order to keep their haphazard lives in check.

Let the Fellows do as they please, the Lady must work on her dis-ease – she remembers Frisky Emilio, a singing star in a distant sky ...

'The Lady is out of control, she begins to move to the initial beats of *Cinco Altos! Ocho, marchar hacia adelante,'* point out some gawking munumunuppu-mongers.

'Cinco, seis, siete, ocho
Marchar hacia adelante, Sofia!

Five, six, seven, eight
March forward, Sofia!'

'No,' the munumunuppu-mongers clarify, 'her name is not Sofia. The Lady with the Slender Hands will not reveal her name.'

The Lady on her part continues to step forward and backward with Frisky Emilio playing in her head until the refrain of *Cinco Altos!* can be heard by all the Fellows of the Footpath.

How can the Fellows of the Widest Footpath of Cottonpettai hear a song that is playing inside the Lady's head?

Well, the Scouts and Guides of St. Alphonsious Pre-University College, all dancing to the perky beats of *Cinco Altos!* blaring from the high class Bigbose speakers of their Superior College Open to the Sky Truck grab the attention of the Fellows and the Lady's, at once.

'Whoa! What a celebratory matter of coincidence,' says the Lady with the Slender Hands as she imitates the sound emanating from the Bigbose speakers, '*Cinco Altos*!'

Whoa ... the Lady's larynx has come un-choked, she sings the *Cinco Altos!*, this time louder than the posh Bigbose speakers, until the Scouts, Guides and all the Fellows of the Footpath choose to repeat the refrain, first separately, then together.

The Widest Footpath of Cottonpettai is a party zone. Young

Suitable Somebodies are tripping on music from a foreign land with the Fellows of the Footpath and an unsuitable nobody who is fondly called the Lady with the Slender Hands.

'What will the Master of Sports for Suitable Somebodies say about this most unsuitable act?' there are munumunuppus in the air.

The going to be Suitable Somebodies do not care. 'The Master of Sports has gone missing,' they declare, stepping up the momentum of *Cinco Altos!* without a care.

Instantly stepping down the momentum of *Cinco Altos!*, the Lady stops short in her sway – she declares that the Originally Solali Kesar, hidden from public view in a closed enclosure upon the Highest Hill in Solali, must be protected, what with the Master of Sports on the prowl!

The Scouts and Guides scowl, they have no idea that a Master of Sports on the prowl can harm the Originally Solali Kesar in any way, leave alone get to the top of the Highest Hill uphill Manmanali in faraway Himachal Pradesh without being noticed!

'What on planet earth is this Originally Solali Kesar that can be harmed by a Master of Sports on the prowl?' the munumunuppu-mongers, the Scouts, the Guides and all the Fellows of the Footpath excluding the Lady, wonder aloud.

Si, the Originally Solali Kesar can be harmed by the Master of Sports for Suitable Somebodies, I know from experience. Si, my *experiencia* tells me that Senor Singh Mono must find my pouch immediately. My pouch has a vital clue. No sacrilege can be resolved without the vital clue, this too, I know from experience ... mi experiencia extends from the Widest Footpath in Cottonpettai to the top of the Highest Hill in Solali, also many other terrains in between where my private parts have been touched by random men without my consent …

EIGHTY-EIGHT

THE MINISTER FOR SHELTERS has a private life – it has been kept meticulously secret to his public profile.

'Of course, there is no harm in having a private life if the man in question is the Minister for Shelters, and uses his power to abuse a woman in her intimate areas without her consent, populate her womb with a son, usurp the offspring they have jointly begotten, and thereafter unscrupulously vanquish her from OneKmBungWow simply because she is not his wife,' contends an expansive-minded saha-monger of Chandinigarh – he has just received a heavy bribe from the politician in question.

But what is now amply apparent to the citizens of Chandinigarh is that the Minister for Shelters has committed a sacrilegious act. 'We are certainly not about to stop our gossip until the Minister has spoken about his private past publicly,' the citizens contend.

The citizens have decided to take the matter into their hands, thanks to the intervention of a certain sanyasi – they will most certainly saha until the private life of the voted to be public servant – yes, the deep dark secrets of the Minister for Shelters become so apparent that the women in his life, dead and alive, will turn around and ask him to go take a long walk.

The Minister for Shelters is all set to take a long walk. This time, he will walk barefooted from the base of Solali, all way up to the Highest Hill where Sanyasi Snowmountainwala keeps a constant third eye on the Originally Solali Kesar.

Sanyasi Solali Snowmountainwala's third eye is alert – he sees the Minister for Shelters approaching the base of Solali – the politician is presently lodged at a latitude of 30.90396 degrees north and longitude of 77.096943 degrees east. The Sanyasi is technically sound, he is well-versed in using the Global Positioning System aka GPS to trace both necessary and unnecessary people, no matter which intersection of latitude and longitude they have taken refuge in. The Minister is an unnecessary man, he does no good unto his people. But right now, it is absolutely necessary for the Sanyasi to keep track of the Minister given that the latter had conveniently abandoned the Caretaker's body to its own fate, and vanished to the Deccan Plateau to relive memories of passionate days with a former lover.

Why is the Caretaker's body being referred to as 'it', pray? The Caretaker breathes despite her death for heaven's sake. The Caretaker breathes for Sanyasi Solali Snowmountainwala's sake!

With GPS locators making unknown locations known, time is running out for heaven's sake. For the Originally Solali Kesar's sake, I choose to start my trek up the Highest Hill despite the rising chill. This chill is piercing my pale skin, I do not have my pheran to keep me warm – the near muerto novice is also calvo, he needs it more than I do. By the way, the near muerto novice is viva, his comrades have caught pace with him despite the rising chill. By the way, Senor Singh Mono has gone to locate my missing pouch, he is adept at using the GPS locator. By the way, I know from experiencia that each time my foetus somersaulted in my womb, I read out the latitudes and longitudes of places that I would like to visit with the flesh of my blood.

EIGHTY-NINE

THE FOUR ROYAL RAGAMUFFINS who have been divested of their identity cards are certainly the flesh of their father's blood – they choose to take a walk in the interim between sahas and waiting-to-be-unravelled facts. These facts will reveal details which are certain to bring to light romantic and biological connections that have so far been concealed from the left and right human eye of every single citizen of Chandinigarh.

Please note that the third eye, unlike its left and right counterparts, has been well-attuned to connections that transcend states, continents, even physical dimension.

Perumal Arokyaswami is in Serendib with a person who has so far been considered dead in the physical dimension.

Of course, it has been concluded, for lack of evidence otherwise, that Pascal Rebello de Fonseca is indeed dead. The case has been concluded sooner than the stipulated period of seven years as prescribed by the Indian Constitution to arrive at a definite conclusion because a certain Minister has been involved in the disappearance of the Good Man of Cottonpettai. The missing man in question has connections in

Serendib and Spain, apart from a house with a legal address in Cottonpettai.

Those who have gone missing from Cottonpettai, both alive and dead, seem to have been found in Serendib.

The Fellows of the Widest Footpath of Cottonpettai are livid, they have wind that Perumal Arokyaswami and Pascal Rebello de Fonseca have exchanged niceties on a distant hill in a less-trodden forest in Serendib – they have connected en route to the Murugan Temple.

'By the way, is Pascal Rebello de Fonseca alive or dead?' probe the Fellows, hoping for a conclusive response from the Lady.

The Lady is known to be silent when she rests in her customary place by the cycle rickshaw upon the Widest Footpath of Cottonpettai. The Lady is also known to abandon her silence as soon as a query is posed. So, the Fellows take an additional step forward – they intrude upon the Lady's resting place, and confess aloud: *'Aadyy* – the Lady, *adi karapambuchi* – she has disappeared!'

The Lady's disappearance is strange given that she was just seen dancing to Frisky Emilio's *Cinco Altos!* in step with a bunch of Scouts and Guides escaped from the camp for the Braver than the Best uphill Nilgiris.

Gossip is rife all over the Indian Subcontinent, 'Why oh why upon planet earth's name have all the women, the Lady with the Slender Hands, the Caretaker's body included, going missing?'

So what, even Pascal Rebello de Fonseca is missing.

Senor Singh Mono has gone missing as well. No one in Chandinigarh, even its aware citizenry, knows where the Senor, son of a certain Suitable Somebody who has decided to embark upon a barefoot sojourn, gone.

I know where Senor Singh Mono has gone. He has gone to look for my missing pouch, of course. But I do not know where the Himalayan Cat has gone – I *preocupación*, si ... I worry about the Originally Solali Kesar as a mother would about her own daughter. I also preocupación about the near muerto novice as I would if my own flesh and blood were to go missing. I do not preocupación about the Guides who have gone ahead of me to ensure that the Originally Solali Kesar has not been messed around with. The Guides are brave, they have undertaken this mission with a fellow Scout to unshroud the mystery that surrounds Senor's biological mother, after all. I am a madre ... a mother who has found her way to Solali to ensure that daughters do not meet their unbecoming fate in the tattooed hands of snãyuňcã purusha.

NINETY

THE DAUGHTERS OF ROZGAARNAGAR are dressed in their brightest synthetic saris, an assortment of plastic bangles on their skinny wrists, and the most sparkling shade of reddish orange lipstick available in Algauv. These wives of Algauv, all dressed to be scrutinized by beady eyes and selected for the flesh upon their bodies, have been told by their respective snãyuñcã purushas that the ruling coolie of the Grand Nizamuddin is travelling all the way from the Undeniable Capital of India to meet, greet and pick one of them to spend the night with by the stinking gutters surrounding Big Ben.

Jhoru Kanbi Badshah, the brightest coolie of the Grand Nizamuddin, is all set to give Bhima and the other fellows in his trade a bad name. He can only give them a bad name by concealing his own identity – for this, he must pretend to intrude with lust upon feminine space. Yes, as shocking as this truth is, Jhoru the Saviour will have to scrutinize the wives of Algauv, their synthetic saris, reddish-orange lipsticks, plastic bangles, et al., and pretend to intrude upon their feminine space, including private parts of their sacred bodies, which are not up for public discussion.

The wives of Algauv and their lives in the gutters by the Big Ben, which remain secret to their parents in Rozgaarnagar, can easily be broken, torn and damaged if the matter is not handled with delicate aptitude for tender beings. It is indeed a delicate matter – Jhoru's pretence must not alert the scoundrel snãyuñcã purushas who are putting their wives up for sale before the perpetrators are brought to their tattooed knees and dragged to the courts of law to be locked up for life.

Jhoru Kanbi Badshah is well-versed in the art of putting people in their places – he has an aptitude for disguise – he will take a train from the Grand Nizamuddin to Algauv with a seemingly pleasant surprise to launch upon the delicate mission by the gutters of Big Ben.

Here comes the surprise – Bhima, who has been taken by the scruff of his sagging neck on the delicate mission, will lead Jhoru Kanbi Badshah and his fellow coolies from the Grand

Nizamuddin to unearth clues about the plight of the wives of Algauv on the pretext of fulfilling their lustful desires.

There is wind of an entourage of well-dressed coolies in Algauv – they all wear gold embroidered scarves around their necks. Algauv is in a celebratory mood – such a large entourage of customers sporting gold embroidered scarves is sure to make the snãyuñcã purusha rich, that too overnight. The tattooed men of Algauv instantly beat the dholaks aka drums of their forefathers, they sing:

'Ame hepi che, dhool dhool dholak
Ame very hepi che, dhool dhool dholak
We are very, very happy, there's paisa on the way'

There's paisa ... there's money on the way, the snãyuñcã purusha say, dhool dhool dholak.

To make them *samrddha*, yes, these snãyuñcã purushas will be rich overnight – *dhool dhool dholak*.

The snãyuñcã purusha are happy to become rich. These snãyuñcã purusha who have not moved a limb in toil will be called the samrddha men of Algauv who became rich overnight, that too by the toil of their wives as the skinny women sleep with unknown men in the dingy gutters by Big Ben – dhool dhool dholak.

'Thambha, yes, stop, this is no time to squash the egos of respectful snãyuñcã purusha for their disrespectful approach to money and fame,' invervenes an all-knowing voice. Jhoru Kanbi Badshah instructs his coolie comrades who are finding it difficult to stop their verbal disdain for the disreputable purusha, snãyuñcã and otherwise, residing in Algauv. The coolies, Bhima included, hide their smirks in time.

The time is ripe by the sea-wind seasoned asbestos hands of the tall and overbearing Big Ben for the wives of Algauv to assemble by the gutters which surround its majestic frame.

The time is ripe to give Bhima a heart attack. His heart is too weak – it cannot survive another piece of news, I hear. The bald novices are messengers of news from around the world in these snow-endowed regions of deep valleys, sudden rivulets, mysterious mountains, manzana trees, Sanyasi Solali Snowmountainwala's open to the elements abode, Buddhist monasteries with red and yellow flags for calvo boys, the Hidimbi Cave Temple dedicated to the rakshashi aka devil by the same name. Hidimbi from hearsay, married the big Pandava Bhima who finds place in Indian mythological texts to have her rakshasa brother Hidimba slain, and together, they had a son called Ghatothkacha. These snow-endowed regions are also home to the Apple Mundi – grand market for the Himachali-bred manzana fruit of the Gods, the frisky Rio Beas, and, according to hearsay, the heavily guarded abode of the Originally Solali Kesar. We have digressed from the calvo novices who believe in precise, evidenced communication, and not hearsay. I have precise, evidenced *noticias*, si news from the calvo novices that Bhima is on the loose in Algauv. I dread this noticias, it is indeed bad news. Bad noticias is a good omen in snow-mountain Solali, I hear from sources found languishing at the much-worshipped bare feet of Shri Shri Shri Shri and Shri Sanyasi Solali Snowmountainwala. Senor Singh Mono is back with my pouch, and an elaborate noticias about a certain

Bhima on the verge of the noose in Algauv. I am elated at this good noticias, I grab the pouch from Senor Singh Mono's outstretched hand. By the way, I have precise evidence that the Bhima on the verge of the noose, is not Hidimba's husband – this noticias is true.

NINETY-ONE

THE THENTODAS HELD BHIMA captive for two nights and three days by the banks of the life-giving Pyraka before turning him over to the Saviour – Awoom, Awaam, Awoom.

News travels fast where gossip-mongers flourish – there's saha about the Thentodas in Chandinigarh, it reaches the Minister's ears. 'Awoom, Awaam, Awoom – the Thentodas cannot be pinned down for their nature-abiding lawful act because they are mostly found hanging downside up from steep rock surfaces upon which no other two-legged living creature bothers to hike. Buzzing bees, however, build their hives on these difficult to GPS pry locations where the Thentodas meditatively hang downside up to teach scoundrels like Bhima a natural lesson.'

'I will deprive the Thentodas of their abodes in the jungle – the scoundrels have had the gumption to steal my most loyal man Bhima,' growls the Minister for Shelters – he has been caught unawares by this saha in the outer premises of OneKmBungWow just when he is about to slink away on his sojourn.

'Please note that no one, not even the Minister for Shelters, can deprive the Thentodas of their jungle homes – their abodes are open to the sky, their homes kiss the ground they walk upon ... Awoom, Awaam, Awoom,' the sahas within and without OneKmBungWow make it amply clear.

The citizens of Chandinigarh are smart enough to saha the truth about the Thentodas and their natural homes. The citizens have all learnt about the beatitudes of the Thentodas from the Scouts and Guides of St. Alphonsious Pre-University College – the future Suitable Somebodies have all arrived in town to lend a shoulder to their comrade at the Caretaker's impending funeral.

But the situation has reversed, the Scouts and Guides all need a shoulder each – they are shocked beyond speech to learn from sahas in the air that their comrade and the Caretaker's body, have both gone missing from Chandinigarh.

'The Scouts and Guides are speechless,' the citizens of Chandinigarh all wag their tongues, they need to tie up this mysterious matter, asap.

The Minister for Shelters cannot stop the citizens who wag their tongues from damaging his reputation. His reputation has already been damaged beyond repair. The Minister for Shelters hangs his reputation on his turban stand. The turban he hangs is a golden cloth, 5 metres long – it has been the crown of all his ill begotten glory, and has diligently covered his half bald head for close on two decades. The Minister stops to think of his lost glory no more – he leaves the boundaries of Chandinigarh on his barefoot sojourn.

The Scouts and Guides all come tongue untied – they decide to follow the near-bald Minister for Shelters on his barefoot sojourn – they have the Double Superintendent of Police for Company. But, unlike the Minister, the Scouts and Guides decide to keep their boots on – they do not want to suffer frostbite when their warm limbs can come handy.

The Scouts and Guides of St. Alphonsious Pre-University

College have all been suitably trained by the Thentodas while on their night crawls to be ready to redeem the world of mess at all times, be it day, night or twilight.

The Scouts and Guides decide to hail the Thentodas – Awoom, Awaam, Awoom, they say, they repeat the refrain to the Minister's disdain.

'The jungle-savvy Thentodas have taught these impressionable girls and boys to hail life in all forms, Awoom, Awaam, Awoom,' the saha-mongers discover, they repeat the refrain over and again.

Despite the doom of death and disappearance, Chandinigarh wears a celebratory air – sahas hail the Thentodas as a rare and undeniably pertinent people who have been responsible in moulding impressionable nobodies to be Suitable Somebodies in the Indian Subcontinent.

'What then has the Master of Sports for Suitable Somebodies been doing all the while until the Thentodas intervened to impart the impressionable Scouts and Guides with lessons on the natural laws of life?' the saha-mongers wonder.

The natural law of life as the Thentodas preach it, is to live and let live despite the increasing lure of bounded shelter, binding religion and unbinding lust for sacred bodies which are not up for sale by personal choice of the ladies in question.

My *carne* ... si, my flesh, it is not for sale in snow-mountain Solali. My flesh was once on sale – the silk-turbaned man who bought my carne became my lover. Soon, the silk-turbaned man and I, we both conveniently lost track of the sale – we made love between the hours that break into day when the night is still young. By day, we danced in tobacco fields blooming with yellow flowers – we lay locked in bone-tight embrace until noon met twilight in a territory far away from our respective homes. My home lay south of this tobacco territory, his abode in the northern direction with a GPS address geographically above the same fields. Suddenly, my home with yellow cushions disappeared from my life, Bhima had chosen to intervene, introducing my carne to trade ... my flesh, for years, was sold to one man alone. The man who danced with me in the tobacco fields – the leaves of this naati plant the raw material for succulent Vignesh Beedi. My pouch wears the faint essence of Vignesh Beedi. My pouch is evidence of my past. My present has brought me my lost pouch. This pouch nestled between two nearly mated rocks in the belly of Rio Beas where the azul-eyed Scout found it. Senor Singh Mono is my present, I know from the look in his azul eyes – this shade of blue matches the colour of my own ojos.

NINETY-TWO

PERUMAL AROKYASWAMI'S EYES, A shade of sun-dried rambutan, meet Pascal Rebello de Fonseca's azul windows to the world for the first time since the latter's body, cooped inside a gunny sack, has disappeared into the heaving waters of River Pyraka uphill Blue Mountain Nilgiris.

Perumal Arokyaswami's eyes have found the Good Man of Cottonpettai – they brim with tears while his chest heaves with the twin emotions of gratitude and fear. There is gratitude in the rickshaw-puller's heavy heart to see his benefactor breathe. There is fear in his pristine heart, which otherwise beats for the Lady with the Slender Hands, and her alone – the rickshaw-puller now stares into the eyes of his benefactor's ghost on top of a distant hill in the inner sanctum of a Murugan Temple in Serendib.

Suddenly, the ghost sounds of gata berayas from a time and date that has been hidden from Perumal Arokyaswami's hippocampus ever since that fateful day when his parents fled Serendib in a coracle tossing across the Indian Ocean like grapefruit in a blunt-bladed juicer, now seem so real – there is din.

The din is indeed a pounding sound inside Perumal Arokyaswami's spinning head. The din unearths a true-coloured vision of his mother stringing a garland of Nil Manel, the Blue Water Lilies of Serendib for the Boy Lord Murugan. Perumal can hear his mother's mellifluous voice rendering the *Thiruppugazh,* song of the Kururuva woman in praise of the Boy Lord. Perumal's head translates the song of the Kururuva tribe inclusive of the men, women and children who inhabit the regions where the Neelakurinji flower blossoms every twelfth year in Serendib, also in Blue Mountain Nilgiris. The Kururuvas are distant cousins of the Thentodas – they too, praise the earth and sky, also the purple haze of the Neelakurinji from which bees draw honey. This honey the Thentodas' harvest hanging upside down from slippery rocks kissing the clouds uphill Blue Mountain Nilgiris.

Perumal Arokyaswami's head continues to spin – his true-coloured vision brings back recent memories of the Thentodas carrying freshly harvested honey to the foothills of Utahkamand, and further ahead to the Mettupalayam Railway Station for Erstwhile Steam Engines. Here, traders bought the freshly harvested honey for pittance and resold the nectar for supreme profit at the city's Main Vegetable Market.

Perumal Arokyaswami's head spins some more – his true-coloured vision takes him back to that year in his childhood when the uphill path to the Murugan Temple on the distant Serendib hill was smitten with Neelakurinjis in near blossom, a supreme sight to behold. The flowers swayed to the tempo of the rhythmic gata berayas performing a tribute to the Boy Lord Murugan, until the tender purple Neelakurinjis froze to the sound of a shot from an aged yet powerful AK-47.

The single shot from that day had left a pool of blood – Perumal Arokyaswami's sister, aged four, now lay as dead as the delicate Neelakurinji she held in her small palm, both flower and girl child devastated by the anger of a fellow citizen in Serendib.

'Why did the fellow citizen kill one of his own kind, that too a girl child who spoke three tongues – Sinhala, Tamil and Spanish with equal ease?' screams Perumal Arokyaswami louder than the din inside his spinning head.

Outside the Murugan Temple on the Neelakurinji-smitten hill, six percussionists sound their gata berayas louder than the din inside Perumal Arokyaswami's head.

Pascal Rebello de Fonseca must finally speak to put an end to the din inside and outside Perumal Arokyaswami's head, before the melee renders the rickshaw-puller insane.

He speaks, and Perumal Arokyaswami listens to his benefactor who is certainly not dead.

Pascal Rebello de Fonseca chose to be Perumal Arokyaswami's benefactor at the sight of rojo on that fateful day when the latter's sibling was shot dead by a citizen, a man who spoke the same tongue as the Kururuva's of the region. 'I, a man with ancestors of Sephardi Jewish connections in Spanish territory dating back to the twelfth century AD, belonged to a family in Serendib which raised me to praise Yehovah, the Buddha, Lord Murugan, messengers of God Christ and Allah in equal measure. I often visited the Murugan Temple on the hill in the not-so-trodden forest in Serendib to hear your mother and sister sing praises of the Boy Lord, song learnt from your ancestors the Kararasa Diyas … the coastal folk, their existence in Serendib dating back to first century BC. Your mother and your father, too, were secular – they visited the Buddha Temple once a week, also the synagogue by Galle in Serendib where the remaining Jews of the land offered their prayers, to sell garlands of freshly harvested Nil Manel to worshippers. Your father was a farmer – his green fingers grew the largest, bluest Nil Manels in all of Serendib, and your little hands were fast blossoming into his. It was all a serene world of Nil Manels and green landscapes until the mojo was drowned in rojo that fateful day. The man who shot your sister dead that fateful day was a Serendib Tamil – his ancestry dating back to second century B.C. The Tamil spoke the same tongue as the Kururuvas, and wanted a separate territory for people of his lineage in north-country Serendib. The Tamil wanted your mother and father, who spoke the same tongue as he did, to express solidarity with the language, and pick up the gun to win exclusive land and territorial rights. But your mother and father belonged to every bit of the land, all of Serendib was their universe until they were forced to flee in the coracle with me to India to escape death. My wife and daughter later joined me in Cottonpettai with all the wealth we had, and we set up a respectable home in India. It is here that I raised you with my daughter when your parents returned to Serendib to harvest more Nil Manel for prayer and communal peace, until they had a respectable death, both shot in this same temple as you sister when she was not quite four. Your peace-loving parents left behind a Kumaru – yes a prince to befit my princess,' explains Pascal Rebello de Fonseca, at length.

Perumal Arokyaswami lets the tears roll, he weeps until he remembers Pascal Rebello de Fonseca's daughter, his princess – Princesca Erendira. The Kumaru wipes his tears – he is homeward bound with a lost and found identity to hold Princesca Erendira de Fonseca in his arms, and kiss her rojo lips smitten with passion.

My lips are azul, they have lost their blood rush in snow-mountain Solali. Senor Singh Mono has turned his azul eyes towards the top of the Highest Hill in Solali – he witnesses a scuffle. Go forth and save your *hermana*, si, your sister, I urge Senor Singh Mono, my voice so loud, the peace-loving novices shudder. Does Senor Singh Mono have a sister? He does, the hermana in question is his half-sister born of a union between the Minister for Shelters and the Caretaker. The novices are perplexed, they have never heard of half-hermanas in their young lives – they run helter-skelter until they hear the sound of firm, bare feet making a distinct sound in the snow. I am slow to turn my frozen neck in the snow, but when I do, I see calvo novices prostrated at the bare and Nil Manel worshipped feet of Sanyasi Solali Snowmountainwala. He promptly blesses the bald novices, but speaks to me. I quietly accompany Sanyasi Solali Snowmountainwala to the top of the Highest Hill in Solali, dressed in a rojo-hued pheran he produces out of his empty jute jhola ... si, a country variety cloth bag that levitating godmen sling around their bare shoulders. Warmed by the pheran, my azul lips regain their lost rojo.

NINETY-THREE

THE WIVES OF ALGAUV have all painted their lips red to lure the coolies to bed them in the gutters surrounding Big Ben. The coolies are lured – they each take a wife, a daughter of Rozgaarnagar for a walk around Algauv Mandi, instead.

They must all walk

They must all talk

About their lives with the snãyuňcã purusha who have strictly instructed their wives to keep their reddish-orange lips pursed – they cannot talk to strange men they bed.

The coolies have all been strictly instructed by Jhoru Kanbi Badshah to walk with the daughters of Rozgaarnagar and woo them with reassuring words until they all find the courage to talk about their painful plights.

Latha, Sarla, Kamla and Vimla, all daughters of Rozgaarnagar, walk around the Big Ben by Algauv Mandi hand-in-hand with the coolies until they feel free to un-purse their reddish-orange lips, and talk.

The daughters of Rozgaarnagar have spoken against their husbands, they will tell their parents that they are breaking all ties, legal and otherwise, with the snãyuňcã purushas they have been married off to.

Amidst all this revelation, Jhoru Kanbi Badshah has a vital clue about his missing parent's whereabouts – he and his coolie brethren must now hurry to the Highest Hill in Solali. Bhima leads the way – Jhoru Kanbi Badshah, his coolie brethren and the daughters of Rozgaarnagar, all take the train to Chandinigarh from where they will ride the Superior College Open to the Sky Truck with blaring Bigbose speakers parked in front of OneKmBungWow to the Highest Hill in Solali. Bhima has just 48 hours to live as a caught free man before he finds himself confined behind iron bars with the other snãyuňcã purusha of Algauv.

I see iron bars from close quarters – Sanyasi Solali Snowmountainwala and I are almost on top of the Highest Hill in Solali. My corazón almost stops, then beats haphazardly for the Originally Solali Kesar at this highest point. This Kesar has been kept behind solid steel bars in a lone cell on top of the Highest Hill in Solali and guarded by Manu Gaddi along with his core people ever since the time she was handed over to them two months from the day she was born, up until now – eighteen years later. Senor Singh Mono and the two Guides are shell-shocked by the vision as Manu Gaddi and the People of the Highest Hill close in on the cell, the strong men shooing the eighteen-year-old boys and girls away from the Originally Solali Kesar. In fact, the Kesar might have been training to be a Suitable Somebody in Utahkamand had she been let out of the guarded cell on the Highest Hill in Solali by her rogue father. It is not too late to be let out, Manu Gaddi suddenly drops his weapon – he has been mesmerised by Sanyasi Solali Snowmountainwala's third eye. I *ver*, si, I see the Originally Solali Kesar smile for the first time – a lone tear trickles down my left ojo, while another pools in my right eye.

NINETY-FOUR

THE MINISTER FOR SHELTERS has arrived barefooted in the valley – he can see an entourage assembled by Sanyasi Solali Snowmountainwala's Nil Manel worshipped feet. The Minister on his barefoot sojourn is perplexed to see the Blue Lily of Serendib in Solali. The Minister is more perplexed to see the closely guarded Originally Solali Kesar given prime place in the front row. This ground-level seating arrangement has been made by the closely monitored bald novices on the snow-cleared banks of the now gentle and handsome River Beas downhill Solali, in Gracia, off the main road from Kulkulu.

We, Senor Singh Mono and his Guide comrades included, are all seated at a latitude of 31.58 degrees north and a longitude of 77.20 degrees east near the Fur and Animal Breeding Station in lowland Gracia. Sanyasi Solali Snowmountainwala has especially chosen this location to rescue animals and girls bonded and bred in captivity for fur and flesh, respectively.

The Minister for Shelters is understandably displeased – he has braved the snow-mountain terrain on bare feet which are now numb, to seek a private visitation with Sanyasi Solali Snowmountainwala, not a public gathering meant for all and sundry! Justifiably so, given that amongst all and sundry members of the gathering, two of his own offspring – Senor Singh Mono and the Originally Solali Kesar – are seated right at the Sanyasi's feet.

Suddenly, the Minister for Shelters feels weary from his barefoot sojourn, that too with a bunch of chitter-chattering Scouts and Guides, all children of his prestigious friends in the Undeniable Capital and otherwise, even his own son Senor, keeping constant eye on him. The Minister's head spins, his feet hurt until he loses balance – he falls upon the snow-cleared ground with a thud. This thud is louder than the sound of a half-ripe apple landing upon a bald novice's head – the all and sundry gathering look at the fallen Minister with utter aplomb.

The Minister for Shelters has feigned a faint given the circumstances, worse shock is yet to come.

One more entourage has come, Sanyasi Solali Snowmountainwala observes with his third eye. Misfortune, yes Bhima arrives with Jhoru Kanbi Badshah, his coolie comrades, the daughters of Rozgaarnagar, also their parents who have given CheapOO the slip, causing the Scouts and Guides of St. Alphonsious Pre-University College to leap out of their newly acquired and grounded seats by the feet of the tri-eyed Sanyasi. These eighteen-year-olds are excited – some spring up in the air, others stand, and still others feign a faint, their actions causing a mild melee for all three eyes of the Sanyasi to see. The sole eighteen-year-old who remains unaffected by Bhima's arrival is the Originally Solali Kesar. This snow-mounatin flower remains calm in the face of all these comings and goings.

While the world turns upside down all around me, I choose to remain calm like the Originally Solali Kesar. There are more matters of social concern, which need to be addressed by the gathering assembled by the thoughtful waters of Rio Beas even as the *mundo*, si, the world around me spins in frenzy. The mundo around me is all topsy-turvy.

NINETY-FIVE

MATTERS IN THE INDIAN Subcontinent are topsy-turvy – in no time, the perpetrators will be punished and traded women will own their bodies, their libertad.

Saha abounds in Chandinigarh that the Minister for Shelters' life has turned all topsy-turvy – the Caretaker has been found, she is full of life.

The Thentodas need to celebrate, Bhima has been found by discerning Suitable Somebodies, who have all, thanks to their stealthy night crawls in Blue Mountain Nilgiris, learnt a thing of two about trekking in sloping terrains to rescue maligned souls.

The Fellows of the Footpath do not know whether it is indeed time to celebrate – Perumal Arokyaswami has returned from his holy sojourn with an identity, while the Lady with the Slender Hands has absconded between the hours they shut eye and shout out for dinner.

On the rare occasions that I have absconded during the waking hours of the Fellows of the Footpath, my out-of-body experience aka OBE has landed me in a place of prime importance. OBE itself is a floaty sensation outside the physical constraints of one's own body comprising flesh, blood, bones, tissues, the hippocampus, et al. I am currently experiencing an OBE – I am in Gracia with the gathering. *Yo … soy*, si, I am where I ought to be right now – see you later, Perumal Arokyaswami …

Perumal Arokyaswami receives a telepathic message – he has been instructed by Pascal Rebello de Fonseca to join him in Gracia along with the other Fellows of the Footpath. Perumal Arokyaswami follows his benefactor's instructions, he arrives at the exact location with the help of a Thentoda locator called sixth sense – it is more accurate than the GPS in these snow-smitten parts.

Perumal Arokyaswami's arrival is accompanied by another thud – a half-ripe apple has landed upon the fainted Minister for Shelter's near-bald head. The Minister shrieks an abuse unmindful of the location, all eyes in the august gathering turn to see a bald novice, the perpetrator, run for cover. Ten more bald novices, all suitably bored with the proceedings of the august gathering, follow suit, the bats-novice dropping his playmate, which as all eyes can see is a piece of drifting wood.

Sanyasi Solali Snowmountainwala is suitably pleased with the novices – they have managed, albeit their game of snow-mountain cricket, to awaken a sleeping mound of breathing flesh from its pretended stupor.

This mound is the flesh of the Minister for Shelters – his other name is Baron of Extreme Excess – call him the Moustached Traderman if you wish. Once a mound of flesh has been aroused from feigned faint, he needs to speak up before the gathering decides to beat him back to pulp.

The Minister for Shelters decides to win Bhima back to his side before he can speak up for what will bring him down and divest him of his political title, his parenthood, his legal and illegal husband-hood, his lover hood, his snãyuňcã purusha-hood, et al.

Bhima cannot be won back, his maligned soul has been cleansed – the owl-eyed Master will perpetrate the flesh trade no more. The Master will join the other snãyuňcã purusha in counting iron bars to absolve his soul of sin – there is a thunderous applause causing din.

'You unscrupulous Master of Sports for Suitable Somebodies, how can you let me down when all I have is about to be silenced by this applauding din ...,' bellows the Minister for Shelters through his faint and sinking larynx.

It has now been established in the eyes of the august gathering that Bhima is indeed the Master of Sports for Suitable Somebodies – call him Misfortune if you please. It emerges in front of the august gathering comprising women who have kicked flesh trade in the shin, that Bhima began his foray into pimping at the behest of the Minister for Shelters upon a moonlit night over twenty-five years ago. That same night, as Jhoru Kanbi Badshah gaped through the slats with the Badtameez Baap, his mother was traded, her flesh abused by the Minister for Shelters. His mother was taken away, and abused until the Minister for Shelters was found out by his respectable parents, and asked to marry the maiden in question, instantly putting sahas to rest in Chandinigarh. Yes, Jhoru Kanbi Badshah's mother is indeed the Caretaker, and the Originally Solali Kesar his half-sister in flesh and blood. The Kesar, upon her father's greedy behest, had been locked away in the well-guarded cell upon the Highest Hill in Solali when she was barely two months old, and left to blossom into an innocent adult to be traded to prime customers from foreign lands alone.

The Originally Solali Kesar who was forcibly taken away from her mother, the Caretaker, only two months from the day she was born, remained in the cell until Sanyasi Solali Snowmountainwala, a godman with rumoured foreign connections, stepped in barefooted and azul-eyed, to salvage her identity.

Ever since Sanyasi Solali Snowmountainwala intervened, Manu Gaddi and the People of the Highest Hill have been guarding the Kesar like a pearl in an oyster. Even the Minister for Shelters is allowed sighting of the pearl only on those rare occasions when Sanyasi Solali Snowmountainwala is feeling benevolent towards the snãyuňcã purusha.

The Minister for Shelters is indeed a snãyuňcã purusha – he wears a Tobacco Flower, permanently tattooed upon his hairy chest. He has, in fact, personally trained the snãyuňcã purusha of Algauv to trade their wives to businessmen and locals in the same town while Bhima kept an eye on the proceedings and collected daily cuts to fill up the Minister's coiffeurs.

At this point, the coolies, Jhoru Kanbi Badshah included, squirm, each turning to the former wives of the snãyuňcã purusha seeking their plastic-bangled hands in wedlock for the sake of love.

I smile at the victory of love, si, amor. Seeking Perumal Arokyaswami's hand, locking mi azul eyes into his sun-dried rambutan-hued ojos, I rest my rojo lips upon his blackened instruments of kiss … I feel love, I feel amor …

NINETY-SIX

THE THENTODAS HAVE WIPED the curtain of smirk from the eyes of the parents of Suitable Somebodies – Awoom, Awaam, Awoom.

These parents still stranded in the first class bogie of the Erstwhile Steam Engine in Hillgroove, all have word from the Thentodas that their children are in distant Gracia. Their children, all Scouts and Guides from St. Alphonsious Pre-University College, are now indeed suitable – they have all been certified by none other than the all-knowing Shri Shri Shri Shri and Shri Sanyasi Solali Snowmountainwala.

Hail Sanyasi Solali Snowmountainwala, Awoom Awaam Awoom declare the Thentodas who are in touch with the godman via telepathy.

'Hail Pascal Rebello de Fonseca – he who has survived the murderous attempt by the Minister for Shelters and his aide Bhima when they dumped the gunny sack with his near-dead body into the heaving waters of River Pyraka in Blue Mountain Nilgiris. Together, the Minister for Shelters and Bhima hatched the plan to murder the benevolent man who had given shelter to Perumal Arokyaswami – the rickshaw-puller had won the heart of the Lady with the Slender Hands. It is the same heart, which the Minister for Shelters wants, but cannot have,' a bunch of munumunuppu-mongers who have word from their phusphus cousins declare.

Mongers from all over the Indian Sucontinent, including Serendib, continue to hail.

'Hail the Thentodas for rescuing Pascal Rebello de Fonseca and reviving his heart to fight for the redemption of flesh-traded women in the garb of Sanyasi Solali Snowmountainwala!

'Hail the Caretaker, she is alive, Pascal Rebello de Fonseca, aka Sanyasi Solali Snowmountainwala has breathed life into her near-dead arteries. In fact, the Caretaker nearly died when the four Royal Ragamuffins gave her a mighty push. The four Royal Ragamuffins had been instructed to kill the Caretaker and the Lady with the Slender Hands before all hell broke loose for the Minister for Shelters.'

Amidst all the hail, Jhoru Kanbi Badshah's heart stands aside with gratitude – he is more than glad to have found his long-lost mother they now call the Caretaker.

I am more than glad that my azul-eyed son has not turned out like his four half-brothers, the Royal Ragamuffins. I am glad that I am no longer in amor with the arrested Minister for Shelters who took me as a lover, his flesh uniting with mine in the tabaco fields of the Deccan Plateau when I was barely an adult. I am glad that the Thentodas who I constantly met on my lone sojourns uphill Utahkamand taught me their native art of OBE. I am glad that my father Pascal Rebello de Fonseca still loves me despite my status as the much-traded Lady with the Slender Hands upon the Widest Footpath of Cottonpettai, kidnapped from my home when I was sixteen-years-old to be traded by Bhima. I am elated that I, Princesa Erendira, can now return with Kumaru Perumal Arokyaswami to the yellow cushion in my father Pascal Rebello de Fonseca's home with an address in Cottonpettai in the Indian Subcontinent. Si, I Princesca Erendira, invite you dear son Senor Mono to groove to this delight – give me a *Cinco Altos!* and feel free to call me your madre.

ACKNOWLEDGEMENTS

A DROP OF RAIN, a tiny step, an unwavering sparkle in the heart of her eye ... Sayontika – that may well be her name as any other, walks in step with mine, and we enter the eye of this monsoon Kolkata twilight hour. Sayontika has taken a short break from her supervisory duties at Ruhamah Designs to connect the threads of her life. A life plucked in the monsoon of her childhood. A life blemished by hungry men who craved her near-adult flesh. A life now worth living given her respectable job and imminent wedding. Rescued and rehabilitated by Freedom Firm, Sayontika thrusts her wedding invite into my hands – she is marrying the love of her life. My heart brims with pride for the work my friend Catherine Raja and her ilk have undertaken through difficult rescues in brothels, also dingy hotels across the country, giving Sayontika and her sisters in trade, reason to call life their own. I feel pride for the gentle finesse with which each trafficked girl, now adult, finds worth in her womanhood.

Another drop of rain – there's gentle finesse in this monsoon cloud. Another step – there's a ray of sunshine negotiating her way through the storm clouds. I step into Sayontika's shoes, I lose my identity and hers. I transpose my identity to write the story of Erendira and people of her ilk. And *Taboo*, the rebel in identity, is born.

Taboo, the pulse of my stream of conscious mind. *Taboo*, an unshackling of all norms, literary and otherwise, in an endeavour to give a traded woman, a good name.

Taboo, a journey into realms I did not know existed, given wing in her impulse by Picador India via the sensitive and intellectual Editorial Director in Prasun Chatterjee, the talented cover designer in Misha Oberoi, the seasoned Managing Director in Rajdeep Mukherjee, the ever accessible Head of Publicity in Bharti Taneja, and all the professional and friendly team members of this famed publishing house.

Taboo, a breathing work of literature as I tided the tenure of her birth, thanks to the emotional and intellectual support of my dear friends – Yogita Dakshina, Ranjini Prabhu, Srividya Hangal, Zahid Javali, Prem Koshy, Manohar Prabhu, Darius Taraporvala, Nausheer Hameed, Sridhar DS and the other Knights of the Square Table, Angela Sudharshan, Rohit Sudharshan, Tina Joseph, Christina Daniels, Manjari Ranasaria, Meghna Chaurasia, Vishal BS and Dr Jampa Yonten – also my extended family of aunts, uncles and cousins from around the world, and in spirit, my late guru Peter Colaco and departed father V. Govindarajan.

Taboo, a tribute to the woman who believed in it from the time I transposed into Erendira – my mother Chandra Govindarajan from her place on earth, and now in heaven.